FANG

VOLUME 4

Edited by Skip Ruddertail
And Graveyard Greg

Bad Dog Books

2012

FANG Volume 4
First publication 2012

Edited by Skip Ruddertail
and Graveyard Greg

Cover by Blotch
screwbald.com

Published by Bad Dog Books
www . baddogbooks . com

CONTENTS

PREFACE

Well, here we are; at last Fang Volume Four is seeing the light of day after a great many years of work. Now not to bore you too much, but this little book is the Swamp Castle of furry erotic anthology collections. I started editing and approving and rejecting submissions. I even had cover art commissioned for this book as well as the previous volumes. Things were moving in the right direction and then I proceeded to nearly drop off the face of the Earth while taking care of things in the cruel "real" world and the book languished. Things looked dark for volume four, and indeed perhaps for the whole Fang anthology, but then a wonderful thing started to happen.

Fang, Bad Dog Books, and later Fur Planet started becoming a real team enterprise, and dare I say it, a family. The amazing Graveyard Greg came on and in a flash changed the whole dynamic of how Fang is created. He and I called in special favors to our favorite authors to corral some more stories to round out the collection, and with an absolutely marvelous stack of work in hand we sat down and got to it. I've really enjoy working with a partner, figuring out which jobs we are best suited to, and at last getting things moving along. We both read each story, vote, and Greg manages the writers, dates, and administrative brilliance while I do most of the editing. And it works!

And boy do we have a great collection of stories here for you folks! It's a healthy mix of both new and established authors, and it's an honor to put their fine work in print. Fang Four is the first volume of Fang to have a tight topical theme rather than the genre based themes of Fang One (Erotica), Fang Two (Horror), and Fang Three (Fantasy), and this volume's theme is "Life After High School." We were hoping that it would be a concept focused enough to generate ideas for writers, yet open-ended enough that we'd get a great variety of approaches, and our writers didn't disappoint! We have a healthy mix of stories that explore the ways in which we define ourselves in relation to our past—stories that ask if one can go home again, and stories about moving on. Fang of course remains our erotic anthology, and we also have some purely fun stories that just get straight to the porn, but they do so in a way filled with a smart playfulness that makes them a joy to read.

I do want to take a moment to thank all the people who helped make Fang Four finally happen. First off Greg, you're the hero here. You keep me honest, and I'll try to do the same for you! Then there's Toonces, (who has his first story in print in this collection) my partner on the Bad Dog Book Club podcast. Fuzzwolf and Teiran over at FurPlanet deserve special commendation—FurPlanet is our new parent, and we couldn't be in better hands. Whitefox and Harvi over at Rabbit Valley are the best con table buddies around and masters at selling books. I also want to give a huge thank you to all the authors who submitted their brilliant stories to this volume.

Last but not least, I want to pay a particular complement to the head of Bad Dog Books, Alex Vance (aka Khaki Dog). Alex gets way too modest when it comes to Bad Dog Books, but we wouldn't be here today if he hadn't thought up the "Little Black Book of Furry Fiction." Thanks for always being the consummate CEO Alex. You found the team, nurtured the talent, and I hope you feel it's finally paying off. This one's for you.

And thank you readers! I've gone on much too long here, and it's past time to get to the stories. Enjoy!

Skip Ruddertail
Your Otter Editor

Our pasts have a certain measure of power over us. When a figure from Ray's memories shows up one night unannounced, he learns that his seeminly monotonous existance in rural Colorado is more than he gave it credit for.

FOR OLD TIME'S SAKE

Whyte Yoté

**SOME THINGS NEVER CHANGE. SOMETIMES THEY
CHANGE TOO MUCH.**

T ime is a paradox like that; you may leave a familiar place, the town you grew up in or the campus on which you earned your degree in Liberal Arts, and come back to it a number of years later and find yourself lost in what you thought was your home. It's unsettling, the way you grow up and get older and you think you haven't changed at all, but there is something about driving down your old street and by your old house, perhaps with an addition or a second story or just painted another color—it shakes you up.

Or you can get the hell out of Dodge while you're still alive, tool around for the same number of years, come back to visit and find that the only thing that's changed is your reflection in the windows, the windows that carry the same faded sticker of a fireman rescuing a child, the same sticker that was on the window you looked out of when you cried the day your goldfish died less than a week after your eighth birthday. Except now you're old enough to get drunk and drive home in a blind stupor, and it won't have been the first, or the fifth, or even the twentieth time you've done it.

Green Hill, Colorado was one of those out-of-the-way, unincorporated towns far enough from any major highway that it didn't need to (or want to, really) change to survive. People just kept on doing the same thing they had been doing for years, the seasons changed, prices rose and nothing exciting really happened except for the weekly sugar beet pricing index over the radio. It was just as easy to sleep through life in Green Hill as anything else, and you just might if you weren't careful.

Ray McCormick watched his own dirty, fingerprinted reflection through the bottom of his glass as he drained the last club soda from around its ice. The Ray-flection tipped the tumbler away from itself, swirled the remains around (it was a habitual gesture after years of "real" drinking) and set it down between a pile of cheap white bar napkins and cheap white stir straws. Morrissey's ears pricked at the sound, a sound Ray could barely hear eight inches away, and he sauntered over to the grey-brown wolf to refill the glass with practiced feigned interest.

"Hotel California" started to play on the jukebox. Ray mused how fucking depressing a song like that was on a night like this, a night where you had nothing better to do than get a little older.

His eyes turned once again to his reflection in the bar's mirror, lined with booze and long overdue for a cleaning. His slim face was centered between a bottle of Johnny Walker Black and another of something called 99 Bananas. Only for the girlfriends, that one, because a lot of the women nowadays liked to dress up in clothes so ugly they were expensive, carry around the same-looking, shoddily-made bag as everyone else on the block, and drink things like 99 Bananas because Entertainment Weekly told them it was the thing to do this week. Ray rolled his eyes and, not seeing anything different in the mirror (he didn't much like the way he looked at this age), he watched the wedge of lime make lazy circles around his rocks glass as he moved it.

Someone came in the front door; Ray could tell that much from the change in air pressure, and he didn't bother to look up to see who it was. He would find out in due time; in a town the size of Green Hill, you pretty much had to hole up in your house twenty-four hours a day to not know every one of your neighbors.

Besides, the wolf recognized the heavy double-clops, a pause and more steps directly over to the pool table. Big ol' Chuck from just out of town must have been feeling the itch to play tonight; he was early. Ray stifled a chuckle into his glass, not knowing whether it was admirable or sad that he could tell all this.

"Chuck's early tonight," said Morrissey from directly above the wolf's head, and Ray looked up, just a bit startled. The scraggly jackrabbit wasn't looking at him, but across the room with the kind of attentive disinterest only a bartender can have. He stood there, polishing a glass (Who does that anymore? the wolf thought) in his white shirt, pleated pants and ratty vest. Ray wondered if Morrissey had planned his life out this way, and then wondered why he cared at all.

"Yup."

"Wonder why?" The uplift at the end of his statement was the standard Morrissey used to spread gossip.

Ray took a sip of his club soda, the lime coming to rest against his upper lip and making him almost snarl. He licked it away and said, "You know why and you just want me to ask."

Showing no sign of irritation to the wolf's accusation, the rabbit continued: "'S his wife, you know." Ray knew. Well, not knew, he suspected. "People been sayin' she's in with some business guy horse from up Fort Collins. Chuck knows, but they don't jaw about it. Shame."

"Gail sure likes 'em big, that's for sure," Ray said, not expecting Morrissey to laugh at that, and Morrissey didn't. Chuck being one big bull, in all areas (Ray knew this thanks to a one-time locker room change after laps in the community pool), it must have been a blow to his ego when he found out about the affair. But he was here to shoot pool, and forget about it for a while, and he would do just that. None of anybody's business but Chuck's, anyway.

"Speaking of wives, how's yours?" The rabbit wasn't a sympathetic ear as much as he was fishing, but Ray didn't have enough drama worth repeating in Green Hill. What secrets he did have, he took pains to keep.

"Same old. Ferries the kids to the bus stop weekdays. Runs errands weekends. Does her volunteer work Saturdays and church on Sundays, and that little fuckin' Do-Your-Own-Clothes thing Wednesday nights." And it was all the truth, the boring, uninteresting truth. Janie kept busy, and she seemed like she was satisfied (she sounded like it in bed most nights too), but Ray had his doubts. It wasn't that their marriage had stagnated, really, it was like they were just two people, with two kids, living their lives instead of an American family living the American dream. Their life was far from that idyllic faux pas, but still.

"Dang, dude," the bartender said, "there ain't nothin' new happens with you, izzere?" If there had indeed been some dirt worth digging up, Morrissey would have brought it to Ray's attention. There were some things the rabbit didn't know about, that he would never find out, but that was beyond the scope of this conversation.

"Not really. Every day like the day before, except I'm a little older, and hopefully a little wiser."

"Keep drinking that shit and you'll just get dumber," Morrissey pointed to the wolf's almost-empty glass.

Ray smiled a weary smile, a practiced smile around his friends and family, and said, "You know my rules. I'm allowed to come in, just not to partake." And the rules were Ray's and Ray's alone. He'd been sober for almost a hundred days since completing Alcoholics Anonymous (his counselor had said you never were totally recovered, but that, along with the "Pray" portion of the program, Ray had regarded as a light frosting of bullshit), and he figured since he'd gone this long it wouldn't hurt to keep going. He knew very well that one drink wouldn't send him off the wagon, but it was all about control. Ray reveled in that control, and it made more sense of his life when he could take hold of something and call it his.

"Yeah, well, at least you still tip like it's alcohol."

"You'd kick me out if I didn't," Ray said, and even though they both knew it wasn't true, they shared a laugh at the expense of mildly-interesting small-talk. "Save my stool, won'tcha?" The wolf slid backwards to the floor and walked to the door, fishing for his Swisher Sweets in his shirt pocket.

"Don't think you can switch one sin for the other and you're still even-Steven," called the rabbit to Ray's back, and the wolf waved it off.

"Gimme a break, I gotta live for something!" Ray yelled back without turning his head, twirling the red pack of cigarillos in his left paw, searching for his Zippo with the right. Just one guilty pleasure, two smokes a day... What was the harm in that, considering what life throws at you?

It was almost startling the way the brash country-bumpkin atmosphere died once the wolf opened the door to the outside world, to a podunk rural town near one in the morning on a random weeknight. The music was still there, but muffled as if in a pair of headphones buried beneath a pillow. Weak neon light shone into the crowded parking lot, reflecting off all four vehicles, and Ray thought it was some kind of twisted metaphor for his life, just another image to add to his substantial mental collection.

He brought a smoke to his lips and held it there before touching it to the tip of his lighter. The tobacco was bittersweet, a planty flavor that would taste so much better once set to burn. Yes, it was bad for his health, and yes, he wasn't addicted to them like others were to Marlboros or Camels or even fucking Misty 100's, but it was something he could enjoy in the privacy of his own personal space, and nobody would bother him about it. Nobody except Morrissey, and he had bartender's privilege.

Ray lit up and watched the night go by. The music kept on playing. The neon kept on buzzing. The wolf kept on shooting puffs of blue-grey smoke into the moonlit March sky.

Somewhere off in the distance came a soft flatulation that reverberated off the hills surrounding the little bar and made Ray's ears come to full-mast. This he did without moving any other part of his body, because it was thus far so inconsequential as to not require a more comprehensive response. The sound died out and became part of the background noise, not disappearing completely but making Ray unsure whether its source was moving toward or away from him. Then it came back again, stronger, so whatever was making it was closer.

It sounded like a truck, though the wolf admitted to himself that he'd been fooled too many times to assume anything. "Assume makes an ass out of 'u' and 'me,'" he mumbled aloud, something he'd read in a book recently (some Stephen King thing about cell phones), and allowed a giggle at his own inane ramblings. Insanity along with misery, now that was a good combination. "Misery, huh," he said, recalling another King favorite, and that brought another self-indulgent giggle.

Now a beam of light played over the hill opposite the bar, across the street, and the flatulent roaring sound was just about to crest the top and make its way right into town, passing out front. The piercing glow of high-beams burst into Ray's adjusted night vision, searing twin trails of phantom blue into his retinas. The cloud of smoke around his head glowed like a chaotic halo, and was gone in the next instant as the semi-tractor rumbled toward the bar.

Really not that much of a bother to the residents, who had grown accustomed to living alongside a through truck route over the years, it was easy to see how such a gathering of clanking, screeching, vrooming parts would be heavily regulated in cities. The flatulating noise, the wolf now knew, was the backfire from the engine retarder, or jake brake, helping to slow the truck as it came down the hill (fine for cars but steep for behemoth towing machines). Its shape materialized from around the headlights as it emerged into the weak streetlamp glow, and by the way it was slowing Ray knew the driver had planned a stop in little Green Hill. He took another drag and pretended not to notice while watching at the same time.

Not stopping for gas, the wolf thought, because everything in town (including all two gas stations) had shut down hours ago. Possible he (or she, you wouldn't want to be sexist in this day and age) was coming into the bar for a drink? Sure, it was probably against company policy, but who the fuck was really going to care? Fleeting images of a slender vixen or wolf, clad Daisy Duke-style with her hair and tail all fluffed out and shining in the meagerly-lit parking lot entertained Ray for the time it took the truck, which was minus a trailer, to swing around and park near the street, sending up a cloud of fine dust as its air brakes were engaged. The diesel rattled to a stop, shaking the cab, and the door opened.

Ray looked down and chewed on the end of his smoke, getting little bits of tobacco leaves in his teeth and on his tongue. It really was bitter when it wasn't lit. He turned his eyes up at the crunch of gravel, saw the vague silhouette of the driver and shook off the little disappointment he felt. No way that could be any woman.

The footsteps approached, as they would have to in order to enter the bar, and Ray waited to mutter a cursory "howdy" without moving. The tips of boots appeared near his own, stopped. There was a sudden silly awkwardness, and an acute feeling of violation, but the wolf stood his ground, being on home turf, so to speak.

"I didn't think you'd stay around here, all these years," said a voice so smooth and concretely familiar that Ray was actually stunned. He kept staring at the ground, even though he knew it was embarrassing, because he didn't want to look up and confirm what his ears had already told him. He wasn't ready... He hadn't been expecting this, he had just come down to the bar for a drink, such as it was. Already he could feel the man's power over him, coercing him to obey, just like it had done over seventeen years ago.

And Ray realized he wanted it anyway, and it made him want to throw up.

Light beige fingertips came up under his chin and lifted it, with no thought of people exiting the bar, and there was so much history in that motion it made Ray almost break into tears. He couldn't move. And then he was looking into the wallaby's face, and it was just like he remembered it, just like he had almost forgotten it, and it had come back to remind him at just the last second. The fingers released his jaw and it went slack; his smoke tumbled out and into the wallaby's paw. No, don't do that, it'll burn you, the wolf shouted in his mind, but the wallaby just smiled slightly and took a drag of his own, wincing as he exhaled.

"When did you switch over to these?" Conversational, as if years had not passed between them. "This isn't a real cigarette. If you're going to get cancer from something, it might as well taste good." The wallaby handed the Swisher back to Ray, who dropped it on the ground and smoldered it, having lost his appetite for much of anything.

"We promised each other we'd quit, Steve," the wolf managed, though it seemed as if he were providing the voice from miles away. Steve Schilling, he repeated to himself. Steve Schilling. Now his legs were weak. Ray put his paws in his pockets and leaned up against the side of the bar, realized Steve would see right through the façade, and didn't care. It was no use trying to fake the wallaby out. Even in the short time they had known each other way back, they had learned lots of little things.

"Promises are made to be broken. You can take the West out of the wallaby, but, you know..."

"How'd you find me?" Ray tried hard not to sound incredulous, or dumbfounded.

"I wasn't lookin', Ray. I'm on my way down through Denver from Coeur d'Alene, I had some extra time, and I figured, why not stop by the ol' stomping grounds and put back a couple? This is a pleasant surprise, though." Ray wanted to say the same thing, but his stomach was roiling too much for it to be completely truthful. The wallaby may have been nonchalant, but he was still checking the wolf out. If there weren't a pair of jeans in the way, his tail would have been curled up to his navel. Thank goodness he was leaning on that wall.

Steve, with the exception of age, was basically the same person he was in 1991, minus the Benetton T-shirt and Converse All-Stars. There were a few wrinkles here and there, and he'd gathered himself an appreciable belly (which Ray found cuter than the slender wallaby he remembered), but the person inside that body was still Steve, the only man he'd ever loved (hell, the only man he'd ever found he could love at all), who'd loved him in return with just as much gusto. He was a virgin back then, and far too stupid to know the difference between love at first sight and erection at first sight.

Leaning against the wall as well now, just as stiff as a truck driver would be in the tight Wranglers he was wearing, Steve pulled a pack of his own from a shirt pocket, a brand Ray didn't recognize, and lit up with a flick of his wrist. The wolf had, by now, gotten over the initial shock of the ghost of an almost-forgotten lover just happening to stop by his hometown, but the way his body was responding could be described as traitorous to say the least. Memories that had been all but repressed were now bombarding his thoughts like artillery fire, so much so that he couldn't pay attention to what the wallaby was saying.

"...higher than ever in nicotine, so no wonder it's so damn hard to give 'em up," Steve finished a sentence Ray hadn't heard him start. "Can't believe the paper, though."

"Tell me about it." He wondered if the wallaby was able to smell the fear and arousal coming off of him in alternating waves, and took his pulse with two fingers. It was something he did as an anxiety-triggered regulator, ever since he'd had that heart attack six years ago. Steve didn't know about that.

Steve puffed into the night air. The smoke seemed to dance insanely along with the muffled beat from the jukebox inside. It pooled against the rim of his cowboy hat and leaked around it in a little tsunami between long marsupial ears. In that moment it seemed that Steve could dress up any way he wanted to, and it would be right. Even the simple red-plaid-shirt-and-jeans combination looked bright against the neutral fur and complemented the masculinity he had always displayed, especially around the wolf. Ray thought he heard the Righteous Brothers, but he couldn't be sure and he was too preoccupied to care anyway. He caught himself stealing a glance at the wallaby's fly, toward the bulge that could either be the cut of the fabric or the object he'd desired so much as a young man.

"Do you want to talk about it?" asked the wallaby around his cigarette.

Ray averted his eyes and looked toward Steve's face. "Whaddya mean?"

"You spaced off. There's a lot I don't remember from the past, but I still know when you're feeling uncomfortable. I'm starting to regret stopping off here. Seriously, I didn't figure you'd still be around, and I'm happy to see you." The wallaby's mannerisms indicated nothing of the sort, but Ray knew better than to judge his emotions by his actions. "If it's me, I want to know it's me. I guess both of us shouldn't be expected to just sit here and make jovial conversation." Steve flicked ash onto the gravel and spit to the side.

Swallowing audibly, the wolf replied, "It wouldn't be fair to you if I lied. You just...go down to the bar for a drink and you're fine, and then something crashes into your life again..." He was rambling, and his voice was creeping up in register, and by the time he finished his thought he sounded like he'd gone back twenty years. Ray bit around his cigarette and listened to Steve's gentle, understanding chuckle (that in itself was unnerving, and unraveled his psyche a bit), fanning it away through his nostrils.

"It's this town, isn't it? Hasn't changed you a mite, because you haven't ever left. I'm probably not any better." Ray felt like airing a gentle protest, but for all he knew it was the truth. There was a lot of time lost between them, and part of the wolf wanted to catch up like friends, but they weren't exactly like friends. They never had been, in the strict definition of the word; at least he'd never considered Steve a friend as much as... Well, there were better words to describe their relationship.

Another part wasn't so keen on the idea of digging up a treasure trove of confusion, expectancy, and an emotion Ray still struggled to include in the "love" category. He couldn't believe he was standing here, when less than ten minutes ago life had been proceeding just as normally as it always had, as slowly as it always had, and now...now what? More fear? More excitement? More discomfort?

All three. And Ray didn't know where to go, or what to do, just like back when he relied on Steve to lead him around and give him advice.

"Come on, puppy. What do you say we go inside, throw back a few, and jaw some, huh? I feel kind of responsible, and it's fuckin' cold out here." The wolf's decision was made much easier then, but he couldn't tell whether it was Steve's natural talent for persuasion, the use of his old pet name, or the words whispered so close in his right ear the wallaby's warm breath rustled the fine hairs inside its concave surface.

"Ayuh," he heard himself say, and pushed ahead from the wall so Steve could drop the paw that was leading him by the wrist. The wallaby got the idea (he probably didn't mean to keep that up inside the bar, for sure) and instead opted for holding the door open. Ray nodded curtly, Steve snubbed his smoke on the doorframe and they walked through into the dimly-lit din.

No one turned to stare at him and his new companion; no one dropped a glass and pointed an accusatory claw in his direction. No one even seemed to notice Steve's entrance behind the wolf, and that suited Ray fine and dandy. His heart was in his throat again, fighting for space beside his uvula. Could anyone in this place recognize the wallaby from so long ago? He didn't see anyone.

Ray sauntered as best he could to his well-worn stool and found it easy and comforting to slide his narrow frame onto its cushion, minorly dismayed at the rush of air as Steve did the same next to him, as if Steve could have magically changed his mind and decided to run away like a part of the wolf wanted him to.

Now, sans glass but marrying liquor, Morrissey side-stepped from watching the far-end television to the two gentlemen now occupying the opposite corner. "'Nother soda for you, Ray? Hi, Steve," nodding to the wallaby. Ray's jaw dropped, it felt, almost to his groin, and he fought to control it before Steve could put that to rights with a finger as well.

"Just gimme a bourbon water, don't skimp on the bourbon, don't upsell me but don't give me shit in a bottle either."

"Maker's Mark it is." Morrissey nodded.

Steve continued, "And Ray here'll have a margarita on the rocks, no lime, with a sugar rim instead of salt." The wallaby turned to look expectantly at the wolf, who was becoming mildly angry— at Morrissey's recognition of his ex-lover (was he really an ex?), at Steve's ordering him a drink when he was clearly (to himself, at least) trying to keep dry, and at the way Steve remembered his favorite drink all the way down to—

The wallaby was still looking at him, studying him.

Ray raised a single eyebrow.

"That's it," snapping his fingers, then, "Cabo Wabo or nothing. You got that here?"

"Uh-huh," Morrissey said, almost embarrassed by the fact.

"Good man. Any other tequila messes with Ray's stomach. Doesn't it?" Ray nodded deliberately.

"You want me to go ahead, Ray?" Morrissey asked, knowing all about the bandwagon himself.

Ray slumped down to the counter, ears lowered in defeat. "Sure, whatever." And Morrissey went back to the television for a few moments. It's not like anybody was ever in a hurry down at the bar, and if you were then you didn't belong there in the first place. The wolf turned wearily to Steve. "Why did you do that?"

"What, order you a drink? It's a simple gesture of good will; besides, we are in a bar. I didn't mess anything up, did I?" The wallaby's long, slender ears twitched toward Ray.

"No, you remembered it fine." There it was again, the beginning of a swelling in Ray's jeans, unprovoked and unwelcome... well, not entirely; a half-erection felt good any time of the day. He was patently certain that Steve wasn't trying to seduce him on purpose; was also certain that the wallaby hadn't been trying to seduce him ever since he stepped oh-so-suavely off that truck and sauntered back into the wolf's life, purposefully or not. Ray was using Steve to seduce himself, and though he didn't like it he found it difficult to stop.

"Then what's the deal." More a statement than a question; it had more gravity that way.

"I'm just out of AA, Steve. You're makin' it pretty hard for me to stay straight."

"You never did react well to alcohol," said Steve without a trace of empathy. Which was good, because Ray wasn't looking for any, though the wallaby made no indication of wanting to take the drink back. "Then again, back in school you were a thin wolf. Still are; beer got the best of me. Wife likes it, for some reason." Steve patted his belly with his free paw, and the wolf had to bite his tongue to keep from saying he liked it too.

Morrissey returned carrying the drinks, his fingers set up in a complicated pattern learned with much practice and, indubitably, many errors, threw out a couple napkins and presented the males with their spirits.

"Payin' now, or running a tab?" he asked.

"Let's wait and see," replied the wallaby. He swirled his glass, leaning back and crossing his legs as he studied the amber liquid before him. "He did a good job," taking a liberal first sip. "Very good." Steve twirled the glass between long, delicate fingers before replacing it on the bar. Morrissey obviously wasn't invested much in whether or not Steve liked what he had prepared, engrossed as he was in marrying liquor. Looking over at the wolf with a casual tilt that seemed meant to further tease Ray, he started, "What the hell you been up to for all this time? Seriously, I thought you would've gotten out of this town as soon as you could after we split up."

Split up. Is that what they had done? Or was Steve just calling it what it was, which was they had gone their separate ways, because life was happening, and Ray had never voiced his opinion (or his love, for that matter). Steve had never been in it for commitment, and the wolf had come to know that over the years, but he felt slighted anyway. It seemed, however, that Ray was the only one who held that view. The details of their relationship were fuzzy, so many actions and words forgotten, that the wolf really didn't know what to think anymore. He hadn't been thinking, not until that truck had pulled into the parking lot.

Ray swallowed dryly, chased it with some alcohol, fought back a coughing fit and spaced his words carefully. "You know, Steve... I don't have much to tell you. I mean, yeah, seventeen years, but...I'm not good at this stuff. Ask me a question."

An enigmatic smile creased the thin fur around the wallaby's eyes. Ray was waiting for an expression he could trust. "You never were good at conversation. Well, where do you work? You already know what I do."

"Same old. I was gonna go to college, but Dad got sick and I helped out on the ranch. That was for about two years, and then he got better. I moved to Denver to try and get out again, but Dad got worse and they needed me. When he died, I..."

"Your father passed away? How old was he?"

"Forty-seven. Throat cancer."

Steve shook his head and lay a paw on Ray's shoulder. He could feel its warmth even through his heavy coat, and when he glanced up to continue, there it was—the honest expression he was looking for. He seemed so much older now.

"I'm sorry, bud. I liked the guy."

"Yeah. Yeah, so did I," the wolf replied, and actually felt pressure behind his eyes. It was only the second time he'd felt like crying over his dad. The first was at the funeral. "So yeah, I was stuck on the ranch, taking care of the family, and I just kind of grew up. Mom's at a retirement home, on her own, and I have the house. Janie keeps it nice and clean, plenty of room for the kids and dogs. I guess I just never felt a reason to leave. What?"

"You're married...with children." The tone of disbelief was unflattering, but not disappointed. Steve had taken a cigarette from his pocket and was manipulating it with his fingers. He wouldn't be able to light it in this place.

"Raymundo Jr.'s seventeen and Eve turns thirteen in about a month. You seem surprised."

The wallaby looked across the bar at their reflections, squinting as if trying to find something that wasn't there, or partially hidden. "Just never figured you for the marryin' kind."

"You thought I would keep chasing cock?" And then Ray bit his lip, hard; it was a joke, but it was the first mention of sexuality either of them had made. The wolf immediately regretted airing it so blatantly. Blame Steve for making him uncomfortable, then tearing down his reserved guard.

"I just knew you were a loner. You can't deny that, after all we talked about way back when." No offense taken, so good.

Ray watched the wallaby, even as the wallaby kept staring at his own reflection. "You can't help who you fall in love with."

"No, you can't, and I don't blame you." I didn't think you blamed me anyway. "That's why I'm sure my wife and daughters appreciate me when I'm home." Steve looked back at the wolf, because he knew the look that was going to be on Ray's face. It was there. "Didn't think I would, did you?"

"Touché," said Ray, and found it easier to drain his glass, easier than it had been before AA. The burn in his gut had turned to a comfortable warmth, and a slight detachment that somehow still made him feel more in tune with the conversation. It was false thinking, but maybe a bit of false thinking would do him more good than harm right now. "So, what does that say about us?"

"What do you mean, us?"

Ray backtracked; this could take a wrong turn very quickly. "I don't know. Are we failures because we had dreams and they took off for somewhere else, and we talked about it so much, and none of it's happened? I mean, life gets in the way when you're trying to git 'er done, and then you go off on some tangent and then you're all grown up and you're complacent."

"Are you satisfied?"

The wolf had to stop and think when he heard Steve ask that. Part of his brain was telling him no, not in the least, that he wouldn't—couldn't—be satisfied until he told the wallaby he loved him and wanted to be with him for the rest of his life. But that was the part of Ray that was still seventeen and immature, the part that could leave everything and follow the pursuit of the day. He wasn't that person anymore. If anything, by now he'd surely grown up. The mortgage was paid, the wife was happy, the kids were in school, and he was good at his job. Was he satisfied with things as they stood?

"Yes. Yes, I am."

"Then that's why you stayed." Ray felt, as the wallaby swiveled on his stool, their legs brushing, and Steve's denim-clad knee slid halfway up his thigh as he turned. The wolf's erection was suddenly there, aching dully and probably not well-hidden.

"Are you?" As he asked the question, trying to see if his bulge was noticeable (it was), he automatically went to Steve's fly, and fought to keep his ears forward as he saw the material twitch.

"I am, really. I love my family to death. Hate being away from them so long, but this job pays too well for such little work. That's what cell phones are for, right? Nothing like being able to read a bedtime story to your kids while you're working." The wallaby tipped his head back, ice cubes piling around his muzzle. Licking his lips, he said, "I got my wallet in the truck. Wanna break out the baby pictures?"

"Sure." Ray had plenty of his own, and he was getting tired of the slow country music in the bar. Steve put some bills down, patted the wolf's leg and stood, stretching. Ray followed suit, keeping quiet about having his drink paid for (when Steve took care of something you didn't contest it), and sauntered into the parking lot. A thin veil of steam rose from their bodies as they walked, dancing for a second or two before winking out of existence.

Ray waited at the passenger door while Steve opened up, cranked the engine until it purred throatily, and threw up the locks. It was more of a hoist up than the wolf had been expecting, but once he was firmly planted in the chair it didn't seem that high at all. The air coming from the vents was very warm, almost hot, and he shed his coat without thinking of it.

"Pardon the mess; I haven't stopped at a travel center in a few days because I'm all stocked on food. That means the trash piles up wherever I can throw it," said the wallaby, twisting his frame around the pilot's chair and into the narrow space between the cab and the sleeper. "Seems I'll always be a packrat."

"Just as long as your wife never sees it," said the wolf.

"Never." Steve motioned for Ray to follow him into the sleeper, and the wolf winced when an overhead fluorescent light flicked on above him. The sleeper was basically all a trucker could want for on the road, and nothing more. There were storage bins on either side stacked floor to ceiling, more storage around the top of the sleeper, and two bunk beds. The bottom bed was made up, and the top had been folded halfway to prevent head injuries in the dark. Ray presumed there was more storage underneath the bottom bed. It was nicely laid out and, had it been clean, it would have been nicely organized too.

"This looks comfortable," Ray said while he waited for the wallaby, who was bent over, to retrieve his wallet from the crumpled bedclothes. He admired his view of the thick tail swaying to and fro, and the way Levi 501's had just the right cut to grip a nicely-shaped rear end. He was just about to adjust himself when Steve pulled up, and his paw quickly detoured to his back pocket, and the wallet within.

Looking around, visibly embarrassed by the state of things, Steve said, "This is how things get when you leave 'em too long." He began to open his wallet, but swore when a bunch of cards fell to the floor. "Shit, hold on."

"I'll get 'em." Ray was already bending to help even before the cards had reached the end of their descent. As he began to pick them up, he saw the names—Petro, Pilot, Flying J, TA, Love's, AmBest—and realized they were fuel cards for truck stops. He faced the cards in the same direction and was about to straighten back up, but found he couldn't so much as breathe when he felt fingers around his tail base, curling and tightening and pulling his tail up just enough to be indulgently gratuitous.

The wolf was still facing down, his gaze fixated upon the "J" on the Flying J card that was tilted to look like a plane taking off. He bore a hole into that letter while another paw bunched up the hair between his ears and gripped it, hard but not painfully, and a grunt filled the sleeper. Ray's head was pushed up against something hard and warm, and it slid off to one side. His nose was filled with the aroma of wallaby; it had grown much stronger in the last few seconds. He was let go from both ends and he shot up to find Steve breathing deeply, looking down at him from his two-inch advantage.

There were a lot of things on Steve's face, too; one thing the wolf could tell was that neither of them had seen it coming. The possibility had always been there, yes, but never in Ray's imagination would he have expected the wallaby to make a move. But in doing so, he'd opened up a can of worms the wolf was afraid could not be resealed. He was too horny now to just ignore it, and the opportunity was too damn convenient. It was two feet from him.

Conflict was apparent within Steve, though it didn't show much. One of the things you don't forget about a lover is how to read their face, even if it's more wrinkled than you remember it. A little conflict, a little doubt, a lot of lust. The wolf knew which one would win out; it was always the winner, even in the later days of their sexual relationship it had seemingly been the only thing they had in common. Steve leaned forward, Ray leaned back until he could go no further, and he watched, breathing as shallowly as possible, until Steve turned sideways and their lips met.

* * *

It was like dying, a little. The French had a word for orgasm: *le petit mort*. "The little death," they called it, but this wasn't an orgasm. This was a kiss, just a simple touching of lips, but never

29

before had Ray, seventeen years old and a virgin, experienced the array of emotions he had just gone through in the last few minutes. Oddly enough, anxiety about being discovered behind the sheep shed at the Northern Colorado Rodeo Fair was not one of them.

Steve was a great kisser, as far as the wolf was concerned. Sure, he'd only kissed a couple of girls before (both of them wouldn't put out fast enough, but he had a feeling Janie'd come back eventually), and that was okay, but the wallaby kissed like he meant it, not like it was something you were expected to do. He kissed like a man, with purpose and passion, and for some reason it set the wolf's system on fire.

Ray had been in various stages of erection since he met Steve at one of those stupid carny games, trying in vain to throw a dubiously-sized baseball through an even more dubiously-sized hole. Wandering around the fair and watching people was what Ray did, because he didn't much like to participate, and it was a hell of a lot cheaper. Besides, he was saving his money for funnel cakes and fried cheese and other assorted unhealthy fair fare.

"Fuckin' gay-ass ball," muttered the wallaby as Ray came within hearing range. He was bent over the fence separating the players from their futile goal, far enough that he was cheating, but the carny operating the game was turned away. Like it mattered. Perhaps feeling a bit overly confident (Ray had a way of sticking his snout into things that weren't necessarily his business; you couldn't very well describe him as shy), or perhaps because he was getting bored, the wolf stepped up behind the wallaby and tapped him on the shoulder. He got a look of aggravation for his troubles.

"Whoa dude," Ray put his paws up. "May I?"

The wallaby looked at his two remaining balls, sized up the shorter wolf, and kind of sneered. "Sure, why not? A laugh at somebody else's expense would cheer me up right about now." He handed a ball to the wolf.

"Stand back," warned Ray, making a show of massaging the ball, breathing on it, winding up nice and big and throwing it—overpaw—right into the hole. When the carny heard that, he whipped around so fast a cloud of dirt appeared at his feet. The ball was in the bucket, Ray was finishing his follow-through, and he was well behind the line. He was also trying very hard to hide his own astonishment.

"Motherf—" mumbled the wallaby.

"Sorry, gentlemen," sung the carny, a dirty-looking ferret with yellow teeth. "The one who pays gets to play, any other winner gets nary a prize, so why don't you move along, youse guys?" It was horrible and improvised, and it grated on both men's nerves.

"Gimme my toy," said the wallaby with just a trace of threat.

"Tough luck, kiddo," said the ferret, who went back to taking the money of a seven-year-old boy.

The wallaby stepped to the fence and said, "I have Greg Wilson's number on speed dial on my portable telephone, and I'll pay the outrageous fees just to report you." All at once the ferret looked stricken, as if Greg Wilson owned the fair or something. Ray had a feeling. "Unless you want me to make a strongly-worded call, I suggest you give me my toy like a good boy."

Abject fear gave way to cautious annoyance as the ferret grabbed a large plush husky from the collection hanging above, and stiff-armed it out. "Couldja just go now? I got kids waiting."

"I'm sure you do," he said, smiling and taking the toy. Ray followed him as they started walking.

"You're welcome." After all he'd done, even though he didn't care about winning a stupid toy, Ray hoped this guy wouldn't turn out to be an asshole.

"Thanks," said the wallaby quickly. "You're a showoff."

Yes, Ray was. And yes, he'd been lucky. But he wasn't about to admit to that. "I dunno, I just thought I would try." And that's when the wolf realized he was hard, just enough to notice himself. "What are you going to do with that silly thing, anyway? You look too old for stuffed animals."

Clutching the husky to his chest, the wallaby said, "I'll probably cut a hole underneath its tail and use it for masturbation." That stopped the wolf in his tracks, but the wallaby's step never faltered. He stopped a few feet ahead and continued, "What? Jacking off gets old."

Ray waited for the wallaby to follow up with an "I'm kidding" or something, but nothing was offered. "Okay," he said in a small voice, and kept walking. He was even harder now, and although it made him vaguely uncomfortable while talking to a guy he didn't even know, there was always that taboo arousal. "I'm Ray."

"Steve, formerly of Bixby High, currently of the Double-R Ranch."

"You went to Bixby? Wow, I go to Crocker! I bet our teams play each other all the time."

"Huh, go Crusaders," chuckled the wallaby. "So why'd you want to play with my balls?" What was this guy's deal with the sexual innuendos, anyway?

Ray played it off. "I was bored, and figured even if I made a fool out of myself I would at least be entertained for a minute." They were walking a little faster now, and the wolf swung his tail to compensate. Plus, he was genuinely having fun. Conversations usually didn't start this easily, no matter who he started them with. "Plus, I spend my money on food, not carny games."

"You hungry?" Steve asked, canting his head Ray's way.

"Yeah, actually." The wolf hadn't thought about it until Steve mentioned it, and now he was irrevocably hungry.

Over heaping and expensive plates of unhealthy food, the two males talked. It was just guy talk, too, something he didn't do with his dad very much even though they worked together on the farm. Having that much in common was a great benefit to Ray as well; he found himself talking up a storm about his family, his school years, the farm and general small-town Colorado things to which Steve could fire right back with his own stories. A relatively boring day was turning out to be worth the four dollars he paid to get into the fair.

Ray finally realized how long they had sat and talked when the midway lights came on above them, showering everything in a seizure-inducing rainbow. Both expressed regret at having to get home in time for an early morning, but hey—that's farm life, right?

"I plan to get out of here and to a college as soon as I can," the wolf said as they made their way to the front gate and their respective trucks. "Dad's guilting me into working for him, because he's got some problems. Beyond high school, parents can be a nag."

"That's why I left early," replied Steve. "You just gotta have a job all the time, you know? That's what life is...paycheck to paycheck." There was a certain sadness to the wallaby's voice, and Ray found himself hoping it wouldn't turn out the same for him. Knowing his dad, though...

They were walking in the 4-H compound, in between the showing stadium and the sheep shed, the faint smell of manure preceding them. Sunset had come and gone, leaving a dull glow behind the trees which marked the beginning of the gravel parking lot. Halfway down, Ray was in the middle of asking if Steve drove a Chevy or a Ford (turned out he drove a Dodge after all), when he realized he was walking by himself. He turned around; Steve was standing in the dark, holding the husky to his chest, looking really a lot younger than twenty-four.

"What's up?" walking back into the shadows. Soft bleating came from the other side of the shed.

"Come here." Steve's voice was urgent.

Ray came up close to the wallaby, looking around warily in case it was something he couldn't see. "What?" He leaned in so his ear was close to Steve's mouth, so the wallaby's warm breath rustled the fine hairs inside its concave surface. Instead, he heard nothing but felt a finger underneath his chin, turning his head so smoothly and swiftly he did nothing but breathe as shallowly as possible until Steve turned sideways and their lips met.

It was like dying, a little.

The wolf's legs just about gave out; it was silly how weak he felt, but how much could you expect when you were being kissed by a man? It just wasn't something that happened every day. Intimate contact was so rare for the wolf anyway; he swiveled against the wall of the shed, triggering a round of startled bleats, and let Steve push into his mouth. It was warm, it felt damn good, and the half-erection that had been pushing at his fly was now a screaming, swelling distraction pressed tightly against the wallaby's thigh, which drove relentlessly forward.

Neither of them talked, or even so much as moaned; Ray didn't even really know how to react to the wallaby's forward actions. Steve kept pressing and the wolf kept letting him, trapped as he was but not wanting at all to move. If someone came by at that moment and saw them, he couldn't have cared less as long as the wallaby's paws kept roaming over his shoulders, down his sides and over his rump.

Steve's tongue was left to do all the work when the wolf just lost control of his mouth, and the wallaby made sure not to seem too insistent, satisfied to maintain languid contact without concentrating, as Steve was busy moving on to other things, like Ray's tail. He would stroke it from base to tip, pulling it up the whole time, skritching right up against the button-flap on the wolf's jeans, and that would make Ray clench and hunch forward. It was oddly pleasurable, and finding a new place his body liked to be touched was always fun. This time he did moan, right down Steve's throat, and he did nothing to stop the wallaby from unbuttoning that button and putting his fingers in places fingers had never been before. An exposed board dug into his back, but it only helped aid Steve's deliberate, lustful touches front and rear.

* * *

An exposed shelf in the side of the sleeper dug into his back, but it only helped aid Steve's deliberate, lustful touches front and rear. Ray's paws were busy propping him against the oddly-shaped cubbyholes where the wallaby's clothes and cold-weather supplies were stored. It's just like the first time all over again, the wolf thought, because Steve's fingers were in the same places— skritching around his tail base, and scrambling over his fly looking for an easy way into the tight jeans—they always had been.

If the wallaby was anything, he was predictable, and whether or not it was purely for Ray's sake he didn't know. He did know what logically would happen next, and ultimately, and the hope attached to that knowledge forced a whimper from his muzzle into Steve's, which the wallaby accepted and swallowed greedily, silently.

Steve's fingers worked deftly, and the wolf's pants were around his ankles, suspended by one upraised foot (Ray'd always done that when they kissed; it was so very gay and he couldn't help it, even with Janie). As the wallaby planted kisses all over the poofed-out fur of his neck, Ray flexed his erection against the inadequate confines of his boxer shorts and into Steve's waiting grasp. And grasp it he did: parting the open fly, then separating flesh from fur, the wallaby was stroking a fully-knotted wolf with all the practiced skill of a man who wasn't married on the side with two daughters.

The only other sound above the thrumming diesel engine was the gentle clacking of Steve's wedding band on the plastic cubbyhole behind Ray's arched back and tail.

At last, Steve decided to pull away from the kiss a bit, and when he did Ray could see just how much he'd been working after all: the wallaby was breathing hard, his lips moist, his blunted snout just as such. He did not look directly at the wolf, but instead seemed to be looking at a point on his upper chest, as if making eye contact meant admitting something distasteful or weak. Then the wallaby tugged on Ray's shirt, and they managed to get that off without unbuttoning it, and it was only then that the wolf felt just how hot it was inside the truck. A flick of some unseen switch and they were plunged into country darkness.

A bar of arc-sodium light, eerie and yellowish and lonely, illuminated the two males in partial silhouette through the windshield. Ray's erection stood out in stark relief, immodest and shiny and throbbing in the small open space between them. The boxers did no good now. With his unrelenting and steady paw, Steve hooked two fingers behind the wolf's knot and squeezed. Predictably, still after all those years, the member twitched and oozed two thick gobbets of precum, which stood at the tip without quite dripping down its length.

Ray stood and looked down at himself with a kind of detached wonderment: I never do that with Janie; she wouldn't be pleased to know what it takes to get me to pre. As if watching from a perspective outside his experience, the wolf saw his paw fall over Steve's, and squeeze gently. This time, the drops of precum (they seemed to glow from within) made their reluctant journey down to his sheath, pooling there and clinging to the short fuzz.

Just like Ray was expecting, the wallaby knelt in the confines of the sleeper, his ears splayed rearward in a rare display of submissiveness, the only time he showed it, really. Steve had once warned the wolf never to divulge his weakness for sucking cock, or else suffer a fate worse than death, and Ray had never seen fit to tattle on his friend. He did enjoy the mounting feeling of domination as he petted the wallaby between the ears after removing his cowboy hat with a flick of his fingers. This would be the only chance he got, if he knew Steve like he thought he did.

Letting Ray aim his wolfhood downward, the wallaby leaned forward and tasted long-forbidden fruit.

* * *

"Never, ever tell anybody I'm doing this for you, or else you will suffer a fate worse than death." The wolf nodded as best he could. Aiming Ray's wolfhood down for him, the wallaby leaned forward and tasted like it was forbidden fruit.

His toes and tail curled against the hay in the stall, blending perfectly with the animals surrounding them on both sides. Steve had drug the compliant wolf through a side door and into the 4-H sheep pens, which at first had reeked of stale urine and manure, but Ray's nose had gotten used to the scent quick enough. He felt more like a kid than the rancher's son he was, partly because he was doing something he knew (or at least it was assumed) he shouldn't be doing.

And it thrilled him terribly.

Not to mention his cock, fairly underused until today, when a random guy (A guy! Ray's brain still reminded him, as if it mattered anymore who got him off) decided to take him into the shadows at the fair and make love to him.

Now his pants and briefs (not to mention the poor plush husky) were discarded against the stall wall, no doubt soiled with sheep matter, but it just might mask the odor of randy wallaby so Ray wouldn't have to answer dubious questions whenever he got home. The wolf leaned against the back wall, Indian-style and effortlessly comfortable on a pile of slightly damp hay.

Steve (how could he stand to keep his clothes on?) knelt prostrate between Ray's legs, bobbing at the torso in a comical sort of prayer fashion. Ray would get used to the feeling of the warm muzzle on his cock long enough to notice the way Steve's tail would tilt to and fro like one of those weeble things and find it amusing, then the wallaby would do something new and unexpected with his tongue to send the wolf's eyes rolling again. "Erf," he said as he felt Steve lapping at the edge of his knot, and gyrated his hips against the straw in approval. He petted the wallaby's head in dominant complement to Steve's show of submission.

But Steve wasn't really the kind of person you would think to be such a bottom… Bottom, that was the word Ray assumed was used in a situation like this. So, when it's a guy and a girl, is the girl always the bottom, even when she's on top, or does it matter what she's doing, or— "Guh!" as Steve actually got his tongue inside his sheath, against the very root of his member, a place he'd never even touched himself…and it was good and weird at the same time. The wallaby gagged a little.

"You like to swell up a lot, don't you?"

"I never noticed," the wolf blushed.

"I bet your girlfriends do." And with that, Steve lowered his head again.

A bass, guttural moan took the place of the blush, and the wolf found himself almost drowning in sensation. Then, like sex had a tendency to do, the wolf completely lost track of the time, or the fact that he had an early wake-up tomorrow. He could sleep when he was dead. He had his eyes closed most of the time, but Steve was so damn good at what he was doing that the wolf didn't even need his usual slideshow of fantasies to get him closer to the edge.

Ray did find that it was most difficult to keep from climbing that ladder too fast, and at one point he actually tried to imagine his mother naked…and that was just gross, so he gave up and focused on finishing what had been started.

It was when he finally did look, when he saw that Steve had taken out his cock and was stroking it into the ground, that he found he could not look away. Mostly it was the fact that this was Steve's bag, and he was not merely doing the wolf a favor but taking personal pleasure from sucking him off. Steve was gay, and Ray was not, but he was a willing participant.

Then the wolf saw a confusing picture in his mind, one that excited and scared him at the same time with its novelty. He could see them as a couple, not a couple of guys but together, saw Steve's delicate fingers around his knot and admired them...saw his closed eyes and what they might look like with tears of joy, or sadness... saw a lot of things he knew he was insane to see, but he could not stop them.

And his heart broke. And the wolf was filled with a love for Steve he could never have mustered for Janie or anyone else. He wanted to give himself to the wallaby, and a second later he was doing just that, biting his paw to stifle the full-throated yelling of a wolf in orgasm, as Steve fought to swallow what must have been an unusually copious load.

When the stars faded from his vision, Ray saw Steve sitting back against the door of the stall, still stroking a little and picking at his teeth. "Tanks," he said around a claw, "I hadn't gotten to do that in, like, a long time, so I thought I was out of practice. Feel good?"

Ray was still reeling a bit, but recovering quickly. Already he felt his desire draining away, and even though he was sure most of the things he had experienced were true and heartfelt, they were fading even faster. "I know it sounds unoriginal, but that's the best blowjob I've ever had. Never shot in somebody's mouth, and certainly not a guy's."

"But it felt good."

"Oh, yeah."

"Then that's all that counts," the wallaby replied, and clicked his tongue.

"But what about you? I'd feel bad if I didn't..." Ray circled his paw.

Steve waggled an index finger at the wolf. "I was just thinking the same thing. Now, since I was the bottom, you can be pretty sure what I'd like." Ray had seen that coming, but hearing it from the wallaby's muzzle was a different thing entirely. Now that his testosterone was effectively leveled out for the evening, it didn't seem like that promising a prospect. It was romantic and all looking at Steve's fingers and such, but now it was, well, really raw and physical.

"And I knew you were going to do that too," said the wallaby before Ray could struggle to make a complete sentence. He crawled over to the wolf and set a reassuring paw over his sheath, rubbing life into it once again. Ray had to admit, it sure felt great when Steve touched him. Maybe he really knew what he was doing? Maybe? "Don't worry. I've done this before, as if you couldn't tell. I can make it so that you don't feel anything but pleasure. If it didn't feel good, there wouldn't be any homos out there. Right?" The matter-of-factness was stunning.

Ray nodded at this absurdity, laughing a little just because he thought it was expected of him. Hell, he was already a couple inches out and growing; that meant another climax was now well within range if he worked for it. "Promise?"

Steve leaned in and planted another of those light, yet deeply intimate, kisses on the lupine muzzle. By the time the wallaby was done, Ray was fully unsheathed, which surprised them both. Steve grinned, "I can see you're a very eager puppy," and broke into a full-on smile when the wolf murred at the term. He was finding—and pushing—buttons Ray never knew he had, and the wolf once again found himself accepting it and welcoming it. This was just a night for weak constitutions.

The rest of the night became a blur to Ray, but would come back to him in sections of uncompromising clarity in later days (before his marriage; after, life kind of just erased it bit by bit), often creeping into his mind during sex with Janie...many times, it was the thought of Steve in bed with him, cuddling him, fucking him that would get him off quickly and intensely. He actually ended up using it to time simultaneous orgasms, and weren't those just about the best things ever.

Later on in their relationship, Steve would teach Ray a lot of what he needed to know about sex. Well, sex with other men. And Ray would soak it all up like a sponge, but that was later on. This one night, this first night, the wolf just lay back and let life happen to him, climb on top of him, and come inside him. It was incredible how the wallaby, as experienced as he was, could muster the patience to let Ray become comfortable at his own pace.

First with a finger under his balls and then a well-placed tongue (rimming would not be part of Janie's repertoire, and Ray would end up hating her in a way for that), the wolf had plenty of time to adjust to the awkward pleasure of it all before Steve actually poked something inside him. Granted, it was just a finger, but for a start it was enough. They must have spent the better part of an hour in the whole act; the wolf found that Steve's naturally slender cock was a perfect fit for a person like himself ("ass-virgin" was what the wallaby called it).

But, even more memorable and clearer than the sex, was what Ray saw while he was on his back, matting down the fur of one paw where he practically bit it in half because he was moaning so loudly. Steve was a man with a purpose, and he was the kind of man who would go after his purpose in a direct, straight line, almost with too narrow a focus, but when he went after it, nobody better stand in his way. The way the wallaby dominated him that first night, with a fragile balance of empathy and selfishness, was a major contributor to the wolf's final climax: he would make sure Ray was okay, and when Ray said yes, his hips would fly. Steve was a silent partner, but nothing could help the sounds of their coupling.

For the second time now, the wolf felt himself being drawn— there wasn't much about this that was voluntary, really, except consent—toward the end, through no manipulation of his own. He was okay with it, because he'd pretty much given up to just experiencing more than anything. Steve was actually grunting too, the first signs of the wallaby's own loss of composure. The wolf's tailhole was almost numb, but the intense pressure there kept him going, going, going.

And then he was gone.

* * *

The wolf was gone.

Steve continued to pound away, his fingers in a death grip on the top bunk for support, but Ray had already checked out mentally. The truck thrummed beneath his side-turned head, and he could hear clearly the rumble through the one ear that was mashed against the grey vinyl wall of the sleeper. He was feeling good, sure he was, but he was also carefully gauging the wallaby's actions through until the end of their affair. He knew, absolutely knew, that Steve had come by purely on accident, but from the time he stepped onto the parking lot it had seemed scripted.

And this was why the wolf wasn't paying as much attention to his cock or Steve's cock in him or anything else external, but why this night—like the majority of nights spent with Steve when they had been together—was turning out as predictable as ever. As far as he could remember, the wallaby had always been a bit repetitive and aloof. When it came to them as a couple, Ray always put, but Steve neither agreed nor disagreed, there was always an air of vagueness. That air hadn't ever bothered Ray, per se, but it didn't feel like that belonged as part of a relationship.

Ray no longer had clumps of comforter in his paws; it was hay, damp and odiferous. The semi's engine became more distant, an old Ford or diesel-powered carnival truck idling in the parking lot just on the other side of the 4-H pens. There was a wind picking up outside, and though there was no conceivable way for it to happen the wolf swore he felt a cool, humid draft enter through some crack or other. Even the soft bleating was audible, so vivid was Ray drawn into the past and his first encounter with the controlled, confident, changeless wallaby who now hovered over him with a grim grin and closed eyes, about to blow.

Of course Steve wasn't in love with him anymore, if he had been at all; they both had wives and families and lives outside of this. It was entirely possible that the wallaby still held some level of affection. You couldn't do what they did, as intensely and for as long as Ray had done with Steve, and not feel at least something for the other person for the rest of your life. There's always something there, something unique and special and shared, and no matter how much changes in seventeen measly years it doesn't go away.

But Ray knew what had changed, and it was him... rather, his view of things. First it was puppy-lust (literally), and that grew into affection and full-blown love in the months the wolf was involved with the wallaby, and it wasn't the simple collusion between love and lust either. But now he saw that Steve had had a different view of things, a more casual view, and it was the wolf's mistake for being too young and stupid and—no, not stupid. Just alive. But he didn't hold Steve's ambivalence against him then, and it would do no good to do so now. Besides, when put into perspective, nothing had changed at all.

A purple velvet curtain drew over his vision, his toes curled, and his tail thrashed against Steve's balls. The wolf wished that Janie would learn to like playing with his tailhole, even if she viewed it as "icky." Ray would do much more disgusting things to her in return, if she would only get over her proctophobia. There was a puddle of wolf drool under his muzzle, a stain that was joined by other multiple stains from his second release. Like most other times, Steve's cock was enough to milk the semen from him by itself. The wolf realized he would stink to high heaven when he got home, but by now it was unavoidable.

Steve came to a crashing crescendo a moment or two later, apparently having been waiting on the wolf's spasming hole to bring him over. For once, the wallaby did utter a couple grunted f-words while he struggled to hold his shaky legs steady. Ray managed to pull the curtain from his vision to watch Steve wipe a heavy layer of sweat off his brow and deposit it onto one quivering thigh, then meet his eyes with that same old I-Just-Conquered-You look. The wolf wondered how many men, if any, Steve had conquered since 1991. He didn't seem as out of practice as he had indicated.

As usual, Steve didn't waste time on pillow-talk after he'd busted his nut, which Ray had also predicted would happen. The wolf had never been one for it either, so no big loss there. Steve did take care to pull out slowly, though, for which Ray was eternally thankful and wrong in his prediction, for once. After wiping down, the wallaby tossed a much-used cum towel (it had the word "Woof!" embroidered on it in garish black lettering) to the wolf, who cleaned his groin and the bed.

"I'm gettin' a smoke in. Want one?" Ray was just finishing up with the towel, but Steve had already thrown on his pants and pulled a heavy jacket from one of the laundry cubbies on the side. Yup, same old wallaby, all the way down to the cigarette after sex. If it were up to Ray, it would be ice cream, but ice cream was a little less masculine. Not to mention, not part of the menu behind Morrissey's counter.

"I'll join you," pulling on his own clothes with more care. There would be no question to stay the night, no offer of another drink, or another round. "But I'll smoke my own, thanks."

"Suit yourself, pansy." Steve hopped outside and closed the door, and it was then that Ray paused, lacing one shoe. He sighed; his rear was pleasantly sore, he reeked of man-on-man sex, and he had just relived an integral part of his younger days and found the answers to some questions he'd never really thought to ask, or needed to anyway. All in all, not the most boring night at the bar.

When he got outside, the wallaby was already two cigarettes down; he could smell the difference between a lighter light and a butt-to-butt light. The wolf leaned against the truck and offered his smoke, and Steve touched it off.

"Thanks."

"Ayuh."

It was getting on time for Ray to be expected home; even if Janie was already asleep he would wake her up coming in no matter how deep she was under. Standing there, against the idling truck with smoke drifting into the half-dead maple above, with nary a wind to disturb anything, Ray knew Steve was thinking. Hard. And the only reason he knew this was that there had been so few times when Steve looked like this. Eyes squinty but focused on an imaginary point on the ground, muzzle drawn down in a painless-pain sort of way, mindlessly flicking his cig after it was devoid of ash.

"Penny for 'em."

"The fuck does that mean?"

"You look like you're thinking hard on something. Penny for your thoughts." Ray took a drag and watched Steve's face carefully.

The wallaby smiled faintly. "Smartass." That was true, to a point. "Not thinkin' about much. That feel as good as ever?"

Ray flexed his cock, still a little hard, and his knot throbbed in response. "You don't know how much you miss something until you've gone without it for so long. It's like poison, the way it felt."

"Poison? Huh. I guess so."

"As much as I love my wife, there are some things she just can't do."

"So she says."

"So she says."

43

"She'll come around if you make it worth her while." Steve drug in an extended breath, drawing the glowing ember line on the Marlboro down past the filter, and blew it out rather forcedly. "I gotta beat feet. My load picks up in La Junta, last night. A few hours ago. I'll be fine, but I have to get rollin'. My clock's running out."

"I understand. Didn't expect you to stick around too long anyway; it's not like you." Ray's thoughts faintly touched on the raw truthfulness of that for a split-second, but he really didn't mean it that way. If Steve noticed, he hid it.

"Get tired in one place. You're different; you can do it no problem. You know, sometimes I wish I were you." And Steve gave Ray a hug that fell somewhere between homo- and heterosexual, patting him on the back while their crotches ground against one another.

"Nah, you don't want to be me. Wishing is good, but it only gets you so far. You got family waiting for you."

"So do you. You going to tie one more on or call it a night?"

The wolf ground his cigarette under a boot. "I'm tired, no wonder there. Got an early day tomorrow."

"Every day here is an early day."

"Right."

"See you around, puppy," slapping the wolf's shoulder before climbing back in, and it sounded so damn expected. Ray was only halfway to his own car before he heard the wallaby grinding into gear and taking off in a cloud of fine night-dust down south towards Denver.

* * *

Ray's Silverado was like Diet Diesel, but comforting nonetheless as he made his way leisurely home. He selfishly relished the rough ride against his rump, and he couldn't stop his tail from waggling against the bench every time he hit a set of railroad tracks and jounced over. Regret and satisfaction fought for his thoughts, and in the end the wolf settled for just letting himself feel good for getting laid like he hadn't been in years. And, unless he met Steve down the line, never would be again.

There had been a point after, when they were smoking, when Ray had wanted to ask a bunch of emotional touchy-feely questions about them, and their relationship, and other things, just to try and get an answer out of Steve. To try and understand why things had gone like they had. But the more he thought about it, the more Ray didn't see the need for questions. He may have been justified, but he also had slowly come to the conclusion that he could live without more questions and answers. He hadn't agonized over it through his adult life, and he hadn't suffered mentally for it either. Not really; that's not the way you lived out here in Green Hill, Colorado. People with issues lived in the city. In Denver. Even Laramie. You could at least still accomplish something there.

No lights greeted him as he turned into the end of his driveway and shut off the engine, letting the truck roll the rest of the way to the garage. Maybe, just maybe, Janie would stay asleep this time. Either way, the wolf would need a thorough shower before climbing into bed.

Guy, his Dalmatian, trotted to the front of his run at the side of the house to welcome Ray home, and the wolf gave him a few pats on the head before checking his food and water. For once, his son had remembered to do his chores...at least one chore. Guy circled himself back to sleep, and Ray eased open the back door and stepped inside.

Every time Ray came home from the bar, most times after two o'clock when his family and most of the town was asleep, he marveled at the difference between day hours and what he liked to call "Oh-Dark-Hundred." Everything that was part of their lives, everything that beeped and whirred and whooshed and moved at all—it was gone at night, and Ray could be the only person on the planet for all he knew, or cared. Then the refrigerator cycled and dropped a noisy load of ice, and the spell was broken.

Chuckling at his morbid romanticism, Ray stripped in the kitchen and threw his clothes down the laundry chute. He would do them in the morning, while Janie cooked breakfast. Jesus, was it only four hours away?

Janie was turned away from him when he sidled around the bedroom door and eased it shut behind. Tiptoeing across the carpet, the nude wolf actually let himself think he was home free to the bathroom when his wife rolled onto her back and mumbled, "Djuvun?"

"What?" Ray whispered back, because not answering would do no good anyway.

"Did you have fun?" She wasn't really talking to him as much as into her pillow, just awake enough to make sure Ray got into bed before zonking out again.

"Lots. Had sex with a guy in his truck. It was nice."

"Wuh?"

"Had a Sex On The Beach for the first time. It was nice," Ray said, smiling at his deviousness. He crawled onto the bed on all fours, an idea growing his smile into a full-toothed sneer.

"Oh, okay. What are you doing, hun?" as Ray uncovered her nude body, still perfectly slim after so many years of marriage, especially to him. He spread her legs, turning her onto her back, and she was so sluggish she didn't even react when he licked long and lovingly over her sex. "Ray, no...oh, not now, Jeezus." But the last words were more moaned than spoken, and the wolf's second lick across her clitoris triggered an explosion of scent across his tongue. What could he say? Steve had left him horny still, and Janie was just as good a lover. Minus a cock.

It didn't take long to complete the act. Ray knew they both had an early morning, and Janie would complain all day long about him getting her all worked up in the middle of the freaking night, but he knew that secretly she would be grateful. It was a matter of minutes, spent pushing each one of her buttons, one by one—much like Steve had done to him—before she writhed on the bed, grinding upwards into his muzzle as she came. Mostly silent, Ray took special satisfaction in getting the whole of his tongue inside her as she twitched herself down from orgasm.

After that, just like Ray had expected, Janie was dead to the world and nothing would bring her back into it except the morning alarm. She would only remember the sex, not the smell of wallaby or anything else out of place. Assuming she did smell wallaby on him at all.

The water would take a minute to warm up, and despite the late hour the wolf had every intention of taking his time...after all, he was good and hard again and he could pump another one out, with just his thoughts and nothing to bother him or tell him all was not right with the world. Because at this moment, it sure seemed that way. When it came down to brass tacks, Ray thought as he stepped into the steaming cascade of his modest but adequate shower, predictability didn't always have to be a bad thing. Expectation could be half the fun. It had been with Steve, and it was getting to be that way with Janie too. And if things changed, they did so with a speed that could be predictable in itself.

Hot water was good on his ears and face, and Ray drank it in with predictable pleasure.

Sometimes things never change. Sometimes they change too much.

And sometimes, but luckily not too often, they get better with time.

Life is messy, unpredictable. Our most cherished plans and deepest convictions can be altered or destroyed in an instant. Still, there's only one way to get through it, and that's one step at a time.

The Long Walk

Sylvan Scott

One: First Steps

Cloudless blue stretched infinitely over the sprawling landscape of South Dakota. Castor licked his muzzle watching heat ripple off the highway. The coyote's fur had thinned to its summer coat but still felt too heavy for July. Feet aching and back sore from his day's hike, he nonetheless felt calm. Carrying a backpack over five hundred miles had hardened more than just his feet. In his dust lay the voices, faces, and troubles of a high school life. Ahead, beyond the Rockies, lay his future. Looking at the sky—so broad and endless—emphasized the twelve hundred miles remaining.

In a town called Cactus Flat he'd deviated from his planned route. The Buffalo Gap grasslands were dry with drought and that morning a walk through the badlands had sounded like an exciting detour. Time wasn't important. The opportunity to immerse himself in the ancient, worn heart of sandstone hills called to his coyote soul like a siren to a sailor. Ten miles further southwest and he was sipping soda beneath a tin awning while the sun set.

Tomorrow he would enter the national park and walk between the buttes and valleys on his way…somewhere.

"Nowhere" was how his father described it. "'Nowhere' is where you're going, Castor; nowhere or an early grave."

The post-graduation hike was his only real act of defiance in an otherwise torpid teenage life. To hear his father speak, he'd practically become a Hell's Angel. The judgment was simple: he was damned for defying his father's wishes. Whether for his collegiate destination or sexual orientation, in his father's eyes he was lost. Castor had come to grips with being gay years before. His father, on the other hand, had only found out recently.

"You'll end up in a bad way," the balding coyote had admonished.

"It's only Washington State," Castor had said. "This isn't about who I sleep with; it's about my education." He didn't mention Taylor, the bobcat he'd been dating online for three months, was also going to meet him in Seattle.

"Oh? And how you going to get there? I will not pay for a sodomite to fly across the country to go to some liberal, hippy college!"

Castor hadn't expected quite so much vitriol. He'd answered with one of his thin smiles. "Well, then, I guess I'll have to walk."

And he had.

Even though he'd gotten the message on his smart phone that Taylor wanted to "keep their options open" and was now eyeing New Mexico, he hadn't let the news change his course. It hurt but Castor faced it with the same stoicism he'd shown when his mother—with a drunk and slurring tirade—had left his father and him a decade before. He was young, determined, and away from home for the first time in his life. He'd deal.

It felt good.

The smell of slowly roasting meat drifted out from the small convenience store. It made his stomach rumble. "Sunday Night Dinner" was advertised on the store window and, judging by the aroma, meant a rib roast. He tried to not think about food and focused on where he was going to sleep that night.

He'd planned his route to follow small, cheap motels. The money from his college fund would see him through if he was careful. Still, he hadn't counted on this detour town being so postage-stamp small. Around him stood only a few old, wind-scoured houses. The population was less than seventy. Aside from the convenience store/

gas station, there didn't appear to be any other businesses in town aside from the local church. His father's relationship with God left him feeling uncomfortable asking to stay there.

From inside the store a lynx with closely-shaved fur strode out into the evening sun. He walked past Castor towards his pickup. He was handsome and muscular; nice eye-candy. An idea sprawled through Castor's head.

"Excuse me," he said. He half-jogged after the cat.

Castor didn't make it a habit of talking to strangers. Still, he didn't know that he'd get a chance to question many others who knew the area before sundown.

Plus, the guy was cute.

The crew-cut lynx turned. His fur color spoke to the upper Midwest where the forests ran up against the Great Lakes. Even though he'd cropped it close and tight all over his body, the soft amber wasn't obscured.

"I noticed your license plate," Castor said, drawing close. "You from around here?"

The lynx nodded. "'Bout sixty miles west, for what it's worth." He shrugged. "I'm on the road most of the time."

Castor smiled. Up close, the man smelled of the dry, baked landscape. His tattered jeans also made him look rugged: something that appealed to the coyote. "I was wondering if you knew where I could find a motel or something."

The lynx shook his head slowly. "Around here? Not much unless you want to head up north to the Interstate. Big tourist trap 'bout twenty miles up that way; lots of motels. On the other side of the Badlands. I guess there's the lodge in the park, but that's mostly cabins that charge through the nose."

Castor nodded. "Thanks; I suppose I can head up that way." He shouldered his pack and affected a sigh. "I appreciate it." He'd rarely hit on anyone in the non-Internet world but thought his tone and body language were good enough without being too obvious. Besides, it wasn't flirting if all you really wanted was a ride. He put on his best, worn-by-life posture, and started north.

A moment later the lynx called after him. "You got a tent in there?" he asked.

Castor looked from his pack to the stranger. He had packed both a miniature tent and sleeping bag before leaving. He'd "roughed it" several times already. Castor cocked his head. "Yeah, I do."

"There are campgrounds in the Badlands. That's where I'm headed. I can give you a lift if you like."

Castor gave the man another look. He was a few years older and his demeanor made him seem earthy. The cat's lean, rough physique spoke of hours working outdoors; his old, worn sunglasses: plenty of time under the bright sun. He was handsome and knew the area.

"You're camping there? Not driving home?"

"I usually do when coming through at night. Don't like the winding roads in the dark," he admitted.

It was a fair answer. But there was something extra in his voice; a sound of—perhaps—interest. The coyote put on the thin smile he'd been told was "enigmatic" and sauntered back towards the lynx. He'd play things by ear. The ride would be a nice change of pace and, along the way, he'd get some nice scenery.

"Sounds good," he said. He put his paw forward. "I'm Castor."

The lynx took it, firmly, and smiled. "Bryce. Pleased to meet'cha."

Castor lingered just a bit on the handshake and caught a gleam in the man's eyes.

The ride was bumpy but relatively short. Baked asphalt roads wound from the base of the eroded canyon walls up to their peaks over the course of just a couple miles. They dove up and down towards the setting sun until the campground sprawled before them.

In less than an hour, outside his tent, Castor learned that the thing he'd heard in Bryce's voice was more than "interest."

The lynx was stocky and powerfully built. He was as sculpted as the windswept hills and as stark as the pale buttes. His paws firmly held Castor's shoulders as he lay him back against a low rise amongst the sage. The wild herbs filled the coyote's nostrils. He swallowed nervously. The scale of the lynx was daunting.

Bryce ripped open the younger man's fly—the button lost in the wild scrub—and exposed his bare thighs and sheathed sex.

The warm night air tickled Castor's tip, already emerging. The big man didn't bother removing any other clothes but his pants and pushed Castor back against the hard, flaky ground with masculine firmness. His own sex was hard and thick and he slicked it up with spit and pre-cum. Before Castor knew what was happening, before he could prepare for it, the lynx's thick, bulbous tip was pushing between his cheeks and squeezing inwards.

Castor arched his back and gasped.

The lynx, his strength in his whole body, not just his arms, pushed steadily. His grin widened.

The coyote's eyes opened wide and his mouth gasped. He strained to accommodate the near-equine thickness of his rough lover.

"God; w...w...wait!" he gasped. His breaths were short and he could barely speak. He wriggled against Bryce's big, blunt paws.

Bryce slowed down but didn't stop. His steady, slow thrusts stretched their way into Castor's rear as he leaned in over the slender man. His sharp, white teeth reflected in the burgeoning moonlight and his hot breath wafted over Castor's ear.

"I'll wait, but not forever..."

Castor caught his breath at his big lover's words. His legs were up over Bryce's hips; one shoe had fallen off and his toe claws had cut through his socks. Coyote paws were large and broad, good for running, and he was so aroused he could feel the whole of the night air through them. He could feel the whole world through every inch of his body.

Each push, each twist of the cock in his ass made Castor gasp.

The lynx's eyes narrowed; his expression of earnest desire. "Ready for more?" His voice made something in Castor melt.

"I'm... I'm ready," he gasped. He wasn't, he couldn't have been—but he felt the thickness halfway into him already. He knew this had to happen.

Bryce nodded. He gripped Castor's shoulders even more firmly and slid his hips forward.

The hard shaft plunged deep into the coyote sending shudders of pleasure with slight pain through his body. He arched his back and yelped, loudly. He panted and gasped through muzzle and nostrils simultaneously. Inch after inch slid into him and then buried itself up to the hilt.

Bryce initiated a slow, steady rhythm that thrust him in and out of Castor's body.

The lynx increased his pace, moments stretching into minutes. Soon Castor felt as if he had become part of some machine: he clenched and strained around the strong man's sexual will. His bare cock was fully unsheathed and throbbing in the night air. Patches of Bryce's stomach fur brushed against its tip.

Ten minutes and then fifteen passed. His lover's powerful face never left Castor's sight; Bryce's eyes locked on the coyote's. Then, amidst shorter and shorter breaths, the sexual thrusting peaked in an eruption of warmth deep within Castor's body. He nearly climaxed from this alone. The fur on his belly beneath his exposed shaft was wet with his own secretions. He howled like his primitive ancestors: high-pitched and strong. Bryce just snarled and lowered himself onto his mate. Finally, he pressed his chest firmly against the coyote, muzzle-to-muzzle.

Warm lynx lips pressed against Castor's. Castor felt as if his body had expanded. He was more than a single organism; he was part of this great, hulking lynx. The two of them were so tightly bound he didn't know where he ended and Bryce began. They lay for a long time, arms around each other, on the dusty clay.

A few hours later the dull orange rays of the rising sun sketched their way across the stark canvas of the South Dakota badlands. Castor sketched it, idly, in his artist's pad. It wasn't much but his hope was to have a visual chronicle of his trip when he was done. He knew he still had a long road ahead but, as he flipped back to examine a drawing he'd done of Bryce, it felt longer, now. The image of the sleeping lynx looked like an angel. Last night hadn't been what Castor had expected. The experience had given him new ideas; new compass points. He wondered whether the traveling Bryce would find the idea of Pacific Northwest appealing.

TWO: GRADUATION

(+5 Years)

Clinking glasses, rowdy conversation, bursts of laughter, a decades-old pop song, and the smell of greasy french fries surrounded Castor like a fog. Big Bill sat across from him nursing a Tom Collins. Bryce had already stumbled out to catch a cab back to the university district. It left Castor with the uncomfortable conversation he'd been dreading ever since his father's old friend had arrived.

"He's a nice guy," Bill said. "I don't think you could have done much better." Clearly he was talking about Castor's boyfriend.

"Thanks; he's been my rock."

The Blue Moon was busier than ever. With classes out for the semester and summer stretching out its offer of parties, casual sex, retail jobs, and impromptu road trips, the area around campus was about to get much quieter. But tonight everyone was celebrating the survival of another year. The blue neon crescent over the door cast its light through the window over Castor's fur. It wasn't a gay bar. It wasn't even one of his usual hang-outs. Normally, when out and about, he'd cruise the scene at Changes. But Bill probably wouldn't have felt comfortable anywhere but a more traditional place. He'd come a long way to visit and, on a machinist's salary, Castor didn't think the high-end drinks at a more trendy spot would work.

Castor's father hadn't come.

Bill sighed. "Castor, your father still..."

"Don't say he still loves me," he sighed. "Five Christmases have gone by without a call. Five birthdays without so much as a card dropped in the mail; if that's love, he has a funny way of showing it."

"Maybe," Bill admitted, "But your father; he's just... conflicted."

The coyote raised an eyebrow. "Conflicted? Is that what they call being ashamed of your son?" He knew that the big bull was trying to help but alcohol and emotions were getting in the way. "Most people get conflicted about whether they'll have the lager or the ale; they don't toss them out because one isn't what was expected."

A puzzled look descended over Bill's bovine face. He cocked his head in the slight way that any of the large-horned races did when in crowded areas.

Castor gritted his teeth. "Ok, not a good analogy. But my point stands: he didn't want to come. He's been ignoring me since I graduated high school. That's not 'conflicted.'"

Bill frowned. "Fair enough. Would you prefer I used the term 'bigoted'? 'Hate-filled'? Come on, Castor; he's your father."

Castor's scowl deepened. "Then he can start acting like it. I have a life, a successful education and he wanted no part of that simply because I like to suck cock and fuck guys." His voice was louder than he'd wanted. A few people at a neighboring table cast a glance his way. "Until he's able to accept that about me, he's not 'conflicted.' He is a bigot and hate-filled! Ok?"

Bill shook his head slowly. "Castor, listen…"

"No, I'm done listening. If my father really wanted me in his life, he'd see that the only thing pushing me away is him."

The bull's face became solid and unmoving. They didn't talk for at least ten more minutes. Slowly, he finished his drink. Finally, he stood. "Coming out isn't just hard for the person doing it," he said. "It's a challenge for everyone." He took his coat off of the back of his chair and shrugged it over his broad shoulders. "You say he hasn't contacted you in five years; that he's cut you off? Fine. But when did you make any overtures after you left? When was the last time you tried to see if he was willing to change other than the email to invite him to your graduation ceremony?"

The coyote didn't answer.

Bill stepped close and patted Castor on the shoulder. "I get it, kid; I really do. But these things go both ways. I've seen your father; I know how he feels. He's trying to process all this, and yes, he could be going about it in a better way. But there's more to acceptance than demanding it. You have to build bridges."

The awkwardness between the two settled into the cracks and crevasses of the surrounding conversations. Despite the crowd the room suddenly felt more private and personal. Castor hardened his jaw but nodded anyway. "Maybe I'll call," he finally said.

Bill nodded. "See that you do," he said, "or we'll have another talk." He smiled at the younger man. "I'm stubborn; I won't forget."

"Neither will I," Castor said. "But remember: I only said 'maybe.' I have to think about it."

"Fair enough."

Bill didn't mince words. He took his cowboy hat off of the rack near the table, put it on, and nodded to the college graduate.

He'd be in town for another day or so, but Castor was pretty sure that they wouldn't talk again.

"Congratulations," the bull said. Bill ducked beneath the door frame and left the Blue Moon.

Finishing his beer, Castor wiped foam from his muzzle. A few minutes later he got his coat and walked out into the night. He thought about grabbing a cab, but this was one of the rare Seattle nights that wasn't damp. Besides, he wanted to try and walk off his buzz. He wasn't a big drinker but the stress of the last few days had been brutal.

By the time he reached home he was still lost. He unlocked the security door, climbed the stairs, went down his floor's dim hallway, and unlocked the apartment door. It was nicely warm— just how he liked it—with the garlic-y smell of a sausage pizza in the air. Bryce was sitting in the living room, an open delivery box on the coffee table.

"You're just in time," he said. "The delivery guy just left."

"It wasn't like in the porno films, was it?" Castor quipped. The joke was light but his voice was tinged with darker emotions from the conversation with Bill.

"Nah. The only tip I gave was cash," Bryce replied. "I just needed something to soak up all the beer in my stomach."

"You know that's an old wives's tale; you're still drunk."

The lynx shrugged. "Well, I left the bar like ninety minutes ago; I've had some time to sober up. Want a slice?"

Castor shook his head.

"Rough night?" Bryce ventured.

"He says I should talk to my father," he replied. "He just doesn't get it. That man has ignored me for five years. When I finally made an overture..."

"Yeah, I know." They'd talked about it quite a few times. "But you went into this knowing that he probably wouldn't come. You even said 'if he refuses me this time, we're finished.' Remember that?"

"You agreed with me."

"Not really," Bryce said. "I just said that you gotta do what you gotta do. That's not the same as approving."

Castor looked at his boyfriend, face darkening. "Look, I don't need people gang-banging up on me."

The words that came from his muzzle were only slightly slurred. Still, he realized how he'd misspoken right away.

"No gang-bangs here, puppy," Bryce said. He rose and walked over to hug his boyfriend. "Unless you want me to call a few people..."

Castor buried his muzzle in the soft fur of Bryce's cheek. He smelled good. The aroma of the pizza laced nicely with the musk of the lynx's pelt and carried just a hint of that salty, Seattle air. It was comforting. He tried to laugh. "Naw; don't call anyone. Let's just see how well you can do on your own." He slid his paw down to caress the firming bulge in his boyfriend's jeans.

"Sounds like a plan," Bryce said.

Sex while drunk, or even buzzed, was never good. The alcoholic haze deadened physical sensation and made for murky memories. The anticipation was always better than (what he could remember of) the experience.

Castor's heart ached. Bill's words still pounded against the bars of his conscience. The choices before him were daunting. Yet here: the man he loved, the man who had pulled up roots to travel to the Pacific Northwest to be with him; wanted him. Castor wanted him in return.

Naked, minutes later they sprawled on the over-sized, second-hand couch. Castor kissed his partner's sex before licking it gently. From between his legs he felt a similar gesture enfold his cock. He moaned at the touch. His hazy mind wondered if it had really been a whole week since they'd last been intimate. He opened his muzzle wider and slowly sucked his way down the length of Bryce's shaft. Impeccably timed, the moist sensation of being swallowed shivered down his cock simultaneously.

He cupped one paw around Bryce's firm rear and pulled himself all the way until his nostrils were buried beneath his partner's large balls. He swallowed and pulled back, varying abrupt suction with pressing Bryce's cock against the roof of his mouth.

The scent of his lover was all he could smell now. The world had exploded in a kaleidoscope of fur and muscle and scent and sex. Rhythm suffused the two as their hands roamed, exploring each other's bodies. Their tongues and mouths caressed the other's hard cock and eagerly coaxed soft sounds of pleasure.

Sex was pleasure; sex with Bryce was… transcendent.

They sucked and stroked; caressed and coupled; moaned and mated as the hours bled into one another through alcohol's blur.

Bryce climaxed last; he always had the most self-control. It was Castor who preceded him each time and, given the lynx's appetites, had to continue past his breaking point a second and—sometimes—a third time to satisfy him. Long after exhaustion had pulled Bryce into sleep Castor found himself trapped between nervous exhaustion and regret. His dark emotions hadn't been soothed, only delayed. His father's shadow loomed over him even in these most intimate of moments.

As dawn spread its smokey, big-city colors across the living room, Castor was still awake. Bryce was snoring softly on the couch. His stocky, naked body lay there as if enticing Castor to curl up against its warm fur.

Castor looked at the clock. Five in the morning.

Two time zones away, his father would be awake soon.

Sighing, he grabbed his wind-breaker and cell phone and headed for the door. Perhaps as he walked to Pike Place to get his coffee his father wouldn't mind an early call. Maybe, just maybe, Bill was right.

THREE: CONVENTION

(+10 Years)

Minneapolis hadn't been his home for a decade. Even when Castor had been a teenager, the urban sprawl never felt comforting or warm. It had its beauty; the stone arch bridge near the old mill ruins overlooking the man-made Saint Anthony Falls was worth it. In winter the landscape took on a stark beauty that he'd never seen anywhere else. During his junior year, when he'd been into landscapes, he'd sketched and painted the natural beauty of the tree-lined Mississippi.

But it had never felt like home.

The downtown convention center was even less welcoming. He had to be there. The bustling buyers and advertising executives at the Consumer Advertising Expo flowed around his booth like ants on a sugar line. Every now and then one of them would pick up a flier or peruse the interactive demo he displayed. The booth for Whitmar Media Group was both prison and fish bowl, with him as the predominant fish. Why his boss had sent someone so ill-at-ease talking to strangers, he didn't know. He suspected that it had something to do with the notion that a "home town boy" would fare better.

He'd come with three others from their office in Portland and was hating every minute of the four-day conference.

"Maybe you'll see old friends," his boss had said. "Catch up with family?"

In the past five years he'd built a life for himself on the West Coast. He didn't want to be reminded of where he'd come from any more than necessary. His bi-weekly calls with his father were enough.

"Hey, Cast." It was Archer: the mongoose from accounting. "Time for your break. Gonna catch a seminar?"

Castor shook his head. "Nah. Those things never tell you anything you didn't already know. It's just an excuse to buoy up the presenter's already over-inflated self-esteem."

Archer laughed at the deadpan response. "Whoa, easy on the cynicism there!"

The two chatted for a moment before the coyote went off to find lunch.

Archer was nice enough. They'd fooled around a couple times back when he had first joined Whitmar. But, like every guy since Bryce, it hadn't lasted.

The lynx had been his first real-world love and Castor relished the time they'd had together. But after graduation they just seemed to have less in common. Castor wanted to see the world; to experience it and maybe meet different guys. Settling down with the first man he met out of high school just seemed… wrong. That Bryce was also constantly pining for the flat Dakotas rather than the deep forests, mountains, and hills of the Pacific Northwest had also been a factor.

The split had been amicable but there had been plenty of tears; most of them Castor's.

After standing in line at the concession stand for far too long, he stepped up to buy an over-priced hot dog with chips. Across the counter appeared a familiar face.

Cats of all kinds had been common in his school but the exotic Analu Tsing had immigrated while a freshman. The lean, muscular golden cat had been a terror both on and off the baseball diamond. Everyone loved how well he played the game and he'd never been without female companionship. His natural physical prowess overshadowed his trouble with the English language and occluded his odious personal habit of beating up the smaller, weaker kids in school.

Kids like Castor.

And here he was, serving hot dogs.

"What do you want?"

The question was flat and uninterested. Castor wondered if Analu even recognized him. He'd been on the receiving end of body-checks and shake-downs enough times that he found it hard to believe the bully had just forgotten.

"Sir? Your order?"

The coyote cocked his head and plastered a thin smile on his muzzle. "Uh, Polish sausage; jumbo. Sauerkraut and mushrooms. Large pop and onion rings."

The cat just nodded, entering the order into the register.

His accent was still thick but there was the faintest Minnesota twang infused with its Asian inflections. Voice alone, though, wasn't the only thing "thick". His body had softened severely since their graduation. If Castor had gone to his five-year reunion, it probably wouldn't have been a surprise. But to see the jock who'd made his life a living hell look so out-of-shape; it made him feel… old.

"Excuse me, but are you from around here?" he asked.

Analu was busy and barely looked up. "Yep; been in the Twin Cities for fifteen years. Guess that's enough to make me 'local'. Why? You too?"

The question dared him to answer it truthfully.

The phrases, "Yes; I'm the one you used to beat up" or "Yeah; you used to take money from me; how's that life of crime working out for ya" both came to mind. The golden cat had been one of the many reasons Castor had used in justifying his decision to go west. He knew that the cat had probably picked on outsiders because he, himself, had been an immigrant and wanted to shore up his own position. But Analu, to look at him, had fallen far from those days. To him, getting the customer's order right was probably the best he could look forward to on any given day. Castor, by contrast, worked on multi-million dollar ad campaigns and was looking to buy his first house in the next year or two.

"No; just here from out-of-town," he lied.

The cat nodded and finished getting Castor's order.

Food in hand, the coyote walked off to the lobby without another word.

He knew that he should probably feel good—or at least better—at seeing his former tormentor doing menial labor at a convention center concession stand. But his pains were years old and the wounds, while once certain to never heal, weren't even a dull throb anymore. Part of him wanted Analu to recognize Castor's success and feel miserable, but that sort of schadenfreude just didn't feel right.

He tried to eat and ignore the chance encounter. Polish sausages were his favorite food-in-tube-form but he barely tasted it.

The rest of the day, attending a seminar on creating ad banners and taking another shift at the booth, passed in a blur.

Old. He felt old.

He knew the saying, "thirty is 'senior citizen' in gay years" and he still had a few to go before reaching that milestone but it already felt ominously true. Hot guys in ample double-digits had filled his bed over the last few years but the flow had trickled from a river to a mere brook.

Then there was his father. He'd considered dropping by his old house for a visit.

Wasn't that what someone who was 'old' did? Visiting estranged and tense relations seemed so movie-of-the-week. He could see it now: going to visit, sitting down, making small talk about everything that wasn't important in his life, and—finally—settling in to watch football with his old man. It sounded… Not terrible.

The fact that he found it even remotely palatable bothered him. What happened to his rage; his passion? Was he losing it?

Or was this something everyone went through?

He didn't want to go to a local gay hangout with Archer nor to the nearby chain sports bar with the other two in their group. Holing up in his hotel room seemed counter-productive and he really needed to get out and clear his head. At the end of the day his feet led him to a small park near the large Basilica. At the edge of downtown, through the twilight, he could see the lights of an art museum and its grounds.

The Loring neighborhood, he'd always heard, was a gay mecca. He'd been too nervous as a teenager to actually check it out in person. Now he was an adult.

The squirrel he met was pretty: slender, athletic, and just a bit effeminate. The sizable bulge in his cut-offs also appealed to several of Castor's Bryce-inspired kinks. The guy wore small, gold earrings and wore a rainbow colored kerchief tied around the base of his tail. They'd started by talking about how no one came to the park to pick up guys anymore but ended with Castor suggesting they renew the tradition.

They shared a quickie right there in the park. The squirrel's muzzle sucked eagerly at Castor's cock and had him moaning for release within minutes. A tease, his one-night-stand made it linger. When Castor climaxed his shouts probably told the rest of the park that cruising wasn't quite dead.

He brought the eager squirrel to a motel he'd found away from his colleagues. There, he reciprocated the squirrel's lusts and tried his best not to gag on the guy's over-sized appendage. He had to rely upon his tongue and hands to tease out as many cries of desire as had come from him.

In his imagination, though, the grey-brown pelt became golden yellow. Feline eyes stared down at him: daring him to step out of line. He stroked and licked his new companion slowly. He lingered on the big tip, unable to swallow most of the shaft. As the night progressed and they pushed their limits, the fellow looked less and less like a squirrel to Castor's aroused imagination.

Analu loomed over the roof of the school, naked and panting as if just crossing home plate. His muscles flexed with each subtle movement and his washboard abs rippled as he stepped one giant paw flat into the middle of the parking lot. His cock, his giant cock, swung heavily between his legs against balls the size of Volkswagens.

Over a hundred feet tall, the titan looked down at tiny Castor and laughed. The low rumble sounded like thunder and, before he could run, the coyote found himself grasped in the golden cat's paw. The naked squirrel who, he realized, had been standing next to him, turned and walked away muttering something about "robbing the cradle."

Castor called after him, begging for him to come back. His voice felt paralyzed and didn't rise above a squeak. He squirmed and begged to be let go but Analu only taunted him in his thick accent.

"You shouldn't have come home, little doggie; you should have stayed where the hippies and liberals could protect you."

Why Castor was naked he didn't know; how he'd come here, he had no idea. The powerful scent of his captor assaulted his nostrils. It smelled like West Coast sea air and the warm fur of a lynx. He was growing aroused despite himself.

"If I eat you," Analu continued, "no one will ever know. You'll have vanished from the face of the earth."

As the giant lifted him towards his sapling-sized fangs, Castor screamed and woke.

The squirrel (what was his name again?) had already left, leaving Castor alone in the motel room. Let the other guys talk about where he'd spent the night; he didn't care. The dream haunted him like everything in his home town.

Naked, he walked over to the small coffee pot on the dresser and turned it on. He knew it would be Midwestern swill but he needed the caffeine.

Castor hadn't thought about his high school friends in years. While he often said, or at least thought, he hadn't had any, that wasn't true. Sue, from pottery class, had been a confidant and friend back when he was first coming out of the closet to himself. She'd understood everything he said about liking boys and how frustrating and unattainable they could seem at times. Then there had been Alex: the geek who tried to get him to like all those bad sci-fi TV shows. At the time, without many people to hang out with, Castor had enjoyed his company even if the entertainment wasn't his cup of tea. And then there had been Hamm. He was the one guy who made going to a hockey game actually interesting. Hamm was one hundred percent German but had come to America when he was just two. The stag had a body that Castor had fantasized over for months but never built up the courage to act upon. He endured all the long, interminable sports that Hamm enjoyed just to spend time with him. Castor's grades and art had suffered that year.

Maybe he should look some of them up. It wasn't as if they'd been enemies; they'd just lost touch. But what about them would they have in common? It had been a decade. What would trying to re-forge old connections really accomplish?

It was especially bad considering the one connection that had been plaguing him for years.

He thought about calling his father and saying, "Guess who's in town?" He could handle it cool and calm as if nothing was out of the ordinary. He wasn't sure what the reaction would be. On the contrary, wasn't growing up all about finding your own way? Why couldn't he just move on?

Still in the hotel room an hour later, he sipped his coffee. He was ready. Dad only lived a few miles away. It was time.

His cell phone rang.

Fishing it out of his pocket he saw Big Bill's caller ID.

"Hey there; Bill?"

The words from the other end doused him like a cold rain.

FOUR: HOME

(+15 Years)

Moans of delight, muffled by a pillow, peaked and fell as Castor rode the wolf beneath him. The smell of morning sex was electric. He lived for times like these; craved them. To come out of sleep to find a warm, moist mouth wrapped around his stiffening cock was better than a half-dozen cups of coffee. Of course he had to turn the slender fellow over and give him what they both really wanted.

Jeremy had the best ass of any man Castor had been with. The wolf took great care of himself, working out daily (but not fanatically) and focusing on his lower half. His legs were great, his calves were great, his feet were great, and his ass was great. Jeremy knew it, too, but carried that knowledge subtly; like a weapon to be produced when he wanted to strike directly at the coyote's hormones.

His sensitive paw pads caressed the back of Jeremy's neck and, with each thrust into his rear, Castor gripped the wolf's shoulders in a tight squeeze. He drove himself in and out, panting with his exertion. The warm inside of his lover's body echoed the warmth of their sheets, now so casually tossed aside.

The bed creaked and groaned. Castor normally would have been concerned. But how could he care about escaping noise when Jeremy was such a screamer? Besides, he liked the sound. Each strain of the mattress echoed his thrusts and made him feel more manly; more like a stud mounting this slender, muscular wolf.

"God, you just aren't slowing... down..."

The gasp from his lover only spurred him on. He wouldn't ever slow down. He'd never grow old, no matter what the years on the calendar said. He'd never grow old, never wither, and never die: that was the credo of the coyote.

He thrust in and out, again and again, his pants becoming snarls. He leaned forward and nipped at the back of Jeremy's neck. The wolf yelped and buried his face deeper in the pillows. Pressure rose within Castor's loins and his racing heart felt like it wanted to burst from his chest. It was the pure exhilaration of early morning sex that made every muscle in his body sing. Only after his cock had pulsed, shuddered, and finally climaxed within his lover did the euphoria begin to ebb. He knew he would have to face the ramifications of their early morning noise. He knew the other person in the house would have heard. He knew he might face an unpleasant scene later on. He knew that it didn't matter.

Not now, not today. Today he was on fire. Today he was alive. He wanted to hold onto that feeling for as long as he could even as it slipped from his grasp like quicksilver. He moaned and buried his face in the fur at the back of Jeremy's neck. The moment was passing and, soon, would be gone.

Castor rolled over. Jeremy reached out to pull him close. His furry warmth beckoned in the cool, bedroom air. He even leaned in and nibbled the coyote's ear, trying to entice him to a second round. Castor wished he could.

"Hey, we've got to wind this down," Castor said. He reluctantly pushed his lover away. "I've got to go and check on dad; make a list of groceries. Bill's coming by for dinner, tonight."

"Those are my jobs," the wolf replied. "Come on; I think I still have a bit more 'oomph' in me."

"I'm sure you do. But how about you save up that 'oomph' for tonight? I've got an interview in three hours." He blushed. "Besides, with all your noise, I should really check on dad."

"My noise?" Jeremy pouted, adopting the look of a wounded lover. "It takes two to tango, hon. As for your dad, you can let me earn my pay, you know."

Castor winked. "I thought you just did..." Jeremy stuck out his tongue as Castor turned and went to the bathroom to shower.

He'd been dating the home care nurse for a year, ever since his father's needs had become more than Castor could handle on his own. Jeremy wasn't like anyone he'd dated before. He was loud, boisterous, overly fond of the Ramones, and had a self-deprecating streak a mile wide. The first wolf he'd ever dated, Castor found the experience similar to riding a souped-up merry-go-round. Every day you could expect the same old views but they'd be sped-up; faster and bumpier than anticipated.

Before he'd met him, he never would have thought he'd want to be with anyone with such a personality. Still, the two clicked

67

better than anyone since Mitchell. And while, at first, he'd been nervous that seeing Jeremy every day while caring for his dad would be too much, it somehow—over time—morphed into something like having a husband. He felt comfortable around Jeremy and Jeremy felt comfortable around him.

When he stepped out of the shower he found Jeremy had fallen back asleep. Castor pulled the blankets over the wolf and went downstairs to check on his father.

Dad was sitting in the kitchen reading the paper. His oxygen tank's hose was pressed under one wheel of his chair. Castor sighed.

"You did it again," he said.

His father looked up with eyes far too pale for a man of his age. "What?"

"Your hose, dad; you rolled on top of it again." He walked forward and found that his father also hadn't engaged the brake on his chair. Rolling him back an inch, he got the hose unstuck and examined it for breaks. It was battered but still usable. "You've got to watch these things."

"That's what I pay that nurse for," he snarled. "How is he, anyway? Tired him out so he can't tend to his patient?"

Castor gritted his teeth. It wasn't like the smell of them having sex could be hidden from a coyote's nose; not even a sick one. His father rarely came out and said anything about the relationship but stewed in a slow burn.

"He comes on duty in another hour; he's just fine." Castor checked the drip hanging from the pole on the back of dad's chair and then the shunt that connected it to his father's arm. It wasn't properly attached and a small trickle of I.V. fluid had pooled on the floor. Sighing, he tightened the hose and went to get a paper towel to clean up the puddle. "I wish you'd wait for one of us to come get you out of bed. It's what we're here for."

"It's what he's here for," his father responded. "I don't know why you're here." He made a show of sniffing the air and scowled. "Then again, maybe I do."

Castor bit back a caustic remark and counted to ten. A rustle of newsprint told him that his father didn't have anything new to add and had returned to his paper.

Chopping up some leftover chicken Castor tossed it in a skillet with some peppers and eggs. He retrieved one of the six bottles of hot sauce from the fridge, took his plate to the table, and sat down across from his father. Dad, as always, had gotten his morning shake but not opened it.

"Dad..."

"Don't start," the coyote snarled. "The stuff tastes like ass."

Castor hid his chuckle behind a fake cough. He had bitten back the question, "And how would you know what ass tastes like" and felt his mood improve infinitesimally. He reached across the table and pulled the tab for his father. Sometimes, he suspected the pain in his father's joints was severe enough that even opening a can was difficult. Dad's pride, of course, would never allow him to admit it.

The two said nothing as they continued their breakfasts.

Jeremy came downstairs a half hour later and brightly checked on Castor's father. Their conversation was considerably less toxic. For all his father's disapproval, he carried on with Jeremy in a manner befitting the nurse's professional capacity in the home.

Castor cleaned up and left the house with a perfunctory farewell. He rode his ten-speed to the park-and-ride a mile away and caught the number twelve bus into downtown.

Dad had hung on better than expected. He'd lasted much longer than the original prognosis. His doctor had confided that it was probably a combination of stubbornness and good, old-fashioned coyote adaptability. Still, the decline persisted. In a way, that made the whole illness more cruel.

No one was expecting dad to last until Christmas.

By midday, the interview was over, having gone as well as expected. Amidst promises of a follow-up call next week, Castor felt confident that his days as a contractor were nearing an end. One of the guys who interviewed him had also asked if he had plans for lunch.

"To talk, more, about your qualifications," he'd said.

The guy was at least ten years younger than him and Castor knew all the signals. He politely declined and made up a story about how he had a doctor's appointment and couldn't eat anything for the next twenty-four hours.

It was nice to know that he still had what it took to turn the young guys' heads.

He got home about an hour before dinner, bag of groceries in hand.

Jeremy was sitting on the front step.

"Oh, thank God," he said. "I tried calling you but I think you left your cell at home and..."

"What is it? What happened?"

Jeremy stammered. "I was taking out the trash and, like an idiot, locked myself out. I knocked and knocked, but I think your father can't hear me. I've been out here for a half hour and..."

"That's Ok, that's Ok... I'm sure he's fine." Castor fished out his keys and opened the front door. The two entered with the coyote's shout, "Dad? Hey, dad? I'm home!"

The television was on in the living room but the wheelchair and its occupant weren't there.

"Dad?"

Jeremy went to check the bathroom and main floor bedroom. Castor headed to the kitchen.

His heart leaped into his throat. Dad was sprawled on the floor beneath the cupboard; an open jar of peanut butter several feet away. The unlocked wheelchair had slid back and was up against the kitchen table.

"Dad!"

The old coyote shakily lifted his head. He snarled and glared with a visual rebuke. "Gonna fire that pansy-ass kid," he spat. He sounded weak, despite his ire. A shadow of embarrassment fell over his features as he struggled to lift himself. Blood flecked his muzzle and he'd clearly not strapped himself into the chair when he'd attempted to retrieve his favorite, now-forbidden, snack.

Castor tossed the groceries aside and came forward, trying to salvage some of his father's dignity by appearing not to do too much work lifting him back up to his chair. Jeremy came in and gasped. "Oh, Jesus..."

"It's only thanks to Jesus I'm still alive," Castor's father said.

Any further insult was swallowed by a wave of coughing. Jeremy re-attached the I.V. and started to wheel him over to the table. Castor waved him off.

"Listen, I'll hang with dad right now," he said. "Why don't you go see if you can find your keys, Ok?"

Jeremy paused for a moment before nodding and leaving the room. He looked stricken and shaken to his core.

Castor knew he'd have to do some serious hand-holding with Jeremy later that night. The situation hadn't been his fault; it was just a mistake. But it was something Jeremy wouldn't forgive himself for without help. Until then, he had his father to deal with. He pulled out a chair and sat down.

"Feeling any better?" His father's coughing fit had died down.

The older man nodded. His soft, yellow eyes stared in the direction that Jeremy had gone. He seemed less angry than expected. When he looked back at Castor, tears were visible.

"I'm… I'm sorry."

"Dad, I don't think…"

"I won't fire him, Ok? I won't to do anything to get him sent away from you."

Silence settled between them. Castor watched his father's muzzle struggle to form the right words. Something seemed to have broken; like a wall coming down in chunks. Dad's aloof demeanor was crumbling before Castor's eyes.

"I… I've never been disappointed in you, Cas," he said. "I know what you must think of me, but I only want to see you happy."

Castor's heart began to race. For nearly half his life his father had withheld approval and love. Now, today, it suddenly dawned on the old man to end that? It struck Castor as selfish audacity. He grew angry.

"Oh, really?" he scowled. "You wanted me happy? Even though I'm fucking your home-care nurse?" Dad winced and looked away. Castor felt a dam of his own starting to break. "You think you can just say a few words and magically wipe away the last fifteen years? Is that what you think?"

Castor's father looked into his lap. His face started to harden. "I had my reasons."

"Yeah, I know! You were always disappointed that I didn't settle down, find a big-breasted bitch to marry, and pop out a dozen-or-so kids! And now—what—you think you can just say 'sorry' and think I'm going to forgive you?"

"I just didn't want you to make the same mistakes I made," his father said, voice cracking.

"Yeah? You ever think that you driving mom away made me the ass-pounding, cock-sucker I am, today?"

He regretted the words the instant they left his mouth.

His father looked him in the eyes, his expression unreadable. The fur around his cheeks was wet and matted. He looked so old, so fragile, that Castor worried his hateful shout might just strike him dead that minute.

Dad let out a long breath. "Your mother left because she found out about Bill an' me... She was never much th' maternal sort and... and, I guess, figured you were part of the whole, stinkin' package of 'wrong' that her life had become."

Castor's heart skipped a beat. "What?" he gasped.

His father fought back new tears and straightened his jaw. It was clearly not going to be a clean, Hollywood resolution.

"You heard me," he said. "I didn't want you ruining your life the way I had."

"Are... are you serious?" Castor's world spun. He felt as if he had been pushed off a cliff. His stomach knotted. "You ... you and Big Bill?"

His father coughed out a wry laugh. "There's a reason he's called 'Big', you know..."

"No, stop! Just... stop! I don't need to know this!"

"Yes you do..." His father fell into a new coughing fit before finally catching his breath and leaning back in his wheelchair. Eventually, he just shook his head. "You needed to hear this years ago. Hell, I needed to say it, years ago."

"But how could you?" Castor finally managed.

His father shrugged. "I wish I knew. I was so ashamed; so broken up over your Mom leaving that I just sort of called it off with Bill and never spoke about it, since."

"What, you thought that it was... some sort of failing? Did

you think it was a curse?"

Castor's dad looked somberly at his son. "Whether or not I knew who I was—what I was—when I met your mother, I still made some pretty serious vows. I broke those promises, Cas. I broke them and have regretted it ever since."

Silence filled the kitchen. In the distance Jeremy turned on the vacuum cleaner in a fit of stress-reducing work.

"So, Bill..."

"He never left me," his father confessed. "God only knows why. He stuck around despite me chasing him away. He became a friend of the family more than anything else."

The younger coyote cast his mind back on all the times the big bull had come to visit. Even when he'd come to Castor's graduation ceremony in Seattle, the signs had been there. The family friend; the single, life-long bachelor who spent an inordinate amount of his time with a single father and his son. Castor felt tears stinging the corners of his eyes.

After a while he said, "He still loves you, dad."

Castor's father just shrugged. "Don't see why; not after how I fucked up all our lives."

Castor closed his eyes, counting to ten. When that didn't work he tried twenty. Finally, he gave up. Life was too complex to be captured and bracketed by numbers. Standing, he went to his dad, leaned down, and hugged him.

"I get it, dad," he said. "Sometimes you love someone hoping that they'll wake up and see it."

When Bill came over the four of them had dinner and talked about life.

Five: End Times

Confession, in addition to being good for the soul, seemed to be bittersweet. If anything, Castor believed that it had helped his father persist longer than the Christmas following his revelation. Two more Christmases and three birthdays had passed with Bill, Jeremy, and Castor spending what time they had together. Castor's movie-of-the-week didn't end with a euphoric closeness. The rifts, however, had been healed.

Castor stood with Jeremy in the Fondulac Gallery. The painting before them had taken two years to complete. He'd started it shortly after the funeral. From blank canvas to framed piece it still felt like he should be perfecting it.

"Art is always abandoned," Castor muttered.

"Huh?"

"Art is never finished, only abandoned," he said. "An old quote; one that is yelling at me to rip that thing off the wall and take it back to the studio for touch-ups."

Jeremy stifled a laugh behind his hand. "You artist types... Who says it's not how it should be?"

"Well, I do," he answered. "It was supposed to represent—well—my life. All the twists and turns I've taken have really been… expansive. This just seems so small."

"Size-queen," Jeremy teased. More seriously he put his arm around his partner's shoulders. "Yeah, your life has been complicated. So's mine. But if you were to write it down, it would fill several books." He walked around in front of the coyote and looked into his eyes. "If a picture is worth a thousand words, you'd need at least a dozen more paintings to do your life justice."

Castor smiled. It wasn't a thin smile, either; it reached across his face with the fullness that came from having a full life.

"Flatterer," he said.

"You know it."

The two kissed and turned back to the painting. It drew the eye with flecks of implied motion and broad, vibrant colors. As far as realism went, it was like looking at a photograph. The rest of the collection ranged from the abstract to the fanciful. This pedestrian piece, though, he'd insisted on being centerpiece of the exhibit.

"The thing is all of these paintings are about my life," Castor said. "Every experience and encounter is there in one form or another. And, y'know what? You're right. All together they still don't make up everything I need to say."

"And that's as it should be," Jeremy answered. "When you have nothing left to say, life's just not worth living."

A triptych of beer steins beneath neon crescent moons hung on one wall while a looming portrait of a naked, giant golden cat was on another. A series of advertisements from his Whitmar days made up a collage that formed a spiraling labyrinth. Faceless, anonymous, half-naked men lined a painted park path looking for love they could never find.

Seeing them through Jeremy's eyes Castor felt newly proud. It was a life after all.

Jeremy cupped his hand against Castor's rear at the base of his tail. The coyote smiled and cocked his head. "Art not riveting enough?"

"You forget: I've seen all these before." He winked slyly and nodded towards the exit. "There are other things I'd like to look at, at the moment."

Castor adopted a faux look of indignation. "You've not seen enough of me yet? What's the difference?"

"I can't make love to a painting." Castor laughed and pulled himself close to Jeremy. The smell of his husband's body suffused his nostrils as he pressed his groin up against the wolf's. It felt hot and alive and compelling. Nearly forty and he nonetheless felt young. Their muzzles brushed against each other and they kissed. Castor could feel just how aroused Jeremy was. It would be hard to hold him off during the drive home.

Still, anticipation made the heart grow stronger. Castor could only hope the same was true for other parts of his anatomy.

The two turned to go, the sparse crowd at the showing walked between the paintings and discussed them in quiet voices. In the center was a landscape. In it, wind-eroded buttes stood in striking contrast to a blue South Dakota sky. Clouds on the horizon were on fire with a range of reds and oranges that spoke of sunset… or sunrise. Just off to one side, a coyote sat with his back to the viewer, staring out at the expanse as if unaware of just how long the road ahead was. A beat-up pickup with the licence plate "LYNX" was next to him. Small, yellow flowers poking out here and there along an old, cracked highway implied hope jutting through into the harsh, uncaring world. The road curved, rose, and fell, winding between the badlands heights and depths throughout the whole painting. At no point did it truly fade into the distance. It eternally wound among the hills.

It was a road that never ended.

Those letters in trashy mens magazines are sure fun to read, but there's never any truth to them—or is there?

SPECIAL SAUCE

Scott Maddix

HILL CITY MEN
April, 2005
Lecherous Letters

I could hear Francisco, no matter how he tried to keep his voice low.

"Yeah? Yeah? F'real? Yeah, yeah, I can do that. That'll be hot. Thank you. Thank you."

He walked around the grill, tucking his cell phone back into his pocket, and I noted a bit of a protrusion in the front of his khakis.

"What's up?" I asked.

It was my first year out of high school, and I was working at the local burger joint to start saving up for college. Francisco usually worked opposite shifts, so I only saw him in passing, but tonight he'd been scheduled closing shift because a coworker was sick.

I didn't mind at all. I'd had the hots for him since I'd first laid eyes on him. He was tall, athletic, and wore a military-style crew cut. I had never before been attracted to a Rabbit, but something about the way Francisco moved, the way he spoke—he tried to come across as some kind of a bad boy, but his long lashes and big brown eyes had me fantasizing about finding his softer side. And his ass looked fantastic in the tight khaki uniform slacks.

Sometimes when he shifted I caught a glimpse of his boxers through the tail slit.

I must have masturbated in the employees' john while thinking about him a million times.

He was upset to work that night. You see, it was his twenty-first birthday, and he and his girlfriend'd had some pretty big plans. They were going to go to all the bars in town to celebrate his turning 21. Now he had to work the closing shift on his birthday.

He stopped fuming about it after that call, though. I could tell he was now looking forward to the evening with excitement.

"That was Veronique. We can't have our date, but she has a kinky little plan."

"Oh?"

"Well…" he paused and looked around. "Just between us guys…"

I kept a straight face and leaned in, hoping it would stay dead tonight. It was just the two of us in there now, and weeknights were usually empty.

"Veronique won't go down on me. She says it makes her feel cheap and stuff. But tonight she'll make an exception, to make up for my birthday sucking and all."

"She'll go down on you tonight?"

"Well, sort of."

I waited for him to explain.

"See, she got the idea from a trashy magazine. See…"

He lowered his voice to a whisper.

"She's going to order a Superburger with special sauce, and I'm going to give it to her."

It took me far too long to figure out what he meant. "Wait, what? That's nuts! If you were caught…"

"That's why I need your help. I need to make sure no one catches me, and for God's sake, no one else can get that burger."

"Oh, I see. I'll guard the front while you fill her order, and keep anyone else from accidentally getting the special burger."

"Uh, yeah. That's about it. Will you do it? Because I'm about ready to bust a nut just thinking about it now, and it's great that she's thought this up for me. She never does any kinky stuff."

I hesitated for a bit, and he said, "Come on, I'll owe you one. My birthday will totally suck otherwise."

I thought quick. I was getting turned on at the thought of Francisco behind the grill, his fly open, pounding his meat into the meat. The idea also tickled my funny bone something fierce. We all hear stories about kids spitting in the food of customers that tick them off, but this wasn't mean-spirited revenge. Frankly it was hot.

"I'll help," I sad, "but on one condition."

"What's that? Anything?"

I looked him straight in the eyes. "I want to watch."

It was a risk, saying that. I wasn't out to Francisco or anyone at work. It was a college town, but it was still a conservative city. And a bad boy like Francisco might just punch my lights out for suggesting such a thing, just to keep up his image.

But my instincts were good. He thought about it for a second, and smiled.

"You're crazy, man," he said and laughed.

"I know it. So is it a deal?"

"Yeah, yeah, okay. As long as no one else is in the shop. She's gonna come in right before closing."

"Perfect."

We spent the rest of the shift quietly. We served a few customers, and as we got closer to closing time, I had to adjust myself more than a few times to keep my wood from showing too much. It was ten 'till, and in walked Veronique. She pretended she didn't know Francisco and ordered the Superburger meal "with special sauce" and sat down at a back booth. I could see Francisco sweating.

The company policy was that the customer would get their burger in five minutes or less, or it was free.

"C'mon," he said, and we walked back behind the grills. I stood to one side so I could see the counter (and Veronique waiting patiently for her order), and Francisco was completely hidden from view—except for mine.

He was already hard, and he actually couldn't get his thick meat out of his fly until opened the button and dropped his pants to the floor, where they puddled around his high-tops. He was wearing no underwear.

His cock was thick and pink, and slid ever farther out of its sheath when it was freed from his pants. I let out a shuddering sigh as I saw a thin strand of precum drop from the piss slit and hang, just for a moment, before breaking and hitting the toe of one sneaker.

He leaned past me and glanced out front at his girlfriend and started stroking, breathing heavily near my face. I watched his paw cover, uncover, cover, uncover the slick head of his cock.

I stared.

"Get the burger, numbnuts," he said, startling me out of my reverie. I scrambled to assemble a Superburger before he came, and less than a minute later I returned, open burger in my hand. I looked around—still no other customers.

I held the burger for him to aim at. The thought that he might miss didn't worry me. I can lick my fingers clean.

After a minute he stopped.

"Shit" he said, staring at my hand holding the burger under his cock.

"What's the matter?"

"I don't think I can do it."

"You don't think you can cum?"

He shook his head.

"Are you just nervous?"

"Yeah, I guess."

I had the answer. Only three minutes had passed since Veronique had given her order, two minutes to finish, according to policy, but at that age we could all come fast, right?

I said, "let me help."

He didn't look surprised. He looked me in the eyes and said, "Okay."

I knelt on the tile in front of him, and his cock bobbed in front of my eyes. He was still leaning sideways, peeking around the grill at his girlfriend as I reached up and gently stroked the soft fur of his balls with my fingertips. He shivered and his balls pulled up a bit and another drop of precum dripped from the end of his cock. From that vantage it was easy to catch it on my tongue before it fell.

I grabbed his cock firmly by the base and gave it a squeeze, before leaning up on my knees a bit so I could lick the end without straining my neck.

My own cock was about ready to burst out of my pants, and there would be a wet spot on the front by the time tonight's adventure was over.

He moaned a little when I enveloped the head with my mouth. I could smell him, the hot smell of a man who works. Not dirty, just… smellable. I love the smell of a man's crotch. I squeezed his shaft gently, making it swell a little, stretching the skin slightly so it would be just that much more sensitive. I and swirled my tongue around the head.

By this time, maybe four and a half minutes had passed. We had earned a warning from the supervisor—but he was the one out sick. And besides, this was a special burger. Worth waiting for.

I took his whole shaft in then, deep-throating him as I had longed to since I'd first met him, nearly gagging on the thickness of it. It was heavenly. He gasped as I pulled back a bit and started stroking the shaft with my hand. With my tongue I felt as the head was covered, uncovered, covered, uncovered with my strokes.

I could taste more precum oozing out over my tongue, and I swallowed, moaning for more against his cock. I was muzzled so the sound didn't carry, but I know he could feel the vibration of the back of my throat.

I picked up pace a bit, and I felt his hand in my hair—not pushing my head, but almost caressing me as I built speed, stroking with hand and lips. He moaned again, and I knew he was getting close. His balls pulled up again and with a cry I'm sure our customer could hear, he unloaded five, six, seven jets of hot cum into my mouth. It was all I could do to not swallow it, but my free hand still held the cooling burger.

I held his cock in my mouth as the last spasm died, then withdrew, slowly, eliciting further shivers from Francisco, who was now leaning back, eyes closed, hands still in my hair.

The head of his cock dragged a stripe of spit and cum down my chin as it withdrew, and I leaned and let his load slip from my mouth and pool onto the burger.

I stood and looked Francisco in the eyes. "That was fun," I said.

"Yeah," he said. "Thanks, man."

"Any time," I said.

"No, I mean it," he said.

"So did I."

He pulled up his pants and managed to stuff himself back behind the fly, and took the burger to the counter to put lettuce, tomato and the top bun on it.

"Your order's up, miss," he said. And she came to the counter and took it with a smirk, and I stayed back, knowing my mussed hair and foolish grin might look suspicious. I hadn't yet noticed the wet spot on my pants or the stripe of spiky, sticky fur down my chin.

She ate the burger, and when she came up to the counter to "compliment the chef." I told Francisco I could close alone, so she took him to a bar for his first legal drink. I cleaned up and locked up, after jerking off in the john.

I chalked it up to just a "dear diary" moment, a one-time thing that was fun but meaningless. But the next day, Francisco came in on my shift to talk to me.

"We broke up," he said.

"Oh shit, Francisco, I'm sorry. Was it because …?"

"No, nothing like that. She was planning on breaking up anyway, but wanted me to have a nice memory. I think she wants me to be so sad about her leaving I'll never want to fuck another girl again."

"Well, that's crappy," I said.

"Yeah, but it's not too bad. We had fun, but…"

"But what?"

"What we did last night."

"Yeah?"

"D'you think we could do it some more?"

I swallowed. He was looking me right in the eyes, standing close and smiling. I forgot I was at work and put my hand on his arm.

"Yeah, I think we could. We can do it as often as you want."

* * *

The clipping from the trashy magazine shared the page with our wedding photos in the big blue album. I know those stories are usually made up by the editors, but this one was true. I know: I wrote it.

I know some people might not think that's a romantic way to meet your husband, but we do. Our friends are tired of hearing that story, but we have a lot of fun telling it. We've been together for seven years now. I went to college the next year, and now I am a professor there, literature and Romantic poetry. Francisco's been taking some art courses, and his sculptures have been shown in a few places around town. We're terrifically happy.

And we still go to that burger joint every year on his birthday, but sometimes he gets the special sauce now.

Becoming an adult is hard, and sometimes you need help to get out of a rough situation. Also, sometimes you find your help isn't enough for the ones you care about.

THE GAME

Tym

I t was a dumb bet. And it was really the best thing I could have done.

It's surprising how much you forget, of all the things that seem to be so important: names and dates, formulas, even things like football. I couldn't tell you a single pass or play, or what the score was on any particular game... Except for that one game, the one I'd bet on. The Crosstown Classic.

The town where I went to college is strange: it has two universites, University of California, and California State University. I know, they sound pretty much the same, but they certainly seemed different enough at the time. As far as I can tell, looking back, UC was focused on theoretical issues, a big medical school. CSU, on the other hand, was more practical, teaching real-life stuff. I went to CSU.

In high school, I had been on the football team, in a tiny little town in the middle of the Valley. I was the only panther on the team, and was the fastest runner by far. Three years as a running back netted me MVP when I graduated. It wasn't really anything special; I was just a really big fish. But my grades were pretty decent and I did manage to get a scholarship. So freshman year I moved into the dorms, joined the junior varsity team, and struggled through harder classes with more students in each lecture than had graduated from my entire high school.

It would have been a lot more difficult, being away from my family, if it hadn't been for the dorm. After graduation, I never saw my high-school friends again—this was a little before Facebook and all—and really hadn't had that much in common with them. They didn't know I was gay, for one thing. Not that they needed to.

I had seen how much drama was stirred up by "romance" in the four years between starting the 9th and finishing the 12th grade, how silly it all was. My mom had left when I was little, and my dad seemed pretty happy being a bachelor again. I guess it had kind of rubbed off on me. So I moved into the dorms, figuring I would probably be single for the next few years: I would rather focus on school and football. You know, important things.

Besides, I had all the eye candy I could want, every day after practice in the locker room. There was quite a difference, I can tell you, between the bucks and hogs and ponies I had graduated with and the men I encountered in the CSU showers. Oh, nothing like that, I never did more than ogle; they were my *teammates*. It would be like…trying to get it on with your sister or something. Well, not quite that bad, but anyways, off the table.

Being college, there was always a pep band at our games, and they often practiced in the field next to ours. It was pretty cool watching them go through their paces, and I know they watched us. That's how I met Trevor Carnarotti. I probably shouldn't use his name, but I don't really care after everything that happened.

He was short, maybe two feet shorter than I was, but it was the easiest thing for him to pick me up—the sort of guy that could easily grow up to be a "fireplug." He played the tuba…or was it the Sousaphone? Anyways, I saw him one practice, and recognized him from my dorm. The short cocky lion was a freshman, too. So I waved at him, and he waved back, and I figured it would pretty much end there, but that night at dinner, he sat next to me.

The dining commons was half empty (I always got back late from practice) and there were plenty of empty seats. But I look up and there he is, with a burger and fries and a slice of pie, asking if he could sit across from me. I guess I shrugged, or said "ok," and he sat down and started talking. I don't remember what we said, but he had a very nice voice, smooth and suggestive. He had this way of talking that could make weather statistics sound sexy. And, well, I liked him.

He invited me to come over to his room that night to show off his computer, or play video games, or something; he was a floor above me and down the hall. His roommate—a little Corgi, I later found out—spent most of his evenings studying and that night was no exception. Not a month into the school year, and he already had everything figured out.

That night was my first time. It wasn't his first, though. I found out later that he had quite a collection of popped cherries. But it was good…he knew just how to treat a nervous little virgin. That deep voice, those strong thick arms, and the way his cock just wormed its way in, it all added up to a very rewarding first fuck.

And it wasn't the last. He was always finding excuses to meet me in his dorm room or mine, usually when our roommates were out. Of course, we did eventually get caught: my roommate, a lanky Arabian named James Kemerer, walked in on us once. His eyes went wide, his nostrils flared, and he spun around on his dainty hoof and left. It was pretty funny, especially when he called my phone three hours afterwards, wondering if we were done yet. Months later, James and I laughed so hard he literally shot milk out of his nose. Normally though, Trevor and I had better scheduling.

And then September rolled in, and the whole school started preparing for the Homecoming game. I don't need to mention the long extended practices, for both the football team and the pep band. Obviously neither of us had much time for anything fun. We made a bet, in the week before the game—it was his idea, really—if our team won, I could top him. I hadn't done anything like that yet…he said he saved that for special guys. If our team lost the homecoming game, however, he would not only "stuff" me, but would try out one of his secret kinks, something he had never done yet, with anyone.

As I said, I don't remember much: I couldn't tell you what plays we made, how many touchdowns, or if I even touched the ball. What I can tell you is that we lost, badly. That night I found a note pushed under my door; Trevor must have been too tired to see me, or maybe he just wanted to increase the…tension or something. It read:

Cody, I order you not to paw off at all tonight. Tomorrow, at 9:30 I'll meet you at the northwest staircase of Ralston Hall. Be Ready.

Or something like that. I should mention that after the first time, he had started getting more dominant. I hadn't seen it then; I didn't think it was strange that he would order me around.

Sometimes I would have to go a whole day without an orgasm, because I had done poorly on a test, or at football practice. And other times, he would order me to climax, sometimes while he was inside me, sometimes while he was jacking me off. And boy did I try. After two months of this, it's not exactly surprising that I looked forward to doing what I was told. It sure helped with my classes, and Coach said none of his players tried as hard as I did—not that it matters now.

He had this habit; whenever passing me in the hallway or on the quad or after practice he would grab my butt, right under my tail-flap. "My kitty," he would say, and then ran his paw along my tail as he walked away. It always left me adjusting my pants, and trying to smooth out my fur. I loved it.

But Saturday morning, when I showed up at Ralston Hall as ordered, he wasn't there. I waited, looking around, sniffing and listening. I was a little early, and somewhere around 9:45, I caught a whiff of his cologne, and his arousal. I turned around, and looked down: his mane was fluffed, his ears directed straight at me, and his eyes were little slits. He looked high. I don't know if he was, but I wouldn't doubt it, from the way his claws extended as he grabbed my arm, dragging me up the exterior staircase.

Ralston Hall is a big concrete monstrosity. Built sometime in the early 90's, by some famous European architect, and winning who knows how many awards. No one who had to take a class there, or work in an office there, ever liked it. It looked like something from *1984* or *Brazil*: all planes and angles of cold dirty concrete, intersecting floors, outside staircases and walkways. Yuck. It did, however have one popular feature; I soon found out.

He dragged me up five flights of stairs, hardly panting by the time we reached the top. I had never been that far up Ralston before, and didn't know what to expect. The fourth floor was the highest part of most of the rest of the building, but the staircase kept going up. At the top, for no reason I could see, there was a flat place, bigger than a normal landing. It had no chairs, no roof, just walls all around, a few cigarette butts, and a little slit in one of the walls, giving a nice view of the parking lot north of campus. It felt like being in a castle.

I didn't have much more time to look. Before I could even catch my breath, Trevor was on me. The more aroused he was, the sloppier his kisses got; and by the amount of tongue that lapped at my cheeks and nose, I could tell he was ready.

"Down." That was it, just that one word, and I was on my knees. He was such a beast like that. He liked it when I sniffed him, liked my nose nuzzling his sheath, taking in his musk. He always smelled like vanilla and pine, I don't know why; but I did like it. He had trained me well.

I had a sequence I had to follow if I was going to have any chance of cumming. Wow, you know, I had never really talked about this, not even to James. But yeah, first I had to sniff his sheath, right where it joined his belly. It didn't matter what we were doing, how horny he was, I had to do things in order. Next was a good tongue-washing on his balls, which moved slowly up to his cock. By then he would usually be pretty much unsheathed. He wasn't too long, maybe 6 inches, but he knew how to use it. Isn't that what they always say?

After that, I would usually suck on him for a while, teasing the little nubs around his cockhead—he didn't have barbs like some felines I've seen, we had that in common, just little bumps around the head. But that Saturday, he pushed me away, saying, "Down," again. I looked up at him, I couldn't tell what he wanted…and then I saw the look in his eyes and the snarl distorting his tawny face.

That was when I realized two things: one, that he wanted to fuck me, right there on the little roof platform thing. And two, that anyone could come up the stairs, at any time. At most we'd get a few seconds of warning, a hoof or shoe on the concrete. I tried to plead with him, to ask him to wait, but I couldn't say anything. He had trained me well.

What I could do, however, was exactly what I did do. I bent over, pulling my pants and boxers down, my tail lifted high. I knew what he would see back there: black fur spreading out from a little pink "panther puss," that's what he called it, I swear. I could hear him clearing his throat, a long low rumbling roar, and a wet sound. He hadn't brought lube. I'll always wonder why he didn't, since he always insisted on something, even Vaseline.

"Open."

And I did; what else could I do? Just picture it: there I was, just 18, lean and tall, on all fours, getting plowed by this short hunk of lion. In the open. I think that was what he had wanted, fucking as though it had been spur of the moment, as though neither of us could keep our hands out of our pants. But I could tell that he had planned it out. From the way he was humping and grunting, I knew that he probably hadn't cum all the day before either, maybe longer.

That was another thing I had learned quickly about Trevor: he didn't cum like most guys I've known since then. He didn't cum like I did either, for that matter. He would shoot a little, and keep going. I know this because I jacked him off once, all the way. Any time I tried to shift position or even change paws, he would snarl at me, the paw gripping my shoulder extending its claws as though saying "don't even dare." So I didn't. By the end of it, I had lost all feeling in my pads, and it felt like my arm was going to fall off. Two hours is a long time to do anything.

So when he gripped my neck—left little holes in the collar of my jacket too—I knew it was going to be just like every other time. We would be there for two hours; I could feel my own cock withdrawing, from the cold Autumn air as much as from....Well, yeah, I didn't want to be there.

I looked it up a few months later, and found out that my fears were correct: public indecency could result in exposure of the students involved. Ha! I meant *expulsion*. How's that for a Freudian slip? But yeah, expulsion. Or worse. And yet, there I stayed, for two hours and 15 minutes—I checked afterwards. Sex with Trevor was...different. It was easy enough, all I had to do was lay there and after all the practice we had gotten in my "tail star" was used to the pounding, which left me free to do other things. Depending on the position, I would paw off, taking my time. Sometimes we would leave the TV in our dorm room on, with the sound off, and I would watch that while he hunched over me. Sometimes I would just think, letting my mind wander, running football plays through my head.

That day, the only thing running through my head was the thought: "We're gonna get caught. We're gonna get caught." It was a certainty, not a possibility. I'm getting nervous just talking about it now.

So yeah, he finished, patted my ass, and said, "Good boy," while he zipped up. And he just left. It took me a few seconds before I realized he was gone, probably as long as it took the breeze up there to blow away his scent. I staggered to my paws, pulling my pants up, and checking to make sure we hadn't left any mess. I'd heard rumors around the dorm, about how good the bloodhounds on the Campus PD were at sniffing out culprits. There were no telltale blotches I could find on the cold concrete, so I left, walking back downstairs as fast as I could.

Have you ever tried to run after sex? After two hours of sex without a chance to clean up? It's not fun, no matter how much hot porn you read on the internet. I hated the way it leaked out, the way it clumped up my fur, chafing and pulling inside my boxers. And I was always glancing back under my tail, to see if it had started darkening the seat of my pants.

It probably was the one thing keeping me sane. Some people pinch themselves or pull their whiskers to keep focused. That Saturday I had to run across campus with a full load of lion spunk inside me. It kept me from thinking about what had just happened. I probably would have just stopped and broken into sobs if it hadn't been for the very real need for a shower and a change. By the time I reached the dorms, stripped, and stepped under the steaming water (because who's showering at one in the afternoon?) I was able to not think about it at all.

Of course, I missed practice that day. I don't know if Trevor went to his practice session, probably did, if I know him. He was never really affected by sex afterwards, just a little grin usually, especially if it was good.

I did go to practice on Sunday, if only to keep the guys from asking questions. A little "24-hour flu" always does the trick. All that week, I kept avoiding him as much as I could. I would dart into the locker room as soon as practice was over, would avoid his glance in the dining commons, would step to the other side in the hallways. By Thursday, he was groping a new guy—a buff deer I had never seen before—as though he were doing it to spite me. It was hard to keep myself from running up and begging Trevor to take me back. It still is.

Another week went by, and he didn't even try to catch my eye on the field. So much so that I started staring at him, remembering how he had looked when I had first saw him, lugging his tuba with such ease, as though it were just a part of his mane. It wasn't that hard, really. He looked so unaffected by me, as though I hadn't existed, hadn't been his fucktoy for the past two months.

You know, it's funny, I never thought about it like that: it always felt so much longer than that. I guess everything seems to be more…more when you're that age. I was almost furious at him, seeing the way the buck hung around, watching Trevor practice with the rest of the pep band. He should be looking at me, looking at me with begging eyes, or something. I didn't even notice that I was still walking, I was so mad at him.

And I tripped over someone sitting on the grass. My practice pads probably saved both of us some bruises, as did my reflexes: all five limbs spread, my tail in the air, my paws propping me up. I sprung back onto my heels, dropping to my knees beside the sprawled black form. I had tripped over my roommate, James.

I helped him back up, apologizing and asking him if he was okay. It seemed like something out of a movie, a bad one now that I think about it. He was fine, but I'd knocked the pad of paper out of his hands, scattering sheets across the grass. It was early afternoon, so there wasn't any dew even that late in the year, but I didn't want someone's cleats tearing up the drawings he had been making, so I helped him gather them up.

They were really quite good, quickly sketched figures in football uniforms. They looked like fashion illustrations, like they belonged in the 50s magazines my mom used to collect. I asked James what they were for, and he said he was working on a "football ballet." That was when I realized I had no clue who he was or what he did or anything. He was my roommate, but we hadn't had anything else in common.

Practice was over, so I asked if he would wait a minute and meet me at the dining commons. I even offered to treat, to make it up to him, not that he needed the meal point. But he smiled a big toothy grin and said, "Sure, I feel like I don't even know you." Can you believe that?

So I changed and we walked together to the DC. I asked him what classes he was in, and he asked me. We split to get food, and when we sat down with our trays, I asked him about what he had been working on at the field.

"It's a football ballet," he had said. "Well, it's gonna be. I told you, I was in a drama class, right? Well, they're trying to teach us to write our own plays, and I really wanna make a musical. Like *Oklahoma!*, you know?" I mumbled through my mouthful of salad that I hadn't seen it. He put down his burger and stared at me, his long handsome face open-mouthed in exaggerated shock. "Never?" When I said yes, he listed off a bunch of other titles, to which I had to reply that I hadn't seen—or even heard of—a single one.

"Well, what are you doing tonight?" he asked. "Why don't we have a movie night? It's not like we don't already share a room. Besides, I'm sick of having to watch them on my computer with headphones."

"So that's why you're always tapping your hooves!" I replied with a laugh. So we watched *Oklahoma!* that night, and I liked it. James paused the movie during the dream sequence, explaining his own project between handfuls of popcorn.

"It's gonna be pretty cool, I think. I don't have the whole story worked out, but how awesome would it be to have a whole team— maybe two teams!—of football players on the stage, dancing like that," he gestured at the frozen screen. I had to admit, it did sound pretty cool.

"Especially if you have the uniforms kinda scanty," I said, and then looked away. I could feel my ears drop down: I didn't know if he was even gay or not, if he would want a bunch of buff guys prancing around in half-torn uniforms. Besides, I thought, I don't know anything about theater.

"That's a great idea!" I heard, and felt him jumping off our small couch to dive for his sketchpad. It was amazing, watching him scribble, seeing a few deft pencil strokes change a normal football uniform to something risqué. As he sketched, he talked, telling me about the scene he had in mind, how each team would symbolize one side of an argument in the main character's head, how they would duke it out to help him reach a decision. "It's never been done before, I think," he added, looking up at me.

I glanced down at his drawings again, and I could see the whole scene playing out in my mind, and I told him so. He had such a winning smile. "I bet we would have gone the whole year without really knowing one another," I finally said. "I'm glad we didn't."

We stayed up late that night, finishing the first musical and then watching another—I don't remember which one—before we realized what time it was. No, we didn't sleep together that night, though I'll admit that I wanted to. He was cute, slimmer than I was then, always bouncing on his taut legs, always grinning that toothy grin. He was sweet.

Of course, the next few days went pretty much as they had all the weeks before. It's not like we were an item, and we had very different schedules. That week, though, I noticed that Trevor's buff buck buddy wasn't hanging around anymore. I was tempted to go up to the little lion and gloat, but it wasn't my style. Plus, he could have whipped me any day; he was strong, real strong. I was in the locker room a few days later, getting ready for the game—we were playing a SoCal school, nothing major—and I felt something behind me.

There was Trevor, without his instrument, without his uniform, his mane a mess and his eyes fiery. "Why aren't you ready?" I had asked, or something like that. The pep band played at every game—Trevor and I had managed to have some very steamy sessions at some of our away games. Oh, we didn't fuck, nothing like that; just groping, teasing, getting ourselves warmed up for the trip home and a nice long private session in one of our dorm rooms. But we had always put the game first. That night, though, I knew he wasn't going to play.

He pressed up against me, his fuzzy chin up-turned against my chest pads, one strong paw gripping each of my wrists as he ground his crotch against mine. Well, just below mine. I knew he was drunk, I'd seen dad get soused once or twice, and knew what it looked like. Trevor might have been high as well; it certainly would have explained what happened next.

"Down"

Yeah, he was at it again, forcing me back against my locker, pulling on my wrists. I glanced around, knowing that there wouldn't be anyone there. There wasn't. The team was out on the field, doing some quick warm-ups before Coach's on-field pep talk. There wouldn't be anyone in the locker room for at least another hour, probably two or three—long enough for Trevor, and far too long for me.

I managed to free one arm, trying to push him away with a paw on his forehead and a stiff arm, like in the cartoons, but he was so much stronger than me. I could feel myself wanting to give in to him, especially when his scent wafted over me. Vanilla and pine, as always, even with the under-scent of booze. I'm sure I don't need to tell you how strong scent memories are, how just a whiff of him could make me go weak at the knees. And here he seemed to be puffing it out, like cigarette smoke, blowing it at me.

Before I knew it, I was on my knees again, trying to unzip his jeans with trembling claws. I felt like an addict. I probably was addicted, it would explain those nights of crying myself to sleep, trying to stifle the sobs with my pillow, so James wouldn't hear. And there was his paw, his claws digging through my fur, scratching my scalp, just like they always did when I gave him a good blow job.

Then I felt them tighten around my ears, was sure he was drawing blood. "You did this to yourself, pussy. You ignored me. For weeks you ignored me. Don't fucking ignore me." He was growling now, but in him it sounded like a purr. He was enjoying this as much as he'd enjoyed doing me on the roof. He must have felt me trying to get up, to pull off, because he grabbed me harder. It was all I could do to keep from biting his cock when his claws pierced my ears "No one ignores me, pussy. You're mine, and you know it."

95

He growled again, and started humping my muzzle, and I could taste the first spurt of cum.

I think that was what did it. In that first little taste—which was not, I should add, the same as his smell—I knew all the hours I had spent servicing him, realized how easily I had become a pet and a fucktoy. "No."

My voice was muffled by the lioncock in my mouth, and masked by his grunting and the rustling of my uniform, but I know he heard me. The paws tightened even more on my ears and he snarled, literally snarled, "What was that, pussy?"

I still don't know what came over me, or how I ended up breaking free of him and pulling away from his groin. But there was a good foot of space between us when I said "No," again. He rushed towards me, and I punched him. I think I actually hit him in the nuts. I hope I did. I'd never taken boxing, never practiced with a punching bag or anything; I'd only done football, but it was enough. I ran away, not caring that I was in my uniform, not caring that he was doubled up on the concrete floor with his cock hanging limp from his pants, not caring that a string of cusswords followed me out the door. I ran.

I ran to my room, half hoping James would be there, half hoping he wouldn't. It was empty, and I flung myself on my bed—cleats and all—and cried. I didn't think, didn't wonder, didn't do anything but cry. I was scared, and hurt, and confused. I was only eighteen, you know?

I must have fallen asleep, because the next thing I remember is someone knocking on my door. I climbed off the bed, still groggy, still in my uniform. I thought it was the Resident Advisor, or maybe James had forgotten his keycard. That's the only reason I can give for why I opened the door, why I let Trevor push past me, knocking the doorframe against my face. I fought back the pain, tried not to scream as I told him to get out.

"No one does that to me and lives!" he hissed, keeping his voice down so no one would hear, so no one would look as he closed the door behind him. There was red on the fly of his jeans, already starting to darken. He was bleeding. He grabbed my neck with one paw, holding me against the closet door, and spat in my face. "You fucker, that is going to cost you. I'm going to fucking rip your nuts off!" And he jabbed his other paw at my crotch. Thank God I still had my cup on; as it was, I was bruised and tender for a week, but I still have my junk. I don't doubt that he would have done as he said, too. He was crazy. I had challenged his honor, his manhood, and I was going to pay, one way or another.

He started punching me, hitting my pads—which only made him madder. He was just pulling back for a punch that would have knocked out teeth, when the door clicked open and James pranced in, humming something.

We all froze.

And James, he didn't even flinch. Before the door could close, he yelled out, "Help! Get the RA!" and then he was on Trevor. He was pretty strong too, despite being lean and wiry, and those three-fingered hoof-tipped hands of his must have packed quite a punch. By the time the RA, and several other concerned students, burst through the door, Trevor was on the floor, coughing and gasping, and James was holding me up as I wheezed.

The Resident, a big bear and a junior, though I never could remember his name, did his job well. I always make that clear: he did what he was supposed to do. "Alright, what's going on here?" He turned to James, "Mr. Kemerer, what happened?"

"I walked in," he replied, holding me closely, "and saw Trevor beating Cody up, threatening him."

"I see. So you punched him to stop him from doing worse to your roommate, right?"

What could James do but agree? So Trevor and I were escorted to the health center, and all three of us were written up for fighting. I kept telling them that James saved me, that he had just walked in on us. But all they'd tell me was that it would be handled before the Student Disciplinary Council on Friday, two days from then.

That night James and I did sleep together. He offered, actually, all but insisted on it. It was so sweet, and so different from when Trevor and I slept together. Usually *that* was because he had fallen asleep after I had gotten him off. He would roll over towards me, holding me in his strong short arms, breathing in my face.

Sometimes he wouldn't wake up until after I was late for class, he just said it was part of my job. I can't believe I trusted him.

With James, it was different. The dorm beds are small,—really only meant for one person—so any two people will be cramped in them, but that night I didn't mind. He took up a lot less room than Trevor did, and wasn't as keen on sleeping face-to-face. I rolled over, at his suggestion, and backed up against him, pinning him to the wall behind the bed. Then he wrapped his arms around me, running his thick fingers through my chestfur, and nuzzled my cheek with his. Of course, the hot bulge in his briefs nestled under my tail didn't hurt either. I felt safe that night. And the night after that.

The Disciplinary Council was...well, it was boring. They asked a lot of questions: why were we fighting, how did I know Trevor Carnarotti, why I let him into my room, had I used drugs or alcohol beforehand. I answered as truthfully as I could, and tried not to get worked up when Trevor, cleaned up, in a suit, and wearing a phony sling on one arm, blatantly lied to the council. Imagine my surprise, then, when they summed up the case.

"Trevor Carnarotti, as this isn't your first time appearing before us, on similar charges, we have no option but to doubt your version of events." Yeah, I know! We hadn't been in school for four months, and he was already known as a troublemaker. How could I not have seen it? They thanked James for bravely stepping in to "curtail the situation," and warned me to be more vigilant in the future. They expelled Trevor, thank God; you should have heard him whining—actually whining—as he was escorted out. "I'll call my dad, and his lawyers will sue your asses. This is fucked up!"

I couldn't help but throw myself at James, kissing his cheek, right there in the council chambers, thanking him for rescuing me. That night we did more than just sleep together. I hadn't known it could feel that good. James was different from Trevor in so many ways.

As soon as we got back into our dorm room, he was on me. Have you ever kissed a horse? Well, it's just about the best thing I've ever felt: those thick flexible lips, that long heavy tongue. I've been with a lot of studs over the years, and that's one thing they have had in common. Of course, until that day, I had only ever kissed my mother, and Trevor, so I didn't have much experience to draw on. But with James, that was okay. The way his fingers held me, the way he kept looking at me through his long eyelashes, I knew he must have had plenty of experience.

We stood there, just inside the door, holding one another. It's so wonderful to make out with someone your own height, not having to stoop or stretch. I can still feel his body pressing up against me. Ahh. I miss him. He was a dry kisser, lips and tongue leaving hardly any dampness where they touched, just his cool minty breath, and the sensation of needing more. Eventually a hand reached up and started undoing my tie and another started unbuttoning his shirt. We were so close together, black fur against black hair, lean muscle against lean muscle; I couldn't tell you whose body was doing what.

Our shirts gone, we pressed our chests together, now and then a pad or hooftip would brush a nipple, stroke a spine, grip the base of a tail. That led to pants being unbuttoned and unzipped. And we were still making out. I had closed my eyes by then, letting my senses fade, apart from the scent of him that rushed in with every breath, the taste of his tongue on mine, the occasional rustle of fabric. I was just one big touch.

I think it took me a few minutes to realize he had stopped kissing back, and I opened my eyes in surprise. I tried to speak, but he put a finger to my lips; it was all I could do to keep from licking it, sucking on it. He smiled, showing those adorable buck teeth, and said: "I'm kinda glad Trevor was such a jerk."

If he hadn't'a been holding me so close, I probably would have socked him one. But he was strong and held me, as he kept talking: "Hey, hey, easy, Cody. I only meant that I wouldn't have found you if it weren't for him." He blushed, and tucked his long chin against his chest. "I mean…"

I kissed the top of his muzzle. "I know what you meant, it just surprised me…I still hurt from him."

"I know. I wish I could help."

"Sometimes the best thing you can do is the same thing, but different." I don't know where I'd read that, or heard it, or if I made it up, but it kept him staring for long enough. I dropped to my knees and pulled down his briefs, pulling his cock down with them. It was like a do-it-yourself striptease, revealing inch after inch of that horsemeat. It wasn't huge, but it was hefty. Easily twice the size of Trevor's little stub. At least, that's how I always remembered it, the way it flopped into my paw, half-hard and flexible. It smelled like him too, warm and musky, but subtle. The skin was soft against my muzzle, twitching where my whiskers tickled it.

I started sucking on him, going slowly, just the head at first. Letting myself stretch out just like, well, just like Trevor had taught me. Soon, I had the whole head in, and several inches more, and then I started to lick. You should have heard him whinny! It's a wonder we didn't get caught, but after that first outburst, he managed to keep quiet.

I guess he'd never had a feline tongue on his cock before, from the amount of precum he was leaking. It was like someone had turned on a faucet, just a little. A steady dribble of salt across my tongue and down my throat. Once I'd gotten him all worked up, I pulled off. He looked worried, and hurt, and horny, wondering why I had stopped. "I want to try something," I said before he could ask. Going down on all fours, I reached back and pulled my boxers down, letting my tail snake out and leering up at him. "I wanna try this," I said as I crawled around, wagging my butt at him.

I felt his weight shifting, his knees hitting the carpet behind mine, his hands resting on my hips, smoothing my fur. "Are you sure, Cody? I mean, do you think you can, you know, take it?" He was so cute like that, thoughtful and sometimes very shy about his endowment. I didn't want to kill the mood with stories of how Trevor had once used his whole collection of "toys" on me, jerking off while he stuffed me with one dildo after another, so instead I just told James to take it slow, as slow as he could stand.

He did exactly what I had said, and it was agony. Oh, not the size, that wasn't the issue at all. It was how damned slowly he went in. He must have been watching me for twitches or signs of pain, slipping in a quarter of an inch at a time. And then he hilted, finally. I could feel his whole body tense when his balls touched mine, and his hand gripped my tail, right at the base. Best feeling in the world, having someone hold you there, using your own tail as a handle while they fuck you.

"You ready?" James asked, and I could tell by the tone of his voice that he wanted nothing more than to plow me hard.

"Yeah, go ahead," I had tried to say, but as soon as he heard "yeah," he started to withdraw, only a little bit faster than he had gone in. I swear I could feel every vein and ridge. And then he started getting a rhythm up and—just like with Trevor—all I felt was motion and heat and the occasional bump against my balls. I started thinking, just like with Trevor. He was gone, out of my life, and I still couldn't stop thinking about him, until I felt the lips brush against my ear. Trevor hadn't done that. Hadn't ever been tender or whispered things in my ear.

But James had. Every time he thrust in, so slowly, he would say something. Nothing major, nothing earth-shattering. Just little things. "You feel so good," and "I can't believe we're doing this, Cody," and "I couldn't ask for a better roommate." Of course, he didn't keep that up for long: soon the whispers became soft grunts, his mint-cool breath curling my whiskers on that side as we both panted. His arms were wrapped around me, one over my shoulder, and the other around my hip. His chest was pressed against my back, barely moving as he rocked his hips back and forth.

And, well, for once I didn't think of other things. I guess that's what Zen feels like: your whole being, your whole consciousness, focused on one thing. It was the most perfect sex I had ever had. Just…part of a machine. Until he flared inside me. I gasped at the feeling of his head dragging all along my insides, completely unlike the way Trevor's had. I felt the carpet between my knees, damp and sticky, clinging to my fur. I didn't even realize I'd cum, it all felt so good. And then James grunted, "In or out?" I didn't know what he meant, and was about to ask him, when he repeated his question.

"In or out? Come on, man, I don't have long." I could tell that his teeth were clenched; flecks of foam dripping down onto my back as he raked his flared cock though me.

"In, in!" And his hands gripped my hips, pulling them against his, as though he were trying to join us together. I felt like we had already been merged, two parts of one great beast. I think I shouted when I felt him cum, felt his whole body tense up, pushing jet after jet into me. A few years ago, I tried an enema for the first time... that's what it felt like, James getting off inside me. I felt so full, so warm, so happy when he collapsed on top of me.

We stayed there, knotted up on the floor, for I don't know how long. He seemed to wake up a bit, running his hands over me, stroking my ears, making me purr. And would you believe it, his cock actually jumped inside me? He was getting hard, again! I laughed and told him.

"Yeah, I know," he said. "That happens sometimes. It thinks it's in charge, I guess." It sounds kinda dumb now, but curled up on the floor, covered with sweat and cum, it was just about the funniest thing either of us had heard. While we were laughing, he did go soft, and flopped out of me. He rolled onto his back and looked at me, smiling, with his forelock plastered to his forehead. I'll never forget the way he looked, right then. Sometimes, I wish I could draw, just so I could, you know, preserve that.

After that, we were pretty close. Not actual boyfriends or anything: we both agreed that we weren't ready for that. We were just freshmen, and we'd heard all the stories of how easy it was to change in college. No sense in getting all dramatic about it. But I doubt many roommates—at least, not in our dorm—had arguments about which bed to sleep in. We became very good friends, with very good benefits.

He even wanted me to help with his project. This was after the end of football season, and honestly, I doubted whether I would even continue in it. I'd only been good in high school because it was a tiny little school. At CSU I was barely making the cut. So I figured I might as well give something else a try. And if I *could* get into drama, it meant that much more time spent with James.

That spring—after a long winter break spent at our separate homes—he was putting the finishing touches on his script, and wanted my help with it. He called me a lot that winter, though not always with questions about technical football stuff. We would talk for hours, about anything. He told me about his hometown in Pennsylvania, and I'd tell him about living in the Valley. After just over a month of that, I felt like I knew everything about him.

When we got back, after a long kiss, we started talking about his play. Not only, he said, did he still need me to help with all the little football-y details, but he wanted me to model the costumes too. I will never look at a football uniform again without getting at least a little hard. That horse was talented, or maybe you just have to be good at everything to make a good play. Either way, it seemed like everything he touched, well…

Like the costumes, for example. He had me stand in our dorm, just wearing my pads, and then just the jersey, and then mixing and matching the different parts, sketching me every time. It was pretty hot, being dressed and undressed like that. When he had me stand there in just my knee-high socks and my cleats, I couldn't help myself: I started jerking off. It ended up being my first time topping him. It was good, but not as good as being on all fours, having him sweating and moaning on top of me. I loved bottoming for James.

The final result was really breathtaking. I know there are pictures somewhere from the dress rehearsals. Anyways, they were deliciously risqué: orange and black for the one team, purple and white for the other, helmets that obscured the dancers' faces, and "torn" spandex that did nothing to hide their bodies. You could even see their jockstraps in the back. He said he wanted to make it look as though they had been fighting that battle for years and years, ragged, roughed-up, but no less strong. He put pads in, of course, to make the guys look buffer, but that's just part of theatre, I guess, like fur dye.

His play wasn't just about the metaphorical players, but sometimes I wondered if it was all just an excuse to have hot guys dancing around on stage wearing next to nothing. Not that I minded. It was a coming of age story, inspired, in part, by me. That's what he told me one night, while we were polishing his dialogue. "I really have to thank you, Cody," he said as he nuzzled up against me. "It wouldn't have all come together like this without you."

"What do you mean," I asked.

"Well, I had a few ideas, but with that…trouble…we had with…you know…" He was always hesitant to bring up Trevor. I'd told him I was over it, but he worried that I would break down. "It really made it all come together." And it had. His story was all about a guy on the football team who can't help but look at teammates in the shower, and who agonizes over it every night, alone, in his room, while the purple and orange teams played their unending game in his head. Of course, the main character ended up killing himself. So *that*, at least, wasn't inspired by me.

It's funny how things click like that, sometimes. I just wish it had gotten better reviews. The school paper ran a horrible article about it, totally missing the point. Even I could understand the metaphors and symbolism; all they could see was a bunch of guys dancing around in torn football jerseys. Afterwards, I saw *A Raisin in the Sun* and *Death of a Salesman*, and I really think that James' *The Game* was on the same level, if not better.

But the review stuck, and by the end of the run—it was only scheduled for three weeks, Fridays and Saturdays—there were hardly any people in the audience. I was always there, and so was James. It was horrible, seeing his whole body sag when he counted the heads in the theatre from our seats in the back. The actors played their parts well, no matter how many people were watching, and James' professor gave him an A, probably for "audacity." I wish I could find the script, it really was a masterpiece.

It changed him though, that kind of rejection. Maybe he would have gotten a better review at UC, or one of those art schools. But I know that, if he *hadn't* been at CSU, if we hadn't been roommates, the musical would never have ended up the way it did, and things for both of us would have been completely different. I tried over the weeks after the curtain dropped on the last show to talk to him, to suggest that he take it somewhere else. There had to be plenty of drama buffs who would love to put on his show, somewhere it would be appreciated. He wouldn't listen.

"Look, obviously there's something wrong with it," he said one night, "I'll be in bed soon, ok? You go ahead...get some sleep." The way he looked at me, as though he were looking right through me, I wanted to climb out of the bed and wrap my arms around him.

"James," I wanted to say, "come to bed, it'll be ok." I knew he would stay up all night, sitting in the dark, his computer screen turning his face dark blue, reading and re-reading his script…and that review. I asked him once, towards the end of that semester, what he kept doing night after night. The bags under his eyes, the way his mane looked—rough and un-brushed—and most of all the sag of his shoulders, told me everything.

"Just reading," he said. And I didn't question him.

We didn't talk much during finals week. I could tell he was struggling just to pass, but we didn't have any classes in common; there wasn't anything I could have done to help. I spent most of my time in the library, and when I got back to the dorm at night, either he was already in bed, asleep and facing the wall, or he was gone. Sometimes I'd wake up and he'd still be there, sometimes not. It was hard; we hadn't had sex for nearly a month by then, and when I tried talking to him about it, he just shrugged it off as "finals stress."

And then finals were over and there was the rush to pack everything up for the move back home. He had my phone number from our months together as more-than-roommates, and I'd given him my address. We said goodbye with a long hug, and I can still feel him squeezing me, as though he didn't want to let go, as though he wanted to apologize for being so distant. But he did let go, stuffing the last box into his hatchback—he wouldn't let me help—and driving away. I tried calling him that summer, but he never picked up and never called back. E-mails never got answered, and I don't know if he opened any of my letters. By about July, I'd pretty much given up.

That fall semester, I had started in the university's Nursing program. I was done with football, after all that happened. Besides, I wasn't very good, and it had stopped being fun. I moved into my first apartment with some other med majors, and…well, I guess I just moved on. I still look for him now and then, online and on campus, hoping to see that long black Arabian face in a crowd. I even checked the obituaries once. But he hasn't turned up anywhere. I guess for all I've forgotten, there's still some stuff I just can't let go. So sometimes, when I'm lonely, I put on my old uniform, and think of James.

Keeping your eyes open can lead to intense experiences. Even things that seem tawdry can be torrid and teach us things about ourselves.

Rock and a Hard Place

Toonces

They use you up, like a chain of condoms or a bottle of lube that might become too gummy and discomforting to handle long before it's empty. That's what they were buying, too. At the pharmacy near this upscale gym where I also see them come and go, this place out on the gentrifying fringes of the city where brand new high rise condos spring from the ground around crumbling schools and clinics. They were buying condoms and lube.

I too was buying condoms and lube. We eyed each others' goods as they walked out, exchanging a glance. Without paying—swear to God. I was the only one to notice, and they didn't seem too worried that I'd watched them do it.

I stashed my items on a shelf and followed them into the crisp night air, and tailed them as they passed through islands of fluorescent streetlight. They sported the same tight-fitting trunks and tanks they could be seen in at the gym, which looked like products of a fabric shortage. They were fixtures at the gym and had made the style fashionable—although it might be more accurate to say the style was infectious. As chatty as the two seemed to be, you'd imagine their opinions—as well as other things—would spread.

Not that I was privileged to most of it. The tiger, he stayed exclusively in the weight room, with a certain forwardness of passion that you could see kind of annoyed the raccoon. The tiger never ventured into the fitness room or the pool with the raccoon or myself. He had once earned a certain local fame as a guard on the basketball court, but his aggressive playing style proved a bit too dominating for the hobbyists. His reputation had only just begun to sour when he stopped lacing up his shoes. He remained barefoot in the weight room and nothing could drag him out until—I always guessed they had a predetermined time—they'd meet in the locker room and make a display of nuzzling their glistening, perfect bodies against each other in the showers. And for all the vanity in the show nobody could pin it quite down as lewd. They certainly didn't seem crass compared to the coyote who'd been tapping his toes in the bathroom stall for the last twenty minutes. Most of the men, when they saw the couple in the showers, stopped and stared with dumb amusement. They'd scan the locker room for a compatriot to share the treat with.

That's actually how I first saw them. An eager look called me over through a pouring fog of blazing steam, and there they were in the shower. They weren't fondling each other. They weren't in the throes of passion. I mean—they were clearly a couple. Was anyone going to complain to the management about a committed pair sharing a showerhead? The tiger scrubbed the raccoon's taut, hewn body with dramatic tenderness, the raccoon coyly swatting away the tiger's more adventurous advances, though I guess eventually he figured those places had to get clean, too. Their cocks hung like great hocks of restaurant meat. The small crowd grew and nobody disliked the scene. The two seemed as if set off by a velvet rope—like a piece in a museum. The guy who called me over leaned next to me and half-whispered, "They treat this place like their harem. And it may as well be. Look at them." The tiger had his beefy arms around the raccoon's fresh-scrubbed body. They seemed to nestle perfectly into one another.

One of the gatherers seemed to try to call their attention, but he was simply trying to stir the thick mist of steam. They wouldn't have seen him anyway, their eyes were welded shut. He held his hand out, as if either directing our eyes through the steam, or to puncture it directly. He whispered to us, and it stuck in my mind for a long time: "If you were them, would you have to fuck anybody twice?"

People spoke of them as a pair, and they may as well have been. Their combined personalities commanded a gravity of permanence, like a memorial flame. A person who saw them together could only see them together. Closer than a couple, even, because they seemed to live a single life, always arriving together and leaving together and splitting only to take to their respective exercises.

Not that they weren't separately social. In the fitness room I often saw the raccoon surrounded by a group of friends, if not admirers, with whom he gossiped constantly. About the tiger, even. Juicy gossip, really. I always had to extend my ears for it, but I got what I could.

But that all seemed natural at the gym. Whoever didn't have a spotting partner found a trainer or cruised the locker room. When I saw them working as a team to steal extra large condoms at the pharmacy—the effect was much more striking. What had been a guilty indulgence at the gym burned like an addiction once in the rarefied air of the general public. And so I felt myself divined to them.

I was relieved to find them stopping for a smoke at a streetlight. The goods had been hidden away, I presumed, and now the raccoon was leaning back against a lightpole as he enjoyed his cigarette. The tiger found some real estate on the pole for himself, and I don't think either saw me as I approached. The raccoon plied the tiger to steal a drag or two, but my interrupting ended the little game.

"Hey—" my voice cracked with meekness. They turned to me so directly, and looked at me so intently, that my jaw dangled on a string. In the moment of my confusion the raccoon butted in-

"You're from the gym!" He pointed his cigarette at me, the confidence in his guess obvious in his face. "He didn't believe me. Tell him. Tell him, you go to that gym on 42nd. You run a lot."

"You're telling him where he works out, now? Did you pay this guy?"

I spit out "no," trying to take the raccoon's side but feeling only as if I were defending myself. "I've seen you two there. You seem like a very nice couple." Complimenting them put me at ease, for some reason, as if I were deflating any possible offense. And they seemed to appreciate the praise, too, so I stammered a few more sincere if awkward tributes.

The tiger especially seemed to beam at this. "You exercise with this guy at the gym?" he asked the raccoon.

"Yeah, we run together," the raccoon answered. "Not so much together, though, I suppose." His glare screwed me down to the sidewalk as smoke curled into the night from his forgotten smoke. "He's a bit shy."

"Is he?" the tiger asked, a tinge of something like hopefulness in his voice. He turned to me. "Don't talk much?"

"I, ah—" I choked on my words. Mostly I was trying to speak through the kind of grin you give the principle when you want him to think an experience has taught you a very valuable lesson. They were some kind of charming, these two guys, you couldn't deny that. They made you at least want to appear to be enjoying yourself, even when your stomach knotted with anxiety and fear. Every word they spoke came out inoffensive, and with the kind of authority that stems from acclimation to control. Their benign teasing tickled me in a funny way. Less like tickling, more like itching. They already had their hands on the scruff of my neck—in the figurative sense. I would have felt horribly insecure if they didn't beam with such open pride at my stammering affection.

Finally, I explained: "I—I tend to keep to myself."

Finding no room for disagreement, the raccoon nodded his head soberly. "Is that so, sweet cheeks?" he asked as he flicked the cigarette away. The streetlight turned on cue, and the raccoon motioned for me to follow them. Of course I did.

The tiger led the way. His domineering person would have made an excellent masthead to clear a path for us, but the sidewalk had been largely abandoned so the three of us walked in public privacy. I knew they were taking me to their place. Where else would they take me? They were taking me back to their place, and we were going to fuck. The flushing of my cheeks, half from cold, half from anxiety, must have served as a beacon of our intentions.

I turned my head at every corner, hoping to shine a light on some chance passerby who might either save or console me, since the stone-silent walk through the city did nothing to cure my nerves. We're going back to their place, and they're going to fuck me. I must have said a hundred different ways in my head to try to make it real. They could have been taking me out for ice cream, they really could have. They might have wanted to show me the new library that opened up. They might have wanted someone to talk about their problems with. None of it would have been so surreal, or so unbelievable.

The last few minutes had already been so lewd. I'd cruised them at the pharmacy, I was now realizing. I'd stalked them down the sidewalk. They couldn't have possibly imagined I wanted ice cream. They couldn't have possibly missed that my dick was tenting my pants like the revival had just rolled into town. I slipped a hand in my pocket and tried to control the beast, or at least keep him hidden from view, but neither of the pair ever tried to steal a peek, and no other soul ever materialized on our quiet walk.

"Are you a top or a bottom, squirrel?" the raccoon chased my worries and invited in my insecurities with one question. I didn't answer as immediately, hoping to goad the raccoon into a phrasing that was a little more open-ended. But he didn't repeat the question.

"I'm—I'm a bit of a bottom, I guess."

"But not exclusively?" the tiger butted in now, not turning his head but rather shouting the question so that it could bounce off the brick walls of the apartment buildings to reach my ears.

"Exclusively?" I repeated the word.

"As in..." the raccoon added, "Only." He spoke the word with a grave finality to it, as if it encompassed something truly vital.

"No," I answered, considering the question now. "Not—not only. I do what I need to, usually. I'm, you know—I'm nothing if not accommodating." That made them smile, all right. It made the tiger turn around, finally, to share a grin with his boyfriend. They shared something in that glance that made my cock twinge.

"What about you guys?" I asked, feeling as if I were interrupting.

"Exclusive top," the tiger stated like an honorary title.

"Exclusive top," the raccoon agreed.

The tiger opened a gate to an apartment complex and led us inside. My mind tried to put something together about the two, about their look they shared, as if there were some code I had but moments left to crack. Some unknown-unknown I wracked my weary mind to decipher. But their good natures swept me from the sidewalk and into an upscale, well-appointed apartment in an almost insensible blur. The scene seemed to change as on a stage, and only a moment after I'd been trying to put something together about them while we walked together, I was on their living room floor with their pants pulled down just far enough to let their fat cocks loll out in front of my nose. My eyes were still peering out from behind glass when the tiger's long, uncut cock pressed against my cheek.

"You weren't lying," he told the raccoon. "He's awful shy. You didn't pick us a virgin, did you?" The question stung a little. I might have a stammer, but my lips had always been more comfortable around cocks than words, and I wanted nothing more than to dive onto either of the cockheads- both overripe and plump like a fruit that will fall to the ground and spoil itself any moment. From my knees I gazed upon the tiger—so much finer now without the steamy veil of the gym shower, so that the rich orange of his fur was as recognizable as a swatch of paint. And I looked up at the raccoon, whose subtle muscle tones—hidden further by dark grey fur kept trimmed short- now revealed themselves in full relief. What had those muscles done? What labors had carved them and which pleasures had polished them to a smooth, gleaming finish?

"You're not gonna gag on this fat cock, are ya squirrel?" the tiger asked. I'd have to prove it to myself before I could to him, so I took the half-hard rod in my mouth and jammed it brusquely into the back of my throat so that my chest heaved and I coughed. Barely even got a taste of it. I peered at the tiger, burning with shame, but he was grinning ear to ear.

"Don't forget we've got a three strikes policy. Two more and we'll just have to cut to the main feature," the burly tiger threatened with a voice of limitless patience. My tail twitched uneasily behind me. I wondered what it must be like—to have a dick so big it demands its own usage policies. How many men hadn't been able to fit him down their throats? And if that got struck off the list, how many even let him try to stuff his cock up their ass? And what was I supposed to do about it, how was I supposed to embrace this demand? I licked my lips, a gentle groan seeping from between them as I studied the prick like a puzzle, turning it mentally this way and that, trying in desperation to find a way it could be worked into my lungs, and continually came to the same conclusion: Either it'd fit in my throat or it wouldn't. Either I'd be able to blow him or not. There wasn't much I could do but count the strikes.

I didn't falter again, though, so it proved unnecessary. I guided the stout cock onto my tongue and let it glide gracefully past my tonsils. I could taste him, then, really. He didn't taste like anything—but in the future, I was certain things would taste like him.

He rifled his fingers through my hair like he was rummaging through my pockets, tossing my head from side to side, making it a slight struggle to keep my bearing. All the while his cock grew in my throat and the raccoon's swelled before my eyes. He padded it against my cheek, as if impatient for his turn, but the tiger gave no ground. The raccoon loomed over me for quite awhile, until well after the tiger's dick had grown rock hard in my gullet. I tried to placate him by stroking him, and he used the occasion to pepper me with a few teasing quips that burned the back of my ears. "The little cock-hound," he'd call me. "All stuffed up with dick," he'd say I was, and all with the same dulcet, cool tone, as if they were still just friendly flirtations.

That didn't last too long, though. He could see the tiger had gotten comfortable, and wanted to get himself similarly well situated. The raccoon knelt down with me and gripped the base of my tail, using his free hand to admire it along its curved length, which made it twitch like an amateur's whip. I didn't feel uncomfortable, but after being stripped by two pairs of hands working in

113

tandem, like being ransacked, I didn't feel entirely at ease, either. Maybe he did it to satisfy himself, maybe he did it to relax me, but the raccoon put his hands on my sides and the touch soothed like a salve. My nose buried in the tiger's short and curlies, my view was dominated by washboard abs under tight fur so deep an orange it warmed you like an ember.

I couldn't follow the raccoon's movements as he guided his fingers over my body. At times he would drag the lightest touch along my spine, as if trying to tickle me, and when my body started to tremble like an unsound bridge he'd steady it by groping my ass. He wrapped his fingers around my stiff cock, the nimble digits caressing along the length of it, which made me blush. It excited some of my rawest insecurities to feel him measuring me up, gauging my manhood—and I certainly couldn't have compared to either of them. I'm just not built the same way. It made me go crimson, or at least I imagined my cheeks burning. It was a response I couldn't have avoided with the proud pair. It's a response I could've expected with anybody. But what made me actually whimper like a sick dog was the slightest grazing of fingertips along the inside of my thigh. My knees would quiver when he did it. The tiger, even, would voice his approval of the raccoon's finding. Or at least, he would straighten me back up by taking a firm hold of a mat of my almond hair.

The pair labored mutually. The tiger didn't look down at me much; his eyes were deadlocked with the raccoon's as if they were in a staring match. I'd say they took cues from each other, but that would make it seem too much like a play, too staged. No—They moved too naturally for that. When the raccoon would slap my ass, and clamp his hand down onto the cheek and knead it vigorously, the tiger knew to immediately stifle any yelps or murmurs by stuffing his cock well past my tongue. They'd share only little comments which largely concerned each other. "He can hardly fit your cock in his mouth," the raccoon would say, and each time the tiger would say something to the effect of "What can you expect from varmints?" In his humility, he'd give the raccoon some adulation, "He could hardly fit yours, either." He was right. The tiger was bigger, sure. "But something tells me this fella would make it work. Wouldn't you, you little cocksucker?" I didn't take the dick out of my mouth to answer.

That was some of the shame of it, but a thrilling kind of shame. A big dick is supposed to be an impediment. Guys with big dicks are supposed to rub the backs of their heads as they find a way to apologize for the oversized wrench in your plans to get fucked. Big dicks are supposed to be difficult. But these weren't. I wasn't just ashamed because they must have thought I was a slut—I was wondering myself. The fact that the cock had intimidated me like a court summons made it all the more shocking when the tiger found a way to fuck my lungs without causing me to so much as gurgle—at least, not after that first abortive attempt.

And then I could tell: They were fucking me like someone they could trust to handle it. They were fucking me like a slut.

Or maybe that's how they'd fuck a virgin, too. I can only say for myself.

The raccoon had settled on stroking my dick in long, almost curious rolls of his supple wrists. He didn't seem to want to rub me off, or even to keep me hard. That was incidental to the process of sizing me up. He explored my body like a surveyor overlooking a new parcel of land, and the journeys his free hand took over my body projected his plans for me.

The tiger didn't seem quite so inclined to exploration. He had taken instead to peppering me with dirty talk— "You love to sniff big guys' jocks, don't you, slut?" —and it brought a whimper out of my throat. (I would sniff his jock. He wouldn't have to ask me twice. I was hoping he'd let me, but didn't have near enough courage to press the issue.) The raccoon seemed to float above it, and if the tiger's words brought me down, the raccoon's hands brought me up. He pawed at me in a manner of appreciating quality; like a king running his hands over silk robes. He pressed his firm body against mine and ground his cock between my rump. After completing whatever mental maps he'd wanted of my body, he disappeared for a moment, leaving me alone with the tiger, who now was allowing me to rest my jaw with his fat cock draped across my face.

The raccoon returned shortly with the stolen goods from earlier and—promptly greasing his paw—slid a digit into my ass. I could moan freely now that my lips weren't stuffed, and I certainly availed myself of the liberty. There was no urgency in his actions, unlike some guys who'll just as soon jam their hand up to the wrist just to make sure you're loose. The raccoon didn't seem to think I needed much loosening up, though. I heard him tear into the box of condoms, and after minimal fussing; he knelt behind me at the ready. He propped me up on all fours and ground his slicked-up, girthy cock under my tail, in the crack of my cheeks, as casually as a golfer taking practice swings.

The tiger knelt down with us, since of course my lips couldn't spend a second away from his fat cock. I never remembered having been so attached to a cock. By that point my jaw had long since cramped and now simply operated out of a machinelike duty. And if my jaw were numb, my tongue was all the more sensitive for it. I was in love with that dick. I'd seen bigger, but only on guys who wielded them with a self-conscious humility. They all spared me the difficulty. But this cock didn't shy away; rather, it perfectly pushed the limits of my experience. I could always just feel a rush of being overwhelmed, though the tiger always seemed to know the perfect moment to pull me off for a breather, let me look up at his burly chest as I wiped drool from my chin, and push me back on before I could get too lonesome. I had no reason to separate myself from that dick. I saw no reason why I should. And in fact, another, particular in itself but just as intimidating, bore against my soft, slick hole. My stomach churned with anxiety, with fears of disappointment, but what voice did I have to express them?

The raccoon dipped his hips, hit his mark, and sunk his cock deep into my ass. His sigh was as much in disbelief as in pleasure. I don't think he gets so easily into most guys, with no more than a grunt that stays choked up in the chest. The raccoon plowed his hips into my cheeks, drew himself back, did so again as he pulled me by the thighs, and from there seemed to settle into a comfortable mainline groove.

I wanted to say something, but I was never much for talking in bed. "Oh, your dick is so big," I could have blurted out stupidly to the raccoon. "Goddamn, your balls smell so good," I could stammer to the tiger. But why? Their unflappable confidence had been their attraction; I shouldn't have to flatter them. And besides, as the dicks speared me from both ends, I got the feeling I was almost incidental to the whole thing. The two arched high above me, lofty and inaccessible, sharing a long kiss. They were talking dirty, but to each other, tones that grew and waned in intensity, as if playfully competitive. I caught only snippets. They were exceptionally personal things. Private things.

His dick in my mouth, his dick in my ass, and they're sharing a moment of intimacy. The guys at the gym were right, I knew it. I was a thrill, and they would burn me up like oil in an old sports car.

Some of the things the tiger said made the raccoon dig his fingers into the meat of my rump and drive himself powerfully into my ass, until I was lifting my chin to the ceiling and panting with lustful, impassioned cries. But those cries neither egged him on nor cautioned him off. They were superfluous. They started with an unheard word from the tiger and ended with another.

My dick twitched underneath me. I could've jerked myself off. I can't think they would have even noticed, let alone had reason to discourage me. But I didn't. My dick had never twitched like that before. I craved it, and waited with servile patience for the raccoon to ply my ass and plow me like a wheat field again.

The tiger grabbed my mat of messy hair and yanked me off his cock. I whimpered as I looked at his cock longingly, feeling as if I'd never have it on my lips again. He hooked his great paws under my shoulders and, with the raccoon tugging on my hips and my ass speared deep on his cock, lifted me up so that the raccoon was sitting back on the couch he was formerly leaning against, and I was upright on his lap, rooted on his dick like a skyscraper's foundation. I didn't bounce in the plush, dark grey lap—I rather bucked my hips, using the raccoon's studly cock to touch off nerves so deep in my gut I'd hardly remembered they existed. And, with the tiger just a step in front of me now, I could admire his physique, like an uncut orange jewel. His cock was rock hard, pointing eagerly up at me as if it were laying down a duel. I could have thought he was admiring me in return, but I knew he was looking right past me.

He leaned over me to kiss the raccoon. And when he did— almost as if he were trying to pull a sly trick on the man—he slid his beefy hands under my ass, lifted me off the raccoon's prick and, with practiced grace, spitted me on his own. I howled a thin, tinny squeal of delight as his fat prick pierced me with a gratified air, already happy to be stuffed again after the sudden lift. The patience he had shown in waiting his turn had been replaced with an active zeal, and he bounced me on his cock with rough, brutish strides, as if he were really engaged in some struggle against my ass. I took it like a good soldier, too.

The raccoon stole me back just as quickly, and the game was on. As they wrenched me from each other's laps they became more possessive, screwing me down on their cocks with determined, deep thrusts that ended only when the other could pry me away. And when the raccoon proved indefatigable—his position on the couch too much an advantage—the tiger merely bent me backward, lifted my legs, and slowly, without hastening himself for my beleaguered moans and yelps of concern, spread my ass around both their dicks at once.

My jaw hung agape. It may have been for awhile before, but now I was especially conscious of it. And I had my eyes shut tight, trying to push back fierce white spots from my vision. A bedraggled whimper or sigh drooled from my mouth as the tiger got himself comfortable. He seemed to be fighting for the territory, and every bit he carved out for himself resounded in a spark of static that coursed through my throbbing cock. The raccoon's rod stirred only slightly as the tiger broke into my ass like he was forcing himself through the windows.

"There we go," the Tiger said, maybe the first words I could have thought directed at me. "There we go," he muttered to himself again, like a mantra, something he might whisper to himself in the weight room. "There we go," he said and pushed himself past my face to assault the raccoon's hungry lips.

Oh God- Oh God- was the mantra in my own head.

I didn't care that neither of them had looked me in the eye for the past hour. I didn't care they might never find it proper to say another word to me ever again. I was fine with it. I might have preferred it. This was the kind of thing I wanted to bear alone, anyway. Writhing around the two cocks I felt ridiculous, silly. My cheeks burned like sulphur. The only thing that gave me the confidence to bear it was the peculiar sense of my struggle being private.

Oh God- Oh God- Goddamn- Goddamn- Goddamn

I realized I was clinging tight, very tight to the tiger's body, my cheeks was nestled up against his broad shoulders. I opened my eyes to see that I'd bitten him, though I had not the slightest recollection of digging my teeth into his shoulder. And he certainly hadn't told me to stop.

I loosened my grip a touch. I loosened up, generally. But they were only just getting started. The two were getting into it now, thrusting together, always seeming to know when to stop or go for the other, as if guided by kinky internal traffic lights. They beat into my ass with the urgency of morse code and my teeth clattered with untransmittable words. Mostly I groaned and squealed. Not for their sake, certainly. Wedged between them I was surrounded, muffled, by warm fur. I felt more as if enveloped in an impersonal furry shroud than by two thrusting men. What they were doing didn't even feel much like fucking; much the way a play doesn't seem too much like real life. It felt too perfect. Every fiber strung sang out too pure a note. The timing of every thrust, every tight grip somewhere on my lithe body, was obsessively punctual, as if read from magnetic tape. As if it could never falter.

My own voice, breaking through exasperated cries, seemed woefully flawed, and though I felt my insecurities ought to have been ignited from so humbling a display, I was drunk on something like confidence that they were too absorbed in each other to notice, judge, or care. My cock blew. It burst in thick white ribbons as if it had been built structurally unsound. It twitched in spastic, irregular beats, soaking my fur in cum. And for it all, the two didn't let up their dynamic, syncopated rhythms. They might have taken hardly any notice at all, as my broken voice didn't reach to any triumphant tenor, but climaxed in a breathy whine, a thin reed of my voice cracking through as I wheezed "Ohh-"

And as my cock still spat and leaked, my stretched ass telegraphed every thrust directly to the base of my spine. This raw energy, a fleetingly pure sensation, kept my mind from becoming hazy and my body from going limp. My muscles instead ached with an intense desire to cling to the tiger's trunk and drag my claw over his impenetrable back. To dig my heels into the raccoon's toes. To force myself closer to them until they recognized me like they had at the pharmacy. But nothing worked. They clamped down on me between their bodies, squeezed the breath right out of my chest. They polished my ring with their dicks until it felt like burnished silver.

"Hrk-!" grunted the tiger, whose chest and stomach fur had been soaked and matted in my cum. It seemed to have been struck out of him, like by a blow to the chest. It sounded strangely as if directed at me and, as if on cue to confirm my suspicions, a burly orange paw grabbed me gruffly by the chin, and the tiger's stout muzzle pressed against mine. His wide maw dwarfed mine, and he kissed me as if assaulting my lips, as if he were sucking their rosiness out for himself. He rolled his thick tongue into my mouth as if he wanted it to bully my own. And all the while he buried his dick in me. There was no doubt he was pumping me full of his cum. The raccoon burrowed himself until he was balls-deep with the tiger, and I knew he was cumming, too. Their hips inched forward in vain attempts to pry deeper into my gut. They pulsed together like that for a few moments, their breaths deep but as controlled as a marathoner's.

I realized my claws were digging into the tiger's back, and as I slowly let my body relax, as the tiger and raccoon seemed to doing, it seemed as if every vein and ridge came into full detail. I felt, even, that I could tell the exact curve of their stout cocks. My own, which had always been and was now straight as a ramrod, was luxuriantly warm sandwiched between the tiger's stomach and my own. But he was the first to pull out, and the cold electric sensation of it shocked me out of my hard-won moment of bliss. In fact, now that he seemed to see me again, and saw me freshly admiring his cut body, my old insecurities came back to a boil. Of course, he was all teeth.

While I was telling myself I couldn't be the first person they didn't fuck and toss aside, the raccoon lifted me off his tool. He pointed me to the bathroom and told the tiger to call a cab.

Toonces

Life doesn't turn out as we expect—not for any-one. We are forced to confront adversity and pain, desires we are uncomfortable with.

Twist the Blade

H. A. Kirsch

A day shy of his eighteenth birthday, on the last day of school, David Van Der Horn was walking out towards the student parking lot after picking up his diploma. Passing the computer lab, the cheetah realized why he was actually there. He ducked into the lab to say goodbye to his favorite teacher, but the room was empty. The cheetah picked up on a smell, a cat, familiar. The source of the smell stepped out of the second lab: a cougar, clad in a black motorcycle jacket, black jeans, cowboy boots, a scowl on his face, splayed ears, ruff of head fur that looked unkempt. Tomasz, who was rumored to be human-born, hence the odd hair-ruff, the awkwardness.

"Uh, hey, have you seen Mr. Parker?" David said, head ducked down a little. "I wanted... never mind," David said, and turned to leave. Tomasz didn't do anything immediately, only leaning against the door to the second lab.

"You are David? In some of my classes. Were in some of my classes. You always look at me."

David stopped. "What?" The cheetah backpedaled. "I... I mean, what? You stare at people, it's hard not to notice."

The cougar crossed the gap between cats, boot heels thumping the carpet, eyes locked on David. David started to back away, oblivious to the easy escape of the hallway door to the right, and quickly got stuffed into the corner where the teacher's station was. "What—"

David turned away from the approaching cat, reached out to grab something, but the cougar pulled him back. Tomasz muzzled the cheetah with a hand, a hint of unsteady nerves in that powerful grasp. It happened so fast; David's pants yanked down just far enough, the smell of sex and leather and feline, the warm push against his rump. Tomasz's low and Slavic-accented voice growled into David's ear, but the words went unheard. The cheetah was too preoccupied by the unique sensation of penetration, body frozen no matter how much the young cat tried to will himself away. Pain, more pain, then the sick break of pleasure through violation. "Do you want this? Do you?" the cougar rasped.

"I don't know," David mewled into the hand that gripped his mouth, the cheetah's own hand braced against the desk in front of him. The cheetah sobbed dry, the emotions swirled away before they could form tears, urged by the relentless push at that one sweet spot deep inside.

"That isn't, 'no,'" the cougar growled, and his body started to lurch. Hot flesh pumped into David, followed by damp frantic breaths against the cheetah's neck, then nothing but the ungodly haze of reflex pleasure into him. Tomasz pulled back and David slumped forward, the cheetah's passage vacated. David turned; Tomasz was walking away, towards the other lab, tail lashing hard enough to bang against anything it came near. David yanked his pants up and ran out, hitting the outside doors hard enough that his body crashed against the hard metal, side finally crushing the push-bar and dumping him into the relative safety of the half-empty parking lot.

The cheetah was halfway home when he realized the crotch of his jeans was soaking wet. He wiped at it and sniffed his shaking fingers; semen. His own.

* * *

David never told anyone what happened, leaving time to bury the memory of sudden violation, cover it over with metaphor and symbol, wishful thinking and the sting of shameful memory. It still came back now and then, those few minutes when Tomasz and David had collided after four years of furtive glances and next to no words spoken. Someone would grab David, and the cheetah's heart would turn over. David would try to have sex with one of the virile sluts in the LGBT social group at college, only to balk when it was his turn to be on the bottom. Masturbating late at night, the memory of Tomasz would return. Sometimes it made David go soft. Sometimes, it made him harder.

Soon after graduating from high school, David was well on his way to making something of himself. Thanks to being born in South Africa, he won a scholarship for African-Americans, even though a cheetah of Dutch ancestry wasn't quite what the stewards had in mind. He started on an engineering bachelors and hoped to get into medical school to work on bio-med engineering.

In his junior year, David's life fell apart. Several weeks after having been given I.V sedatives for a wisdom tooth extraction, David's left arm developed a sore, crooked lump. The campus doctor said it was an inflamed vein from the injection and gave him ibuprofen to cut down the swelling. The tortured blood vessel rebelled thanks to the accidental overdose of ibuprofen, and threw a blood clot that lodged somewhere in his brain. As he walked into a review session for his engineer midterm, David suddenly saw everything to the left turn gray. When he reached out a hand to grab at a chair, he grabbed at nothing and fell over onto his side. When a group of students gathered around him, David opened his mouth to tell them to call for help, but he couldn't even remember how to make a sound. Hours later, he woke up, unable to comprehend where he was. It took a week for him to be able to understand that he'd had a massive stroke.

In the wake of the stroke, the brain-work of school dissolved into grueling and humiliating physical therapy. Engineering and neuroscience homework was replaced with lessons on how to put food from a spoon into his mouth. After a couple of years, David had made great strides and was released to the rest of the world, where he got a job working at a nearby city hospital as a janitor. Another year of drudge work and David had worked himself up to a computer technician position with hospital IT, something that would have been no sweat as a student. While he had to take notes continuously to fend off the unexpected moments of brain fog that would waft over him, the job satisfied his animal need to

125

move around. David was quite content to jog—with a slight lurch unless he let his mind go and let instinct take over—around the hospital to 'put out fires.'

The stroke would have killed a human; the doctors chalked his stunning recovery up to being a hybrid. There was one significant complication, which only surfaced after a year and a half. While watching television, David felt the room start to spin, existence itself closing in around him, pressing on his skin like wet fabric. The sensation intensified into the literal sensation of clinging wet clothing, and the cheetah could barely will himself out of his chair. Panicked, he crawled to the phone and dialed 911. The terror-stricken cheetah found himself CT scanned, MRI scanned, EEG'd, poked with needles again and again. Nothing particularly was out of the ordinary.

The revelation came while David was in the waiting room. As an educational program on Celtic culture came on the TV, wet cloth dragged over his body, compressing him. More profound than the terrifying sensation was deja vu; something was the same as before. It was the television show, specifically a segment on the haunting uilleann pipes. It took one of the interns working for the neurologist to piece together the diagnosis: physical synasthesia. As David's brain came back from the stroke's damage, neurons rerouted themselves into patterns that never existed before. In David's brain, sound became touch. A baby crying felt like Kleenex on the fingerpads, a trumpet solo felt like cool wet grass underfoot, "Moonlight Sonata" felt like someone was literally sitting on David's chest, a blood curdling horror scream felt like he was chewing on meat.

David learned to live with the cross-stimulation just as he did the bouts of fog that clouded his mind from time to time, the weakness down his left side, the slight aversion to anything on the left. He could mostly blot out the world of felt sound with some odd ambient electronic music that made him feel like he was inside of a cloud. For five more years, David jogged around the hospital, eventually becoming lead desktop technician. While it wasn't his first choice in career, it worked. David always thought of going back to med school, but it just never materialized.

* * *

The cheetah became friends with one of the other neurologists, and started helping him out after work for extra cash. The doctor needed some photo paper as part of a cataloging project, and sent David out to pick it up along with some food for both of them. David jogged downtown to the store the doctor had told him about, "Jay's Printing". The cat milled around the aisles, ears distracted by the rhythmic synthetic drones and blurps pumped into his head by his iPod. The cheetah held out his PDA, trying to match the badly-taken picture of the right paper with the shrink-wrapped packages. The doctor was a little anal-retentive; David knew that any brand would work, but he didn't want to be on anyone's bad list.

Sound started to invade David's music, a voice. The cheetah couldn't help but try to listen in, especially as the speaker was agitated.

"...these prints, this is the sample you gave me, see? Very nice. This, this is what my client received, different paper, somehow it's too dark, why is this? Why?"

David fingered his iPod in his pocket, stilling the music and leaving only the agitated voice. The sound froze him in place, a spike of electric tingle down his lower back.

"Look, okay, so one of the guys screwed up. It happens, we'll do it over." This voice was a slightly-thuggish inner city accent. It made David feel like he was touching a fresh strawberry with his right palm.

"I don't think you understand. I am an artist, I take pictures of moments, moments of life, and my clients expect this to be flawless! What do I say, 'I'm sorry, someone else fucked up,' that isn't forgiveness. You don't charge me," The Bad Voice said. David tried to concentrate on what he was doing, but the sound drilled through his brain and spine until his tail fluffed out. The sensation was so familiar and so unexpected that David didn't place what it was, only that it was Not Appropriate.

"Hey, I can't do that. I can make it right, but I can't... this is the top of the line stock, it's expensive. It's a big loss."

"I don't care if it is loss! You are here to make money, you want to rip me off! Asshole!" The Bad Voice growled, escalating in pitch. Familiar. Paralyzing. More than that; the crawling miswired feelings moved from the cheetah's spine to between his legs, and there was no way to avoid the feeling. Sex. David's heart started to pound in his chest.

"Sir, I'm gonna have to ask you to leave, you can't, you can't yell like this in the store—"

Something fell off the sales counter and made a loud bang on the floor. David spun his head around just in time to see the maker of The Bad Voice grab the salesperson by the shirt. The angry customer was feline, a cougar, wearing an expensive-looking black alligator leather coat, black leather jeans, black cowboy boots. Everything flawless and glossy black. Past connected with present; David knew exactly who the cat was.

The mind-crossed cheetah dropped the package of photo paper on the floor with a splat; both other heads turned to look at him. David panicked and looked around. Luckily, the supplies were at the front of the store, no doubt to put the expensive things farther in the back where street kids couldn't rip them off as easily. David simply bolted out of the shop, his task failed.

Almost back to the hospital, he realized he actually had to get paper or he'd get a very long lecture about how he had to be more careful about writing things down. He turned and ran back towards the store, flustered at the thought of seeing the cat... and then finally found another camera shop. Back at the hospital, he came in panting and dumped the paper into the doctor's office along with his sack of take-out. The doctor wasn't there. David got out his food and started shakily chewing on an egg roll. He went to slug his PDA into its little cradle, but his pocket was empty.

"Oh shit, oh shit, oh shit," he hissed, muzzle twisted up on the right. David frantically searched online for the first store's telephone number and called them up. "Hi, I was just in your store, I think I left my PDA there. I was over by the paper. Yeah, I was, I ran out, sorry. I thought that guy was going to shoot you or something. Is it there? It's not, shit, can you, can you look under something? It's not mine, it's work's, I guess I can call the cops. Did—did that c-c-cougar pick it up? You didn't see? Isn't there a camera? Not on the paper! You're kidding! What, you want to give me his number? No, I'll— thanks." David hung up. The cheetah scribbled a note for the doctor, left the change from dinner under it, and took off for home.

* * *

That night, David tried to relax after his evening run but was jolted by his cell phone. The number was unlisted. He sighed and prepared to interrupt some script-reading sales person with the fact that it was illegal to telemarket to cell phones. Instead:

"Owner name, David van der Horn. Phone number, what I am calling. If found, please call." The Bad Voice. David wanted to put the phone down, but he couldn't.

"Who are you?" The cheetah said, voice coming out with a startled rrwrl.

"I have found your device. Your name is familiar... You went to school with me." Tomasz. The cougar's voice was instantly recognizable; condescending and stilted, accented, always a hint of upset. "You have spots."

David felt that crawling sensation descend down his spine again, then creep between his legs. At the store, he hadn't wanted to put a name to the cougar, in hopes that it would be a cosmic coincidence. Now, he had to. Prickles and tingles and running water sensations were normal, things that he didn't like but were used to. Occasionally the sensations felt comforting instead of upsetting, food in his mouth, the soft cloud of his music, warm flannel sheets for rustling newspaper. Never before had it felt sexual. David's memories of Tomasz made the cheetah far more scared and humiliated than they did excited, but the voice forced pleasure into the mix.

"I want to return your lost thing, there is no address."

"Don't call me! Don't call me again or I'll call the police!" David yelled into the phone, then hung up. He put it on silent and tossed it across the room onto his desk. He sat in bed, tail swishing on the covers, staring for nearly twenty minutes to see if it lit up and started buzzing its way across the desk. Nothing. The cat buried himself under the sheets, panic welling up, then subsiding, then welling up again. He remembered the brutal violation, in such a public place, how he could have been caught, what the cougar had said. "This is the last time I see you. I make it mean something," a second before the cougar had pushed inside. David heard those words again, and even in memory, his cock leaped to attention from the helpless surge of synaesthetic pleasure.

* * *

David didn't have work the next day. He spent most of it nervous, trying to ease his mind, running around town and keeping up on his exercises. When he imagined the phone call, that twinge of sexual excitement came back and the cat fought to get it out of his mind. The cheetah couldn't get over the coincidence, the incident in the store replaying over and over again. Tomasz was pissed off and about to... what? Punch the sales clerk? Stab him? Claw him? Bite his neck open? David thought back to high school, the few times Tomasz had been in fights. The malcontent cat was left alone after the second one, and for good reason; the aggressor had—rightfully—been mauled.

Dinner left the cheetah drowsy, and he fell asleep to the burbling synth sounds of his sound-blocking music, only to be jolted awake by the ringer of his phone. David unplugged an earbud and held up the phone. "Mrruh?"

"I still have your device, David," the voice on the other end said. David squeezed out a breath, chest feeling tight, hands prickling, vision posterizing as he started to faint. Then, the electrical jolt of sex.

"Stop calling me!"

"There is nothing interesting on it. Your schedule, I see, which looks boring. You play with computers?"

The cheetah started to breathe harder, and each of the words came into his ear only to send warm waves of electricity down towards his groin. After the initial shock the previous day, the sensation was more manageable but still profound. David took the phone away from his ear and looked at it. The call was at exactly eight o'clock at night, the same as the previous day's. "Why are you doing this?"

"You are the David van der Horn who was at Park Ridge High School? You don't go to school reunions. I remember you used to look funny at me all of the time. We did a project, you were bright, sullen, quiet. Maybe you still are bright. Are you well?"

The phone's distance from David's head didn't cut down the bizarre, helpless prickles of arousal at hearing Tomasz speak. "I... I guess."

"You are upset."

"Do you, do you even remember what you did?" The cheetah sighed. "I don't want to talk to you. Please stop calling me, or I'll call the police."

"That never works, they just tell you to change your number, then you have to tell everyone," Tomasz said.

"Then I'll change my number," David said. The cat's ears reddened as he realized that changing his number would be a minor inconvenience; he had barely anyone to tell.

"I don't believe you," Tomasz said, and hung up. Shaking, David curled up and felt his resolve slowly weakening away. He clutched a pillow to the side of his head, then started licking his wrist, grooming the fur down in even straight lines. The regression was humiliating, but at the same time it made the terror of anxiety go away, leaving the last ripples of helpless erotic pleasure behind before he yawned and fell asleep again.

* * *

Another day, more work, more worrying. At home in his apartment, David kept looking at the clock while he ate dinner. The nervous anticipation escalated until he staring even as he pushed food into his muzzle. 7:57. 7:58. 7:59. Just seconds after his clock reached 8:00, his phone rang.

"David, I am still holding your device," Tomasz said, a hint of play in the Slavic accent.

David tried to walk around his apartment, but found it difficult unless he went around in counter-clockwise circles. Walking subdued the filthy tingles, but only slightly. "Are you stalking me?"

"I liked you in school. Are you the same person you were back then?"

The cheetah shuddered and turned his head to the side, clutching the phone to his head as he went to lick at the fur on his arm. "I don't know, I don't think so."

"Something happened," Tomasz said. "Something bad, you are upset."

David was naked, and his cock quickly slid free of its vestigial sheath, words stroking it like a hand. "My plans for the future got w-wrecked, but I'm fine." The cheetah caught himself and slid back to being defensive. "Why do you care? You're a creep."

"I am broken, but I know this," the cougar growled. "You talk to me, so I talk back."

"Every day at the same time?"

"To make you relax, I did not think of you for at least a decade. I have other things to think about, my soul, my career, whatever there is in my cat-head. Now, I have something from you."

If David had been attacked in a park, knifed and robbed, raped and left for dead, it would be easy to simply hang up on Tomasz. Instead of brutal rape, David had just been fucked. Tomasz had even asked if the cheetah wanted it, complete with a pause for an answer. That, along with the titillating trembles from the sound of the cougar's clipped Polish-American words, made David realize that his nervous waiting for the cat's call was not out of dread. "Oh, I see." David sighed it out, breath shuddering a little.

"Are you doing something right now?" The cougar asked.

"What do you mean? I'm, I'm just... I just sat down," David said, depositing himself onto the bed. The words came through his head and made him want to lie back, hold himself, touch, feel. The cheetah's ears grew hot.

"The way you breathe, it sounds... like you touch yourself," Tomasz said, voice preceded by an amused mrrwrl.

The cougar was right. David chirped and hung up the phone. Not from anger, but shame. He rolled over in bed, again and again, urged on as a cat to roll his scent around. The cheetah let out a mrrwrl and a chirp. Then, horrified, he started stroking himself again. All he saw in his head was Tomasz violently holding the hapless store clerk from the print shop, but it was enough.

* * *

The phone calls stopped, leaving David to get increasingly worried about his missing PDA and the repercussions at work. While heading out to lunch a few days later, David took a shortcut to avoid a mass of onlookers gathered around a traffic accident. His phone startled him halfway down a side street.

"I can see you," the voice said. Tomasz again.

David froze, blanching before the warm trickle of sex could take hold. "You can see me?" He said, eyes looking around, trying to spot where the cougar could be.

"Yes, I am up in my studio. I will flash a camera at the window," the cougar said. A little glint caught David's eye and he turned around. Then again, a flash strobe up in a third-story window. Next to the flash was the outline of a cat wearing a black suit.

"Are you following me?" David said, afraid to move.

"I decide to stop calling you, but what happens? Then you walk past my window. I look, there is a spotted cat. Would you like your device back? I can come down and give it to you," the cougar said. He moved away from the window. David quickly jogged to the end of the block, where there wasn't line of sight.

"Look, keep it, I don't fucking care!"

"In that case, perhaps you want dinner instead?"

David looked at his phone like it was a foreign object. "What? Dinner? Are you f-fucking kidding?"

"Dinner, lunch, breakfast, coffee. I would suggest drinks but that might be frightening to you."

The cheetah kept walking, looking around, panicked that the cougar might appear on the streets. Only the usual pedestrians. "I, I don't know why you think I would want to do that—"

"It could be something fast, I don't know, I do not like fast food as in American trash, it is foul. Do you like sushi?"

David stopped by a bus stop enclosure. It was simply too distracting to walk and talk on the phone, especially with the crawling sex that was moving over his back, stomach, crotch as the strange cat talked. "Yeah, sushi is okay."

"There is a place, Midori, not far. If you come there at eight o'clock tonight, I return your device to you, and we could eat together. Goodbye," Tomasz said, and the line went dead.

* * *

David's curiosity got the better of him. The last day of high school was years in the past, and he needed to get the PDA back.

Filing a police report and admitting he had dropped it out of fear would be awkward, just another mistake, just another unfortunate situation.

The cat took a seat at Midori at ten to eight, heart pounding, tail curled around the legs of the chair. The restaurant was nothing visually fancy, although it ranked high according to some reviews. Midori smelled like fish; the salty smell of a meat market, not the rank smell of fish gone bad. The interior was also alarmingly green.

David busied himself with a ginger-dressed salad. Another side effect of the stroke's brain-mangling was that crunchy food was abnormally comforting, even if it was something un-catty like a salad.

At one minute after eight, Tomasz showed up. He was dressed exactly the same as in the print shop: black alligator blazer, white dress shirt unbuttoned to mid chest, black leather pants, black cowboy boots. He fixed eyes on David and beelined for the cheetah's table, then sat down. "You look the same," he said.

"I guess, you do too?" David squeezed his knees together, feeling the stir as Tomasz spoke. He had a little control over the sensation now; It felt like the flush from having a strong drink on an empty stomach.

"I now wear fancy clothes," the cougar said, and picked up the the little check mark order sheet. He ticked off a few boxes with a stubby pencil. "I still eat raw meat, even if it is only fish." David produced his own sheet and the cougar ran them up to the sushi bar. Tomasz returned and sat down, muzzle tipped down.

"I just fix computers," David said. "You don't need a suit to do that. They'd outsource my job to the other side of the world if shipping wasn't so expensive."

"I'm sure Mr. Parker would be proud," Tomasz said, leaning just the slightly bit closer. David squirmed and looked away. He was about to stand up and leave when one of the sushi chefs dinged a bell.

"Hey Fancy Coat! Sushi is ready!" The chef waved a knife as he put the serving tray onto the top of the counter and rang the bell again.

"Do you see? That was fast, efficient," Tomasz said, stalking over to the bar and taking the two trays with a bow. "Fucking gourmet, no McShit." The cougar's tray was lined with only sashimi. David's was a mix of colorful nigiri and maki, half vegetarian, one of the rolls looking like it had glistening green twigs sticking out of it.

"Yeah. I heard this place was fast and uh, colorful," David said, trying to speak slowly to keep from stammering. His face felt weak from nerves, cock hard in his pants from the sound of Tomasz's voice. The cheetah dipped the fish-end of a nigiri into some soy sauce, then put it away in his muzzle, right hand cupping under it, left resting on his thigh.

Tomasz leaned and sniffed at his fish, then switched his eyes back and forth. "I do a bad thing," he said as a stage whisper, leaning closer to his food. Instead of picking up one of the slabs of fish with chopsticks, the cougar lowered his muzzle down to the plate and grasped it in his teeth.

"Oh my god, don't..." David said, looking around, ears burning red inside. He chuckled with a stutter as Tomasz dropped and licked at the hunk of meat, then picked it up again in his teeth, the cougar quickly jerking his head as he chewed it by dropping it and catching it again, finally putting it down with a swallow. David stared.

"Are you surprised? I am a cat," Tomasz growled, then turned towards the bar and grinned. One of the chefs slapped knives and grinned back. "I come here all the time, they are used to it. It is like watching the animal show for them."

"Oh," was all David could manage. The cheetah took another piece of sushi and the two sat for minutes with no words, no sounds except eating. Slowly, David's arousal waned, cock slacking inside his pants.

"You see I don't have your device," Tomasz said after a swallow of the last sashimi. The cougar wiped his fingers on his napkin, but not before looking at his hand like it was going to attack him.

"Why do you call it a, uh, device?"

"Why do you turn red in the ear—and your left one wilts—when I talk?" Tomasz responded. David had no answer except to

135

turn his muzzle down. His eyes watched the cougar take out his wallet and put down cash for the meal. The cougar then simply walked out. David rushed after him, bursting out onto the street.

"Hey! You can't just leave—"

"I have it at my home, it is an excuse to invite you," Tomasz said with a jaw snap, twisting on a boot heel to face David. The cheetah trembled and nearly fell over, left arm flailing out and banging a light post before seizing hard around it.

"Invite?"

"I want you to see my apartment, my studio. To prove I am a real person," Tomasz said over his shoulder as he stalked down the sidewalk.

David let almost a quarter block go by before he ran after Tomasz. The cougar didn't slow, or even look behind. "I guess that's, that's... okay," David said. He almost wanted to cover his mouth. No, it wasn't okay, but that didn't matter. If Tomasz spoke, David could not resist the sexual pleasure that came over him. Tomasz said nothing, not even looking back to see if David was following. They reached the same brick building from earlier in the day, and Tomasz opened the door to go inside. Still without looking, he held it for David.

The first part of the apartment was a sort of lounge area that led to to the kitchen through a curtain. Paneling the walls were huge photo prints, all of them starting at 'fashion' and ending at 'creepy'. Nothing X-rated, but there were several alarming scenes that looked better placed in war journalism. "These are pictures I take, I hang them for prospective clients. Do you want a drink?"

"I don't, I don't drink," David said, stroking at his left upper arm. The cougar didn't make himself anything.

"Neither do I, but I ask." The cat walked across the room, boot heels pounding the hardwood floor. "I ask you something else, are you lame?"

David felt his heart start to race; it was something in the way the cougar walked. A subtle, gut feeling. It lifted the fur up the back of his neck. "Am I lame?" The cheetah perked his ears up in disbelief at the rude question.

"Like a horse, broken legs, you walk strange, never use your left arm," Tomasz said as he latched the door. Then he moved past David, towards another door, going into the adjoining room. David carefully followed, looking in through the door frame, left side of his body facing the wall.

"I... I had a stroke a few years ago. It kind of messed everything up, but I'm better now." The room he was looking into was full of an odd assortment of furniture. A leather sofa, all alone, with everything else pushed up against a far wall. A contrived living room. "Uh. This is weird."

"It is my studio. Come in if you want," Tomasz said. Against his better judgment, David stepped in, lured by that patronizing clipped English. The cougar stood near the couch and regarded the jumble of stuff at the far wall. Coffee table, chairs on top of it, end tables, a single bed frame, lamps, rolls of some kind of material. Tomasz walked over to the door and flicked a light switch. Cold fluorescent light gave way to impossibly bright incandescent spots, which the cougar dialed down to a dusky glow. They were all aimed at the couch. The cougar then closed the door most of the way, and walked back over. "I will not take pictures."

"Uh, good. I don't think I'd make a good model," David said, tail thumping against the couch.

As Tomasz stood there, he took out something from his pocket, a pair of black gloves. He slid them on over his broad hands, having to fiddle with the leather so his blunted claws could stick out little holes in the fingertips. "I disagree."

David's eyes fixed on the gloves, staring as the leather fitted over tawny fingers. He felt a stir in his crotch, but not from the cougar's words. Then fear, and he backed up, forced to sit down as his legs met the sofa. "No, really, I don't, I mean my eye sometimes wanders, and I get this far-off look... and my arm has this huge scar on it—"

Tomasz lunged and seized the cheetah by the left bicep. David froze, so panicked he could not move. Moving his left arm was an act of will, and his will was gone. "You are hot, you were hot ten years ago, sheepish and sullen. You are hot now, sheepish and sullen and broken." The last word came with a sneer, a sweep-back of the cougar's ears. The words stroked through David's cock, swelling it inside his pants. "When I talk to you, you get... hard, you get scared. Helpless, aroused. Do you think I can't smell it? I smell everything, all the time, it drives me insane, along with everything I hear, all the feeling, wind in my fur, someone bumping my fucking tail."

David struggled and pulled at his arm, having to lurch his body. "Let me go—"

"No," Tomasz hissed, and grabbed David by the other wrist, the cheetah fighting. "I talk, it runs through you. Your ears are hot, I see your dick in your pants."

The cheetah tried to fight, but the vicious words buckled his knees, body sinking back down to the couch. He tried to kick, but his left leg didn't want to cooperate. He opened his muzzle, but only a stuttered chirp came out. Tomasz sunk down as well, until he was straddling the spotted cat's lap, gloved hands holding David's arms back against the couch. The cougar then leaned forward, rubbing his forehead against David's face, muzzle then touching muzzle. The cheetah twisted his head, chirped, let out a high growl.

"I liked you in school," Tomasz purred. "So scared and lonely, looking at me when you could, tail curling around your chair. Do you think I don't notice? Why do you think I fucked you? What could I say so you like me? I talk like shit, I get in trouble, fail classes, I have to think hard just to keep from growling like a cat or talking in Polish," Tomasz scowled, and let go of the cat's lame arm, reaching over to pet his face. "You still look good, slender. I like that."

"Sssstop," David hissed, ears burning hot as gloved fingers touched his face, nose sniffing hard at the musky smell of leather.

"You don't like being touched there?" Tomasz said, leaning back. He pulled on David's lame arm, twisting the cheetah's upper body. The cougar kneeled off the cat's lap and started turning him to push him towards the arm of the sofa. "Then I fuck you again. Everything is sex and meat, and when I eat some, fuck some, there is only more! Born human, twisted into cat!"

A lame cheetah was no match for a burly cougar. Tomasz was strong, and wielded that strength with little grace. He put his forearm down on David's back and shoved the cat's chest down against the arm of the couch, then drew the other hand down over the cheetah's rump. "Take your pants down," Tomasz growled. "You like this, you like my words, I smell it, so hard."

"No, I'm not! I'm not hard!" David yowled, arms clutching at the sofa, then shoving back against the crushing weight between his shoulder blades.

"Don't lie to me," Tomasz hissed, and stuffed his free hand under the cheetah's waist. David was lying. Tomasz didn't fondle, but simply undid the top button with a yank, pulled the zipper down. The cougar let out an excited rrwrl as the cheetah's tight, spotted rump came free. Gloved fingers stroked from David's shirt down to his tail-base. The cheetah yowled and squirmed, tail lashing, hiking over to the side, back arching to push his rump up. "Ahh, you're a fucking cat too, you can't resist this."

"Stop, I don't want to, I don't, I don't—" David mewled, then shoved his face into the arm of the sofa. The touch was irresistible, eons of cat racial memory eroding the cheetah's human desire to flee as he was petted. "I w-wanted to see..."

"You wanted to see me? Is that what you say?" Tomasz chuckled. The cougar massaged at his own crotch with a black hand, then unbuttoned the fly and reached in to expose himself. Half-feline, tapered point with nubs around the crown, thick otherwise, curved up, already glistening at the head. One hand stroked the length to milk preseed out. The other wiped a little onto a gloved thumb, then grabbed the cheetah's rump-cheek and stroked thumb over tailhole. David mewled again, breath catching in his chest, the hole flexing and squeezing. Tomasz slowly pressed in, until David rrrowrled and slapped his tail around at the penetration. "You are not so tight, you get fucked often?" David said nothing, so Tomasz pulled his thumb back, then smacked the cheetah's rump with a hard swat. The cheetah yowled. "I said, you get fucked often?"

"N-n-nhrhr," the cat whimpered, hiding his face. He quivered and twitched, then let out a stuttering intake of air and a sniff through his nose. Tomasz couldn't see it, but David's face was burning, scrunched up, tears watering down the black trails in the fur around his muzzle. The cheetah sobbed hard, each convulsion twisted with the relentless twinge of sex from being touched, penetrated, not to mention the sound of Tomasz's voice.

The cougar growled, moving so his cock could ride at David's cleft, pushing through the white fur there, the tapered head quickly entering. David's stuttering sobs turned into an alarming cat wail; Tomasz simply shoved in, then tugged back, leathers creaking as he started up into a forceful rhythm. ten years collapsed into no time at all, David in exactly the same place he had been the last day of school, mounted and confused, excited and ashamed.

"Sometimes I think of you, seeing my dick slide into asshole, smell you come into your pants, how satisfied I felt to conquer you, and I touch myself," Tomasz growled. The sound of it stung down through David's body, the cheetah unable to keep from writhing himself forward, cock pressing against the sofa's smooth leather. The penetration stung suddenly, and David reached back to shove Tomasz away, only to have gloved hands latch onto his biceps like metal vices. The cheetah struggled as Tomasz thrusted, the force only growing. Tomasz leaned down, licked the cat's ear. "You come for me again, as I tell you that you are slut for coming here, letting me fuck you, again."

David's face burned as he sobbed for a moment, the convulsions fading much faster into helpless pleasure. 'Letting me fuck you, again'. That was the truth; David was strong, he could have screamed the banshee wail of a cat, bitten and clawed, but he didn't. His tail thumped at the cougar's chest. "Please..." he begged, face mashed against the leather arm of the sofa, lips moving against the wet of drool and tears.

The cougar stopped, mid-stroke. "What? Is this please stop, or please fuck harder, please come into your asshole like you are whore?" Tomasz's gloved hands eased up on the cat's arms, fingers moving to stroke the cat's back, down towards the tail, triggering a shuddering lift of the cheetah's rump, a powerful spasm in David's tailhole. "Do you want it? This time?"

All that time, and David was still bent over and fucked. "Yes," he chirped, head swimming as a wave of dizziness came over him, hole squeezing on the invading cougar.

Tomasz moved from ear-licking and back-stroking to biting at the cheetah's scruff, and that was it. David shuddered and mrrrred, the sound dropping at the end to the throaty and unearthly howl of a female cat in heat. The cheetah shook and arched his back, prickled the fur along his spine, fluffed his tail out; his cock sprayed at the sofa, seed landing in wet splats. His ears splayed, ashamed and terrified, wishing he wasn't a cat so it would take much longer, so he wouldn't come, but it was far too late when the thought came. David gasped and struggled, not to fight away the cougar, but to jerk his body back and forth on the penetrating flesh, push his cock into the wet puddle on the smooth sofa leather.

Tomasz pounded, snarling and grunting around the cheetah's neck scruff, gasping turning rhythmic as his own climax came, seed squirting in through the tight hole. The cougar backed off almost before he was finished, a last spurt pushing out against David's tailhole before the black-clad cat simply stood up and stomped out of the room, a flurry of boot heels and leather creaks. From the other room, sounds filtered in. Water running, a few fabricky smacks. More boot heels on the hard floor.

Alone, David felt empty. Literally, as his hole squeezed tight, trying to restrain the cougar's seed inside. The cheetah looked down, wincing as he saw the slimy streaks of white on the couch. He sniffed, the pungent smell of his own seed. An urge slid up his spine and he leaned down, ears splayed as he could not resist the need to clean, letting out a kitten mrrewl as he licked up the mess. As soon as it was gone, the urge vanished, leaving David hunkered down and panting.

Tomasz re-appeared in the doorway and threw something at the sofa, a silver metal thing landing with a thump on the leather. "Here is device. You see the door, you go out, turn left down the hall, there is fire-escape. Put your dick into your pants or you will be arrested." Tomasz's eyes looked anywhere but at David. The cougar then clutched the doorknob and yanked the inner door shut, leaving David alone again.

The cheetah panicked upon seeing the cat, vision going spotty as he felt shame turn to panic, knowing he was caught licking up his own spunk. Then, Tomasz just left, leaving David with only confused relief. The cheetah looked over to the other exit, hand absently clutching for his returned PDA. David leapt up to his feet, hurriedly yanking his pants up and fumbling the fly shut. Heat flooded his face, but no tears came, just panic.

David found his way out onto the fire escape. He paused, head flicking around, trying to pick out any watching eyes. The ladder went down into an alley, where no one else seemed to be. He quickly rushed down it, and took off as soon as his feet touched ground. David usually limped somewhat, having to think to move his left leg. But a reflex like running, he had no problems with that, and was soon at top sprint, bolting down the street, the world turned into a blur around him as he instinctively retraced steps to his apartment. He flew into the lobby, raced up the six flights of stairs, and nearly bashed his own apartment door down. Once inside, he collapsed into bed, panting for air. He ripped his clothes off, rolled back and forth against the sheets, then sniffed at the air.

Tomasz's scent still clung to him. It wafted up from the heat between his legs, asshole still wet with the cougar's sex. Naked and quivering, David reached back to feel the damage. His hole was sore and wet. When he brought his fingers up, they were smeared with whitish ooze, not blood. David felt thankful for a moment, ashamed the next. He wanted to take a shower, clean off the smell, but then he remembered Tomasz's voice, the sound reactivating all the mixed feelings, sex and fear. He remembered the words, the cougar's claim that he wanted it. He remembered how it felt to be forced to come from inside, helpless. He remembered back to school days, brain finally hitting the full realization that he had a crush on the strange, dark-clothed cougar who stared at him. Being violated twice was no coincidence; Tomasz had wanted it, and David let it happen. Thinking about it made the cheetah mewl and tear up again, but he was hard. He lay back, ears burning hot, tail lashing the bed, and started to imagine Tomasz taking him again. The thoughts kept coming until David came.

H. A. Kirsch

Growing up in the tight spaces of the spaceship Sojourner has made Taylor adept at blending in and sneaking around. Can he make it when circumstance pushes him onto center stage?

The Revelation of Choice

Anima

If there was one sound that all races everywhere could unite in loathing against, it would be the shrill *KREEN—KREEN—KREEN* of morning alarms.

"Off," Taylor mumbled, tugging sharply on his blanket to set it retracting into a slot at the foot of the bed. The alarm stubbornly continued to wail.

Wait, that's not—

"Taylor! Suit! Now!" His father Ulysses' silhouette bulked in the door frame just long enough to bark what his son had just figured out, before thumping down the hall to the next bedroom. Taylor lurched out into the corridor, brown sleep-glazed eyes reflecting the sherbet-orange and phosphorus-white of emergency lights, and careened his way into the anteroom to grab his suit from its locker. The acrid stench of synthetic fabrics and plastic made him sneer, black lips arching to show wet teeth, but he didn't hesitate in slithering into the suit. Hesitation meant death if this wasn't a drill, and hours of lectures and reeducation if it was. It was hard to say which motivated him more. On went the helmet shell, and Taylor swung down the elongated myriplex shell that accommodated his muzzle. Click, hiss. Three green lights glowed to life, and he could relax a bit.

By now his siblings were all roused and suited up as well, and in the emergency strobes he could see frightened, bored, and barely-open eyes through his brothers' and sisters' respective face-plates. Their father thumped in a few seconds later, glancing at the status lights on each young canine-type's chest.

"Good. You all live today, assuming our section wasn't holed or blasted or sacrificed, blah-de-blah-blah." He flicked the status monitor beside the airlock for a time display, and the family watched it tick down from 05:59 to 06:00. The alarms fell silent, and the suits came off, strobing lights replaced with the unwavering sunshine hue of WakeUp mode. An image of the fleet, three generation ships in formation around the fourth 'sleeper' ship, sprang onto the monitor. A communications officer recited the Sojourner status report, tuned out by the family as background noise. It sounded like just another morning.

Taylor stowed his suit, following the dozens of necessary steps without a conscious thought, but ran nose-first into Ulysses' thick arm when he tried to return to his room.

"This is it, pup. You're moving quarters today. Get your padd; you won't need the rest." His tone was gentle, but Taylor's ears and tail still drooped.

"Today? I just reached completion yesterday! I thought..." The big, brawny canine, a constant in his life for so long, was uncharacteristically somber. He made no move to relent, and his expression didn't budge. "Yes sir."

Taylor ignored his personal cubby filled with trinkets and awards from the past eighteen years, and spared just a glance at the poster of fog-wreathed mountains he'd stuck to the ceiling above his bunk. He scooped up just the sleek slab of his personal padd and its padded sleeve, and resisting the urge to linger, toggled the lights off for the last time. Back in the anteroom, he punched up his assignment and synced his badge so he'd be able to find his way to the new quarters. Movement reflected in the screen made him turn his head to see his family assembled, and everyone had a hug, a slap, or a nip for him to send him on his way.

* * *

When the door opened on the assigned quarters, Taylor was sure there had been a mistake. *This can't be for four people! True us canines need just about zero personal space, but...* His childhood room had been just large enough for his bed, a tiny desk, and a cupboard for coveralls. This spartan, steel-gray chamber, intended for four, hardly seemed bigger!

Of course, I would be the last one here. Taylor sighed to himself as three pairs of eyes turned on him.

"Welcome to the press!" His male bunk-mate grinned, not bothering to roll out of his rack.

"The press?" Taylor cocked his head, then glanced around for some sort of nameplate.

"Chris was just telling us he's convinced they're putting us in progressively smaller quarters to turn us into puppy-bricks," one of the females explained, grinning. "It would be in keeping with their ruthless exploration of resources, anyways."

"Karin, it's 'exploitation,' and did you bite the hand that feeds you the second you were out of the womb, or did you wait until after your first breakfast?" The second girl chided with a smile, poking Karin in the ribs and eliciting a yelp.

"Well excuse me for not being perfectly, uh... indoctrinated like you and the other lapdogs, Heather." Karin fended off more pokes from Heather while turning to the newcomer. "And you, muttly? Got any politics yet?"

Taylor scratched briskly behind one ear, and broke eye-contact to toss his padd onto his bunk. "No, not really." *It's just a giant mess of old men arguing.* "I'm Taylor, by the way."

"Welcome Taylor. I'm sure I'll have you converted in no— Yelp!" Any further proselytizing by Karin was prevented by a more determined assault from Heather, giving Chris a moment to mumble to the newest bunk-mate.

"'Muttly.' Geez. Don't sweat the ancestry, pup. Karin's poodle stock, Heather is an Australian kelpie whatever the hell that is, and I'm German shepherd, but who cares? Maybe it used to mean something back when these tubs first launched, but these days it's just a sign your ancestors were xenophobes. Anyone who tells you different is a dinosaur." Chris winked, and gave his bunk-mate's shoulder a comradely squeeze. Taylor managed to relax a little, just in time to be embarrassed by a deafening stomach-growl.

Heather took mercy on Karin to applaud Taylor's midsection. "Hear hear! I doubt any of us got breakfast. Let's see where we'll be eating, chow-hounds."

* * *

Taylor noted that Heather took to the role of 'den mother' quite well, herding her three 'pups' out into the broad, ribbed corridors of the massive generation-ship. They soon found themselves in a busier artery than Taylor was used to, and he found himself struggling to keep from tucking his tail between his legs. Avian communications officers darted and wove between slower pedestrians, bearing sealed orders and signed rosters and who knew what else to the furthest reaches of the spherical ship. Taylor turned his head to follow one stunning blue, yellow, and orange bipedal bird, its bright hues warning other foot-traffic to let it and its vital messages through. Security officers, created by blending human and wolf genetic material instead of 'watered-down' canine DNA, loped by occasionally. A single reptile-type stood by one of the simulated 'window' slots in the corridor, staring, literally, off into space.

"Have any of you ever seen a navigator in person?" Taylor had always wanted to meet one of the hulking whale or sleek dolphin-types.

"Nuh-uh," Chris responded, twisting sideways to let a broad-shouldered equine-type pass by, "just seen 'em on the monitors like everyone else."

"I saw one once, when father took me to a high-level officer's meeting." Karin grinned, secure in her superior knowledge of the cetaceans. Heather tweaked her ear for her, and expertly dodged the retaliatory nip.

The mess hall was functionally identical to the one Taylor had grown up with, but all its facilities and seating were doubled to serve a larger population in this portion of the ship. There was nothing new on the menu, but the novelty of eating in a new space with new people made every bite seem exotic. Other canine-types happily made room for the four at a table when they approached, and Taylor and company squeezed in. There was hardly room between them all to move his arms enough to handle the utensils, but a little nudging in either direction got him just enough space to manage.

By contrast, the wolves sat quite far apart at their own tables, and the avians ate so quickly few of them even bothered to take seats or perches. Then there were the hoofers. All the heavy lifting aboard the ship tended to be done by equine-types and their relatives, and being descended from herd animals, they tended to close ranks against all but their own kind. A clatter from behind the serving counter drew his gaze, and Taylor watched a cow in food service gear stare at the floor while the canine kitchen manager scolded her. What could she possibly have done to deserve a tirade like that? You can't hole the hull or steer us into a star by overcooking beans.

A nudge brought Taylor's attention back to his own table, where Chris was nodding across the table at a pretty Irish Setter female. "What do you think? You into red-heads, Taylor?"

Taylor looked, and had to admit she was a striking girl, but just a glance was enough for ingrained mental habits to tell him she would never give him a second look. Chris tilted his head as Taylor's eyes slid off of the girl, the shepherd's ears pricked, then frowned.

"Taylor, not all the pure-breeds are like Karin. Not all of them are even pure-breeds, they just have some seriously dominant genes. I probably have plenty of other breeds in me," he grinned, resting a hand on his chest.

Taylor shook his head, but at least Chris had him smiling again. "Maybe, but at least a handsome one came out on top."

The bigger dog planted one paw on his own chest, and laid the back of the other across his forehead. "Reign in that silver tongue sir, before I swoon into my pudding!"

When Taylor had gotten his snickers under control, he wobbled a paw at the German shepherd. "You know what I mean. You're tall, you have a great build, a regal muzzle..." Chris made a half-swoon towards his dessert, finally putting an end to the mutt's gushing.

Taylor gestured to himself, wearing a wry smile. "In primary they called me the amazing jumble-hound." Taylor was rather patchwork, it was true. His coat was cocoa-brown all along his back and most of his limbs, but his chest, belly, and face were all splashed in a white and black speckle pattern that would've been striking—if it had been symmetrical. Even his paws' pads weren't uniform, the left being pink and the right paw's black. His build was strange too; most of the canine-types were either wiry runners, barrel-chested workers, or diminutive and nimble technicians. He was short and heavy-chested, making him an awkward fit almost anywhere.

"You're a s'more dog, Taylor. If anything, you look good enough to eat!" Chris gave him a slap on the back, and rose to dispose of his tray. Taylor should have been doing the same, but he was too startled by Chris's words.

Good enough to eat?

* * *

Back in their quarters, all four bunk-mates found their padds blinking. Taylor set the slender slab of plastic and silicon across his thighs and tapped the screen, bringing up a short video message. A portly Border Collie matron smiled up at him.

"Taylor of Fortitude Level, Section 3? I'm Suzie-B, and you have a career counseling appointment with me tomorrow. I've uploaded some forms and questionnaires for you to fill out and drop in my e-basket, so take care of that and I'll see you tomorrow! Toodles!" He tossed the padd aside, a whine escaping his muzzle.

"Oh come on now muttly, I'm sure they've got a lovely inventory clerk position all ready for you! Probably in a nice out-of-the-way cargo bay." Karin got about halfway through the sentence before Heather stuffed a pillow into her face, but she gamely continued on, and Taylor was only too able to fill in the muffled words. Chris dangled his head down from the upper bunk, peering upside-down at Taylor.

"Are you really that worried about what you'll end up doing? There's no shortage of work, especially with all those activists refusing their positions. I'm sure there will be something you'll like to do." He let an arm drop down as well, reaching beneath his own bunk to ruffle Taylor's ears. "What are you interested in?"

Taylor leaned into the ear-ruffling a bit more than was really called for, while a warm little thrill floated down his spine. "None of the stuff we learned in primary, or secondary, or tertiary. I mean, the engineering stuff looked like fun, but you need so much math, and I'm terrible with numbers. And growing things in the hydroponic bays sounded fulfilling, but the hoofers do that. When I was younger, I wanted more than anything to be an explorer... But not even my grand-pups will live to see the world we're bound for."

Chris considered a moment, and consulted his padd before sliding down off the bunk. He sat on Taylor's bed, hip and thigh pressed flush to the mutt's. He showed Taylor some open positions on his padd, but it felt like an excuse to get closer. The mutt felt a growing tightness in his shorts, and tried not to breathe too deeply of Chris's scent lest that snugness get any worse! I... I had guessed a couple of times, but this proves it. No breeder, I...

Chris tapped his padd and spoke. "What about supervision? You could work in an engineering or hydro section, doing part of the teamwork without needing the nitty-gritty skills necessary to do the specialized work."

This time, Heather spoke up for him. "Chris, I'm not sure it's in Taylor's temperament to herd gear-heads or farm-hands around, and it's the work itself he thought sounded fulfilling if I heard him right."

Taylor nodded, after a brief surprised silence. "Pretty much, yeah." I guess I must be pretty transparent.

"Well, the counselor's are pretty good at what they do, so keep an open mind and ask lots of questions. That goes for all of us!" Chris raised his voice, but got raspberried for his trouble by a petulant Karin.

"Princess poodle probably already has a job lined up as the captain's slipper-fetcher anyways, right?" Taylor ventured, grinning, and was well-rewarded with various yells.

"Oooooooohh!"

"Burn!"

"You damned runt!"

* * *

"The career counselors are 'pretty good,' huh?" Taylor tried to make it come out more joking than bitter, and failed utterly. Chris sat up in his bunk and watched while his roommate shrugged out of dust-covered coveralls and limped toward the cleanser unit at the rear of the room. He spotted the patch on the mutt's discarded coveralls and winced.

"Ore processing? Earth and sky, that's horrid!"

Taylor just waved a dismissive paw, mumbling "Life's a bitch," still shedding clothing, and finally stepped into the tiny cubicle set into the wall. He held his breath while abrasive powder jetted through his fur, stinging the skin beneath, and shivered as vacuum vents sucked every trace of it away again. Chris was standing outside the cleanser when he emerged, and gave him an awkward lick on the cheek, one paw resting on the mutt's shoulder. The welcome contact eased the sour twist of the mutt's lips, but couldn't erase it entirely.

"I'm sorry, Taylor. You couldn't... There wasn't another option?" The incredulity in Chris's voice made Taylor sigh.

"Karin and the activists may be right about some things. That counselor, who seemed so sweet and motherly? She is very, very good at kindly killing off your aspirations and convincing you to aim low. No one wants to do ore processing, but it's one of the most essential departments on board. 'We keep the ships moving,' you know." Taylor reached up to Chris's paw on his shoulder and gave it a squeeze, his eyes resting on the other male's. The shepherd whined once, quietly, before Taylor felt himself flush and changed the subject. "What about you? Did you get placed today?"

Chris nodded, and jerked his head at the uniform jacket hanging off his bunk. It was the familiar royal blue with red stitching of management. "I'm overseeing one of the sick-bays. The reptile-types make excellent physicians, but they need a lot of prodding."

"Whooooooo needs a lot of prodding?" Karin snickered, stepping in. "Are you two boys joining the anti-breeder movement?"

Taylor's tail tucked well between his legs, and he backpedaled from Chris, fairly diving into his bunk. He shot Chris a pleading look and the shepherd answered with an ear-flick.

"We could hardly be blamed, when the folks we're supposed to be humping are shrill harpies like you." Chris growled, and Karin actually shut up instead of firing back, her eyes wide.

Taylor wriggled into clean coveralls, and before Chris could climb back into his bunk, grabbed the taller male's paw and towed him out the door into the ship. He felt Karin's eyes on them all the way out. No one stood in their offshoot from the main corridor, so the canines had a moment of privacy. Taylor swallowed and blinked rapidly, willing his stomach to settle. "When you asked me about that setter yesterday, it wasn't just guy-talk, was it?" Gods, this is too soon, but I need this.

Chris leaned over the mutt's shoulder to murmur in one flopped-over ear, "I'd hoped you were more like me. You're a sweet little guy, Taylor." This close to the shepherd, Taylor could get his scent properly, something the Sojourner's filtration system was designed to prevent. Arousal, and the exotic spicy musk of a strange male teased the mutt's nose.

Feeling a shiver race up his spine from tailbase to neck, Taylor whispered back in a hot burst of breath, "And you're gorgeous, Chris. I want—" A trio of canines turned into their offshoot, chatting and laughing. Chris dropped Taylor's paw, but the mutt beckoned subtly to the other dog, walking quickly towards the main corridor with his eyes straight ahead, trusting the shepherd to simply follow. A glance behind him after a few dozen feet showed him that he was indeed pursued, and in more than one respect! Another shiver rolled up his spine.

Fewer and fewer crew-members passed them in the corridor, until the broad artery split into capillaries, service passages which in turn lead to maintenance tunnels.

"Taylor, where—" Chris began, reaching for his friend's shoulder. Taylor stopped short outside a maintenance hatch, and threw the bolts.

"Here. I learned about these while on one of my 'exploration' expeditions on my old level, and if they're the same..." He ducked his head inside, then raised a knee to the lip of the hatch to crawl forward and in, disappearing into the dim tunnel beyond. Chris glanced around for bystanders, then followed suit, tail cautiously a-wag. The cramped passage soon opened out into a section about four feet wide, lined with a soft springy material instead of the usual synthetic rubbers and plating.

"What is this? It's as nice as our mattresses, maybe better!" Chris was too involved in trying to solve the mystery of the wonder-foam to see Taylor turning around, and bringing his nose in to touch the bigger dog's.

"It's a filtering moss. I would come to a junction like this every afternoon I could and read." He grinned, tongue lolling out. "Or nap." Taylor drew the tongue along the clean dark lines of Chris's lips. The shepherd reached for him, turning to rest on one hip. Taylor gladly wriggled in belly-to-belly against his bunk-mate, letting the bigger canine wrap toned arms around him and slip a firm thigh between his legs. Their breathing, closer to panting now, seemed to die inches outside their embrace as the sound hit the muffling filter.

"Am I...?" Chris murmured in a floppy, chocolate-colored ear, and Taylor's head bobbed beneath his chin.

"My first. I haven't caught many eyes, you know. Most look at me and see 'runt,' not,"

"S'more dog," the two chuckled together, tails thumping on the living foam. Somewhere a blower started up, and warm air ruffled the pair's fur. Chris reached between them, pulling down the zipper on first Taylor's coveralls...then his own, while snuffling down over the mutt's ears, cheek, and neck. Taylor shuddered, sucking in a great lungful of the stronger scent released from behind those clothes, and struggled completely free of his own. He sent fingers questing down his own stomach to brush along the rigid length of his shaft, its length nicely swollen, a trickle of needy nectar working its way ticklishly down its taut underbelly.

I thought it would be harder... It always was in the dreams. Must be nerves. He tried to clear his head and think bold thoughts, and Chris let him reach down into his open zipper, palming the heavy tip of his own bone-stiffened cock. A whine threaded its way through Taylor's nose.

"Found what you want?" Chris smiled, planting moist kisses between Taylor's ears. He was quivering, and breath whistled through his nose, just shy of a whine of his own.

"Ever since your quip about eating me up," Taylor whispered, wrapping his paw around the throbbing spire of heat that was Chris's thick shaft, "I wanted to be at your mercy. No wonder they made you management," he growled, grinning up along Chris's chest, into his eyes.

"I excel at handling all situations," the shepherd smirked, wrapping his own paw around the mutt's cock to deliver a brief squeeze. Chris rolled to his knees to shrug out of his coverall sleeves, grunting when one stuck at the wrist. Soon he was as bare as Taylor, crimson cock-flesh bobbing above a handful of balls the color of graham-crackers. Taylor's own pink shaft spurted slippery need at the sight of his crush in the buff, and as if he'd done it a hundred times, he wiggled down to brace his chest on the floor and hiked his rump into the air. The white and black speckled fur intruded between his thighs and even blazed over his surprisingly large sac, but left the cleft of his rear uniformly chocolate-brown.

Taylor hunched at the feel of Chris's hands on his hips, then buried his head in folded arms with a louder whine at the feel of the shepherd's wet bone nuzzling beneath his tail. Chris had to seize the wagging appendage to make any headway. Slippery, fire-poker-hot cock kissed the silky star framed by soft-furred cheeks, and though Taylor clenched anxiously instead of relaxing, Chris forged onward. Taylor's whine jumped up to a yelp, before quite by accident, he discovered how to relax back there. Still wincing, he took comfort in the throaty growl that rumbled in Chris's chest where it rested atop his back. The feel of rigid flesh filling him grew as Chris sank deeper, Taylor's tongue lolling out over his lips. That delicious feeling of slithering intrusion helped him forget the hot pain of a sphincter too swiftly stretched.

"Chris... so perfect, oh..." Taylor's half-coherent pants got a chuckle out of the bigger male. Soon the shepherd's hips cupped his rump, and Chris's hot panting breaths stroked the back of his neck and head. Chris pulled slowly back to the tip, burrowed back in with a shiver and a whine, then began to thrust in earnest.

Taylor moved with him, pain gradually replaced by pleasure. His eyes slid shut, and trembling croons squeezed out as if displaced by the heavy shaft sliding home. Chris's hips slapped his ass and his sac bounced into Taylor's own, beads of leaked precum dampening the fur covering both pairs of balls. The mutt unfolded an arm from beneath his head, sliding a sweaty-padded paw down to grasp his shaft, squeezing and pumping it in time with the thrusts of the shepherd. Now he was as hard as his dreams had promised, almost as if Chris's shaft had slid deep enough to fill out his own, swelling him to the utmost. Not a word passed Chris's lips, just growls and heavy breathing.

"That's some good prodding!" Taylor panted, grinning. "Is this that positive reinforcement technique I've heard about?" He leaned back, grinding his ass into Chris's hips at the bottom of one of the shepherd's thrusts. He received just a grunt in return, before needing to yelp himself! Chris's knot had swollen and was battering at his stretched sphincter. "C, Chris, try not to, okay?"

Chris wasn't listening. He forced that bloated bulb of flesh home, making both cry out for perfectly opposed reasons. The shepherd's hot seed surged within the mutt, who'd bitten his wrist to muffle any further cries.

He must not have heard me. I must not have said it loud enough. Taylor un-wedged his wrist from his jaws and subtly brushed tears from the corners of his eyes, while Chris let the mutt take most of his weight while finishing off his climax within him.

"Thank you, s'more dog." He sighed, reaching beneath Taylor to stroke his belly and, a bit shyly, brush a finger along his pink shaft. "Need to do something about this."

Taylor moaned, letting the sound fill out his throat in a column of audio bliss, spilling between teeth and over wet lips. The feel of Chris's paw around his shaft was half-familiar from his own private explorations, brief moments snatched in restrooms and in his bunk. He couldn't feel his own shaft through this strange appendage though, losing half his awareness, half his control over the experience. Chris gripped him strangely, fingers spread in a way Taylor had never tried before, and the pumps he delivered were too quick and—the mutt winced.

"Slower, softer!" He pleaded, and this time Chris listened, grinning as Taylor's muzzle fell open in wordless bliss. A klaxon wailed to life, startling both dogs into raising their hackles, and killing all desire left in Taylor's heart and loins. Chris swore, and pulled, trying to work his knot free of his partner's rump. Taylor yelped and groped behind him, clutching for his lover's hips. "No! You can't, not yet!"

"Have to, have to get to my station. Have to!" Panic tinged the shepherd's voice, and he pulled harder still! He popped free, leaving a whining and smarting Taylor behind as he scrambled back to the hatch and his duties. Cum with a definite hint of pink soaked into the moss beneath the mutt's rump. Taylor felt hot tears dribbling down the length of his muzzle, a saline burn in his nostrils, and slammed a fist into the foam again and again, creating no sound whatsoever.

* * *

Taylor avoided his quarters, and simply reported to his duty station. The emergency was virtually over by the time the alarms had been sounded; a hoofer had screwed up the placement of a pallet of chemical drums, and several had toppled and burst open. Minor chemical burns and lung irritation afflicted half a dozen workers before safety seals sprang into operation.

"Late response to an emergency recall. Extra duty shift for you, to be completed before the end of this week." Taylor's supervisor didn't even look up from his padd when he paused in front of his newest recruit to deliver the reprimand. If he had, he might have seen the evidence of recent tears, and a shimmer in Taylor's eyes that promised more, given just a little encouragement. He didn't look up, and those tears never fell.

After haunting a mess hall and an observation lounge for a couple of hours apiece, Taylor finally returned to his quarters in the middle of his bunk-mates' sleep cycle. He crawled into his bunk and sank into a deep, exhausted sleep. It took shaking to rouse him.

"Taylor! You'll be late for your shift. I don't think your padd's alarm is working." Heather straightened from her crouch beside his bunk, and glancing over her shoulder at him with wrinkled brows, returned to the mirror beside the cleanser to finish her grooming regimen. He fumbled his padd out from beneath his bunk and saw she was right; he hadn't set the alarm last night, and he had just minutes to report to his station. He dressed quickly and quietly in clean coveralls and hustled out the door, feeling Heather's eyes on his shoulder blades. A thought turned him around, and back through the hatch.

"Thanks Heather. Have a good day." Taylor received a sunny smile in return, the earlier tension above her eyes erased, before he jogged back out. Out in the corridor his brisk trot slipped into a trudge, eyes on the soothing blue foam of the corridor floor. He nearly ran right into a familiar barrel-chest.

"Taylor! I thought I hadn't made it in time." His father turned and fell into step with his son, ruffling the s'more dog's ears. "I read they'd placed you in ore processing, eh? You're doing the ship a great service, keeping us fueled and sailin' along."

Taylor managed a sickly grin for his father's benefit, and nodded. "Yes, we keep the ships moving." That earned him a laugh and a slap on the back that nearly sent him down into that blue floor.

"How are the bunk-mates? No friction I hope? Were you lucky enough to end up with a couple cute girls or are they..." He glanced both ways before ducking his head down and muttering, "dogs?" Whether it was his own joke or Taylor's shudder that did it, the mutt's father laughed until the entire section heard him. Taylor turned from Ulysses to stare at a monitor suspended from the corridor ceiling, tail low with embarrassment. The monitor was displaying a news-feed of a ship council meeting, where all crew-types were represented. The hoofer representatives happened to be speaking, and it was hard to miss how sparse their delegation looked beside the other types; even the reptiles, by far a minority on any of the ships, enjoyed better representation on the council. Before Taylor could think much on the strange imbalance, the pair reached the lift down to ore processing. Taylor gave his father a good hard squeeze around the middle, nose tucked against the big dog's chest. The scents of home in Ulysses' fur nearly made him break down.

"Here's my stop Dad. Tell everyone I miss them, okay?" *You have no idea how much.*

"I will, pup. Your mother would have been proud you're doing such vital work. Come join us for dinner some night, okay?"

Taylor waited for the lift doors to shut before allowing a shuddering sigh to escape. Motors hummed, and the fragile mutt was whisked down into the bowels of the ship where all the life-saving, fleet-moving, back-breaking, soul-sucking work got done.

* * *

Heather was again the only one in the room when Taylor returned from his shift.

"Chris and Karin went ahead to dinner. I thought I'd stay behind, do a little paperwork, then walk over with you." She pointed him to the cleanser with a wink. "Don't take too long, or Chris will clean them out. He's been eating like a hoofer lately."

Taylor smiled, wagging just enough to raise a small dust cloud around him, and hurried to the cleanser. When he emerged, he felt like hiding behind a towel while getting dressed, and couldn't figure out why until he realized Heather was casually glancing his way now and then. Privacy was a rare luxury aboard the Sojourner, and he'd spent most of his life dressing and undressing in front of family and strangers alike. It's not just that she was looking though. It's how she was looking, he decided, warmth spreading through him at the realization. Next time he caught her peering over at him, he managed to peer right back.

She was a pretty girl, with coloration similar to a doberman's but far better-defined. Her coat largely resembled black velvet, a soft darkness, while light honey-colored fur covered her limbs from the knees and elbows down and spread across the lower half of her face and jaw, cascading past the neckline of her uniform. She lacked the 'slippery' sleek impression pinschers give, possessing a stockier build. Her ears stood tall and proud, and faithfully trained on him whenever he spoke.

Do I like that she's looking? Would I like to return the favor the next time she steps out of the cleanser? He decided to make an experiment out of it. His eyes darted to Chris's bunk, one of his management coats draped over the pillow. He left you in that duct like a used rag, you goofy mutt. No one will ever care for you. Ears down and tail tucked, Taylor fumbled his way into fresh coveralls.

"I know you're not enjoying your work," she murmured, not needing any great volume in their tiny quarters. "It's hard to imagine who would enjoy nudging asteroid chunks around. We have an opening in my traffic control office..."

Taylor's ears and tail both perked.

"...but it requires a level two math rating." She hurried on when Taylor tucked his tail. "I can help you study!"

"Thanks Heather. That means a lot to me, and I'd love to study you." He blinked when she giggled, then groaned. "With you. Let's get something to eat; I must be running on fumes." Taylor brushed the door controls and let Heather lead the way to the mess hall. They spoke about work on the way, and she shared some of her own rough moments from the first week guiding and approving courses for the mining tugs and repair vessels that the Sojourner and its two sister ships carried.

"Hattie had just finished reminding us about our tag-out and lock-out responsibilities, lecturing to us while we stood in nice orderly ranks, when one of the mechanics got blasted out of a maneuvering thruster she was working on! She rolled fifty feet, finally fetching up against a stack of lube drums, but on the way she bowled over half the working shift! In formation, they were ducks in a row!" Taylor couldn't stop giggling in spite of himself, and Heather's wicked grin only encouraged him.

"Was she alright?" He managed after a moment, brushing a tear from his cheek.

"She hasn't been able to get her fur to lie flat since, and she ralphed on the deck chief who reached her first. Other than that? Sure, she's fine. She had to retake the tag-out training though." Their laughter preceded them as the pair entered the mess hall, the happy sound dying out as they stepped over the threshold.

* * *

Two hoofers lay bleeding on the floor of the mess hall, and Chris stood over them, arm hanging broken at his side. Blood oozed from his left boot, adding to the nearly-black puddle he stood in. Every other hoofer in the hall was grouped in a semi-circle around the scene, some simply mute and horrified witnesses, while others gripped tools or serving trays and glared

160

at the injured canine-type. Behind Chris, the other canines had arrayed themselves, but there was no more unity among their ranks. Whatever had happened, not everyone backed the German shepherd.

"Chris...?" Taylor heard himself say, and the shepherd locked eyes with him, one filmed with red.

"I don't know you." Chris turned from the mutt, and growled at the defensive line of equine, caprine, and bovine types. "Sit down and finish your meals, or your next one will be through a straw, I promise you."

Just as a beefy donkey lunged towards Chris with a screwdriver, a black-furred blur hit him in the ribs, throwing him onto the bodies of the first two unconscious hoofers. Before the herbivores could react to this fresh assault, eight lupine-types, massive wolves with frozen eyes, moved to flank the hoofers. Security had arrived in force.

"Look at this! Look! They don't even care about the dogs, just us! That deviant, boy-breeding Shepherd chews a pair of us to bits and we're the villains!" The donkey on the floor brayed, one arm clutching his bruised or broken ribs. One wolf pricked his ears at this, and snarled once, a sound like a uniform being torn in half. All eyes on him, he spoke.

"Violence will never be tolerated on this or any other vessel in the fleet. It is not a part of our mission. It is not a part of our breeding." The donkey looked about ready to challenge that last statement, but a glare from the wolf cut him off. "Everyone involved in this incident will be punished exactly as law dictates." More and more of the security officer's teeth grew visible as he spoke. "Departure from the law leads to chaos. I will never abide chaos on this ship." Both the canine and hoofer sides of the confrontation shrank from the display. One type was bred for strength and endurance, the other for loyalty and management, but the creature putting on its show between them was bred for a position requiring violence and intimidation... and it was exceedingly well-suited for it. The situation was defused.

Taylor and Heather retreated well out of the way of the security detail and their prisoners. Chris didn't so much as glance at his former lover again. Heather wrapped a paw around Taylor's arm above the elbow, and squeezed.

"Brawling... that's four months in the brig at least." She sighed, turning to watch Chris's back retreat down the corridor. "Let's get out of here, Taylor... find somewhere else to eat. I don't want to eat anywhere with blood on the floor."

"I, I think I want—" His mind raced for an excuse, any excuse that would cut this exchange as short as possible. "I need to visit my father, Heather. I'm sorry, I forgot I was supposed to meet him for dinner. I'll see you back at our quarters." Taylor mustered a genuine-looking smile with a soul-cracking effort, and slipped out into the corridors. He nearly ran over Karin, who turned an accusing glare on him.

Stammering half an apology, he continued his flight, ears burning with the one word the poodle had hissed at him.

"Whore."

* * *

Hours later Taylor found himself in another mess hall, a much smaller one. It seemed to be a temporary addition to accommodate some maintenance workers involved in the reconstruction of a large chunk of the Sojourner's outer hull. No one he knew would be here, and no one would remember him when he left.

While spooning up the pasty beef stew he'd grabbed, he read the first sentence of a plaque on the wall again and again without absorbing it. 'Mission year 126: An asteroid later identified as SO8950311A struck Sojourner because of Navigational error on two levels, causing loss of life and equipment.'

A seat beside him swung out on its anchoring arm, and an old goat filled it, his shaggy hands wrapped around a mug of coffee. His uniform declared him a high-ranking maintenance worker, probably a supervisor even, a level very few hoofers climbed to. Taylor dropped his eyes from the plaque and concentrated on his soup again, spoon clunking on the dull beige plastic of the bowl.

"Don't wolf it down and hurry off on my account, pup." The goat chortled, holding the mug beneath his chin as if bathing in the steam rising from the brown brew.

Taylor winced, and lowered his spoon. "Please, don't say wolf. Had enough of them today."

The goat took a leisurely sip. "You were there, over on Solidarity deck. You couldn't have been at the other ones; no matter how disturbed, no pup would wander more than eight decks from home."

"There were other incidents today? Between..."

"Hoofers and yappers, yep. First was the ugliest, but the w— pardon," the goat winked over at Taylor, "the security officers came down so hard and fast on the other two that everyone seemed to get the message. The only peaceful ship in the fleet is the humans', and only because they're all hibernatin' deeper than bears with mono." He took another meditative sip, then nudged Taylor gently with an elbow. "You're too quiet. Everyone else has been crazy for news about this." When Taylor had no immediate retort, he set his coffee down and nodded, slot-pupiled gaze softening towards the canine. "Yeah. I thought so. I'm sorry, pup."

Alarmed, Taylor's fur bristled all along his neck and shoulders. "Sorry? About what?" The mutt checked the exits for security, undercover Social Relations officers...anything.

"You're the one that other pup was protesting so powerfully about today... First with his tongue, and then with his fists and fangs. Don't make a puddle kid; they don't install monitors in temporary messes like this. And don't give me that look either, I happen to be as 'deviant' an old goat as it's possible to be on this star-bucket." He wagged his bearded chin at Taylor, and the mutt couldn't help but smile weakly, fur smoothing out again. "I take a quiet interest in situations like the one that exploded today, and I saw you. I have access to the monitors. It just so happened you wandered into my neck of the woods, and I just so happen to know that when we most want time alone is often the time we need someone's ear or shoulder instead."

Taylor's shoulders sagged. He was so tired, and didn't have the energy left to worry about this being a trap. He shrugged at the goat, his muscles bunching with an abrupt surge of anger. "He used me. I thought I'd found a friend, and more, but he used me and threw me out." He stared hard at his soup bowl, imagining how good it would feel to dash it off the table and into the wall. Maybe he could splatter that plaque if he angled it right.

"I don't know him, but he's management, right?" The goat mimed a snappy salute, rolling his yellow eyes. Taylor nodded, still calculating soup trajectories. "I know his type then. I lay odds he liked you, and was as excited as you at first. No one has much 'experience' just out of their educational period, no matter what you heard in the cleansers, and I would bet he was discovering himself anew just as you were. But then he got to thinking about life, and his career. You dogs, and don't take this the wrong way pup," he warned with a shaken index finger, "have a lot of built-in loyalty. It works on you in strange ways, and the purer the breed the more pronounced... or strange, the effect. He is denying himself, and he probably has the will to do it for the rest of his life."

"And I'm not pulling my fur out over not being a breeder because...?" Taylor wondered aloud, swiveling to face the goat completely.

"Because you're a hopeless, mixed up, homogenized, shaken-not-stirred, melting pot of a mutt. Hell, look at your chin!" The caprine reached over to fuss with the fur about Taylor's jaw. "There might be some goat in there somewhere." The billy-goat smiled as the mutt let a laugh escape, and continued. "That instilled loyalty must've faded over the generations somewhat. I don't excuse your lover for dumping you and his true self the way he did, but maybe you can understand why he did it, and take any blame off of your own head. Trust me, liking your own sex doesn't make you an asshole." He tapped his chest. "I'm not one, though you'll have to take my word for it. You don't seem like one. That's already two out of three that lay outside the overlap of 'deviant' and 'asshole.'"

Nodding slowly, the mutt started to address his dinner companion, then winced at an oversight. "Ugh, I'm sorry, I'm Taylor. What's your name, sir?" He asked, tilting his head.

"I'm Reggie, head of maintenance for this quadrant." Taylor's eyes must have bulged, and Reggie laughed 'til his glasses nearly fell off. "Yes pup, you can climb the ladder and keep who or whatever you wish in your bed, so long as you're smart."

No wonder he could get at the monitors. "Reggie... thanks. I'm lucky I ended up here. The stew wasn't great, but the company and advice really hit the spot." Taylor slid out of his seat, and saluted, then had to duck as the old goat swatted at him.

"Ohhh, quit it and get on home. Drop by again and tell me how you're getting on. I'll be here 'til I keel over I bet, trying to patch this bucket."

"I will, though I might grab a bite somewhere beforehand where they don't use liquid-weld to thicken the stew." Taylor gaped his jaws in a grin, waved, and trotted out of the mess with his back straight and tail proudly arched.

* * *

Taylor found the two girls asleep back in their quarters, and undressed by the glow of his padd. It took his tired mind a moment to realize Karin was in Chris's empty bunk. Gods... She had a thing for him? I should talk to her—sometime.

Exhausted, the mutt crawled right into bed and fell asleep before his head settled into the Taylor-shaped dent in the pillow. In a flash, he was aware of a presence looming over him, then a paw stretching out towards his face. Panicking, Taylor swatted at it, but his wrist was intercepted and caught in an implacable grip.

"Hush, lil mutt. It's just me, your friendly local kelpie-dog." Heather's face resolved in patches above him. The honey-colored jaw and the cute comma shapes above each eye seemed to float in the darkness of the rest of her coat. Taylor opened his mouth to ask what was going on, when Heather ducked beneath the top bunk and slid a very warm, very unclothed thigh across his body to rest against his opposite hip. She straddled him, planting her palms on either side of his head, the upper bunk's height pressing them close enough that she forced him to remain staring up at her.

"Heather... you want me?" He whispered, tentative paws sliding along her sides, fingertips sinking into the inch-thick coat.

"I'll show you how much," she panted, tongue pouring back and forth an inch from her muzzle. Her hips began to stir, sliding up over his stomach, then down again...leaving a stripe of his pelt slick and carpeted with her scent. Any question of whether or not females could stir his loins was obliterated in a great flush of heat, as his cock plumped and slipped from its sheath. Heather slid forward once more, trying to muffle a giggle, and parked her sopping groin just north of his navel. She wagged furiously, and their positions being what they were, Taylor found his cock assaulted by that enthused tail! With mixed motives he seized her hips, pulling her further up his body and simultaneously scooting down until her slippery folds kissed his nose. Her yelp at the cold of his nose melted into a moan when Taylor smothered her flushed sex with his tongue. She put up with it for just seconds before pulling her hips from his grasp, and squirming back down his body.

"Next time. Tonight I want to be filled to the brim with s'more-dog." Her breasts pressed in around his nose as Heather planted her dripping cleft atop the tapered spear of dog-cock below. *Ohhh stardust... I've never appreciated being short 'til this second.* Liquid velvety heat rolled down around his straining shaft, swallowing every inch, Heather laughing breathlessly.

"Ohhh Taaaa—"

"Taaaaylor. You forgot to set your alarm again, didn't you?"

He blinked awake, turning his head to see Heather smiling at him from her bunk, where she was lacing up her boots. Taylor blinked harder, trying to clear the sultry after-images of the dream from his head. He bunched the blankets to try and hide the tent he'd pitched beneath them. "Yep, got in late and forgot."

"I know, I was worried." Her smile faltered. "I got in touch with your father, and he hadn't seen you all day."

Taylor winced a little. "Yeah... I lied yesterday. Sorry Heather. I was..." He found himself completely at a loss. What could he possibly say that would make any sense? As the silence stretched out, Heather shook her head and stood, looking smart in her uniform. *If I'm ever going to catch a glimpse of her stepping out of the cleanser, I really need to set that alarm.* Her pants clung snugly to her legs and curvily-flared hips. He found himself looking forward to her turning and leav—

"I guess no excuse is better than another lie. Just tell me you don't want to hang out next time, okay? I thought we had fun chatting yesterday, but whatever."

Taylor looked, but couldn't properly enjoy the kelpie's backside; not when she'd left on that note. The mutt's shoulders began a familiar slump into weary resignation, when Taylor halted mid-wilt, set his jaw, and bolted out of bed. He darted out into the corridors after Heather. Other crew-members on their way to work smirked and pointed at his nearly-nude state, and though his ears and nose burned, he strode past them all to reach the kelpie.

"Come back to the room a second? I can explain. I really don't want to go through the whole day knowing you're upset at me." He spread his paws, pads up, tail twitching with a few hopeful wags.

Heather shook her head, but smiled, leaning down to lick at the mutt's muzzle-bridge. "I'd be late, and so would you. We'll talk tonight, okay? Maybe Karin will have a hot date and we'll have a bit of privacy even." She winked one amber-colored eye, turned and bounced off. This time, Taylor could fully appreciate her departure. Then he realized he was enjoying it too much for the amount of clothing he was wearing!

Hurrying back to his quarters, the mutt mumbled to himself. "Well... let's get to work! We keep the ships moving after all."

* * *

Taylor's muzzle itched behind his mask as condensation from his breath beaded and dripped back into his fur. His eyes itched behind his goggles. His paws were overheated and clammy inside his gloves. Standing before a waist-high conveyor belt, he nudged chunks of rock off on their way to the furnaces, and raked gravel over grates where it could fall into collection bins. Those molecular furnaces would break down the ore, extracting trapped gasses and valuable minerals to keep the ship stocked and fueled.

Others like him, misfits or layabouts or perhaps simply unlucky, performed the same mechanical tasks up and down the belts shifting ore left by the mining tugs. He had tried striking up a conversation with one or two of his coworkers, but the responses were wooden at best, and more often he'd just been ignored.

After doing this for a few months, I doubt I'd want to acknowledge the new guy either—just get through the day and escape.

He winced as a clumsy shove down the line sent a large chunk of rock to the floor, earning the worker responsible some rough words from the shift supervisor, a stodgy bulldog whose brain's contents would have fit in a daily log binder with room left over. Ore-processing drones were micro-managed and treated like sub-normals. I wonder if Chris's underlings feel like this.

The supervisor, Richards, pulled a squawking communicator from his belt and stopped to listen, eyes jerking back and forth as if he could read the spoken words. He turned and waddled towards the operations office, and the laborers exchanged significant looks. No supervisor had ever left a chewing-out unfinished. Taylor felt a sinking sensation in his gut. He set his Ore Sorting Implement aside and pursued his superior into the office.

"...believe this! What were those wolves doing, sitting down to tea? So no one can get in or out? No, we'll be fine until about 1800 tomorrow, then we'll need another load. Cripes, this is—you! Get back to work."

Taylor squared his shoulders and stood his ground in the office doorway, facing down the glaring bulldog. "I need to know what's going on. A friend might be involved." I don't see how, but...

Token protest lodged, Richards simply waved Taylor towards a memo displayed on the terminal on his desk. Taylor walked over and stooped to read. "Herbivore revolt? Space docks six through ten are blocked by protestors... Security forces were poisoned?!"

"None of 'em died, but they'll be laid up for hours yet. The hoofers have too much to do with food production. It was easy to target the security shifts, though they got a lot of other canine-types too." He snorted and whipped a paw out towards the receiving bay, getting on to the really relevant news. "Our ore deliveries are halted until further notice. They're going to park a passenger shuttle in our bay because the main ones have been shut down!"

Shit. "Heather." The hoofers wouldn't hurt her, would they? She is a symbol of their 'oppression' after all though. If they're going to hurt anyone, it'd be her, and any other canine management they can get their big calloused hands on.

"I need to go. I have, er, wagging pneumonia."

168

"Wagging... pneumonia?" Richards squinted, looking the mutt up and down. "You look fine."

"I know! That's the thing. You look fine in the early stages, walking around and spreading the bug, and within two hours," Taylor winced and rubbed his own belly, "your prolapsed stomach is hanging from your jaws."

"Euugh!" The bulldog backpedaled, tripping over a chair and rolling off the edge of the seat into a cabinet. The meaty impact sent a cascade of mask filters and tension sheets down upon his head, and Taylor decided his early dismissal was granted.

* * *

Ominous announcements about remaining in quarters and reporting to duty stations reverberated through the corridors, but Taylor flattened his ears and pelted towards the contested sections. He'd had quite enough of authority for today. *If they'd just treated everyone more or less equally we wouldn't be in this mess.*

He hadn't made much progress towards the docks when a familiar poodle shoved a maintenance worker out of the way a few yards ahead, and looked ready to do the same to him.

"Karin! Stop! Where's Heather?" He put up both paws, ready to catch her shoulders and hold her if necessary.

"Taylor? Out of the way, slut!" Her snarl held panic and malice in equal measure, and the salt-tang of tears was strong in her fur.

"What happened? Is Heather behind you?" He gentled his voice, but the fur was raising all up and down his back, puffing out beneath his coveralls.

Karin scowled, refusing to meet his eyes. "No, she got herself penned in by those stupid plant-munchers. They almost murdered me, but I got away! I'm going to my father right now and telling him to override the bay's controls and blow the reeking lot of them into space!" Her eyes narrowed, lips curling over her needle-like teeth. "I only wish you were in there too! I'll never forgive you for seducing Chris!"

Taylor's eyes widened. "I didn't! He–" Karin lunged at him with a snarl of fury, but he sidestepped and made a grab for her. Taylor got a sharp nip for his trouble and a desperate shove. Karin wasn't huge, but she didn't need to be to knock down the mutt. She disappeared back the way he'd come at a dead sprint. Fear pushed him up and got him moving again, jogging towards the bays again with his heart in his throat. *She can't tell anyone, can she? Revealing me would reveal Chris.* Before he chased his mental tail through too many circuits, Taylor got ahold of himself. *Stop worrying about something you can't change, and focus on what you still can.* With a clearer head, he pressed on.

Twice, gruff management personnel stopped him to ask his business, apparently filling in for the ill security force. Instead of sticking with his pneumonia story, Taylor claimed to have an important message for the chief of security. This got him past the first figurehead, but the second seized his arm.

"Excellent, we've been waiting for an update! Chief Compatii is just down here, c'mon c'mon!" Dragged along by the thrilled golden labrador, Taylor soon found himself staring up into the face of the wolf who had made that little speech in the mess hall the day before. Security Chief Compatii might as well have been a cargo-lifter covered in fur. Every limb was hard with muscle, a result only possible with religious conditioning and little desk work.

"You're not sick?" Was all Taylor could think to say, tail tucked so far between his legs he could have clutched it in his paws, and almost did, for something to do with his fidgeting fingers.

"I never eat anything I don't prepare, unseal... or kill myself. Where are the orders?" Compatii's cold stare drilled into Taylor, and the mutt fought to keep a whine from escaping his throat.

Two or three precious seconds passed while the mutt juggled the tasks of formulating a lie, retaining bladder control, and resisting the urge to show Compatii his tummy. "You're to open formal negotiations with the protesters, and take no one into custody."

Every jaw in the room but Taylor's and the wolf's dropped open.

"You can't be serious!"

"Who is this kid?"

"Where are the damn birds! They should be delivering communiques like this."

170

"The communications officers can't get through. The protesters are detaining them. I got through because of my... unglamorous position." Taylor slapped the ore processing insignia on his coveralls, raising a puff of dust in the process. This whole lying thing must be momentum-based; it's a lot easier to roll on once you get started!

"Who sent you, undercover-pup?" The wolf was stone-faced. Taylor struggled to control his sweating and fear, knowing the scent would, if not give him away, at least trigger further suspicion! The superb air-handling system on board was his ally, this time.

"Quadrant-head Reggie. I didn't presume to ask where he got the orders, sir." Take that and chew on it, loyalty-programming.

Compatii pushed back from his desk and strode to the far wall, every movement making Taylor feel like stalked prey. The wolf punched buttons, calling up a communications menu on the inset monitor. There was a murmur from the other gathered officials as the wolf punched for Reggie.

"I will not discuss the nature of the orders," he reassured the murmurers. "I simply want to confirm their messenger." Compatii stood at parade-rest and waited for the video-call to go through. In seconds, an image resolved of a cluttered office and a rumpled-looking Reggie. Every single surface in the goat's room was covered in padds, parts, tools, and plastic film printouts; except the desk behind him, which was suspiciously bare.

"What?" The old goat snapped, panting. "I'm very busy just now." Taylor couldn't be certain, but at the edge of the camera's coverage he thought he saw a hoof dragging itself beneath a massive pile of old-fashioned paper manuals.

"Sir," Compatii nodded in what seemed like real respect, "I have a canine crew-member here who claims to bear orders from you, and I wanted to confirm your relationship." The wolf stepped aside to allow the pickup to include Taylor. Reggie adjusted his glasses to cover any shock at seeing the young mutt.

"...I'd be happy to confirm our relationship. Goodbye." Reggie terminated the call.

Smartly done, you old hornball. Taylor managed to avoid wagging by digging his claws into the pads of his palms. When he flicked his eyes over to Compatii's face, however, the desire to wag swiftly faded. He wasn't positive what an entirely-convinced lupine-type looked like, but he was sure it looked nothing like Compatii.

"Crew-member—" The security chief raised one brow.

"Taylor, of Fortitude level section 3, sir."

"—Taylor, I'm sending you on into section 8A to open negotiations with the disaffected hoofers. Report back to me when you've made some progress. Here's a portable comm." The huge wolf gaped his jaws slightly in a grin that made every hair on Taylor's body attempt to shoot off and escape. "Good luck."

* * *

Corridors near section 8A weren't quite deserted; there were hoofers roaming around, either under orders to keep a watch on the perimeter or aimlessly wandering, as confused by recent events as certain speckled mutts. With every yard he drew closer to the docking bays, it grew harder to avoid being seen; his unimpressive stature and the occasional doorway or wayward equipment crate were often his only savior. Activity in the corridors rose steadily, and too soon he was pinned down between two large fuel canisters, hunkered down in their shadow, while listening to a raised voice ringing through the nearest open bay.

"—every day we show up for work, and heave and ho until we're permitted to leave. We don't get ill like the dogs, or the lizards, or the birds! We always show up! But when one of us is gravid, do they lighten her load? Do they give us fathers even one shift off to tend to our mates?" The answering chorus burst from throats that had held in their complaints for not just years, but generations.

"NO!"

"We're muscle to them, and expensive-to-feed muscle at that! Have you looked around in the mess halls lately and wondered why the tables seem emptier every year? They are thinning our herds, my friends."

Could that be true? It would be easy enough to slip something into the herbivore diet to reduce fertility. Look how easily they managed to do it back to the security force...

Taylor shook his head, and set his jaw. Peeking around the edge of one fuel canister, he could just barely see past the massive shoulders of the gathered hoofers to the other side of the bay and the control offices. Burly guards were stationed at the office hatch. Taylor dropped his gaze down to his paws, experimentally curling them into fists. Maybe. If they were all drunk, blind, and I was armed with a p-wand.

He scrutinized the immediate area for an option that wouldn't result in a s'more-colored stain on the deck-plates, and did a double-take. There, just twelve feet away across the corridor, was a duct access hatch. After a quick whip of his head to and fro to make sure the hoofers were still fixated on their charismatic leader, Taylor scurried to the hatch, threw its bolts, and dove within. He closed the hatch as stealthily behind himself as possible, then set out at a swift crawl through the dimly-lit passages. The hum of air scrubbers and the sound of knees and paws skimming across cool metal could do nothing to drown out the booming voice of the hoofer leader in the bay below.

Through a combination of guesswork and the occasional helpful evacuation diagram, the mutt managed to cross over the bay unseen and ended up right where he wanted to be: the docking bay control offices. He dug with his claws to peel filter-moss away from the vent it serviced, wincing away from the sudden jump in light levels. Peering through the louvers, he could see only an empty conference room. Removing the vent made quite a bit of noise, and Taylor's heart beat against his ribs so hard he thought it must surely drown out the clanging and scraping of metal on metal. Finally he wrenched the vent free, stowed it on the poor abused moss, and dropped through the hole to the floor. He waited, crouched, for the thump of his landing to bring raging bovine guards running but he heard no change in the noise levels outside the door. Taylor wrapped his paw around the door handle, eased it down, and opened it a crack. An eye was there staring right back at him! Taylor yelped, backpedaling from the door, as it opened to admit...a corgi. Well, that explained how she was at eye-level with him; corgis weren't exactly the most statuesque of the canines.

"Who are you? How'd you get in here? The hoofers have us penned in like...well," she rolled her eyes, "cattle."

Taylor straightened to his full height, and gathered the scraps of his dignity about himself. "I'm Taylor, and I'm here to help. I'm Heather's, um, roommate. Is she alright?"

The corgi reached out and took his paw, towing him out onto the work floor of the office. Heather, with two other canine-types, lay on the floor with blood-stained bandages wound around their limbs. Taylor crouched by the kelpie's side, eyes wide, fumbling for and squeezing her nearest paw.

"Oh space-rocks," he breathed, cold sweat standing out on his pawpads. *Hearing the hoofers are revolting is one thing. I didn't think about casualties.* "How did this happen?"

"The hoofers aren't what you'd call a disciplined force. They're panicky, in fact. Stupid brutes trampled a few of us when we got growly with them, trying to intimidate them into letting us go, there at the start." Miss corgi sniffed, paws on her pudgy little hips. "I can't wait for the security forces to prowl in here and make hamburger out of them."

Taylor grimaced, and turned back to Heather.

"Hey you, anyone home? It's your mutty roommate, here to save the day." *Never mind that I feel like an idiot now. What did I expect to find? A tea party?* He used his free paw to brush the backs of a few fingers across Heather's forehead.

She blinked slowly up at him, before finally seeming to resolve his image.

"Taylor? Did you get promoted? Are you in medical now?" She began to stir, and he gently pressed her back down.

"No, I'm in the diplomatic corps. I'm going to get you out of here, Heather." He raised his head and glanced over the half-dozen crew-canines still standing. "I'll get you all out, but I'll need your help with the wounded." *Wow, that was great. Sounded just like something from the old vids. If I can keep my teeth from chattering, I might just convince them I know what I'm doing.*

In minutes, he'd assembled the sole male, five unwounded girls and three wounded ones in the conference room, and makeshift slings were being made out of the girls' uniform jackets.

"Alright, could you," Taylor asked a well-built black labrador female, "go up first, and haul the wounded into the duct as we pass them up to you?"

"Roger." She brushed past him rather more sensually than necessary, making sure Taylor felt the curve of her hip and just a brush of breast against one ear as she passed. Whoa. Where'd that come from?

"Taylor, I need a hand up. Even with the conference table..." The labrador pointed up at the vent, standing on the coffee-stained little table they had dragged beneath the opening. The mutt scrambled atop the table and made a stirrup with his paws, while the shapely lab stepped up and grabbed the lip of the vent. The fact that she ground the crotch of her snug uniform pants into Taylor's nose was surely accidental, but the big buck and stallion that busted open the door just then didn't have the context to agree.

* * *

Everyone froze in place, and Taylor found himself thinking that things couldn't possibly get more awkward...unless the lab trembling against him lost a specific sort of control out of fear. Slowly, he lowered his cupping paws, and Suzy (he finally noticed her nametag) obliged by releasing the vent and sitting on the table.

The two hoofers stared at Taylor, the silence in the room stretching out until the stallion finally erupted into neighing laughter. "You dogs sure go to great lengths for a sniff, don'tcha?"

Snorting, the buck joined his partner in the laughter, but stomped forward to round up the canines and shove them back into the main office. He shut the conference room door, then used the pry-bar he was toting to ruin the handle, effectively locking it. The pair of leering hoofers looked all set to tease rather than interrogate, but a grizzled giant of a bull shouldered his way through the main hatch, bringing silence with him. He was all too willing to fill that silence with the stentorian tones Taylor recognized as the leader's who'd rallied his forces earlier in the docking bay.

"Who is this, and who are the boneheaded hay-munchers that let him get this far?" He shoved aside the giggle-twins, his own bulk making them look like gawky teenagers, and craned his neck down to peer at the mutt who'd dared to infiltrate his lines.

"Tell me everything you know, everyone you know, and you may just come out of this horribly maimed. Hold even a breath of information back, and they'll be scraping you off my hooves for the rest of the day."

"I'm Taylor, mutt of no consequence, working a job as shitty as yours. I'm here to protect my mate. If you still think I deserve death or crushing, or goring, get on with it." Brave speech from such a small dog, even if every word trembled so much coming out it sounded like he was sitting on one of the ore grinders back at work.

Snorting so harshly plastic print-outs scattered from three desks, the bull scowled at the shaking mutt. "You expect me to believe that? You're a spy! A saboteur!" The huge bull raised a fist that probably weighed half what Taylor did. The little dog's eyes fixed on the knuckles, the huge mitt quivering with the tension building in the bull's bulging arm. "The glorious leaders ignore our diplomatic overtures and send their very best..." The bovine blinked slowly, then let his fist fall again to his side with a sigh that just about knocked the mutt over on its own.

"Not even they are cruel enough to send such a defenseless shrimp in first. You're not my enemy. You're fortunate you encountered someone who could realize that, when most would hate you simply for being canine." He waved over the buck and stud. "Bind him and the rest. We can't take any more chances. Have Greta see to those three wounded as well."

Taylor stepped back from the advancing hoofers, finally finding his voice again. "Sir, hold on a moment. I heard you speaking in the bay, and I agree—ouch!" He winced as the buck pinned his arms behind his back, more hot, grassy breath gushing down through his headfur. The bull waved the buck off and cocked an ear, and Taylor tried to ignore the stares he was getting from his fellow canine-types. "I agree you herbivores are being mistreated. I don't know much of anything about the issues you were discussing, but from my own dealings with those 'glorious leaders,' I know that they're pragmatic to the point of being, well, cruel. We face some of the same challenges, you know."

"And how would you know that, pup? You're just out of training, aren't you? The only place you've even seen us is across the aisle in mess halls. Have you ever even turned long enough from your yapping pack to speak to a creature with hooves instead of paws?"

Taylor nodded, trying not to let the condescending tone raise his hackles. "99% of the time, you'd be right about all of that, and a month ago you'd even have been right about me. But I recently met a wise old goat named Reggie, and I'm proud to consider him a friend."

"There's no way he knows Reggie, Marcus. The guy works every minute he isn't sleeping." The stallion mumbled to the bull, rolling his eyes. Marcus casually shoved the horse away from his ear, almost sending him into the wall.

"If you know Reggie, then you can get him on the comm, and help us straighten this out. We tried to get ahold of him before this all happened, but he seemed to be blacking out all communications." He held out his hand to the stallion, who dizzily dropped Taylor's comm into it. Taylor blocked Marcus with a palm as the bull extended the comm towards him. Trying to halt the bull's motion felt like trying to stop a speeding lift.

"I won't deal for you until I get some promises."

"Where the hell did they issue pants big enough to fit this mutt?" One of the girls whispered, incredulous, frightened and giddy all at once.

"You lying runt," the bull ground out, stuffing the comm into his coveralls. "Bind them. I'll be back." Marcus rose and stomped out, hooves making the deck-plates ring. In minutes every unwounded hostage was bound with plastic strip-locks. Wriggling his way over to Heather, Taylor set his muzzle down beside her ear to whisper.

"Heather, I never got to explain this morning, and I want to do it now before anything else happens. I broke SR code, and tried to make Chris my mate."

The kelpie blinked, and began reaching across herself to cup the mutt's cheek, but aborted the movement with a wince and gasp. "I... I'm sorry pup. What happened in the mess... You must have felt like..." She just shook her head the slightest bit. "No wonder you ran."

"I didn't think you'd get it, Heather. Then, after, I started wondering about you and me. Do you still want to try with me? Knowing that I..."

"That you what? Reached for something you wanted?" Heather let her eyes slide shut, and tipped her muzzle towards Taylor's, lips parted and inviting. The office hatch crashed inward, a cry of pain squeezing in the door ahead of Marcus as he stormed back in. The huge bull was dragging a buffalo with one arm and simply toting a blubbering goat beneath the other. Bovine eyes were wide, with rage or fear it was hard to say. Greta darted to his side, helping guide the wounded to the deck.

Taylor couldn't make out the quiet, grunted conversation between Marcus and the guards, but caught a word or two: "wolves" and "sealed off." When his gaze happened across Taylor again, Marcus stepped between bound hostages, reached down and scooped up the mutt. Holding him in one fist before his face, the bull's big liquid eyes reflected the stunned canine's image.

"You mentioned promises. Such as?" Marcus ground out, his tail lashing the deck-plates with thunk after frustrated thunk. Through the open hatch behind him came cries of distress and angry shouts from the massed herbivores.

"Release your hostages. Stop the violence. We can't afford it!" Taylor surprised himself at the passion that crept into his voice. "This ship feels solid under our paws... or, uh, hooves, but all it takes is a bit of rock or a cloud of radiation, and we're just another chunk of cold, dead minerals spinning through the black. Go look at Reggie's quadrant! That stupid little plaque on the wall should read 'we almost bought it 126 years into our trip.'"

"Don't give me that 'don't rock the boat' manure. That's—" Marcus shook his fistful of mutt, disgusted.

"That's not what I'm saying!" Despite having his teeth rattled in his head, Marcus heard and stilled his hand. "The people in charge would say that, but I'm telling you to forget them, and just think of your crew-mates. We're all we have out here. There may be a few thousand of us aboard, and the same in our sister ships, but we're the loneliest island nation imaginable. A war would kill us, and it's so unnecessary!"

"Unnecessary? How else am I to win rights for my kind that they should already have? If they won't deal, then we must fight."

"No, there is something you can do," the other male hostage

spoke up. A tall, awkward Afghan Taylor had been calling 'the gentle nerd' in his head, the hound struggled upright against the wall to better address the bull. "Do one thing tomorrow, and see how quickly the administration folds."

Marcus looked mystified. "One thing? What?"

"Don't report to work." The Afghan shrugged slender shoulders, staring earnestly up at Marcus through the thick lenses of his glasses. "Is that so hard?"

Marcus looked as if someone had gored him, and took one staggering step back to sink down into a totally inadequate chair. He let Taylor slip from his fist, paws touching the floor. "I... I wouldn't have thought so until you said it aloud just now. I'm struggling with the concept of staying in my quarters tomorrow. Just thinking of it feels wrong on a disturbingly deep level."

Taylor nodded solemnly, and behind his back, flashed a thumbs-up at the Afghan. "Reggie told me my kind has built-in loyalty. That's why we're put in charge so often, and why there are so many of us aboard, relative to the other types, I think. We carry the mission directive through by, uh, doggedly following orders and dragging everyone along. You herbivores must have something similar encoded into you. A steadfastness gene? A dependability trait?"

Marcus frowned. "I'm starting to understand our little world better I think. If your compulsion to follow the rules and your superiors is as strong as what I just felt, no wonder you all tend to act like brown-nosed performing pups."

Taylor grimaced, and tapped one foot on the floor, about the only way he could express himself in his restraints. "In the interests of diplomacy, I'll try not to take that personally. Now, will you untie us? Then I'll get to work with that comm."

Eyes still deeply troubled, Marcus nodded to the guards, and Taylor was soon free and back in the loop, so to speak. He punched the button for Compatii on the little comm, and smiled when the wolf answered.

"Yes? Are you dead yet?"

"Not quite. I'm sitting here with the leader of this revolt, and I'd like you to put me through to Reggie."

"...Right. Let me speak to him."

Taylor handed Marcus the comm. "This is the security chief who thought he was sending me to my death when he allowed me to pass through his cordon to come after my girl."

Marcus grimaced and vocally assaulted the comm for a few minutes. Taylor was all set to sit back and watch the show, but felt a tug on his arm and turned to see Suzy.

"Heather's asking for you." She led him back to the kelpie's side, and Taylor scooped up her left paw in both of his own. He was surprised to see Suzy settle on Heather's opposite side, taking her other paw. She answered his curious glance with a smile and a burst of wagging.

"Taylor, what's happening? So much shouting, and..." Heather groaned, moving one wounded leg on the floor. "I should've torn their throats out."

"Heather, I adore you, and I'm thrilled it's mutual, but we can't hold the hoofers as enemies or even at arms-length anymore. They're no less 'people' than we are. You wouldn't talk about tearing out another canine's throat, would you?"

"Just Karin's," she growled, eyes fully open and abruptly quite lucid. "She tagged along with me to the control office today to meet our deck chief, who I'd passingly mentioned was cute. When the herbivores showed up, she bluffed her way out! She said her father was the captain's second officer, and they would gas the whole section and kill everyone with hooves if they held her. They were still unsure of themselves enough at that point to let her go. She didn't come find you?"

Taylor grimaced, "I saw her in the ha–" A heavy tap on his shoulder brought him up short: Marcus, with the comm.

"Captain Compatii is ready to talk now."

Taylor had to grin at that, and accepted the comm with a wag. "Captain. Yes, that was indeed the moon-sized leader of the revolt. Yes, patching me through would be most appreciated. And Captain? If you listen in on the following conversation, we'll have you brought up on charges. Thank you for your consideration."

Reggie was gruffer than ever when he answered this second call.

"What do you people want now? I've got epoxy in my ear and grit under my eyelids and still you wanna yank my cord?"

"Reggie! It's me, Taylor. You wanted to know how things were going in my life? I have an update for you." Taylor verbally sketched the situation for him, and got a gusty sigh in his ear in return.

"I never wanted to be involved in politics. Maneuvering, sure... jockeying for position, inevitable! But capital-p Politics? Never. I managed to gracefully dodge that bullet you sent my way earlier but now you're putting me on the damn stage, under a spotlight, and shoving a straw boater over my horns!"

Taylor rubbed the fur between his eyes, but before he could feel too sorry for himself, the gangly Afghan handed him a cup of water. He smiled his thanks up at him, and then had to stumble his way through a response as the quiet hound surreptitiously tucked a paw beneath the seated mutt and fondled him. Earth and sky, these survival situations really bring the inhibitions down! Mm, he is adorable though. A grumpy 'Hello?!' from the comm broke his reverie. "Reggie, you've been patching this ship together your entire career, yes? It's not just the alloy, wire, and... super structure or whatever else is inside these walls that holds the Sojourner together. If herbivores and canines go at each other, we might as well all roll over and wait to die. The journey will be doomed, the mission a failure. It could spread to the other ships!"

"You hadn't heard? It already did spread. There are dozens dead on the other vessels. Things are at the breaking point all over." Reggie sounded tired, and the mutt could picture the goat rubbing his temple, sitting at a cluttered desk while his world complicated itself. "One herbivore group has commandeered a mining tug full of charges and threatened to suicide-bomb the sleeper ship."

Taylor swallowed, his throat gone abruptly dry. They were all teetering on the edge. It took him a moment to find his voice again. "All the more reason to act quickly—bring everyone off the battlefield and to the negotiation table!"

There was silence on the other end for a few seconds, then helpless laughter. Taylor lowered the comm from his ear and scowled at the little gizmo. *Is he even taking me seriously? I know*

I'm a pup compared to him, and I have no idea how to do the things we need done, but I know they need doing!

"Pup, you're a born diplomat. If I've gotta be stuck dealing with these hard-heads, I'm enlisting you to help. With my even-harder-head and your puppy-dog eyes, we'll have everything ticking over perfectly again before those wolves stop hurling. Now, let me speak to that gorgeous slab of beef."

After a second of confusion, Taylor handed the comm over to Marcus, who he swore began to blush not two sentences later.

Greta, an older mare who apparently knew something of first-aid, had just finished re-dressing Heather's wounds when Taylor knelt by her side again. "Looks like I have a new job, kelpie-dog. Will you hold it against me, as I 'pursue relations' with many others besides you?"

"Word of advice: keep jokes out of your diplomatic arsenal," Heather grumbled. She nodded at a point past Taylor. "Suzy here has been begging me, and I'm too tired to fight about it, so here's the deal. We share you." The black lab's mouth closed possessively over one mutty shoulder, a playful "Rrrrr," buzzing from her muzzle. "She's been a great friend the past week, and an even better one over the last few hours." The look she lavished on Suzy seemed rather more than friendly.

From heart-break to this, inside of a week? He just shook his head in disbelief, but wagged ferociously.

Heather continued, grinning as she watched Suzy lap along her mutt's cheek. "Maybe with your new-found authority, you can have a certain poodle transferred to new quarters, and Suzy can move in with us."

Taylor's eyes glazed over, wagging tail whacking Suzy repeatedly until she trapped it between her thighs. In a dreamy voice, the luckiest mutt in the fleet predicted the future. "Karin will go live with three reptiles, in a room that's a constant 90 degrees. They'll make a shipboard reality drama out of it. And I will live happily ever after."

Nothing about Conner's final summer before college had gone as epxected. First the trip to the islands, then the handsome otter friend—would the surprises ever stop?

BEACHSIDE FUN

Lindskold Janis

The hard part about being a teenager is the inherent conflicts in your life.

Okay, so may be that applies to everyone and not just teenagers, but I'm eighteen and I didn't really notice trend this until I was thirteen.

For example, as a teenager, more often than not, the last thing I want to do is spend time with my family. If I can get out of a family trip or event, no matter how minor, I will. However, not many teenagers get the chance to go to some tiny little island off the coast of Puerto Rico for a month long summer vacation. Therefore, when my dad unexpectedly won such a trip through work, it was painful for me to balance my great desire to go to a beach on a semi-private island in the Caribbean for a month against my desire to not go anywhere at all with my family.

Not that I truly believe I could have talked my parents out of accompanying them on this trip, but to my surprise they asked and to their surprise I said yes. Maybe somewhere deep down inside I acknowledged that having just graduated high school, I'm about to spend most of the next four years of my life in the mountains of Virginia while they continue living in Seattle and that I should get some time in with them while I can.

Maybe.

The trip to Puerto Rico was my first time leaving the continental United States, though hardly the first long trip with my

185

family. We had a tradition of taking a big vacation once every four years, and this one happened to coincide with my high school graduation. Sure, it happened to coincide with my sister's graduation from college too, but I took credit where I could.

Packing for the trip took a week for us as a whole. My packing took about a day for the basics, and then slowly gathering a few things over the next few days. The high point of packing for me was explaining to my mother, whom I love very dearly but has always been a little too deepwoods country at the most inconvenient times, that people in Puerto Rico do speak English and she would not have to learn Spanish to be understood, though knowing Spanish wouldn't hurt.

The flight out took forever and we arrived very late Sunday night, very jet-lagged to boot. The resort staff won major kudos from my dad for helping us get our wearied selves and our luggage into our beach house… bungalow… whatever the term was. A friendly and reasonably attractive tigress lead me to my room, which was technically a sunroom. The couch was very comfortable and I slept like a rock while the waves lapped the shore. I'm not sure if I dreamed her flirting with me or if it really happened, but she was out of luck in that regard.

I woke with the sun and stretched. Or rather, I tried to. I had apparently fallen asleep in my jeans, and they were just uncomfortable after sleeping in them. I generally wore my jeans a little snug, and typical morning behavior of my body wasn't helping. Grumbling, I shucked the jeans, then retrieved my accidentally-removed boxerbriefs before putting on a pair of basketball shorts.

"I may need to get mom and dad to buy me new jeans if that's going to keep happening. I don't think my roommate at school will appreciate naked dalmatian, intentional or otherwise. Though, I wouldn't mind if he did."

There was a tapping at the door to my room. "Connor dear, are you awake? I heard movement and I'd like to see the view."

"Yes mom," I said as I removed my shirt. Much like my jeans, it wasn't particularly comfortable after sleeping in it, despite it being designed to cling to my body.

"Are you decent?"

"Yes mom."

"Can I come in?"

Frustrating as this exchange was to me, I'd spent six months fighting for it and wasn't giving it up now. "Yes mom. You can come in. And you can leave the door open. My suitcase is closed and I'll unpack it later."

My mother, from whom I got my height and my green eyes, opened the double doors wide and stepped into the room, looking for all the world like a displaced country housewife her old-fashioned glasses and holding a large mug of coffee. She was not, I noticed, wearing her usual flannel bathrobe, but instead a fluffy pale green one that looked to be ridiculously soft.

"Oh wow, such a nice room. And the view. Are you sure you don't mind dear?"

"It's fine mom, I promise. Where'd you get the coffee?"

"The kitchen, which seems to be stocked for a traditional Sunday morning breakfast if I wanted." She paused, getting one of those silly looks only a mother can, "Which I didn't—so I asked for a breakfast platter to be brought down from the resort. It should be here in an hour."

My mother, who hated having people wait on her, had taken advantage of super room service on the first day? Maybe she was more ready for this vacation than I was.

"Ah, is this where everyone is?" came my father's baritone voice as he entered the room. "Well, almost everyone. Cheyenne not awake yet?"

My father is where I got most of my looks from: a strong, angular jaw, abs that refused to go flabby, and the pure white ears. He was also five-foot-eight and still not used to looking up at my seven-foot-two form, despite the face he'd married mom and she's six-foot-eight.

My mom started to answer, but my elder sister beat her to it as she swept into the room in a bold yellow sundress and holding a pair of matching sandals. "I've been awake for an hour, showered, and am ready to face the day. Where have you lazybones been?"

She was teasing, and we teased back. Cheyenne's six-foot-four frame was not known for early rising until she went off to college in

Florida and discovered that the mornings were generally far more tolerable than the late afternoons. After a single semester, she'd started taking every class as early in the day as possible.

After a good hour of just relaxing and waking up, not to mention steak for breakfast, Cheyenne announced her intention to catch an early shuttle over to the mainland to evaluate the shopping there. My mother and father had already arranged to be in the spa all afternoon, which left me on my own. This was, after all, my vacation too.

I showered and dressed in short order, trading my boxerbriefs and basketball shorts for a black speedo and dark blue board shorts with a white and green pattern down either side. I also made a point to rub sunscreen through my fur and into my skin, as I was planning on going shirtless all day and doing some swimming, or surfing, or whatever came to mind so long as it was near the water.

You'd think, being on a semi-private island, this would be easy. However, I did not want to go swimming right outside the beach house and the beaches that looked interesting when I got to them had a tendency to develop families with small children that either made a lot of noise, stared at me because I'm tall, or both. The noise had to go.

After the third attempted to find a peaceful lagoon, I frustratedly sought out one of the vendor stands for food. A young male kangaroo smiled as I looked over the food and eventually suggested something I'd never heard of—some sort of fried corn meal stuffed with cheese. I still don't remember what it was called, but I remember it being good. The other piece of good advice he gave me was far more useful.

"Looking for someplace quieter, but with a bit of atmosphere?"

I nodded glumly.

"Are you legal to drink?"

"Nope."

"Eighteen at least?"

"Yep."

He directed me to the center of the island to a freshwater pool exclusively for adults. I thanked him and headed off. Fifteen minutes of walking, five minutes of careful searching, and one,

"Ah-hah!" later, I passed through the entrance I'd mistaken as a gateway to a garden.

"Whoa," was probably not the most intelligent thing I could have said when passed through the vine-draped archway and into the secluded pool, but the appearance of the place has that effect on you. It looked like a postcard painting of a secluded lagoon. The pool was molded into a natural-looking shape and had natural rock outcroppings in and around it to increase the effect. While some of the rocks were fake, the plants were very real. The part I really liked though was the waterfall.

The waterfall poured out of an elevated pool just over two stories above the main pool. The escarpment that it originated from also hid bathrooms from the immediate area which were accessible either by a tunnel in the back of the rocks or by swimming behind the waterfall. To either side of the main fall were numerous small falls the splashed and sprayed about, resulting in rainbows flickering in and out of view.

I spent a couple hours swimming lazily and taking a slide into the pool. Eventually, I got tired and settled myself on to a ledge on one side to rest for a bit. I think I drifted off for maybe thirty minutes, but when I came to I had to shake myself to make sure I was awake.

There'd only been maybe half a dozen people pass through the pool area since my initial arrival, and they'd left when I decided rest. When I woke, the first thing I noticed was that the water was sloshing around a lot, like someone was swimming at high speed through it. When I sat up to look around for the cause, a brown blur I barely registered as an otter shot past me, which was impressive given how narrow the waterway was between my ledge and the miniature island that sheltered me from the open pool.

I followed his motion around the deeper parts of the pool, watching him weave in and out of arches with a grace I couldn't hope for. The otter neatly turned into the open area in the middle of the pool and began to circle, gaining speed rapidly.

With little warning, he banked hard and shot towards a trio of tall arches in the middle of the pool. Again, he wove through the obstacle course with the ease of an aquatic race, going deeper as he did. When he could dive no further, he surfaced fast and shot into the air, spraying water everywhere.

I will admit to myself and no one else that I got hard in the brief moment I saw him airborne. He had to be two feet shorter than me, and he was packed with muscle as otters are wont to be, but he was amazingly toned. And he was wearing a pair of blazing red box-cut trunks that clung to him tighter than I think my speedo was on me.

When I regained my senses, I saw him climb out of the pool and head up the hidden staircase to the upper lagoon. I watched for him to appear at the top of the waterfall and was not disappointed... until he lay down out of sight.

I have no clue what possessed me to go up there and continue staring at him, but I did. He seemed to have fallen asleep almost immediately and was lying on his stomach with his arms propping his head up to keep his mouth and nose out of the water.

The sheen of his fur was incredible, but I kept going back to his build. And his butt.

I don't normally stare at people's rear ends, but when said rear end has a powerful tail resting atop it and it's covered in tight red lycra or spandex or whatever that's showing off muscle definition in the glutes, it's hard not to stare.

Fifteen minutes later I heard my parents coming into the pool area and hurriedly dashed for the slide, grateful that I was not so far gone as to have not heard them.

It's not that my parents don't know I'm in to guys, my mom and I have spent the occasional afternoon discussing who is cute and why. Oh no, the problem was that my mom had no tact, and both my parents were at the stage where they wanted to see me with a steady partner, even if they weren't getting grandpups out of the relationship. The last thing they needed to see was me staring at that hunk of an otter. My mother would probably wake the man and try to set me up with him, assuming he answered her very direct question about his sexuality.

I pretended to be surprised to see them when they arrived, rather than risk such embarrassment. We chatted for a bit about the pool and how nice it was to be away from all the small children.

Mom made an offhand comment about it would be nice to occasionally have small kids around again, but no full-time residents were needed.

When dad proposed going up top to where we could see the area, I turned my mom's manners against her.

"This is probably not a good time to go all the way up."

"Why not dear?"

"There's an otter sleeping up there. He was exercising in the pool and wore himself out I guess. I saw him go up top and lay down. When I went to go jump in the slide, I noticed he was asleep."

"Well," she said with that tone that said her ideas of good manners were being tested, "it's a strange place to sleep, but if it's only us here, it is no real trouble to let him be."

"I bet he's comfortable. I fell asleep on a ledge on the other side of that island for half an hour earlier after I'd been swimming around."

Dad laughed at that. I'd always been good at falling asleep in the oddest positions.

"So," said dad after a bit, "joining us for dinner tonight? They've got these things called canoas I want to try. They're plantain canoes stuffed with meat and covered in cheese."

"Sounds good to me."

"You can show us around the pool tomorrow afternoon. It looks like it has all sorts of secrets."

"Probably. I don't think I've found them all yet. And where would the fun be in showing you all of them?"

Mom laughed at that and we headed off towards dinner.

The next morning I spent walking along the beaches and snorkeling in a nearby cove. I had lunch with my whole family, and then I showed them a few things about the isolated pool. My sister headed back early, because she was going on a midnight snorkeling trip. My parents were going to dinner at a club-style event in the over-21 pool. This left me visiting a familiar vendor cart and walking back to the eighteen and over pool, quite possibly hoping to spot an otter again.

Subconsciously, I swear.

Regardless, the otter did not disappoint. If anything, he was teasing. Now he was wearing white trunks with teal and gold accents in the same style as the day before. And he was in the same spot as before.

On his back.

If his swimwear was accentuating his lines yesterday, I lacked a word to explain what it was doing today.

I guess technically speaking, they were maintaining his decency.

Technically speaking.

And the same could be said of my board shorts and speedo, technically speaking.

In my defense, I spent an untold amount of time unabashedly staring at his whole body, not just his crotch. It wasn't that he was huge, but he was certainly being displayed well. Eventually, the sun began to set in the distance and I looked past him to watch it.

"You know pup," said a soft and deep voice that could only have had one source, "most people will tell you it's impolite to stare."

I started blushing. Quite possibly enough to tan from the inside out.

"Then again, most people consider it rude to tease. And in either event, I did dress up yesterday with the hope of being stared at. And since I rather liked the appearance of the dalmatian doing the staring, and I overheard he'd be back again tonight, I upped the ante."

"Y-y-you set me up!"

"Didn't mean you had to take the bait handsome."

That was about the point I really registered what he'd said and implied. And perhaps was implying. While attractive, I wasn't looking for that and I started to open my mouth to say so when he held up a finger.

"Don't get me wrong, I wouldn't mind, but that's not really my style. I would, however, like to know the name of my admirer since I suspect we'll be seeing each other repeatedly over the next month."

He was going to be here the entire month? My reputation for good behavior was suddenly on the line.

"Connor. Connor Jackson," I said and offered my paw.

"Hi Connor, I'm Jace Smith. And you're wet." With that, he took my paw and pulled me face-first into the water.

"A tease and a flirt and you play dirty? I think I like you," I offered after sputtering up some water and righting myself.

"Figured you might as well know what you were getting in to."

My ears twitched a bit and I focused on his words.

"You're not a local. I've heard that accent before!"

"Yep. The mountains of Virginia currently."

"Oh cool, I'm going to be attending college out there in August."

"Tech?"

"Yep."

"It's about an hour's drive from where I live."

"Small world."

"It happens."

I chuckled. "Yeah, I guess it does."

"Pup," he said, his tone changing, "you're still staring."

"I… err… uhmm…" I did not know it was possible to blush this much.

"Does this help?" he asked, sliding down into the shallow pool and leaning his back against the ledge he'd been resting on.

"Y-y-yes," I started to say, before his spread out his arms along the ledge. Damn his chest was huge for someone his size.

"I'm a horrible tease, I know. You should probably get used to it."

I forced myself to take a deep breath and sat down in the water across from him. We spent the afternoon talking about different parts of our lives. I was getting ready to start college and wasn't sure what degree I wanted to pursue. At nineteen, he'd actually graduated college a year ago with a double major in business management and computer engineering. He'd only spent two years there and took classes year-round to finish as fast as he had, in addition to the advanced courses he'd taken in high school. I'd spent my summers working summer camps, showing kids how to be safe in extreme sports, which he happened to be in to when he wasn't working. He worked for a major internet technology firm, but didn't really say which one or what he did there.

Eventually, he pointed out the late hour and we headed our separate ways. When my mom and dad asked where I'd been, I explained that I'd made friends with an otter who was here on vacation and happened to live an hour from college. The idea that I'd made a friend I'd be able to see at college was apparently enough to make my parents not ask about his appearance, attractiveness, or anything else regarding his boyfriend potential. I could live with that.

By Saturday night, Jace and I had spent most of every day together doing one thing or another. He'd been to the island before and showed not only me but my family around, pointing out some special events and locations that were often overlooked by first-time visitors. My father commented that Jace seemed familiar somehow, and even my mother agreed, but no one could figure out why. I didn't care, I was just grateful that no one asked if we were dating. Hell, even Cheyenne hadn't teased me about him. They genuinely liked him for who he was, and I did too.

This didn't stop me from staring almost every time I saw him. He teased me about that, even once going so far as to threaten to wear a speedo just to see if I'd explode. I couldn't decide if I was grateful or disappointed that he didn't follow through.

Eleven on Saturday evening found Jace and I alone in an underground hot spring. There was a big fireworks show going on on the surface holding most people's attention, but Jace had assured me that there would be better ones before we left, so we'd gone exploring. We'd roughhoused a bit, but mostly just relaxed and talked a while. I was curious about the mountains and things to do around college, and he just seemed to enjoy talking about something other than being smart.

Eventually, we dragged ourselves out of the water and into the showers. The hot springs were treated with a chemical to keep some local parasites down and while it was appreciated, it tended to make your skin itch under your fur if you didn't wash it out. The same substance was in all the isolated pools and lagoons on the island and there were a large number of signs reminding people to wash before moving in to the ocean in order to help protect the local environment. As such, this was not the first time we'd wandered off to the showers at the same time. Nor was it the first time we'd been the only ones in the showers.

We each entered our own shower stall and stripped, as we needed to wash our suits too. I quickly got lost in my own shower. The hot water and soap felt great on my body and was re-energizing me a bit. It also startled me when it hit me between the legs on the hard-on I hadn't realized I had.

"Well hello, where'd you come from?" I said what I thought was very softly as I stroked my length just a little. "I thought I'd been good about not staring today."

It was right then that I felt another person, significantly shorter than me, come up behind me, press itself against my back, and then reach around and take my hard-on in a familiar-looking paw.

"You have been very good about not staring today pup," said Jace in a very soothing tone. "I stole a glance as you got in the shower and noticed your condition though."

"I… umm… mmmrrrrr…" It was very difficult to talk with Jace's warm, soapy paw running along my cock and his left arm wrapped around my waist supportively. Especially since I'd not pawed off at all since going on vacation.

"Shhhh. Unless you want me to stop, just shush."

I nodded my consent, I think. The whole act felt so good I kind of lost focus. I remember feeling his own length poke the backside of my thigh at one point as he wriggled in as close as he could get. I also remember that he stopped me from reaching for it, saying it wasn't time for that right now. Instead, he slipped his head under my arm and braced me as he stroked my length steadily.

And it felt so damn good.

I have no clue how long he stroked me, but I remember hearing someone whimpering softly, then realizing it was me. I was close and it felt powerful. Almost as powerful as some of the worst teasing I'd given myself, and that normally took me an hour or more. I became conscious of the fact he was holding my waist hard enough to discourage my instinct to buck into his paw. He was in complete control, he knew it and I didn't care.

Without warning, he gave a few quick jerks over the tip of my length, making me arch up. Then he gripped firmly and slammed his paw backward to lock down on my knot. The next thing I remember I was on my knees and panting heavily with Jace hugging me from behind.

I opened my eyes to a whitewashed stone wall. Before I could comment on it, the otter reached up and directed the water to wash it away.

"Damn pup, I'm going to have to get you a muzzle."

"Huh?" I tried to say while panting. I'm not sure the word came out, but the idea did at least.

"You let out one hell of a howl. My ears are still ringing with it."

"I… what?" I'd never howled before to my knowledge. If I had, I suspect my parents would have told me a few years ago.

"You're loud, handsome. Now, up on your feet," he said as he pulled up on my armpits. I was grateful he was there to help me up and support me, because I was apparently still weak in the knees.

"C'mon, it's late. We should get you back."

"But what about…" my words were cut off by his finger on my lips.

"I got what I wanted. That's not to say I won't want something else in the future, but tonight was all about you. Now put your shorts on. I can't put mine on holding you up and I'm not interested in walking you home while naked."

With a nod I braced myself against the wall and proceeded to scrub out my speedo and board shorts as he did the same to his trunks. He walked me back to the beach house and I let myself in through the door leading directly in to the sun room. I managed to get myself out of wet clothes and into a pair of shorts before passing out.

Over the next few days we were far better behaved. Still, there was this awkward not-talking about it thing and that was amplified by an unconscious change on my part: where I sat. Up until this point, I'd always sat across from Jace. But now I found that I was sitting as his side. More importantly, I liked sitting at his side. It felt natural.

Wednesday evening found Jace and I alone on a rocky outcropping on the north side of the island, watching the sunset. The weather forecast was promising, and after making sure it was okay with both the resort and my parents, we'd decided to spend the night out under the stars.

Jace had acquired sleeping mats and small pillows from somewhere and brought them out in a pair of waterproof backpacks. We'd timed our adventure so we could walk out to the outcropping and not have to worry about salt in our fur overnight. This meant dinner was sandwiches, but the company meant the food didn't matter.

"So," I began, somewhat nervously, because I knew exactly where I was going with this. "About Saturday…"

"Yes?" he asked in a sly tone that implied his mind was where mine was.

"I was wondering when I got to pay you back for it."

"Roll on to your side handsome and I think you'll find your answer."

I obliged and looked his taught form over, eyes coming to rest on an unusually swollen bulge between his legs.

"I see," I said as I reached over and carefully traced over his sensitive parts with a single clawtip.

"Hrrrf. Tease!"

"I'm learning from an expert."

"No comment… erf!"

I'd palmed his balls at just the right time, and no matter how gentle the touch, if you aren't expecting it, it startles you. As soon as he relaxed, I slid my paw up his trunks and began to rub gently along his maleness, squeezing occasionally. I can only describe the trilling noise he made as the otter equivalent of purring. Between that and his half-lidded eyes, I decided I was doing just fine.

I continued stroking him like this for a few minutes, then paused to tug the front of his trunks down and hook them behind his balls. This wasn't the first time I'd eyed another guy in person, but it was the first time the situation was quite so intimate.

Given that Jace was two feet smaller than me, I judged him to be of normal length for his height, the same as I was. But where

I was built slender, he was unquestionably thicker than average. Fortunately, being tall gives me large hands to work with.

I'm not sure how long I stroked him, but I do know my arm had never gotten sore doing this to myself. He was leaking, but he wasn't panting, and I was becoming concerned I was doing something wrong. Apparently, this concern shifted my scent enough to tip Jace off.

"You can rest your arm you know. Or switch. I'm willing to bet I have significant amount of experience you don't, and that means I've trained my body to resist a bit more."

I switched paw, reversing my grip as a result as I was still on my side. I'd just been given an opening to something I hadn't really considered: his sexual history.

I'm proud to say it took me all of about five seconds to decide that it didn't matter right then.

Once I gained a bit of feeling back in my right arm, I reached over and traced a dull clawtip over his scrotum some before trying to wedge my paw between his trunks and his balls. Given how tight his trunks were, this turned out to be a slightly painful idea for me, but caused him to trill louder when I accidentally pulled on his sack.

"Oh really?" I asked, rolling my r a little, trying to sound playful.

"Mmhmm," came his reply.

"Lift your otterbutt up a moment then so I can get these off you," I said, tugging as his trunks, "and I'll do that some more."

He barked very softly and complied. I tugged his trunks off quickly and set them to the side before switching paws again so I could cup his balls in my right one.

The vocal effect was instantaneous, with the other effect taking a bit more time. I straddled his legs and worked at his sensitive parts gently. Eventually, he began to make a number of happy, needy noises and had to take a deep breath to form words.

"Connor," he side in a rushed, slightly pleading whisper.

"Yes?" I said in what I hoped was a sultry tone.

"There's no place to wash off up here, and there's going to be a need for that soon unless you got a plan."

I actually stopped what I was doing for a moment or two so I could start considering options. Once I had ideas, I started back on him far more slowly.

My options were simple: I could stop, leaving us both unsatisfied; I could muzzle him, but I wasn't quite ready for that; or I could figure out how to jerk him off without getting cum all over him.

I really wanted option three, and looked about for a towel or something. It was then that I got a better idea and withdrew my paws.

"Stand up," I said, glancing back at the shore, and then out opposite it. The shore seemed clear, and even if it wasn't, it appeared to be a new moon: I could see stars, but not the moon itself.

Jace somewhat confusedly got to his feet, having figured out I wasn't stopping but wasn't quite sure what I was doing. I motioned him to the edge of the outcropping, instructing him to face the ocean. Then I knelt behind him on a pillow.

That temporarily made us the same height, and I licked the back of his now easy-to-reach right ear. That got a whimper.

"Oh really?" I said in a more playful tone than before. Or perhaps more mischievous.

"Mm.HMPH!"

I'd anticipated his answer and managed to grab his cock again in my left paw, cross-brace his chest with my right arm, and lap my tongue across his entire ear all at the same time. Not only did he whimper, he bucked into my paw. Better yet, each time I licked, he whimpered more and bucked again.

It took maybe two minutes from the time I got him on his feet until he barked sharply and sent a white stream arcing through the air and into the ocean. It took a full minute of rapid pawing and him asking me to chew on his ear before he collapsed back against me, finally spent.

I carefully eased myself onto my back, bringing him with me to lay atop my body. He panted heavily for a bit, then trilled pleasantly before suddenly stopping and wriggling his rump and tail

"What?"

"How the hell are you not pressing into me with a raging boner?" he asked in the way one does when one is not sure if they should tease about something or not.

It was a good question. I wasn't hard, nor to my knowledge had I been. This made no sense, as I'd pretty much sprung a boner every time I'd seen or thought about him. Now that he was laying on me and nude, and I'd just pawed him off, I wasn't having to have an argument with my subconscious or my hormones.

"Uh…. I don't know."

"Fair enough," he said with a smile. "Probably better that way. I'm too far gone to be of help!"

We laughed at that, and I commented about his drawn out orgasm. He responded that it happened sometimes, and normally meant he was really wired, or hadn't gotten off in a while. When I asked which this was, he just grinned in a way that said I wasn't getting an answer out of him tonight.

Eventually, he put his trunks back on and we went to sleep. I was on my back, and he'd wormed his way between my arm and chest to sleep with his head on my left shoulder and his right arm across my chest. It was quite possibly the best night's sleep I'd ever had.

By Friday, Jace had joined my family for dinner, at my mother's request. By Monday, we'd had four meals and gone to two events with him, and no one had asked me the question I was dreading. I hadn't even been teased by my sister. Life had never been better.

Then my sister mentioned her boyfriend would be here in a week.

This wasn't unexpected; it had just slipped my mind. I'd always known he was coming out to join us for a week of our vacation. Problem was, as soon as she mentioned it; I remembered he was coming for the last week of vacation. Though entirely unintentional, my sister had just cashed my reality check—it sucked.

Two weeks of bliss down. Had I not thought about it, this rollercoaster I was on would still feel like it was going uphill until probably the last couple of days. Now it was on a steep drop. My mood crashed hard and everyone noticed.

They were all either totally clueless as to why, or at the least, being polite enough not to ask and risk making things worse.

On Wednesday night, Jace found me in one of several gyms on the island. As soon as the door opened, I knew it was him. Nothing tipped me off, I just knew. I lashed into a kickbag with a roundhouse and snarled when it swung back into me.

"You know," he said calmly as be brought the bag under control, "these work better when someone braces them for you." And just like that, he broke me. I'd been avoiding him and my sister for two days, and I let loose on the bag with everything I had.

I cursed. I growled and snarled. I got angry. I sounded like a child as I went on about how things were unfair and how I wanted to blame my sister for ruining my illusion but couldn't. I even complained that I sounded like a spoiled child. When I finally stopped beating the bag, he thumped it and grinned.

"You realize that you just proved how mature you are, right?"

No, I didn't. Apparently the look on my face conveyed this.

"A child would have blamed his sister. He'd've probably confronted her instead of finding a kickbag to beat on. And he'd have told me to go away as soon as I came in the room."

I couldn't help it, I smiled at him.

"How the hell did you know exactly what to do and say to make this better?"

"I didn't, but I made an educated guess." He smirked. "Never believe anyone who tells you wisdom comes with age; wisdom comes with experience, which most people associate with age."

"And where did you get such experience?"

"My parents," he answered. "Or rather, watching them and how they handled when I came out to them."

In general, announcing you were gay wasn't as big a deal now as it was ten years ago. Homosexuality had become tolerated, if not entirely accepted by the world at large. By the way he spoke, I guessed his family was an exception. Again, he must have read my thoughts on my face.

"Most of my father's family was raised devout Catholic. My father broke tradition by marrying an Athiest, who was herself descended from Mormons. Still, his family recognized and respected love when they saw it. They don't approve, but they trust his judgment. Mom speaks to her sister once every couple of months, but hasn't seen her family in years. They raised me and my brothers to be who we wanted and believe in what we felt was right. She took my coming out better than he did, but he took his cues on how to handle it from his family. His family was a little less forgiving. For the past five years, we've talked with them less and less, because my father chose to do what he felt was right. Since I went away to college, his family will come by when I'm not around."

"Damn. That's… a lot to deal with at fourteen, and during high school and college."

"Like I said, wisdom comes with experience, not age. I tuned out the source of my troubles and focused on my work. Turns out, I was a lot smarter than anyone thought and once I applied myself, it showed."

"So you have your father's bigoted family to thank for being nineteen, holding two degrees, and working for a major tech firm?"

He nodded. "That's it, more or less."

I didn't realize then that he'd given me another opening to ask about his personal life. Instead, I kept on being a responsible adult.

"I suppose I need to go apologize to my family now. And especially my sister."

"Yep."

He walked me back to the bungalow, but did not come in that night. We did resume spending time together, both by ourselves and with my family, but we didn't do anything more than spend time together.

I was surprised when he met us at the docks on Sunday morning while we were waiting for my sister's boyfriend to arrive.

"Hello Jace," said my father as he spotted him, "what brings you here?"

"Meeting a friend of mine, Mr. Jackson. He called me at one in the morning from his flight to tell me he wanted to ask me a favor when he landed."

"Hell of a friend who calls at one in the morning."

"Jasper has never been good with time zones."

Suddenly Jace had everyone's full attention. Ears had perked and eyes shot open as heads whipped about.

"Jasper Willows?" asked Cheyenne.

Jace blinked and stared for a moment. Quite possibly the first time I'd ever seen him at a loss for words. He recovered quickly.

"Cheyenne, I think your boyfriend and my friend are the same person."

My mother of all people broke that awkwardness by asking Jace if he knew Jasper via the internet, as it was supposedly making the world smaller in ways like this.

"I keep in contact with him that way, but I met him here three years ago. Right before I started college actually."

I couldn't help it. I began humming the obvious choice of song. Cheyenne and Jace raced to push me into the water. I think they decided that double-teaming was going to work just as well after about two steps. By the fourth I was airborne.

On the other hand, my family and Jace were laughing now, so I couldn't really complain.

Jasper Willows was a lean coyote with red-gold fur and amber eyes who was just as tall and just as old as my sister. He got off the seaplane wearing a wide-brimmed straw hat, Oakleys, khaki shorts, and what appeared to be a neatly-pressed loose white shirt with a green and blue floral pattern. Once he was done being mauled with kisses and hugs by Cheyenne, he took about two steps and stopped as he noticed Jace at my side.

"Jace? You know the Jacksons?"

"I bumped in Connor here at the waterfall lagoon three weeks ago. We've been hanging out since."

Jasper gave a quirky smile. "I could see him bumping in to you, but he's two feet taller than you, how did you not see him?"

Jace grinned and shook his head before stepping forward and giving Jasper a hug.

Cheyenne came up behind Jasper and leaned against him. "Heya gorgeous, I'm exhausted. I need some sleep and then perhaps you all can join me for dinner tonight?"

Everyone confirmed that this would work out and we settled on a time. Cheyenne and my parents went with Jasper to his cottage a couple beaches over from ours, while I went off with Jace.

"Didn't he want to ask a favor to ask of you?"

"He did, and I suspect he'll ask me later."

"Did you and he…"

Uh huh, because that's the mature thing to ask. No, I'm reasonably certain that came from a cross between the horny teenager and the protective brother.

"I won't lie, we did. Two or three times a day for a week."

My mind boggled as the implications came together.

"Two or three times a day?" Okay, now I was visualizing all sorts of things I wasn't sure I wanted to think about. And they didn't all involve Jace and Jasper being paired. I was getting substituted… for either of them. Part of me definitely liked the idea.

Jace tugged my by the hand and into motion. I was unaware I'd stopped.

"He was horny and curious. I was horny, aggressive, and knew exactly what I wanted. To my knowledge, I'm the only guy he's ever been with. He was the second guy I'd ever been with. And by the end of the week, we both knew it had been a very pleasant fling, but it wasn't for him."

Okay, I guess that kind of made sense. I'd had a couple of guys ask me what it was like being gay and were confused and at times frustrated when I told them I couldn't answer the question they really wanted the answer to because I was still a virgin. I couldn't describe the sensations they wanted to know about, and I couldn't compare it to what they were used to.

Jasper managed to get enough sleep for all of us to have lunch together. As a bonus, I'd managed to quiet certain thoughts in my head, if not remove them entirely. A powerful thunderstorm in the afternoon lead to us all watching a pirate movie trilogy together and Jace spending the entire time curled in my lap certainly helped me relax a bit. I invited him to stay the night, but he declined, saying that he had plans fairly in the morning and it would be rude of him to wake us as he left. I offered to walk him back to his bungalow and he said it wasn't necessary and that then he'd have to worry about me getting lost on the way back. After all, he'd been here several times and I'd been here once. It didn't occur to me then that the resort was laid out in a manner to make it difficult to get lost.

We were awakened Monday morning not by the sounds of seaplanes like we'd been expecting – the resort had politely reminded everyone that Network Atlantis, the IT firm behind the most successful social networking sites on the planet, would be flying people in all day in preparation for their company's annual week-long event. Instead we were awakened by the gentle chimes of our doorbell and a polite voice calling out good morning.

At the door was Maria, the tigress who settled us in the first night. She was holding a tray with an assortment of breakfast baked goods and what I can best describe as a royal midnight blue glitter envelope sealed with emerald green wax and "The Jacksons" in pearl white on the front. My foggy brain registered that those colors looked familiar, but that hotel's chosen colors were pale coral, sea foam green, and soft white.

When my dad pointed out that we hadn't ordered anything, Maria responded that these were a gift and that the invitation in the envelope would explain. Confused, my father gestured Maria in to the house. She set the tray on the kitchen counter, then handed him the invitation.

He read it through fairly quickly, blinked sharply, read it again, then handed it to my mother who'd been trying to read over his shoulder. Her reaction was much the same. Cheyenne and I were already curious and the intensity of the curiosity increased significantly when our parents looked at Maria and said "Really?"

"Yes," the tigress replied in a soothing, professional manner. "But we do need to get going soon."

My parents nodded even as Cheyenne and I asked "Going?"

"We've been invited to Network Atlantis's formal dinner kickoff event. Tonight. However, the dress code is very specific. I don't think we could pull it off with our entire wardrobes here. Network Atlantis is going to cover that, but we need to get over to San Juan to visit tailors."

Cheyenne and I opened our mouths to ask questions, but apparently our mother could still read our minds. "We don't know why we were invited or by whom, but both Jace and Jasper will be there."

It took about twenty minutes for everyone to be showered and dressed, which was apparently about twenty minutes faster than Maria had planned. Fortunately, the resort staff is used to responding to odd requests on short notice. If they had to have the shuttle ready a little faster than was planned, they did so with grace and skill that showed no signs of being rushed.

The only thing I remember about the boat ride to San Juan is that I'd never been so fast in anything open to the air before and was grateful for my short fur. Maria simply remained below deck for the trip to keep her fur looking proper for her position.

I remember being bewildered with several style choices and an array of shiny and glittery fabrics. I wound up with a suit in a irridescent deep emerald color and remind me of light played across oil, a silk white shirt, the most comfortable black dress shoes ever, and a sapphire blue tie that matched the suit in style.

My dad's suit was similar, but the colors were reversed and he had a bow tie for his black shirt. My mom wound up in mid-necked, sleeveless formal gown that clung to her curves like whoa and made her look gorgeous. It was the same color as dad's suit, but accented with a pearl and emerald necklace, heels that matched the gown, and a gold bracelet watch.

Based on this trend, we were confused when Cheyenne's outfit was revealed to be a silky white sundress with an emerald, gold, and blue geometric tribal pattern on the hem. Sure it was accented with a belt of gold and copper hoops, but it was amazingly simple compared to what the rest of us had been given.

I managed to snack on some empanadas during the day, but we'd been so busy that we'd not really had time for lunch, so I was quite hungry when we arrived at the resort's premier restaurant around 6:30. The wolf who greeted us at the door wore a classic tuxedo, though the shirt was the same sapphire blue as my tie and his cummerbund matched my suit. A glance around revealed that the resort staff working this event all wore the same basic livery.

While our outfits looked like what most of the rest of the attendees were wearing, we apparently looked out of place to the wolf.

"I'm sorry, but El Ritmo del Playa is closed to resort guests for a special event this evening," said the wolf. He was polite about it, but it was quite clear that he wasn't going to let us in.

"I've got it Marcus," came Jace's voice suddenly as he came around a wall to left of the host stand. "They're special guests and not with the company."

If you've ever seen a show where someone's behavior changes suddenly and sharply because the boss of all bosses is suddenly there and knows their name, you've seen the reaction the six foot tall wolf gave to a five foot nothing otter in an iridescent white suit with matching shoes, a potent emerald shirt, and a tie exactly like the one I was wearing.

"Yes Mr. Smith," said Marcus as he recovered.

It was now clear who had arranged the invitation to the party, but the how escaped me. Certainly normal employees could not invite random families to the company dinner.

My father's dropped jaw implied he'd figured out whatever I was missing.

"Now I know why you look familiar Jace," said my father in that tone that says the speaker is still trying to process everything that lead them to the conclusion. "You don't just work for a major IT company, you own Network Atlantis!"

"Founded, actually," said the otter with a smile. "And I am the majority shareholder, but not the sole owner." It was clear he was trying to downplay this.

I stared at Jace in shock. I now remembered seeing him on TV two years ago when Network Atlantis launched its second major service. He was interviewed left and right, receiving praise for his accomplishments at his age, but the stories never really covered the motivation that lead him to success. And I now I knew why, because I knew his past.

"Jace," whispered Cheyenne as she leaned over to me. "Your boyfriend is incredible."

It didn't occur to me until the next morning that I didn't dispute Jace's boyfriend status at all. My immediate reaction was something far more basic.

"Why didn't you tell me?"

"People behave differently when they get introduced to me with my title. A bit less like themselves and more like who they think I want to see. It makes it hard to get to know people."

I opened my mouth to protest, then shut it because he was right. Had I known, I would have acted very differently. I would have never struck up the kind of friendship we had, the kind that led to a relationship I wanted.

And then I thanked my brain for quick wit in the face of potential embarrassment. "I think you just like startling people, because this is at least the fourth time you've startled me like this."

He laughed. "Guilty as charged," he smirked. "But you all must be hungry and there are endless appetizers at the table, along with a coyote. This way."

Jace turned then and lead us through the crowd and tables to the head table, which was set for six. Jasper was there in a soft grey suit with the same oily look as mine, but the shimmers were flecks with emerald and sapphire while his shirt was white and tie black. He stood from his seat and pulled back a chair for Cheyenne while a resort staff member pulled out the one next to that for my mother. This left me to Jace's right and my father on mine.

As one would expect at an official company dinner, the table cloths were white and there were people constantly stopping by to say hello to the company's majority owner and founder. Having been to such dinners with both my parents' companies, I expected this. What blew my mind was that everyone who'd met Jace at least once before, or had possibly been warned by someone who had, called him Jace. 'Mr. Smith' was quickly but politely discouraged for anyone old enough to understand when it would be appropriate to call him such.

As Jace attended his responsibilities, I looked about the room. If the light had been bright, the decorations in Network Atlantis' bedazzled signature colors would have been gaudy, but by candlelight and firelight, they were gorgeous. Granted, the vast majority of the decorations where the people, but I think that was intentional. Sure, the plates had the same pattern as the hem on Cheyenne's dress and the napkins were a midnight blue version of my father's suit, but everything else was lighting and plants.

The colors and the shimmer and sparkle present somewhere on every outfit drew your attention to the people. Married and single men had outfits similar to mine and my father's respectively. The women in green favored gold and sapphire as accents, but most had the same color arrangements as my mother. Pure white seemed reserved for non-employee girlfriends, fiancées, newly-married women, and the occasional dress of a small girl. In contrast, guys in the same situations wore outfits similar to Jasper's. Styles varied greatly without any discernable pattern.

Now, apparently, was my turn for a leap of logic. I think I'd figured out Jasper's favor of Jace and Jasper's plan. I glanced at my sister. If she'd figured out what I had, she showed no sign. As Cheyenne inquired of a server about the location of the restrooms, I caught Jasper's eye and pantomimed putting on a ring. He nodded and I smiled, then decided it was up to me to keep Cheyenne from figuring it out before he asked.

When Cheyenne returned, I struck up small talk. I asked about classes and college and future plans. I'm quite certain my parents at least figured out I was being a distraction, if not for what. Cheyenne was just happy to share the sisterly advice she'd been unable to force on me for the past four years.

Eventually the room was called to order with a classic tapping of knife on a wine glass. That the wine glass contained sparkling apple cider was unimportant. Once people found their seats, Jace gave a speech welcoming friends and family, touting the achievements of the company in everything from finance and technology to employee satisfaction. Apparently, no one had left the company in search of another job in the past 18 months. My mother, the human resources specialist seemed boggled by this.

Jace then called for the heads of Network Atlantis's five child entities to make their announcements, followed by Network Atlantis's CEO doing the same. The announcements were primarily profit sharing and promotions, with a couple of oddball things throw in for humor, like the request that the fountain in the center of the main campus be filled with chocolate had been denied. Finally, there was a call for additional major announcements. It was then that Jasper stood.

"It has been my pleasure to know Jace Smith for three years," he began. "And I'll admit that I regret not taking the job offer he made me three years ago, but really, when a sixteen year old college graduate says that he can revolutionize the social networking industry, who believes them?" The crowd laughed. "I've learned a lot about myself thanks to my friendship with Jace and thanks to him found myself in a place I never thought I'd be: love."

Cheyenne blushed at this, then squeaked as a spotlight settled on her. My mother began to cry as Jasper knelt before her daughter and pulled a golden ring out of his pocket. "Cheyenne Jackson, will you marry me?"

She took a breath and reached for the microphone, then stood. "Jasper Willows," she said holding back tears, "I will marry you on one condition. I want a man at my side, not my feet. If you want to marry me, stand up and kiss me."

There was a lot of oohing and awing for what seemed like forever as Jasper did as asked. My parents were holding each other, my mom crying happy tears, and for once I didn't care how sappy and silly my family looked, because somewhere during the proposal Jace had grabbed my hand and hauled it up on the table in plain sight of everyone, then stood to lean over and kiss me on the cheek. I decided my first kiss was going to be slightly more impressive and pulled him back over for a second on the lips.

The next thing I heard was my dad saying "Aw, look dear, both our kids are happy and in love," followed seconds later by my mom crying again.

"Parents", said Jace.

"Can't live with 'em," I said as I passed a handkerchief the otter had pulled from his pocket to my father, "wouldn't be here without 'em."

Growing up often feels like an endless struggle to differentiate yourself to create your own identity. Can two star-crossed high school sweethearts reintegrate once they've grown?

Differential Equations

Tyler David Coltrane

Part I: Define The Variables

Stuart had a problem. Has a problem. There is a problem in Stuart's life.

In order to properly comprehend what the issue is at this point in his life, we'll have to step back a bit, to grade school, when the entire fiasco that we, from our outside positions, would call 'romance' began.

Stuart Mouhsse, Stu to his friends, was born in the middle of 1969 to a wealthy pair of doting parents, everything a kid wants when he dreams of the folks he doesn't actually have—rich, caring, like something from a 50's sitcom without a studio audience and a morality lesson before the sponsor came on to talk about their frozen dinners. Stu's dad was hardly your traditional Jim Anderson or Alex Stone, and don't even mention Ward Cleaver in the same sentence lest some horrible fate befall you. The man was queer as a three-dollar bill, something that defied most people's perceptions, mingling a sweet spin of Liberace and Paul Lynde, a charming entertainer and eternal bachelor with a smile that could blind and a wit so sharp he cut his meat with it. Darwin Mouhsse was unafraid to be a fop, a mince, even a queen if the situation called for it, and the local atmosphere was more than congenial to him—he was one of their own, even if a bit of an odd fruit on the vine. Virginia Applesire-Mouhsse, Stuart's mother, was a quietly grounded woman, content to maintain her household, health, and maybe a bit of business in the background. It was impossible to share the spotlight with Darwin, and she happily never wanted to try. The good ship Mouhsse kept floating along on crystal-blue waters, with Dad swishing away on the deck, and Stu was perfectly happy with his lot.

Now here at the present point in Stuart's life where we're going to drop in, Stu—no one but his teachers and people who hate him call him "Stuart"—is in grade school, the 6th grade to precise. Days went by without event, leaving Stu not so much bored as a bit ground down, struggling under the monotony of the every day. As much as his houselife was grand, the day-to-day was hard to deal with, and excitement didn't come his way too often. Miracles or tragedies had to come by in order to change that fact.

One of those miracles was sitting in the hallway, sniffling almost inaudibly at the edge of his hearing.

It wasn't him crying, no. It was the paunchy, squat hyena tucked away in the corner with his head in his hands. Whoever he was, it was fairly obvious that someone had expressed their dislike for the fuzzy little guy, likely by trying to throw him in the trash or maybe flushing him down the john. So there he sat, fingers and cheeks wet and probably a bit snotty.

Stu would have none of this. "Here. Let me help you up." He extended a hand, small just by its nature, to the boy on the floor, giving the widest smile he knew how. That was pretty big, too; Darwin had taught him well.

Moments passed, neither party quite sure how to handle the situation, Stu holding the arm out in space while the other lad, still nameless, simply stared at it. But Stu wouldn't be defeated that easily, no sir! He slid down on the floor next to this poor woe begotten kid, and got himself comfortable. "I'm Stuart," he said, "but everyone calls me Stu. Stuart's a dumb name, so only dumb people use it." The mouse grinned at no one in particular, hoping his mood would be somewhat infectious. "You new here?"

It had the desired effect, finally, his partner looking up a bit with oddly golden eyes. "Yees. First day," he managed, voice hoarse. How long had he been crying? His voice was coloured by a distinctly thick accent, making the simple response an exercise in on-the-fly translation.

Stu blinked, just a bit, and mulled things over in his mind for a second before the gears clicked.. "You must be an exchange student. Africa, maybe?" He didn't give the other boy a chance to speak, carrying on breathlessly. "We don't see many hyenas here. Too cold and boring for anyone exotic to want to live here!" A little speculation paid off with a short, slow nod, and Stu continued on. "Explains your accent. I bet you ran into Jacob and his football goons, and they probably found it a laugh." He made a mock punching motion. "Those eighth graders just get on my nerves…"

The other boy, still unintroduced but not quite so full of sobbing, gave a deep sigh and placed his chin on his knees. "Yes. Was not funnay, but they t'ought so." He wiped his nose with a hanky. "Yoo don' laff, dough. Don' t'ink its funnay, or jus' waitin' for me to leaf?"

Stu looked the African import he'd discovered right in the eyes, grinning like a Cheshire cat that was in the process of eating the canary. His father had always told him that one of the best ways to disarm a bomb of a situation was to smile like a madman and knock 'em dead. And brother if this wasn't one of those times, what was? "You? Funny? Naw. Nothin' really funny about you. 'Sides, what's the fun in pickin' on a kid? You know what you need? You need someone on your side. And hey, I'll have the only hyena friend in the school. But what's your name, anyway? I can't just go around calling you 'that fuzzy guy from Africa' all the time. It's, what would dad say, 'undignified.'"

The previously distressed and now substantially more relaxed member of the pair snickered softly, and shook his head. "Yoo 'mericans are odd." He put his hanky away in a pocket on his jacket and started to stand up, Stu right alongside. "I am Harold D'ogu, but jus' call me Harold." Harold was shorter than Stu, just barely, but being an inch shorter than a 4'10" mouse was certainly

215

something that would be pointed out to you repeatedly whether you cared anymore or not.

So it started, simple as that, someone's concern starting up a friendship that had more durability than concrete wrapped in titanium. The boys were absolutely inseparable for the next eternity and half of the next, spending every possible moment with each other, at their happiest when they were together. As much as walking through every moment of those halcyon days would be, that's not really feasible, so let's focus on something particularly special.

Ah—let's stop here, sometime several years later, during the first year of their high school, when big changes come around and the entire scope of the game can turn itself sideways. Both boys had grown, though not by leaps and bounds; neither one was an athlete, both content to be enthralled by Atari and MTV and bad pop music on the radio. Stewart and Darwin had sat down and helped Harold work through his accent, pushing away the worst of it and making the rest sound charming by comparison, the sort of thing that attracted good attention rather than derision.

"Man, where'd you get reflexes like that?" Stu had been beaten again at some nameless racing game. This was the eighth game of the night, and once Harold had gotten the hang of the controls he was unstoppable, leaving the mouse sitting in second place on every lap by more and more seconds. The hyena was a racing dynamo, completely impossible to defeat.

"What can I say? I'm da predator, an' you aren't. An' you know what losin' means!" Harold pointed at the kitchen and gave a little glare before breaking down in snickers.

Stu grumbled as he stood up. "I know, I know! I gotta go get you pizza and soda. You're lucky I'm so nice to you, Scavenger Sam." He grinned, that same proud and unnaturally wide smirk that had gotten him as many friends as it had punches in the arm or pillows in the face, one of which nearly clipped him in the head as he ducked through the door to the hallway.

The house wasn't exactly massive; Darwin liked living fancy but knew full well to keep it within his means. "Can't entertain people if I'm living in a box on the Interstate, now can I, hmmm?"

he'd say when co-workers bragged about things like their indoor pools or how they had amazing art all over the walls. It still took time to get things together, and struggling back upstairs with arms full of pepperoni deep dish and Pepsi made things a bit slower, especially when you're a short little mouse. By the time he got back, Harold had moved on to reading a magazine, sitting on the bed and kicking his feet while the game buzzed its tinny little tune and played a demo race for no one at all.

"Here you g—" Whatever Stuart had lined up after the word "go" didn't bother coming out as he sat down on the bed and went to look over Harold's shoulders at the magazine, not recognizing the cover at all. It certainly wasn't one of his gaming rags, and the guys on the cover weren't on television or in the movies. So what the heck was it? The response just about stopped his heart, and certainly made white cheeks turn the most distinct tint of rose.

Whatever it was called, it was without doubt (or much shame) pornographic. The pages he could see filled with a handful of photos of men, and only men, laid out in a dizzying array of positions, doing things to each other that were reserved for exactly these fake situations. They only got more involved and complicated as Harold turned the pages slowly."H...Harold...where'd..."

Harold didn't look up, eyes wide."I found it in da bathroom. I thought it said 'Joysticks', so I thought it was a game magazine..." The hyena was lost in his own little world of images, continuing to page through the content with a little gasp and his mouth slightly hanging open.

Stu couldn't claim to be any less amazed by the pictures; while no one could say he was a blank slate on sex, even of the gay variety—his dad wasn't subtle about anything, relationships or others, and Stu had a few 'uncles'—he'd never seen it in action, and definitely not this way. It was stunning, overwhelming, his throat dry and a voice in the back of his head quite pleased that the mouse had worn loose shorts that day, though he'd never been embarrassed about anything around his best pal Harold before.

The two sat next to each other close and browsed the pages as if it were a catalogue of fucking, or maybe some sort of Encyclopedia Of Sex, to be learned from and observed, flipping through it again and again. An hour passed, maybe two, neither deeply aware of the game music, the pizza, or anything else, except themselves, right up until the last page closed for about the seventh time. Finally they took a breath, together, looking up from the matte finish back cover.

"W-wow," Stu stammered, shifting uncomfortably in his seat, looking around the room. "Th-that was...neat..." He was at a loss for words, brain a little foggy from everything he'd just seen and the way his body was responding to it. "S—so that's what my father likes to do, huh." He gave a little chuckle, nervous, and looked back to the game. "Wanna play another round?"

Harold was dead silent. He didn't look particularly thrilled or hurt or anything else, just still as he held what was nothing more than a spankrag (and not a particularly good one) in both hands like a treasure unlike any other. After moments passed, he finally cut the silence, looking over to Stu. "Stuart?"

Stu jumped, just a bit, blinking rapidly. "Wha?" He was lost in thought, trying to focus on the racing game but having a rather hard time of it.

The brown one of the pair looked right at Stu with big, golden eyes, his own signature look to counter Stu's grin. "I—I think I pissed myself." If you could blush through thick layers of fuzz and hair, Harold would have, deeply.

Stu blinked again, fighting back an urge to laugh. "Are you serious?" He looked down at Harold's shorts, thinking. "Naw, it looks more like you spilled something. Did you fumble the soda? It ain't a big spill, so..." Something in the side of Stu's brain clicked, almost audibly, and he snapped his fingers. "I know what you did!"

Caught off guard, Harold stammered a little. "I didn't spill nothin'..." Stu was already flipping through the magazine again, the entire contents burned into his brain with a beefcake-powered laser, pointing at a picture of a lion with his cock in his hand, right in the throes of orgasm, the camera capturing what is commonly referred to as 'the moneyshot', cum shooting through the air in a lazy arc onto his chest. "You did that," Stu shouted like it was some great discovery. "You...uh...squirted."

Harold blinked now, and cocked his head sideways at Stu. "I know, ya goof. I was...uh...tryin' t'hide it.'sides." He canted his head the other direction, curiously. "Ain'tcha nevah done that yaself?"

He'd never once thought to, and he was pretty blunt about that. "No...why...would I?" He had a good idea why you would, especially after the last few hours, but for some reason it felt like something he didn't want to talk about, like he should keep it secret.

"Duh! Cuz it's a good feeling. Nothin' like it!" Without missing a beat, he pulled his pants down around his knees. "See, ya kinda..." He stopped talking, and chose instead to demonstrate.

Stu looked less enthralled and more stunned, having a difficult time finding room to breathe, much less the strength to get any air in the first place. Even his loose boxers and shorts were becoming unpleasantly warm as he watched the hyena, the best friend he'd ever had, masturbate there, right in his bedroom, right in front of him! Instinct kicked in, and before he could figure out exactly what he was doing, he had reached over and was giving Harold a few strokes, nervous and unsure.

Harold would have blinked, would have winced, would have done something, if he hadn't been enjoying himself more than he ever had before. Curiosity was ruling the day here in a joint measure; passion and lust had certainly moved into the room and were dominating two minds. All through the night they explored, touched, felt each other. What should have been a sleepover with pop and pizza was spent not in pajamas watching television, but trying to copy some of the poses they'd seen in the magazine. Some were simple enough, though a few weren't reasonable or were just damn painful when they tried. By the time the sun rose, both partners were completely worn out, having moved to their own experimentation with what was available. More than just enjoying their first experiment in sex, though, they were exploring each other, friendship at the next level.

At 8 AM sharp, Stu's mother knocked on the door. The plan had been to take the boys to the mall that afternoon, to do a bit of shopping and maybe pick up some Christmas pointers while they thought she wasn't paying any attention. No one answered, though, with the exception of a few grunts and a mumble. Her eyes rolled; they'd probably binged on sugar until the wee hours and then passed out. Children...

"Now, Stuart, we have plans for today." She popped the door open, quickly, smiling in that angelic way mothers do when they're about to ruin your dreams. "So get your..." She stopped talking, right then and right there, Stu's mother giving a little sigh, and not a particularly happy one, more one of resignation. The two boys were coupled on the bed, Stu on the bottom with his tail pulled to one side. Harold had fallen asleep inside of him, though judging from the appearance of Harold's own tail, he'd been mounted once or twice. She bounced back from the initial shock, having been through this same situation with her husband more than a few times, and was really expecting it one day or another, though she'd imagined somewhere in her heart it would have been a girl on the bottom, not her son. "I suppose it had to happen eventually. Well, they can't lie there all day." She stepped around the bed, picking up a bit of laundry here and there. "Stuart, darling, time to wake up. I know you can hear me. We have things to do today, and you two need a shower. If you let that dry much longer, you'll have to shave it out."

So began the second stage of the relationship between Stuart and Harold: the truly loving one, where they were not just friends, but lovers, sharing time, life, and their bodies with each other. The remaining years of high school were a combination of learning, preparing for college, and spending every minute they could find away from prying eyes in the arms of their chosen, those few moments enough to make the darkest of days more bearable. They became the gay couple of the school, thankfully accepted so long as they kept their fingers under control when people were expecting them to. They were hardly the only people fucking around like that during class, and no one raised more than the slightest of concerns. It was actually charming to see such a thing, and they were only the first of many.

Oh, and let's just say, they were given time alone in the gym showers. Lots of it.

Part II: Changes In Structure

So it went for a few years. Nothing stays the same forever, though, and karma decided she'd have to throw a wrench in the gears to see what happened.

College was one of those things Stu had always planned for and dreamed about when he wasn't fixated on Harold's body and what he could do with it when the hyena wasn't being the more forward one. He wanted to go there, to get his degree and make something of himself, maybe give back to his parents, who were not only paying for things but had given his relationship their blessings many times over. It was a small secret shame of Stu's that he wasn't self sufficient all the way around, even though at 19 not a soul expected that of him.

Harold, though, was rather concerned with this plan. He wasn't exactly a smart guy, and while he could hold his own in high school higher education wasn't in the cards as he read them, so he'd wanted to get work as soon as he could rather than any lofty goals of college graduation in his head. Stuart would have none of that, not a single word, and dragged his partner off to the college dorms, Darwin offering to help the two keep themselves fed and Stu using a little physical manipulation to remind Harold what he'd miss if he didn't come along with. It dinged Harold's fragile pride a bit that the mouse he'd fallen in love with had sunk to sex—or rather the lack thereof—to try and convince him, but the idea was pushed aside. This is love, right? You give and you take, he told himself.

The accommodations were exactly what you'd expect in a dorm, the room tiny and the amenities few, but the two got by perfectly alright at first, spending their afternoons and nights together. But the term dragged on into winter, and Harold grew lonely quickly. Stu was in class, in the library, in the cafeteria studying, in evening meetings with classmates or so exhausted that all he could do is flop into bed and pass out, leaving little Harry Knows-No-One to curl in behind him and try to sleep. He had few hobbies, he had no friends, and without Stu around him, he felt exposed and unwanted in a way he hadn't since he was a small child, drawing into himself and spending all his time in their room. Deep down he hoped Stu would notice one night that something was wrong, but he never did, so wrapped up in himself and his future. Even the sex was suffering, and he didn't seem to care at all.

On one of his few trips out, wandering down to the laundry room to take care of washing, Harold was startled to see another hyena standing by the front door to their building, waving flyers and delivering some sort of pitch. It was a combination of things that kept his attention: the fact there was a hyena like himself here at all; his infectious energy and amazing charisma; and in no small part the male's impressive musculature, something which made Harold shift a bit on his feet and thank whoever was listening for impressing him to come down in more than his bathrobe, more aroused than he had been in quite a while. Was Stuart really ignoring him that much?

"Hey, amigo, step right up!" The body builder, at least that's what Harold assumed he was, had caught the lingering stare and was waving one hand, gesturing his admirer over. "Oh no, hombre, I'm not about to take no for an answer. I need to talk to you. I know I do, one 'yena to another, eh?" His accent was thick, Mexican maybe? Harold didn't know for sure, but he found himself heading in that direction almost without realizing he was moving, the grin on the other's face growing wider, a bit like Stuart's used to when he was on the verge of a grand idea.

"Thanks for coming over. I was afraid I was gonna have to chase you down or somethin'!" he said with a deep laugh, setting his stack of fliers down on a table and leaning himself against it, arms crossed around a broad grey-brown chest. Harold was in awe of his build and keenly aware of their differences, curling up a little and tucking his head away. "My name's Ricky, and I'm from Bullgod's Gym. Sure you've heard of it. And if you haven't then it's my job today to change that. Now lemme take a couple of guesses 'bout you, okay?" Ricky rubbed at his chin, deep in thought, just the slightest bit theatrical. Probably part of a well-rehearsed pitch, Harold though, starting to turn around and leave as his little courage failed him.

Ricky stepped into his path almost immediately, starting to walk a slow circle around his "subject", still thinking. "You're havin' trouble with a love interest...left you lonely, did they?

Self-confidence is battered, and you've been alone an' livin' on Nintendo and Mars bars for while. Don't go out often. Mm hmm." He went back to the table, eyes to Harold's. "What's got Paradise lost for you, brother?"

Harold started to speak, the words muddled and too fast, surprised that he was even talking at all. Why was he opening up to this random person? Because he'd guessed that Harold's love life was shot? That wasn't spectacular, that was just taking a low-risk chance. And low self-confidence? He was an easy mark for that idea as well. But there he was, telling the story to a person he'd known all of five minutes who nodded with every word as if it was the most important thing Ricky had ever heard in his life.

"I have an offer for you, my brother," Ricky said when the tale had been spun, holding a flyer out to Harold, a splashy full-color affair with photos and pitches and an enormous mascot of some kind of bull creature. "Come out to the gym some afternoon while your ratón does his classes. I'll give you a little story of my own: once upon a time, I was just like you. Different town, different partner, different college, of course, but same story: down on my last shred of dignity, left to my own devices and about to call it quits and head back home. Someone told me that maybe if I let him have a few hours a day with him, he could show me that sometimes, if you work the outside, you can find a better inside too. An' he was right." He smiled and handed his business card to Harold, shaking a much smaller hand. "I'm tellin' you the same thing. Don't let one person ignorin' you bring you down, amigo, even if he the one you love. And it's not like you can't spare the time! I'll even get you the first coupla sessions free, just tellin' Ricardo Grey sentcha." It all sounded like a pitch on the outside, like practiced words that were meant to bring in the gullible and the defeated to sap them out of their money. But the whole conversation had an edge of truth to it, something warm that settled in his head and wrapped around his brain, hugging it and whispering how this would work. It didn't help that Ricky was a beautiful specimen of a man…

Ricky cleared his throat as quietly as he could, and very carefully pointed his finger down. "I appreciate the, ah, applause but how about we just work out?" He gave a little grin, and Harold grabbed his laundry basket, dashing back to the room he shared with Stu as embarrassed as any moment he ever had been before in his life.

Ricky stood and smiled for a moment before getting back into his routine, working his arms for a few adoring rabbit girls who had wandered by.

Stu didn't get that wonderful warmth from the story, rolling his eyes at points and staring at the flyer as if trying to find Waldo, or maybe to get what had his Harold so happy. It didn't make sense. "Why? Aren't those things expensive?"

"$200 a year. I have it. What else do I buy? Your father gives me a stipend, and I work a little." He sighed deeply, maybe a little too much, and looked Stu up and down with those golden eyes. "I'd just like to try it. It's something that I think might help. And they've offered me a few free sessions." He took Stu's hand in his, clutching it, hoping for some sort of reaction. He barely got any back, a weak squeeze in return, distant. "Stu, I can't stay here in the room and masturbate all day. It's bad for my health and the sheets."

Under normal circumstances, that would have provoked at least a giggle. Today, it got a weak smirk and a shaken head. "I still think it's just a money trap, and they're drawing you in with a walking erection machine. But..." He gave a small smile to Harold. "If it makes you happy, you're more than welcome to try it. I hope you have fun at it."

Harold was ecstatic, bouncing off the walls happy. It didn't hurt that he'd already paid for a year at Bullgod's Gym and had already been once, taking advantage of the free sessions with Ricky...

At first, he was deeply afraid it wasn't actually helping. Harold's paunch faded of course but that was to be expected--just water weight or "easy flab", but he was still a dumpy, short nerd, the same old Harold D'ogu. It didn't matter. Without any idea where the motivation was coming from, he worked and worked, harder and harder, day after day, spending his nights pressed up against Stu, weak from the effort. It certainly didn't stop their lovemaking, though; his stamina had clearly picked up, and Stu was hard pressed to keep up, having to outright complain that he had other things to do than be pounded in the ass by an oddly hormonal hyena—tests needed him sleeping.

The calendar rolled over to 1991. New Year celebrations were shattered by a frantic phone call during dinner, a nurse telling Stuart that Darwin had crashed his car during an ice storm, and there was no hope of him surviving more than a few nights. When the limo to the airport arrived, it took Harold and the driver just to get the shaken mouse into the car and on his way. Virginia told Harold that as a close friend of the family he was welcome to come as well, but he chose to stay instead, making up some lame excuse about maintaining the dorm room ownership, taking a class, and maybe looking for an apartment for them to move into before graduation. No one questioned it; there were far more pressing matters and everyone trusted that Harold could tend to himself for a few weeks while matters were attended to.

Harold was, in fact, not being honest. But he would certainly take care of himself. He had plans.

Bullgod's Gym was open 24 hours. That was nearly enough for him.

Stu returned six weeks later. Between spending hours with lawyers, trying to negotiate some peace between squabbling family members all posturing for a chunk of Darwin's estate, and tending to his shattered mother, closing the last of his father's affairs had wiped him out completely, leaving him nearly a drunken wreck on the last night before he flew to the college. It was not a welcome sight he came home to. The room was the very definition of devastated, with sheets unchanged, the dishes dirty, and a heavy stink of sweat lingering in the air. He lifted up a rag, cringing at the smell of stale milk, and tried to figure out who had let the place get this far in just two months. Had Harold just run off? Was he on drugs, or worse, dead? Stu had always known his hyena to be a neat freak, so to find his feet sticking to the floor was a shock.

A flick of his ears cued Stu into someone else's presence in the room, the sound of running water—someone showering?—was faintly audible, echoing off the tile and concrete walls. Stu clenched his jaw and reached for the bat he kept behind the bedpost, needing to shuffle filthy laundry to get at it. The room must have been broken into while he was away, and whoever was washing up was hiding out in here. Since Harold never left the room, it would be just fine…

The water eventually shut off, signaled by the whimpering of old pipes deep in the walls. Stu crouched down and got ready to lunge. It was a laughable sight, really, the tiny mouse trying to act all big and fierce with a Louisville Slugger in his hand, but appearances weren't on his mind. He clenched his teeth and watched as one foot came around the door.

The intruder was a massive beast, Stu dropping the bat just from the shock of it, wood clattering to debris and tile. Whoever this was, they took damn fine care of themselves, a behemoth of a hyena with legs like tree trunks and a chest that would require several barrels just to get across. Most notably, he was completely and totally naked, a monster of a member—though suited to his nearly 8-foot-tall stature—swinging a bit as he moved. Stu scrambled backwards, falling into a chair, before his eyes caught the glint off this beast's glasses. Tiny simple frames, perched on a nose.

"H-H-Harold?" His voice was a tiny whisper even for him, almost too quiet to hear, eyes wide and gaping.

Harold, who it really was stomping through the room, stopped suddenly. "What's wrong, Stu? You look like you sat on a tack." He sat down on the bed, the poor thing creaking in agony. "It's almost like you don't know me." The hyena grinned a bit, muscles flexing with every single move, sculpted lines even visible under the skin.

"You don't even sound like Harold…" Stu walked over, steps careful and slow, staring into those golden eyes. They were Harold's, they were his lover and his best friend, ones he knew well. "But you are. What's happened to you, Harry?"

Harold beamed widely, smiling like a kid at Christmas who just got the pony he asked for. "I hit a growth spurt! Ricky and Delilah said it was going to happen, and it finally did! I'm big!" The formerly scrawny man ran off an entire story in rapid-fire cadence, Stu too awestruck to stop him, something about a suppressed puberty and stimulating a 'late bloom' that nearly doubled his height and shot his mass into the stratosphere. He paused for breath after minutes, and noticed Stu's confused face, just staring at him. "I wanted to tell you all this as it happened, but I couldn't reach you. Mail would take too long, and I didn't want to call your house while you were mourning. I know how you were about Darwin." He turned around and bounced on the bed a bit, pointing his hand around. "I had to modify the bed a little to keep it from breaking, and the shower is a little awkward, but I usually use the one at the gym…"

Stu shook his head, hard, trying to clear it. "What have you become, Harold? Where's the little shaky fuzzball I met, the one who always needed my shoulder and wouldn't leave my side? What did you do to yourself?"

"What do you mean 'do to yourself'? I'm what I should have been all along. I'm big, just like my father always wanted!" He grabbed Stu with his massive arms, crushing the mouse into a hug that would leave most folks dead. It almost did, in this case, Stu's face flushing red and eyes bugging.

"Let…me go….you…" Stu shifted back, dragging the breath back into his lungs.. "This isn't natural, Harold. You're not just bigger…you're taller, you're wider…you're…this isn't a growth spurt… this isn't natural!"

Pointed ears flattened at that last word, eyes slitting. "It is, trust me. Ricky says that this is the natural me, and it just hasn't come out until now. I'm still the same me on the inside, just… happier now. More confident."

"But you're not the Harold I fell in love with. You're…I wouldn't have been able to talk to you in school. We wouldn't have been unnoticeable. You're—too big." Stu saw stars as Harold pushed him away, banging his head against a wall as his partner lost control of his strength.

"Oh, I get it now. I don't need you to stand behind me and be my confidence, be my protector, so it's time to leave me behind. What happened to 'unconditional love', Stuart? Did you leave it behind in the car, when you drove home? Did it fall out of the limo when we came home from Prom? Did you bury it with your father, maybe? Was it ever there?" The last word was spat, teeth bared from a huge muzzle. "Maybe you don't like being on the small side of things, huh? Afraid you're the loser now, the tiny one, and I'll have to protect you when that asshole smirk and smoothness won't rescue you? Hah! You didn't love me, you used me!"

Stuart flinched, pushing back up to his feet and rubbing his head. "I never used you, Harold. You were the tiny little flower than clung onto my waist and pouted and sobbed until I kept the bad people away. And now you've gone and shot yourself full of steroids or horse hormones or whatever the fuck they've filled you up with at that meat market you call a gym, and worse yet, you used my father's money to do it!" A thin finger pointed at a broad face, right between angry eyes. "You were jealous, and you ruined the Harold I loved to pad your own fragile ego. I hope you're happy, because I'm not. I'm going to deal with this personally and convince you just how wrong you are." He pivoted on one heel, grabbing his jacket. "I'm going to down to this Bullgod's Gym, and talk to your trainer. You cheated somehow, I know you did and they did too, and I'm going to get it all undone or I'm going to get compensated for my suffering!."

And with that, he was gone. Harold stood there, looking at the door, hands in his lap. "But what about mine?"

Bullgod's Gym wasn't difficult to find; it was a massive complex several stories wide located in the hottest part of downtown. Failing that, you could always follow the billboards plastered about randomly, with their giant smiling mascot, some monstrosity of a bull they called Crete. Everywhere you went, there he was, big Crete, with his stupid stoic face and his stupid fake name and stupid impossibly perfect build. He was obviously a wholly artificial creation that some CGI mill in California had whipped up, or maybe he was the product of a team of artists and a few days in Photoshop. All this to make people believe that 'at Bullgod's Gym, the power of the bull god will get you the body you've always wanted!' or any of their other brainless ad-lines were true. People are intensely desperate to be happy, he thought to himself, driving at just more than slightly unsafe speeds through traffic.

The parking lot was crammed to capacity with a variety of people, the thin, the buff, the flabby, and the sick, all trying to get to that ideal physiology that everyone begs for. It made Stu sick, really, all these people who were 'discontent' over something as simple as scrawny biceps or a saggy ass. Why not be happy with what you have? What is with the endless pursuit of unnatural perfection?

Inside the gym was no better than outside, the whole thing one long ostentatious eyesore. The facility was a mock temple, flooded with gaudy gold trim, fountains, and giant statues of their 'spokesbull', Crete. It wasn't an ill-equipped gym, filled to capacity with what felt like square miles of equipment, aerobics rooms, and all the other things that gymnasiums provide as part of the service. Even the crowd was thick, too, Stu needing to push his way past buxom gym bunnies and hulking beefcakes in every condition you could think of.

"Hey there, li'l guy! Welcome to Bullgod's Gym. What can I help you out with?" The clerk was perky, sure, but beyond a chipper attitude she was another entry in a long list of 'too big' people that Stu had been inundated in this afternoon. The hippo had arms that even made Harold's look diminutive, tied with breasts the size of tractor tires, figuratively speaking. It was all Stu could do to not yell something about her parentage and ask for someone who didn't chug Diet Roids between sets.

"Yeah. Yeah you can. A friend of mine, Harold...Harold D'ogu...he was coming here. I think his trainer might have done somethin' to him, pumped him fulla chemicals." Stu put on his absolute best bravado, which was rather wasted in a discussion between a titan who would floss her teeth with airplane cables and a mouse who could probably weigh himself in a vegetable basket at the supermarket.

"Harold? African guy, hyena? Oh, he's a pretty one, yeah. Amazin' piece of work! And that means you must be Stu." Stu blinked, but before managing to say anything, the clerk continued. "He talks about you all the time, thinks you're the best thing since hot showers and cold beer. You're good people he tells me, mmm-hmm."

"This isn't about me," Stu cut in. "It's about Harold. I'm gonna say it again: I wanna see his trainer. I want to know what sort of drugs they spiked him up with to make him that big so fast." He caught a glance of someone with "Ricky" written in huge block letters across the back of his muscle shirt working on a machine to one side. "Him! That's the fucking drug pusher what broke my fucking Harold and turned him into some bloated freak!" His voice was as loud as it would go and still barely broke the clatter of gear, grunts and shouts, and certainly Ricky didn't notice.

The clerk, apparently named Delphi, leaned over the counter, pressing her bust within inches of Stu's face. Against taller clientele, it would have been her face, but not here. "Right, bubby, let's start with manners. You don't walk into my house an' scream at my staff an' piss off my members, you hear? There's a door over there and you're two breaths and a heartbeat from bein' introduced to it lips first." She held up two wide fingers an inch from Stu's nose. "Second, we don't do any of that 'jucing' here at this gym. I can smell a steroid from 5 feet away, and our boys don't even need none of those funky Chinese mumbo-jumbo herbs to bulk up. Only one-hundred-per-cent pure and natural muscle is made here. Now, if you'd like to make more accusations about the establishment, I'm sure I can show you what sort of things it's done for me." She started to roll up one short sleeve, something entirely unnecessary as her biceps already surged up from her arms.

Stu winced and gave a sharp squeak, backpedalling away from the wall of breast and muscle that was threatening to envelop his head. "It's just not natural. I imagine you worked for years to get that muscular. But Ha...ro..." He stopped as a shadow drifted over his head, completely blocking out the light. He just closed his eyes rather than bothering to look up; it was easier this way. Death would be brief and easy.

"Is this one creating a problem for you, Delphi? I will have him removed at your request."

Delphi shook her head with a bit of a dismissive hand shake. "No, no, he's fine, Crete. This is Harold's lover, Stuart. He wants to talk to you about Harry, and swears you, ah, 'cheated'"

Stu's eyes grew much like Harold had, and he snapped his face up, ignoring the pain in his neck as he tried to figure out if that really was the mascot himself. It was honestly impossible to tell from this angle, but those certainly were horns, and that certainly looked like his torso. "There's no such person as Crete. He's a computer-genera—"

"Let us step into my office, and we shall discuss this matter privately, Mr. Mouhsse. I think we have a great many things to deal with, and Miss Oracle does not need you causing a scene at her counter." Crete reached down with a meaty hand and hefted Stu up off the ground, carrying him about the waist like a bundle of towels towards the locker room.

Moments later, the pair had passed beyond the showers and the lockers, through a sea of naked bodies of all species, shapes, and sizes, none concerned in the least to see a great minotaur tromp through the room, wearing a pair of running shorts and a shirt marked "YES, I AM THE BULLGOD" across the chest. Neither fit well and both showed off things in amazing detail, the minotaur's amazing chest and abs shining through and the fact he was a bull in absolutely no doubt. Stu took a deep breath and gulped, worried about what sort of abuse he was about to go through before he was dumped with unexpected grace into a chair.

"Give me one moment, Mr. Mouhsse, and we will discuss matters." Crete wandered behind his desk and pulled off his clothing, setting it into a bin that seemed intended for just that before coming to stand in front of his desk. It hardly made any difference; the muscle shirt had covered so little and the shorts had outlined so much that bare pectorals and abdominals over an immense endowment wasn't a very substantial change. Stu did sigh inwardly though—today had been 'let's make the mouse feel very insignificant' day on many counts. "I do not enjoy the concept of clothing," the minotaur said in a nearly emotionless voice, slow and steady, exceptionally well spoken with a very slight accent that Stu couldn't place. "But the owners of this facility prefer that I cover myself when amongst the public. I acquiesce in the name of good public relations." He shook his head. "Now, about you and—"

"Yeah, about me and Harold." Stu's initial anger had bubbled back up as he was being toted around a very crowded gym in front of dozens of people and with it an intense reckless streak was burning over top of it. "I want to know, whatever kind of androidy-cyborg-robot thing you are, what exactly you did to Harold to turn him into a mutant wall of muscle from the pudgy little guy I fell in love with. Did you brain wash him too? Out with it!"

Crete didn't even blink; he didn't breathe fast, stutter, sigh, look confused, or anything else. "To begin, I am not an 'androidy-cyborg-robot thing', or any one of those things individually. I am not a computer generated image, and before you even suggest it I am not a 'fucking man in a costume'. I am Crete, I am a minotaur, and I am quite real, with muscle and blood as proof. If you would like to continue to believe I am a facsimile, I will make no further effort to change your mind, but I would prefer if you could stay on the topic at hand. Do you find that acceptable?"

Stu just shook his head, not believing a word of it, and definitely not listening to a majority of whatever Crete had to say. "Sure, yeah, okay. Minotaur, right, right. And I'm the Easter Mouse. But you're right—let's stay on the business at hand. What in the world did you dope him up with? Some of that Chinese shit that Delphi mentioned? Maybe you experimented on him? You got a lab in here?" There was more, a long string of increasingly loud and incoherent nonsense that bordered on conspiracy theories and even a few things that would make them take pause, Stu worked up until his face flushed and his eyes grew bloodshot, waving his arms around frantically like a complete lunatic.

Again, the minotaur showed no signs of anything except a gentle rise and fall of his chest. "I did nothing to your love. There is a story here, and I believe you are reacting without knowing the full details. If you will let me provide you those missing facts, mayhap you will come to accept Harold and understand his decision."

Crete sat down on his desk. It obviously was just for show; the chair was far too small for him, the phone was fake, and the computer was not plugged in to the wall socket. "This is a gymnasium. People come here for a variety of reasons. To be healthy, to gain muscles, to become an ideal that, perhaps, is unattainable. It is nothing more than it appears to be on the surface. The machines are normal, the trainers are normal if not highly skilled, and our methods are sound and traditional. Harold came here several months ago, on the suggestion of one of my assistants who believed that helping his body develop would ease stresses in his mind."

"I don't believe that for a moment. He tells me everything. There's no rea—"

The story continued, around Stu's protest, as if it were just as small to Crete as Stu. "He has always been a small being, a 'runt' amongst his people. He tells me that his paternal ancestry was of mighty males, warriors and protectors of their village. The list of deeds and trials recorded was long indeed. This trait carried into Harold's father and again to his children. Even his mother is, by your standards, exceedingly large and muscular. Do you know how tall his youngest sister is, Stuart?"

"I dunno, maybe four foot tall? She can't be that big, if Harold is—"

"She is seven feet and ten inches tall, and masses easily four hundred pounds. Comparatively, Harold was four foot eight inches when he first chose to exercise here, weighing a mere one hundred twenty pounds. He is twenty years of age, and she is fourteen. This has rendered him as the outcast of his family, his people, and his ancestral home. This is the reason he was sent to America and you were able to meet him. He is immensely ashamed of his failure."

"And you couldn't leave well enough alone, could you? You took pity on *my* Harold, and—" Stu was ranting now, red-faced and completely beside himself, fingers pressed into the arms of his chair until his knuckles were sore. Still, his storyteller was unfazed by any of it and he continued.

"When your studies took priority over his affections, he felt lost again, abandoned and alone. Hephaestus, Ricky to you, invited him to our family with an offer of a way to find himself through bettering his body. He worked unexpectedly hard, trying to produce in himself that which he has never had. It did not come, no matter the effort. Harold simply became healthier and stronger but was still a small being in his own mind. So..."

Crete shifted his weight slightly, looking to the wall. "You observed Ms. Delphi Oracle when you entered, did you not?" He paused, but didn't wait for the still seething mouse to answer. "When she arrived here, she was in no state to even exist. Her weight was extreme, her bulk laying in rolls down her chest and stomach. Her only mobility was in a custom cart, Mr. Mouhsse, which was not unlike a forklift. She could not stand under her own power let alone walk, and her fingers were useless extensions at the end of bulbous hands. Medical science had provided no answers to why this mass grew and grew, so she had come to me, Mr. Mouhsse, as person with no future through no fault of her own. Had she come to me as someone gluttonous, lazy, or any other number of things, she would have been turned away.

"Instead, I accepted her. I am not simply a trainer here, you must understand. I am not simply a 'mascot', though I lend my image to it as requested. I am in some ways its healer, its mentor, and the leader of its followers."

Stu blinked, slowly, trying to make things settle in his rattled brain, the pounding of his blood finally reaching painful levels. "You mean a different Delphi, right? That woman in the lobby could bench press my car with one hand and nearly killed me with her breasts."

Crete gave the slightest little smirk possible on a person's face, hardly even noticeable, and Stu in fact missed it entirely in his angry haze. "No, Mr. Mouhsse, there is only one Delphi Oracle that I am aware of. She had been brought to me by her physician, a man who had exhausted his own abilities and was saddened to think that Ms. Oracle would be lost. I could not allow that to happen, not to anyone. To do so is simply unconscionable.

"I cannot simply touch a being and have them suddenly explode into their perfect image. The effort is strenuous; many do not finish and some fail to even begin. Ms. Oracle completed her training and has become a person I and she are both proud of. She was strong in spirit, and now she has a body to reflect that. It is good to see her smile."

"What in hell does this have to with Harold? What in the world did you do to him? Stop evading my questions!"

"Mr. Mouhsse, you are a poor listener. Harold wished to have all the sorrows of his childhood as the 'runt' replaced with the happiness of being what he felt he was destined to be. He is like Delphi, but where Delphi was physically failing, Harold was emotionally collapsed. I allowed him to support himself by giving him the ability to resolve his concerns with his failures to his people."

Stu scowled. "You can't possibly mean that. He had me. We were in love. You make it sound like that had no meaning."

Crete looked back at Stu, a piercing stare with dark eyes that never blinked. "You were his anchor, yes. Had you not appeared in his life as you did, he would likely have never survived to meet Hephaestus. But you cannot undo his basic fears, Stuart, and when you removed yourself from his days they surfaced with vengeance."

Stuart jumped to his feet. "I know how you can make this right. You make ME as big as him, hell, maybe bigger, and we'll be alright again."

The minotaur cocked an eyebrow, looking not unlike a Vulcan. "I do not understand your logic."

"It's simple! If I'm as big as him, I can love him again, like we used to. It cancels everything out and we're back to the status quo!"

"You do not love him now that he is larger? You are irrational—"

Stu clapped his hands together, sharply. "Hello, Crete. I'm not asking you, I'm telling you what to do. Make me big and buff, we'll have a patched up relationship, no problems. Ding dong done!" He snapped his fingers with each of the last three words,

Crete sighed a bit. "You do not understand what you ask." He looked up. "I can do this for you, but it will cost you. I do not speak in terms of property."

Delpi looked towards her security monitors as something flared in the locker room, sighing as she noted it was Crete's office. "I sure hope he knows what he's doing. Otherwise, I'll deck that brat and wear his teeth." Hephaestus nodded too, face marked with worry, something shared across a number of similarly named titans at the Bullgod Gym's central counter.

Part III: {} - Empty Solution Set

Harold sat alone in his darkened dormitory room. He had moved barely an inch since Stu had stormed out hours before, still naked in a drying damp spot on the bowed bed. There were no tears; he knew Stu would be back, and that everything would work out fine, a weak smile on his lips. They were meant to be together, that he had always believed, and it would still be fine. It had to be. This is one of those rough moments all couples had, of course it was...

The dull thunder came first, growing slowly, making the free furniture rattle around him.. Harold looked up at the ceiling, then down at the floor. One of those rooms with the excessively over-powered stereo systems bought to compensate for a tiny penis must be listening to something with quite a bit of bass, he thought, and ignored it. But it was still growing and getting closer.

And then it stopped, right outside the door. The hyena's heart snagged inside his chest as old fears exploded out from under well-secured doors, rapping at the walls and pressing against the worn latches, threatening to drive him catatonic.

"Harold? Are you in there?" It was Stu at the heart, but it was wrong somehow, tainted and twisted. Harold didn't answer, clutching his legs to his chest, eyes wide in the darkness as he pulled himself into a ball. The bed cracked and splintered under the sudden added weight, but he took no notice.

The door was opened so sharply as to nearly tear it from its hinges and a monstrosity of a hand reached in. At first, the massive fingers had a hard time flicking the light switch, finally meeting success after frustrated degree of trial and error. Then in walked Stuart Mouhsse, clad in a pair of torn jeans and a shirt that had given up the fight hours ago, having fallen away from him before he arrived.

Crawled would however be a more appropriate word. His head failed to clear the doorway without a significant quantity of stooping, and even then he could not entirely stand up. The floor creaked, the concrete construction having difficulty holding up the newly over-massed mouse. "Hi, honey, I'm home..." It was that same Ricky Ricardo impression he'd done a million times, only distorted, too bass, more like a giant calling out to Jack than a lover calling his partner. With a grin, a huge thing that spanned far too many inches, he stomped over to Harold. "I fixed everything," he grunted. "It'll be alright."

It was not alright, Harold would have said, but he was too busy backpedaling madly, trying to climb the walls behind the bed, claws shredding through the sheets and digging long grooves into the wall. His ears flattened against his skull and the smell of urine filled the room. With eyes as big as fists, he dove for the floor and ran into the bathroom, locking himself in, slamming his weight against it as he threw the locks. "Stay out there!"

Stu was, to say the least, confused. "Isn't...isn't this better?" He banged on the bathroom door, his equivalent of a knock, rattling the hinges until they nearly collapsed. "I thought you liked big. Isn't that what you wanted for yourself? I'm just sharing with you!" Stu could not tell how loud he was bellowing, but the entire building was now quite awake, scrambling for weapons, phones, or escape routes.

The only sound, once the rattling subsided, was a dull whimper. "Too big...too...you're—"

With one final grunt, Stu pulled the door free, setting it against the other wall. "I'm wh..." His voice died a thousand deaths in that very moment, looking upon the room. Curled up there, in the corner of the bathroom, pressed into the tiniest ball an eight foot hyena can make, was Harold. He was sobbing uncontrollably, his eyes twitching madly from side to side, fingers digging bloody holes in his knees. "Too...too...too..." The sight was pitiable, and Stu's heart cried, a tiny voice chanting that something had gone drastically and uncontrollably wrong.

Stu leaned down, to pet Harold, to tell him things were fine. And then the fist hit him, taking him entirely off his feet, claws leaving bloody lines down his cheek. The monstrous mouse lay there, not moving, just watching Harold, eyes wide and mouth agape.

The hyena got up, slowly, after a moment, and left the room. The sounds of a closet echoed gently through the air, then the clicking of the door as Harold left silently.

Stuart's world went black, and it would be several hours before light broke its way back in again.

Shaking fingers felt at the dried blood spattering over clean cuts on his cheek. The headache rang through his head above a swollen brow; Stu reminded himself that Harold apparently could throw a mean punch. Finally he dragged himself off the floor and staggered into the living room, crashing down on the floor.

"For a man who claims to love, you are a poor lover." Crete was sitting on the only chair in the room, simply watching Stu try to walk. "I advise and you ignore. I teach and you forget. I warn and am disregarded out of hand. I do not know why I should help you any further. You do not deserve Harold."

The dialogue paused for a moment, Stu choosing instead to take the easier line and simply punch Crete in the head. The experiment was a resounding success in creating response, though it was not the cracking of a skull but more the crunching of an entire hand's worth of fingers, Stu screeching in further pain.

Crete was as unmovable as ever. "Are you finished now? Your 'love', as undeserving of the term as you are, has returned to the gymnasium. I would highly suggest not going there, though."

Stu had already grabbed his keys and a coat which, really, was a stupid gesture as his arm wouldn't fit through it. "And why not, Crete? You don't want me to have my Harold back?"

Crete grabbed at Stu's arm and with no sign of any effort on his face dragged the oversized mouse, actually larger than him, down to the floor. "Because Delphi will most certainly snap your head from your shoulders before your shoulders clear the doorframe and Hephaestus will delight in shattering your limbs. While I do not advocate such violence, there are moments when not even I can restrain my followers and disciples. Now please, for your sake and mine, listen to me this time. I will not advance you a third chance.

"Harold D'ogu was not simply a runt in a village full of giants. He was an outcast, an unacceptable product of his parents. They were cast in a dark light because of his very existence and because they created him. He was not suited to be a member of their group, even in these modern times; the world around him was built for giants of strength and stature, and he was not. This you know, or had best.

"He escaped Africa not long before you met him in grade school, essentially given away to an American family who had met him during a stay there. A missionary group or some such, it is irrelevant. Until the moment he was placed with you by fate, he had been brutalized. His father, whether by anger or ignorance, mauled his own progeny and denied him food, shelter, anything he could think of, in a misguided attempt to make him stronger. When he arrived here, the people around him were no different and in some ways worse with their scheming and manipulation. It is difficult to be...different, as I'm sure your father would have told you many times.

"You, Stuart Mouhsse, were a random chance placed into an otherwise bleak and pointless life. And here we sit, nearly fifteen full years after, and you have abused the man you chose to protect. You have created, in yourself, the very thing which Harold has avoided forever. You are too large, too strong, too dominating. You want him to stay smaller, for whatever reasons you might have. You care about your own future to the detriment of his. I do not understand you. I suspect I never will."

Crete stood up, slowly, and started towards the door. "I do not believe I need to explain you stand a very strong chance of losing him now. I shall intervene on your behalf, but do not believe that all shall be made better." He crossed the threshold, then paused. "Mr. Mouhsse?"

Stu simply looked up, eyes red and damp, face puffy and bruised.

Crete touched his shoulder. "I will undo this foolish thing you have done. In one hour, you will be yourself again. But all is not made better. I will see you, whether you intend it or not, again." And he was gone.

Part IV: Starting Over From The Very End

Days passed. Stu did, as Crete had told him, return to his normal size after a time, the wounds lingering far longer. He cleaned up the dorm room, throwing out sheets and requesting a new bed, feebly dodging questions about the damage from anyone and everyone. The days were lonely, with nothing but education and self-pity to fill them; the nights were worse, quiet and lonely. To call Stu a wreck of a being would be putting things lightly.

He was thin, even more than his species called for. His appetite had fallen away and his stomach worked to reject nearly everything he put in it. He did not sleep, could not concentrate, and barely kept himself clean, collapsing before the eyes of his peers into a shambles. Those around him were convinced he was a drug addict, and several times the college sought to remove him, grades and finances barely keeping his name on the rolls.

The time to graduate came, and to no surprise, Stu had not succeeded in college, nearly so catastrophically as he had failed at romance. There was no place to go now; his mother had given away to charity much of the family fortune, save a fund to get Stu through college, and scaled down her existence after being widowed. She was in no state to have him around, her mind feeble and body weak. With no brothers and no sisters, he was very aware of how simply alone in the great crush of humanity he was. Friends had abandoned him during his downward spiral and few people would have anything to do with a man in his state, even the dregs of society turning away. As one put it to him, "no one loves a nihilist".

He had gone looking for a replacement, someone to fill in the hole in his heart and his being. At first, Stu had been selective, but as he declined so did his standards, dropping to the point where he was simply begging for affection or paying for it outright. When the money flow dried, so did the love, alone again with his memories. Man or woman, he gave everything and offered anything for a moment of their time with some feeble hope that one would think of him as less than a whore and rather a lover, someone so perfect and wonderful they would make all the pains go away. It did not work, no matter how good his tongue was or how wonderful his ass might be known on the streets around his home. As a john had said when he asked about conversation after sex, "no one loves a whore".

He grew older. 22 years old had come and gone, and now 25 was past, with 30 creeping up the doorstep, the never-ending pain in his jaw during cold days reminding him of what had come and gone, what that had left him. It was a tale of selfishness and greed, one of taking things for granted until they left. Now an aging hooker on a dark corner of a seedy part of town, a man with a few dollars to his name with a sore ass, a tired expression, a two pack a day smoking habit and not an polite word to be said about him. He wore bad clothes, lived in a bad apartment in the bad part of town and drove a bad car that ran badly. His reputation quite possibly took the most damage, faces who had once smiled and offered pity and charity now ignoring the situation after their help was used and abused. The addictions had left him alone, but the damage was done nonetheless. He knew, more than ever, that he had needed Harold more than Harold had ever needed him.

He wondered, daily, where his hyena was. He still dreamed of the boy he'd met in the hallway at Fairchild Junior High, back in those simple days. But he shot those dreams down before they grew too warm and inviting. Miracles only happen in the movies.

Stu made a decision as December rolled around and Christmas rang around his ears. It was time to let things go and stop being a burden on the last few people who chose to interact with him. It would be a great present to the world if he were to move on to whatever comes after and say good-bye with a bit of a bang, maybe a lot of a bang if things went quite badly.

And there he was, Christmas Eve, sitting in a bar drinking cheap beer he wasn't sure he could pay for. The plan, such as it was, was to get himself so stupid drunk that he wouldn't be able to drive home safely. It was a good plan; it eliminated him from feeling any guilt while he was doing it, so if he ran over the median and killed a few five year olds in a mini-van, then so be it. He wasn't going to sweat the details. He'd already ruined everything, so why should today be any different?

It would have worked, too. If not for those damn Christmas Cabs. Before he knew it, it was 11:30 that night, and he was in the back of a cab with a beer buzz that was rapidly fading.

"Where you live, bub?" The driver was a big man, fat like a balloon, a gorilla chomping a cigar the size of a billyclub.

"Sssssseventeen Cartridge...Cartway...Safeway...Cartwright street. Apartment ooooone...seven. Yeah. The one with the cardboard box in front. I live in the box. Haaaaah hah hahahaha-haha...that's my summer home! Yesh!" Stu wobbled and laughed maniacally. "Fuckin' schoot me in th' head, man."

"Uh huh. 17 Cartwright? Kay. Youse jus' sit yaself on back dere, an' get some sleep. S'gonna be a loooong drive, an' I'll make it nice an' easy for youse."

241

Stu didn't need to be told—he was quite asleep already.

The cab pulled into a half-empty driveway, crunching snow under its tires, marking its arrival with a signature sound heard in every Christmas movie at some point. The driver slid out, puffing on a new stogie, and went around back. "He's out like a light, boss. Stinks like a damn hobo. You sure that's him? Don't look quite right to me."

A familiar voice came through on the cabbie's radio. "I'm quite sure it is. Bring him inside, Sid, before he grows too cold."

There was no energy wasted as the silverback hauled Stu over his shoulder and wheeled him inside like a floursack. "Here youse go. He was right where ya said he'd be."

"He is nothing if not easy to follow, Mr. Calinto. Set him on the couch." Stu could barely make out voices now. He was coming to, but he didn't know where, exactly. But there was that voice... was that really?

"Crete?"

Stu's vision was mostly fuzzy lights, dancing around his skull, a hand reaching up to try and grab one. But that damn voice rang out like a bullet through his brain, making his teeth itch. Every word was clear, completely piercing his intoxication in a way many wives would pay good money to do. "Wh...where am I, Crete?"

"You are at the gymnasium. I had said we would meet again, but you were making an attempt to rob me of the chance, and others as well."

Stu tried to sit up, having limited success without the assistance of a big hand on his shoulder. "I'll thank you when the room stops moving, but what am I doing here? I have a date with several empty bottles and a bridge." His eyes started to draw together, the light making him wince but several images slowly came into focus around him.

The minotaur was exactly like he'd been that first time, sitting on his desk with nothing on. The taxi driver who Stu presumed was this magical Sid was standing slightly hunched over next to him, oversized arms crossed. "To celebrate Christmas, I believe. It is nearly that time of year, is it not, Sid?"

"Already is, boss. It's two in da mornin.'"

Crete shrugged a bit. "I do not follow time very well. It is a very old habit. But Christmas it is!"

"Don't yell," Stu moaned, clutching his forehead. A glass was placed near his side, with a few pills next to it. They were swallowed, with lots of water, a bit lost down a soiled shirt. "Thanks, Cr..."

Stu squinted, holding up his hand and pointing at each person in turn. "Yer over there. And that's Sid. And I don't hear Delphi. Who's that?" He pointed upwards.

"I thought your memory was better than that, Stuart. Just a few years, and it's like I never met you!" Big hands reached down, quite suddenly, and grabbed Stu entirely, smashing him against a mostly bare chest. It was all he could do to not throw up against the rigid pectorals before he passed out again, the immense strength against his emaciated chest pushing the breath out of his lungs and leaving him dazed.

"Oh no... Crete, he's in such horrible shape. He looks like death on the walk..." Even semi-conscious Stu's radar ears picked up tangents of conversation, too vague and random to put together, but someone was concerned for him. Was he that bad? Sure, he hasn't eaten lately and he was a little ripe, both with filth and cigarette smoke, maybe some booze. But it couldn't be all that bad.

Stu's nose woke up before the rest of him. He smelled all sorts of things—talcum powder, sweat, Harold, metal, expensive carpeting, the couch...

He popped up suddenly, or at least tried to. A pair of brown arms, each sporting their own endorsement from The Popeye Society, held him quite firmly in place. "I know these arms," he mumbled. "I've seen them before. Hell, I think this one over here jerked me off once or twice!" He managed to look upwards along them, head throbbing through a hangover that would make record books if they kept such things.

Golden eyes. The ones he hadn't seen since that horrible night in his dorm room, at least five years ago. They brought back memories, both wonderful and horrible, and Stu simply started crying, sobbing, blubbering and grabbing at the thick muscles with his bony fingers.

"Welcome back," Harold said with a sideways smirk. "It looks like you missed me."

Stu nearly fainted, again, but for once that holiday managed to hold himself awake. "Kiss me, you stupid fool, kiss me!" They kissed awkwardly, Harold's muzzle more than Stu could handle, but he positively did not care, burying himself in the hyena's pelt and crying against him, a big hand running down the back of his head, an arm cuddling him protectively, cooing words of safety in his ear. "It's okay, Stuart. I'm not going anywhere, not anytime soon."

The two spent Christmas day in each other's arms, refusing to be even out of the other's sight.. Stu refused to let go of his big lug, even when it came time to eat or when nature called. If Harold went, there Stu was. Harold laughed it off, letting it go as 'just one of those Christmas things'. The rest of the staff at the gym seemed pretty happy with it, too. And who could deny it was a cute display, a muscle-bound hyena wandering about in cotton gym shorts and a tanktop with a white mouse in his arms, or up on his shoulder? Delphi swore up and down that she even saw Crete smile, and Hephaestus dressed himself up as a rather sloppy Santa and offered them presents. It was ridiculous display, but it was a good way to spend a very light day in the house of the Bull God.

"We need to catch up," Harold said, working his way through an immense salad, watching Stu poke at a very small sandwich, having taken barely a bite. The mouse looked up with an expression that belied unpleasantries that he was trying to keep hidden, and for the moment, Harold allowed it. "Well me, I went home."

Stu's jaw dropped. "To the family that beat you? The one that basically handed you over to missionaries and didn't look back?"

The hyena nodded, swallowing another immense bite. "Yes, them. I had to go and prove I had started as a runt but there was a powerful being inside me." His face fell and he looked down at the table. "It…didn't go very well. No one remembered me, and trying to explain the situation was pointless. Our language just doesn't have the words. So I had to leave." Harold perked slightly. "I dated a bit, though. I met a lovely female who works here on the weekends, we've been dating a little. She's a rabbit, kickboxer. Championship grade!" He paused, and poked at Stu's hand with the tines of his fork. "But I don't want to talk about myself. I want to know where the beautiful man I knew for a decade went." Black fingertips ran over a patchy white face and along three scars and a lump of bone where a jaw had been badly tended to, along exposed cheekbones and thin lips. "Do you not eat? You looked like you had been sleeping on the street."

"I may as well have," Stu said with a shrug. "My apartment was condemned two weeks ago, and I've been sneaking into a warehouse for shelter. Some crackhead stole my pack, and no one wants a whore who doesn't bathe, so I can't afford food. I think I ate last week, but…" He looked up into Harold's eyes. "I haven't had much of an appetite since you left."

Harold was aghast, eyes so wide they might just fall out of his skull. "You…you sold yourself? But…why didn't you do something else? You're a genius! I know this!"

"I failed out of college, and when you already look like you're going to sell drugs to small children, job offers don't fall into your lap. I did what I could." Stu gave another little shrug, looking up as he nibbled at a corner of his sandwich. "I did what had to be done, really. I ran out of money, and I don't have much to offer but an ass, a mouth, and a cock. No one wants to hear me talk."

Harold stood up and looked Stu over, walking around him slowly, examining muscles and bones and limbs and lines. "You… you look like you're about to die. I can see your ribs, Stu, and your cheeks are drawn. Your pelvis, your wrists…" Harold was genuinely on the verge of tears from seeing his lover in this way, a level of concern Stuart hadn't seen in more months than he could count. It made him feel so much better immediately, warming his tired heart and making him glad that miracles worked in whatever reality he happened to live in.

"And there you have it. I've been a lot of unpleasant things, Harold, and I wouldn't be surprised if you didn't take me back." He looked up at the massive hyena, sliding his chair away and standing up, wobbling on sore legs and covered in worn, dirty clothing.

The big hyena would hear nothing of it. "You dope. I love you more than ever. Nothing will ever change that, and I've figured something out about our relationship."

An arm wrapped itself loosely around Stu's waist. "Since we met, you protected me from what wanted to hurt me. Now, I'm protecting you from your own demons which are trying to destroy you. Let me pull you up."

There a raucous round of applause from the small group in the closed gym; Harold wasn't much of a speaker, but he had his moments where, just by speaking honestly, he could get a mighty message out. Stu locked the hyena—no, his hyena—in a kiss to end all kisses, eyes closed and hands on the sculpted muscles.

Crete coughed a bit, before Delphi nudged him in the ribs. "Maybe we should give them a little, y'know, 'alone time.'" She started dragging Crete out by the arm.

"But this is my office...and what alone time? They are together..." He could be heard complaining all the way out into the hallway.

"So now what, Harold?" He drew gentle lines through the chestfur he was laying on, the both of them having given up on clothes as soon as the room was theirs. "This body is...it's different, not what I met and grew up with. But it's still you. Just there's so much more of you. I could learn to love that." He sighed, resting his body against the chest and thighs of his partner, curling up a little. "I...I want to make love to you, but I can't." He looked up, eyes wet and swollen, one looking as though it'd been blackened recently and was healing. "I'm too sick, too broken."

Harold shook his shaggy head from side to side, giving Stu a light poke on the nose. "You're only damaged. I can help you recover. I'm here to bring you back to your old self." He chuckled, deep in his chest. "You may not have the body you used to, but I still see the you inside, and I'll help you bring that back to life."

They laid back on the couch, Stuart spreading himself comfortably over the man twice his size, the hyena who had come to him seeking affection and had found himself as a protector resting quietly under the confident mouse who could avoid any situation with sheer pluck and guile only to nearly lose himself to short-sightedness and blind desire. Together again, different than they'd met, yet still the kind of lovers that songs are written about, sleeping together for the first time in years.

In the hallway, three titans stood, watching the doorway soundlessly, only barely hearing what went on within. Hephaestus turned to Delphi and Crete, a seed of concern on his face. "Do you think he'll recover, Crete? He's malnourished and I think he nearly drank himself into—"

The minotaur ended the conversation with a soft shake of his head as the three turned and walked towards the center of the empty facility, the lights set low and the sun slowly sinking outside. "He will be fine. He has the love of a titan to protect him. As I said to you both, the path towards finding yourself is never a safe one, and the results are not always titans themselves, but…simply people who are complete. " He sat down on a bench that looked crafted for his immense build, and gazed out into the parking lot and the surrounding city. "Stuart has completed his journey, and he has found his destination. I cannot say I am happy to have been the catalyst for such an unpleasant turn of events, but it is what I am upon this blue Earth to do." He turned back, looking at the hippo at her computers. "How fare they?"

Delphi sat down and checked her security monitor. "They're asleep, sound and wholly. What should we do with 'em, boss?"

Crete, completely emotionlessly, shook his head. "Turn off the monitors. Let us leave them be for now, and we will tend to them in the morn."

He stood up, flexing his legs, and began walking towards the elevator to his quarters. "Their only needs for today are each other, and if they need the Bull God again, I will find them."

The elevator doors closed softly, leaving Hephaestus and Delphi to turn off the lights and depart for the night, the gym empty save for the soft sounds of breathing from one small office.

As high school comes to a close, the traumas and dramas of four friends come to a head. It's the biggest night of their young lives, and the fact that it's prom is the least of their concerns.

The Rule of Four

Lycanthromancer

First Step: One's Alone

Rubric's red-brown eyes stared out over the moonlit ocean, watching the silver-edged waves as they rolled onto the sand.

I'm such a coward he thought, and he wished he wasn't.

Here he was, a red panda sitting out prom during his senior year on a big flat rock. And for what? Because he was too chickenshit to come out of the closet and ask a guy to be his date. And almost as bad, he had no idea who he would've invited, even if he had the guts to do it.

On the one hand there was Jaron, his best friend since gradeschool, but Rubric was fairly sure he was straight. Or at least, the Tasmanian devil had never shown interest in anyone but his friends. He couldn't quite imagine the tough-as-nails jock, whose father was serving back-to-back life sentences in the state pen, batting for his team... though he wished he could. Other than the torch Rube carried for him, they'd always had a platonic (if close) relationship, and as much as it hurt sometimes, he'd rather have Jaron's friendship than risk it by pushing for something the devil didn't want.

And who knew what the guy thought about homosexuality? He regularly beat the hell out of bullies and, occasionally, people who pissed him off. They were best friends, but sometimes that didn't mean much. Rubric had read stories by other gays who'd come out to friends and family and had negative—even violent—reactions from people they'd trusted, and Jare had one hell of a temper. The idea of losing him like that... well, it scared him.

Sure, he could've asked innocuous questions, feeling out how Jaron felt before outing himself. But the idea of asking his best friend for a date was just so... awkward.

On the other hand were the twins, Rasputin and Charles, though they went by Raz and Chaz (and people who forgot that fact regretted it more often than not). The two lop-eared pranksters, true to their lagomorphic temperaments, were well known for their shared exploits amongst the female population of Hendrix High. And then there were the unsubstantiated rumors about the rabbits having double-teamed several male members of the school soccer squad. He could've asked one or the other of them out, but again, the idea of asking his friends for a date would be weird, and even—especially—if the rumors were true, he'd just be another notch on their bedposts.

Sure, he was their friend, and he crushed on them more than a little, but how far could he trust them and their libidos? Given some of the stories floating around school, probably not very.

And beyond his worries about homophobia and infidelity, he was just shy, and that made romantic overtures embarrassing. Really, that was the crux of his problems. If only he could be like his friends and throw caution to the winds, refusing to give a damn about what anyone thought...

He sighed, picking at the artificial flower in his black lapel. He'd actually gone to the dance, but turned and fled before he hit the hotel doors. Yeah, he'd inherited his grandfather's giant panda stature and the muscles to fit the massive frame, but he still had his red panda heritage to thank, at least in part, for his spinelessness.

At least he hadn't accepted one of the numerous offers from the girls that asked him out. Rubric might feel like a coward, but he wasn't that gutless. He had to be true to himself, and using a girl like that felt like a betrayal.

But now he was alone, and he hated it.

He sat there on the beach, feeling lonely and guilt-ridden. He should've come out to his friends. He should've asked them to the dance. He should've pushed past those anxieties and fears and done something, rather than nothing.

His head felt full, his thoughts chasing themselves around his brainpan for a good half-hour before he felt the pressure of someone leaning against his back and resting their elbows on his head, and someone else squeezing his shoulders with delicately-fingered hands. The twins had an uncanny knack for knowing where he was when he didn't want to be found, and the soft sand and sound of surf covered their footsteps handily enough for them to ambush him.

Great. The twins were here; Rubric felt his regrets drown themselves in a wash of anxiety as soon as they appeared.

"Hey there, Spazz!"

"Yeah, hi!"

Yeah, that was him alright: Spazz. And the twins often baited Jaron by calling him Taz, but only 'cuz they ran faster than the devil. Literally.

He didn't bother looking back. "Hi guys."

The fingers on his shoulders squeezed at some knots they found there. "Why so glum, chum?"

"Didn't want to go to the party?"

"They've got alcohol!"

"We made sure of that!"

Of course they'd spike the punch. It's what they did. One or both of them had been drinking, at least a little; he could smell it. Probably Chaz, since Raz had allergies.

He shrugged, and the fingers kneaded the tense muscle; if he weren't so miserable, it would feel wonderful. "My parents made me go. They said I'd only get one prom, but they didn't say I had to stay."

"Couldn't get a date, huh?"

"You could've asked us!"

"We don't have a date either!"

"Unless you count going with your brother."

"And we don't."

"Don't we?"

"No."

Rubric tensed; he couldn't help it. "What?"

Raz let go of his shoulders and flopped down on Rube's lap, straddling him so they sat face-to-face. The twins were touchy-feely with everyone, but with him more than most.

Raz wore a white tuxedo that glowed under the moon; Rubric would bet dollars-to-donuts that Chaz had dressed identically.

"We had to walk to the prom!"

"Our parents wouldn't let us borrow the car after last time, so you could've picked us up."

"And everyone would be jealous at you walking in with a handsome rabbit on each arm."

"I know we would be."

"And we're us!"

He shut his eyes tight, trying to ignore the erection growing under the rabbit in his lap. "You're not serious."

From behind, Chaz stopped leaning on the top of his head, wrapping his arms around the panda's neck and nuzzling him instead. Yeah; he'd definitely been drinking. "Of course we are."

"If friends can double-date, why couldn't we hit the prom together?"

"Yeah, then we could find some losers and steal their girl-friends from them!"

The panda relaxed a little. The twins were just being their normal goober-selves.

"Of course, you probably won't want to do that, since you don't like girls." A pause.

"Shit, Chaz! Shut up! I knew I shouldn't've let you have those shots before we spiked the punch!"

The Earth shifted under Rubric, and he felt his stomach drop. He opened his eyes and looked right into the blue eyes staring at him from less than two inches away. "What? I'm not...I..."

"Ohhh, *right*. I wasn't supposed to say anything, was I?"

"No!"

"But, y'know, it's okay with us that you're gay, Rube. I mean, we're bi! Right, Raz?"

"Right, Chaz."

"Sorry, Raz."

"It's okay, Chaz... I think."

"So... you know?" the panda interjected.

"It's pretty easy if you're looking for the signs."

"Yeah, we saw you checking out other guys in the locker room."

"We saw you checking us out once or twice, too."

"You're good at hiding it, but you never pay any attention to girls."

"And we've seen the look on your face when you see Jaron and you don't think anyone's watching."

"We think he's adorable too."

"But we won't tell him if you won't."

"Agreed."

A baritone voice behind them interrupted, sending Rube's brain into Blue Screen of Death mode. "Oh really."

Oh God! I wanted to work up to this! He felt the twins' bodies stiffen around him in unison. Dammit!

The panda fumbled for something to say. "Oh! Uh...hi, Jaron. Err...how much of...that...did you hear?" Yeah, that was smooth...

The devil padded around so Rubric could see him over Raz's shoulder, though he was hard to see in the darkness with his densely-compact frame and black fur and tux, complete with tails. He cocked his head to the side, his green eyes inscrutable in the night. "They're bi, you're gay, and all of you apparently have a crush on me. Oh, and nobody has a date for the prom. So, pretty much all of it."

He could've pushed the rabbits off of him and run, but he buried his face in the tux-sheathed shoulder instead, taking small comfort in the masculine-scented warmth. "I'm sorry."

"Sorry?" Jaron sounded confused.

"Yeah."

"For being gay?"

"Yeah."

"Why?"

"I didn't want to piss you off."

"That... is the stupidest thing I've ever heard."

His eyes jerked up and he stared at his friend. "What?"

"I can't believe you thought I'd get angry at you over that. You should know better. After all," he said, hiking a thumb at the lapin in his lap, "I hang out with these two fruitcakes—"

"Hey!" the twins yowled together.

"—which, of course, I mean in the nicest way possible. But seriously, you two are gayer than Rube here could ever be, even if you do like girls."

"Are not!"

"So are not!"

"Just because we haven't dated a girl since Dahlia—" Raz punched Chaz in the arm with a warning glare. "Ow!"

"Shut up."

"Look, you're both wrapped around him like a jackrabbit sandwich. I know you two have the hots for him, but c'mon."

The panda's world dropped out from under him again. "They... what?"

Jaron huffed and rolled his eyes, shaking his head in exasperation. "How can such a smart guy be so clueless? These two are all over you. Constantly. Yeah, they'd be all over me too, if I let them, but we've already established that they think I'm... What was the word you two used? Adorable."

The twins giggled at that. "Yeah, you are!"

"We just never told you 'cuz we didn't want to get in Spazz's way in case he ever wanted to, y'know, actually make a move."

"See?"

"But they're all over everyone!"

The moonlight glinted off the white in Jaron's raised eyebrow. "Dude. Raz is practically grinding on your boner, and it'd take a crowbar to pry him off. I've never seen 'anyone' get that much out of him, let alone 'everyone.'"

Thoughts of the rumors skipped through his mind, but he pushed them aside. "I... see your point."

The twins giggled again. "Well, I wasn't going to say it."

"And now I'm jealous; when do I get my turn?"

"You can wait 'til I'm done, Chaz."

Rasputin grinned, then grabbed him by the cheek-ruffs and kissed him. And Rubric found himself returning the favor. Other parts of him responded too, and the jackrabbit definitely noticed. Both were breathless when they finally parted.

Raz grinned. "I'm enjoying myself too much to give him up yet, and I think Spazz agrees."

He felt dizzy, and though he couldn't see it he knew he had the ditziest grin on his face. "Yeah..." And then he found his body a puppet to his hormones, rather than his fears; it hugged his friend tight and spoke the question he'd wanted to ask, but was too afraid to say on his own: "Want to be my date for the prom, Raz?"

The pretty rabbit's eyes glowed luminous in the light of the moon. "Definitely. But who's going to lead when we dance?"

The twin at his back bristled. "Aww, man! No fair using biological warfare! You suck, Raz!"

Jaron piped in. "I hope you're right, Chaz. For Rube's sake, if nothing else."

Charles blew him a disgruntled raspberry in response.

Second Step: Two's a Party

They stood outside the doors of the beachside hotel the school had rented for prom-night. Rubric heard the techno bass thumping inside, but he swore his heart pounded louder.

"Why Mr. Jaron," Chaz said to the devil as he nuzzled in close, or tried to. "I don't see why Raz and Spazz get to have all the fun. Will you be my date for the prom?"

Jare sputtered for a second, and Rube saw his ear-tips redden as he blushed. "But... I'm not gay, Chaz."

Oh. Damn. Not unexpected, but he still felt disappointed.

Chaz giggled. "That's okay! You said so yourself; I'm gay enough for both of us. And anyway, it's just 'til Raz's turn with Rube is over."

The devil huffed. "Fine, whatever. But no funny business."

Rubric was already having second thoughts about his hormone-induced decision, and if the idea of jumping into a hotel full of his classmates scared him, doing so while on a date with another guy (even Raz) was worse.

God, you're such a coward, taunted the voice in his head. Raz and Chaz don't care what they think. Jaron doesn't care what they think. Why should you care what they think? Man-up, you chicken.

His date stood beside him, handsome in his white suit. He twined his fingers around Rube's as the panda screwed up his courage to walk through those doors. Raz's hand was soft and warm in his. "You okay, buddy?"

He pulled a deep breath and released it slowly, reminding himself that he was surrounded by friends, and together they could face down anything. A bit melodramatic for a school dance maybe, but it made him feel better. "I'll be fine. Just enjoying my last few seconds inside that closet I've been holed up in the last seventeen years."

"Meh," called Chaz from behind him. "Being closeted sucks. You'll feel better once you're out and everything dies down."

He flashed them all a weak smile. "I hope so."

Jaron's growl made Rube's candy-striped tail fluff out. "And if anyone gives you crap, I'll kill 'em for you. With kindness if possible, and violence if necessary."

The twins snickered. "And we'll give 'em a metaphorical kick to the 'nads."

"I don't think anyone's gonna mess with you with what Chaz and I've done to some of them the last four years."

"Haha! Yeah! Remember what we did to Johnny Dirk sophomore year?"

"Yup! He walked funny for a week!"

Rubric winced. "You kicked him that hard?"

"Nope!"

"Never touched him!"

"We weren't even in the same room!"

"We can't vouch for the debate team, though." "But we did learn something from them!"

"Yup! 'Never enter a battle of wits unarmed.'"

He rolled his eyes. "You two are nuts."

"That's what Johnny said!"

"Something like that, anyway."

"Nuts were involved, at least."

"And super-glue!"

Jaron cleared his throat before the twins could elaborate, pinching the bridge of his muzzle, eyes clenched shut like he had a headache. "I don't even want to know. Now are we going in, or not?"

The rabbits looked to Rube, and he steadied himself with a nod. "Here goes everything."

They pushed in the outer doors and through a large well appointed foyer, then followed the signs leading to the Executive Conference Suite. A few of the hotel staff bustled down the transverse hallways, but they didn't see anyone else.

They hit the suite doors without slowing and Rubric tried his best to emulate Raz's nonchalance, though his bulk and the situation made him feel so... exposed.

The room had to be fifty feet wide and twice that long, with large glass doors leading to an open courtyard on the far end. Inside, students loitered along the walls and near the snack tables, with densely-packed groups chatting around the floor. Nobody danced in here, which was a relief, but he suspected that was an outdoor activity tonight.

The first thing he noticed was the heavy beat of the music hammering on the inside of his skull. Gah! His ears flattened to shut out the noise, but it was still unpleasant. Next came the mandatory disco ball; spotlights shining on the gaudy decoration left it twinkling from the ceiling like a kitschy kaleidoscopic star.

Maybe they could hang here for a half-hour, then do something less... seizure-inducing later? He'd have to ask.

They weren't even five steps in before a squeaky female voice drowned out the music. "Rubric! Over here, Rubric! You came!"

Crap.

A petite gray squirrel in a blue dress waved her hand in the air to flag him down. She immediately ignored the raccoon-girl she'd been talking to as she darted toward them, much to her friend's obvious annoyance. He couldn't exactly ignore the body flying at him, so he let go of Raz and braced himself as she leaped (in a hug if he felt generous or a flying-tackle if he wished to be accurate).

The smell of alcohol wafted past his nose, which certainly wouldn't help matters.

He wanted to push her off, but he considered what happened last time. So instead he held his arms up, careful not to touch her. "Janelle! I asked you before, please don't do that!"

She looked up at him with a grin. "I knew you didn't mean it when you said you didn't want to come!"

He tried to keep his voice as gentle as he could while still yelling over the music. "Actually, I said I didn't want to go with you. I have a date, so please let go."

She released her grip and stood back, looking around to either side of him in disappointment and confusion. "You have a girlfriend? Where is she?"

"No, I don't have a girlfriend." Rube pushed for that last ounce of resolve, reached out, and pulled Raz in with an arm around the shoulders. "I have a boyfriend. I'm gay, Janelle. I didn't have the heart to tell you before. Sorry."

Her confusion swelled visibly. "You're not gay."

Jaron stepped up halfway between them with Chaz plastered to his side and a strangely pleased half-smile on his face. "Actually, I got to watch them making out. Either he's telling the truth or he's the best liar I've ever seen." Rubric got the impression his friend didn't exactly like the squirrel much. That made two of them.

She looked from Jare to Chaz to Raz then to Rube, and her expression darkened. "Don't think I don't know what you're trying to pull, Mr. 'I'm Gay'. If you didn't want to be my date to the prom you should've just told me, rather than using the Doubleslut-Twins to lie." She turned on her heel and stomped off.

"I did tell you! Multiple times!" But either she couldn't hear over the pounding decibels or she didn't care. He looked at his friends, his own anger plain. "Girls are crazy. Almost makes me glad that I'm gay."

Janelle reached her friend, and they exchanged a few very animated words.

The twins glared after her sourly. "Girls really aren't that bad."

"...Most of them."

"Take it from us."

"You just have to watch out for the drunk ones."

"And the crazy ones."

"And the crazy drunk ones." Chaz's expression turned even more bitter. "And the narcissistic vindictive batshit-insane ones."

"I'll take your word for it." He grabbed Chaz with his free hand, pulled him in close, and gave both twins a hug. "What a jerk. She shouldn't've said what she did. I'm sorry."

They each pushed away far enough to cock identical eyebrows at him; sometimes they were so in sync it was downright uncanny. "Why?"

"You didn't do it."

"And besides, we've been called worse."

"Much worse."

An all-too familiar voice snickered at them from the side. "Hey, faggots. Making little girls cry now?"

Oh no...

"See?" As one, the twins glowered at the polar bear leering from the sidelines.

Jaron wasn't far behind. "Go away, Rick. Just because you're team quarterback and two feet taller than me doesn't mean I can't pound you into the floor. Or won't."

Rick Sheer hardly ever backed down when he had the bit between his teeth, and it'd be just like him to make homophobia his new hobby. This could get bad.

Or not. "Whatever. But tell your panda friend to watch himself," he said, ignoring Rube standing less than ten feet from him, "or those two will have him on his knees sucking cock and out the door before he can blink." Rick waved them away as he turned to walk off. "And don't let those perverts fuck up the prom for us normal people."

Janelle and her friend had watched the exchange, the raccoon glaring daggers at him for a moment before turning with a flick of her tail. Janelle turned with her and they melted into the crowd.

"Yeah, yeah." Rubric read the devil's lips as he muttered, "Get bent. Ass."

The odd encounter left Rubric both relieved and mortified for diametrically-opposed reasons. "What the hell was that?"

"That," Raz sighed, "was par for the course." Chaz just shook his head in resignation.

"But you shouldn't have to put up with stuff like that! Why didn't you say something!"

Jaron rolled his eyes. "You know Rube, as much as I love ya, you're too soft. You're the biggest guy in school, and I bet you bench-press twice what he can. None of you would have to take shit from anyone if you weren't such a teddy bear."

The twins hugged him tight. "But we like our big softie, don't we, Chaz?"

"I know I do, Raz. Though maybe not too soft." And they giggled.

Would the twins really do what Rick suggested? Fuck him then chuck him? He'd been their friend for years, and he knew them as trustworthy and kind (albeit vindictive when you pissed them off enough); not at all what gossip said they were. Were the rumors wrong, or did he not know them as well as he thought?

But... Why didn't they deny it?

Rube shook his head to clear it. "He's right. I should've said something. Rick shouldn't get away with stuff like that."

Their shared expression was pointed. "We've dealt with it this long."

"A few more weeks won't make any difference."

"School's almost done, then it'll be over."

"Just let it go, Rube." "Please?" They shared the last word, and it hurt to hear.

"But..." He wanted to argue, to convince them to do something, but the look in their eyes stopped him. He nodded. "Alright."

"It's okay."

"You're a lover, not a fighter."

"If we have anything to say about it, anyway."

He blinked. "Right." He knew where this would lead, if he let it. Time to change the subject before they worked him up too much to walk. "Why don't we hit the snack tables? I'm thirsty."

Raz grabbed a hand and tugged him toward the side of the room, and Chaz seized Jaron by the lapel and followed suit. Raz turned to him as they neared a big glass bowl full of neon-red liquid: "I wouldn't touch that stuff if I were you. It packs a helluva punch!" He laughed at his (admittedly horrible) pun, grabbed a can of Rubric's favorite brand of cream soda from a nearby ice-chest and handed it to him.

He popped the top and knocked back a swig. "Thanks, Raz."

The music switched tracks to a soft rock ballad: slower, mellower, and thankfully for his ears and his sanity, much quieter. The DJ sucked, but his developing headache thanked the guy nonetheless.

Raz grinned as his ears perked up. "You can slow-dance, right Spazz?"

He felt the tips of his ears burn as he blushed. "Err... Not really, no. I've never done the whole 'date' thing before."

"Wanna learn?"

Whether he wanted to or not, he decided right there that he would, for Raz's sake. He nodded. His friend deserved that much, rush of dread notwithstanding.

The rabbit's grin widened. "Goody." And he pulled Rube out the sliding glass doors and into the crowd of boy/girl couples dancing in the courtyard.

He looked over the heads of the throng, and they seemed to be the only gay couple there. Were there others, sitting on the sidelines or hiding behind a girlfriend or boyfriend or whatever? Or were they the only ones? He'd feel more comfortable if they weren't. He wished he knew.

Raz tugged on his arm and Rubric turned to face him. "Okay now, you're bigger, so you lead. See how all the guys are holding their dates? Just hold me like that, and move the way they move. That's it! Easy!"

He mimicked the other couples and held Raz close. It felt so gauche at first. He tried to stop thinking and simply move, and it became easier. He melded into the movements of the dance, and holding the rabbit was suddenly so natural. It felt... good. Better than he'd felt in a long time. He noticed the rabbit's erection as it brushed his leg. Oh yes, definitely better.

Several people nearby broke away in open disgust, but he did his best to ignore them and focused on the young man in his arms;

the fluid grace in his movements, the warm scent of him under his cologne. Others moved in to fill the breach; not everyone felt the same way obviously, and that made him feel better.

His half-closed eyes wandered around the room as he drifted across the floor.

Jaron stood propped against the wall, his gaze following them on their way around the floor. Rubric wondered what he was thinking to put that sad look on his face. Was he remembering his mother before she died? Was he considering his next visit to his father? Was he thinking about the fact that he'd have to go home to that huge empty house of his once the night was over? It hurt to see that look in his eyes, and Rube wished he could make it better.

Chaz, meanwhile, was clearly pestering Jaron for a dance, but just as clearly getting nowhere. Jaron merely huffed and said something Rubric couldn't hear, and ruffled the rabbit's head in a way he knew would annoy him.

A number of other people around the edges stared at them. A few simply gawked, though most of them looked quite disgusted, including Janelle, whose flattened ears were taken by the 'coon whispering into them. The two of them looked out of place together, one in an attractive blue dress and one wearing a black Lycra bikini top and a matching way-too-short skirt, her knee-high stiletto boots completing an outfit totally inappropriate for a formal dance.

The squirrel's expression suddenly twisted in rage, and she nodded to her friend before stalking off into the crowd. The 'coon practically oozed a self-satisfied smirk as she glanced at him and waved.

The panda should've paid more attention to his own dancing, because he stumbled, nearly crushed Raz, and totally broke what mood was left. "Sorry, man. I tripped."

Raz laughed. "It's okay. Not everyone can be graceful as me." The DJ swapped tracks to some annoying pop-song and his ears twitched. This was not something either of them wanted to dance to. "The song's over anyway."

The rabbit led him to the edge of the courtyard by a concession table on the far side of the room from Chaz and Jare for, he assumed, a bit of privacy, and squeezed his hand. "Thanks for the dance, Spazz. It wasn't that bad, was it?"

His thoughts went back to the disgusted glares he saw around the room. Most of which weren't directed at him so much as the rabbit he held, now that he thought about it. He looked around the room and saw several more students glowering at his friend in open revulsion.

Those looks didn't seem to bother Raz, but they certainly bothered Rube. Janelle and her friend troubled him the most; they were up to something. He still managed a smile as he leaned down and nuzzled into the rabbit's ear, making him shiver. "I don't know, Raz. It seemed pretty hard from here."

Raz giggled at the double-entendre. "I should hope so! You're sexy, even if you are a klutz."

Rubric blushed. He couldn't help it. Comments like that took on an entirely new dimension when he knew his friend actually meant them.

He wanted to pull his friend close, but before he could manage it he felt a heavy arm clap him across the shoulders, and a deep gravelly slur bellowed in his ear, "Red! Dude, why didn't you tell me you were queer? I know this guy you'd like. Kind of a man-whore, but you like those, right?"

Rubric grimaced at the muscle-bound bull in a tacky purple suit, and tried to lean away from the cloud of alcohol billowing over him. "Excuse me? What the hell are you talking about, Garth?"

The bull's volume only increased. "You like guys that're easy! I dunno why you'd hang all over those scrawny jackrabbit twins if you didn't. They'll jump in the sack with anyone! I hear they double-fuck the Calculus teacher Mr. Moray 'cuz they were flunking out. That's how they get straight-A's."

He pushed the drunken bovine off him and glared. Why couldn't people just leave his friends alone? The twins didn't deserve to be treated that way. So they had some sex here and there... or people said they did. Who the hell cared! "First, I like them because they've been two of my best friends for years! And second, they get A's because they're smart; they help me on my homework all the time. And the rest is none of your business!"

Garth waved it off. "Well I heard they—"

That did it.

The panda stiff-fingered Garth in the chest, forcing him back on his heels. "I don't care what the hell you heard. Stop spreading rumors about my boyfriends."

The bull looked stricken; Rubric never lost his temper. "Geez, man! I was just looking out for you. With all the gossip flying around, some of it's gotta be true, and I don't wanna see you humped and dumped."

"Garth! Raz is right here! At least grow some fucking tact!" He glanced down at the aforementioned twin, who stared at him as if he'd grown a second head.

"It's not rude if it's true!"

Rubric pinched the bridge of his muzzle the way Jaron had earlier, breathing deeply in an effort to calm down. "Thanks for the concern, but just... butt-out. Please. I know them, and I trust them." He hoped he could, anyway.

"But—"

He opened his eyes and looked into the bull's. "Do you think I'm stupid, Garth?"

Whatever Garth had been expecting, that wasn't it. "N-no. You're not stupid, Red."

"Then trust me. Stop listening to gossip, because all it does is hurt people that don't deserve it, and you're better than that."

Garth slunk away, his tail drooping. Rube hoped the rebuke would stick with him after the alcohol flushed out of his system; he didn't want to have to give up a friend for the sake of the twins, but he would if he had to.

The lop giggled, unfazed by Garth's insults. "You're too cute, Spazz." He nuzzled against him, and Rube draped his arm around the rabbit's shoulder.

They snuggled for a bit, and Rubric's body grew warm from the closeness. Raz looked up at him, and his eyes were such a beautiful blue. He leaned down, shifting so he held his friend in both arms, and kissed him gently. It wasn't the hard passion of back on the beach, but something softer.

The tension between them mounted the longer they kissed,

and Rube found his hand straying lower and lower on Raz's back, until the clearing of a throat interrupted. It was Chaz; he and Jaron stood a few feet away, and the rabbit had his arms crossed. "Not to interrupt here, but the prom is like halfway over, and I still want my turn."

The panda realized they'd been groping each other in public and his blush practically glowed through his fur.

Raz grinned. "Alright, then. 'Scuse me, boyfriend-mine. I've gotta hit the little bunny's room anyway." He turned to his brother with a wink. "Take care of him while I'm gone, Chaz!" And he left, his delightful backside holding Rubric's attention as he darted away through the crowd, pulling out his cell phone as he went.

"I'd love to." Thing One was no sooner gone than Thing Two filled the void, pressing against him in a way totally inappropriate for anyone else. But this was Chaz, so it wasn't at all unexpected.

And oddly, the panda relaxed under the attention. The situation wasn't nearly as awkward as before, despite being considerably more intense than mere hand-holding. Maybe the dancing and the making-out had loosened him up. Maybe he'd finally realized that he loved his friends more than he cared about anyone else's opinions.

Or maybe he needed a therapist.

"Uh, Chaz?" he whispered. "Not that I would normally mind, but isn't it cheating if you grope me while I'm dating your brother?"

Charles's grin widened, his lavender eyes crinkling at the edges. "Only if he actually minds. He did say to wait until his turn was over, and I say it's over. And Taz already said he doesn't care."

"You aren't going to fight over me, are you?"

"Nah. We share everything." His grin held a world of meaning. "And I mean everything. Hope you don't mind."

His head spun. "What, date both of you? Can I do that?"

Chaz shrugged. "Sure, so long as everyone you're dating is fine with it. And believe me, neither of us minds. I still want my turn, though."

Rube felt giddy; his first boyfriend, his first kiss, his first date, his first dance, and his first ménage á trois, all in under an hour. How awesome was that?

And then there was the whole out-of-the-closet thing. He'd already told his best friends, and everyone who saw them on the dance floor knew. Students around them were glancing covertly in his direction, and it was obvious what conclusions most of them had come to.

He would normally feel embarrassed, self-conscious, something. But his hormones were running full-tilt, and he was flying too high to hide now.

Chaz rubbed one hand up the inside of his thigh as high as it would go, squeezed, then pulled away with a shit-eating grin. "I think I'll get myself a glass of punch. Want any?"

He shuddered. "Uh...sure. J-just...please don't get us drunk. You saw what it did to Janelle."

Chaz waved it off. "It's only one glass! This is a party! Live it up!" And he moved toward the far end of the table. Damn, that bunny was cute. He was glad the concessions stood between him and the rest of the room, or his telltale bulge would be visible to someone other than the rabbit.

And Jare, apparently, who stood on the other side of the table, just far enough that Rube figured he hadn't heard their whispered conversation. "You really weren't kidding, were you?"

Both of the twins were so damned distracting in their form-fitting white suits. He couldn't help but be mesmerized by the hare in his crosshairs. "Hmm?"

"I didn't know if you were joking when you told me you were gay. Obviously you weren't. I never noticed before; I must be fucking blind."

Chaz stopped at the punch bowl and looked back, and Rubric turned away to keep from gawking, waking from his trance. He blinked and looked back at the devil. "What?"

His friend rolled his eyes as he often did, but something about him seemed off. Down, maybe. Whatever was on his mind during the dance must still be hanging around. "Nothing. Nevermind."

Chaz returned with his glass of punch, and they spent some time talking and palling-around. This really wasn't any different than their standard modus operandi, except Chaz took more liberties than he used to. Rube had another glass of punch after the first, and he noticed that Jaron continued to be distracted, but he wouldn't talk about it, and Rube didn't press.

He started to relax; this wasn't so bad. The warmth of his third glass of punch definitely helped, and he found himself responding more openly to Chaz's advances, even going so far as to goose the rabbit with his tail when he wasn't looking.

A few of his other friends came by, some congratulating him, some nervous, but no outright rejection. They all seemed wary of Chaz, however, and he saw several of them whispering as they left, agitated. Rubric frowned; were they talking about the twins behind their backs? Behind his back? At least a few did; he caught the words 'twins' and 'slut' more than once.

He tried to stomp on the anger, to push it down, but each time he noticed it got harder to keep his calm. He wanted to yell at someone, to tell them to stop, but all of it was whispered so low he could hardly make it out; it might well have been his imagination.

Jaron sniffed the punch Chaz gave him and wrinkled his nose, setting the plastic cup on the table. "You know Chaz, I really wish you and Raz hadn't..." Jaron began, but he trailed off when he looked up, and his face fell into a scowl.

The devil cut off mid-sentence as something slammed into them from the side, knocking Chaz out of Rubric's grip and into the table, where he landed on several bowls of food, scattering potato chips and ranch dressing in all directions and coating his white coat in dip and crumbs in the process. All that kept Rubric from the same fate was his hand, which managed to grab the edge of the table before he toppled over too.

Several people watching them laughed, including a feminine squeak that sounded suspiciously squirrel-like.

"Oops! Clumsy me!" Rick's voice dripped with sarcasm. It dropped to a growl as he sneered at the rabbit sprawled across the table. "I slipped."

Rubric glared as he helped Chaz out of the mess he'd fallen in. "Like hell you did."

The edges of the bear's mouth twitched as his gaze slid from rabbit to panda. "Oh, like you'll do anything, you fucking pansy. I heard what your boyfriend said about me." He turned to the rabbit. "You'd better come clean you little whore, or I'll make sure the rest of your night is full of pain."

Jaron took a step forward, fangs bared, but stopped when Chaz raised a hand, shaking his head. He stood there, ignoring everything dripping from him, his face blank. Rubric had never seen him so...resigned. "I didn't say anything."

The panda grabbed Rick by the shoulder and squeezed. "He's right. Jaron and I've been here the whole time, and he hasn't said anything to anyone. Leave him alone, Rick."

"Liar." The bear pushed his hand away and snarled. "Fine, if he won't 'fess up..." He snatched Chaz up by the arm and brandished the claws on his other hand. "...he's gonna bleed." He made to swipe the rabbit across the face, but stopped as Rubric caught his wrist.

"Don't." Rubric's voice went low and quiet as anger seeped into the words.

Rick struggled against his grip, then let go of the rabbit with his other hand and reared back. But instead of throwing the punch he intended he screamed as the panda squeezed. Hard.

"I said, don't." He let go of the bear's wrist and pushed him back, hard enough to knock the wind out of him when he hit the wall. "Leave him alone, Rick. He hasn't done anything to you."

The quarterback growled. "Like hell he hasn't! Apologize you little slut, or you're going to end up in the hospital."

Something inside Rubric snapped; he vaulted forward, grabbed Rick's shirt, and lifted him into the air one-handed, pinning him against the wall. He moved in close, glaring into the bear's suddenly-wide eyes from a couple of inches away. "You lay one more finger on him," he snarled, "and you're going home in a full-body cast. Do you understand?"

Rick nodded mutely, his face a sudden mask of fear.

The panda dropped him, and he scurried off.

He heard applause from across the table. If it'd been anyone but Jaron he would've thrown something.

THIRD STEP: THREE'S COMPANY

Jaron's face held the widest grin he'd ever seen on the devil. "I can't believe I just witnessed that."

"I can't believe I just did that." The panda's ears burned, and now that he'd calmed down a bit he wanted to hide under the table. He still wanted to deck Rick, though; the bear could use a good smacking.

Chaz's grin matched Jaron's as he pulled off his jacket; lucky for him his undershirt and pants were still clean. "I'd say I can, but I'd be lying. It was worth coming tonight just for that!" He looked around the courtyard, and peered inside. "Where's Raz? He's got to hear this!"

Rube looked around too, but saw neither hide nor hair of —well—hare. "He left for the restroom awhile ago. Could you call his cell phone? Make sure he's okay?"

Chaz shook his head. "No. I don't have mine on me. Sorry."

"Did he drink whatever you added to the punch?"

"No. And you should know; you've kissed him enough tonight." He sounded a bit huffy.

He felt a sly smile crawl across his features. "Well, we might just have to even things out then, hmm? Let's get to making-out... after I make sure he's okay."

And that satisfied Chaz, if his leering grin was anything to go by.

He clapped Jaron on the shoulder. "Stay here with Chaz, okay? Keep Rick away from him. I'm going to find Raz." The devil nodded. "Thanks."

Rubric checked the men's room in the suite first with no luck. The rabbit's disappearance right before Rick's assault had him worried. Janelle had something to do with it, he was sure, and he wouldn't put it past her to go after both the twins.

Next he tried the publicly-accessible restroom he saw on his way to the ballroom, but the door was stuck. It gave a bit, as though something heavy sat on the other side, but otherwise wouldn't budge.

He noticed Raz's cell on the ground next to his foot. It had more features than he'd ever seen on a phone, and was slim and sleek and covered in stickers, so he knew whose it was. *Uh oh.* He could hear the collection of growls and a conversation echoing inside.

A gravelly voice. "I ain't like you, faggot!"

"Fine, you're straight. I never said you weren't!" Raz!

"You been spreadin' rumors about me, though. My girl dumped me 'cuz of that! We're gonna make sure you don't spread any more. Can't do shit with yer jaw wired shut."

Raz's voice filled with scorn. "Wake up, dumbass. Why would I want anyone to think I fucked you? I'll never be that desperate."

"Oh, you cocky little cocksucker. We're gonna beat the queer right outta you." And a chorus of male voices grunted assent.

He'd heard enough. The alcohol boiled in his stomach, or maybe it was his anger. Now that he'd let it out it wanted to *stay* out, and for once he welcomed it. Rubric shoved against the door hard as he could, and it moved... about four inches. Someone inside yelled, "Hey! Someone's tryin' to get in!" He stepped back, lined himself up, and shoulder-rammed the door. He hit it so hard the wood splintered, the hinges gave way, and the wooden cabinet wedged behind it toppled.

Five of the school's better-known jocks stood in a circle around Raz, one of which held the rabbit's arms wrenched behind his back so he couldn't move. None were armed.

His boyfriend's face froze in shock, which melted first into relief, and then into worry. Clearly he wanted out of the situation, but didn't want Rube involved.

He felt his ears lower, and he bared his fangs. He had to protect Raz. He couldn't talk his way out, and he obviously wouldn't abandon the rabbit. That left one option, so he readied himself to unleash hell.

Rubric tore off the top half of the broken door and held it up with menace. "I'll beat the shit out of you before you can beat the queer out of him. Let him go. Now." The burning in his stomach sizzled, stronger than before.

The gang glanced at him, then at Anthony, the gravel-voiced razorback standing before Raz. Their leader weighed their chances against a man who outweighed the biggest of them by at least seventy pounds (and all of it pure muscle). He must not have liked the odds, because he shook his head. "Let 'im go."

The badger gaped at the boar, incredulous. "But what about your rep, Tony? Are you gonna put up with that?"

Tony hiked a thumb at Rubric with a snarl. "D'you think we could take 'im, Frank? Really? He'd tear us apart. Let the fag go. I'll find another girl. That 'coon was one kinky bitch anyway."

Once released, Raz rubbed at his shoulders, obviously in pain. He walked up to Tony, his eyes narrowed. "Just a minute. Was this girl the one who told you about the rumor?"

Tony glared at him. "Yeah. What the hell do you care?"

"Was her name Dahlia Tolver?"

"Yeah."

"And I bet she told you that after you got here tonight, right?"

The glare deepened. "Yeah. What're you gettin' at?"

"She's using you. She spread that rumor and dumped you so you'd beat the hell out of me and my brother on prom night. Not only is she a kinky bitch, she's a vindictive and crazy one."

The boar studied Raz's eyes for a moment. "Why should I believe that, you dirty fag?" he asked, but not like he meant it.

Raz shrugged. "Frankly, I don't care if you believe me or not. She sicced you on one of her exes like a rabid dog and tried to ruin your reputation in the process. I'd be pissed if I were you, but whatever. I'm leaving." The rabbit stomped away, and to his credit he didn't bother looking at the men who nearly beat him to a pulp.

Rubric moved aside to let him pass. "You okay, Raz?"

He nodded. "I am now. Let's get out of here."

Rubric glared at the gang shifting their feet in the middle of the floor, then threw the broken door to the ground and prowled after him. He itched to throttle those bastards, but he shoved his hands in his pockets instead.

Rubric rounded the corner about fifty feet down the hallway and bumped into Raz, stopped dead in the middle of the aisle. They stood face-to-face with that slim female raccoon, who lounged against the wall in a manner he could only describe as slutty.

He'd never heard a rabbit growl, but Raz managed it. "What the hell do you want, Dahlia?"

Rubric wouldn't normally hit a girl, but he strongly considered the possibility now... for all of a second. He reconsidered and after a moment pulled his hands from his pockets and crossed his arms with a glower.

"Aww, Raz." She looked him over, obviously disappointed. "Tony didn't play with you like I asked him to?"

Raz's glare should've set her fur on fire. "Go to hell, Dahlia."

She trailed a hand down her neck and fondled a breast. "Oh Raz, baby, is that any way to talk to me? You know I want you."

"You sure have a horrible way of showing it. After all those nasty rumors, after everything you've done to us, do you really expect Chaz and me to come running back to you? You make me sick; you make us both sick."

"Honey, you know I don't give up until I get what I want."

"What you want is to slit the throat of a feral dog and watch while we fuck it to death. We're not into that kind of shit, you psycho!"

"But it'd be so much fun."

Rubric's stomach knotted up. Raz was right; this bitch was twisted.

She kicked away from the wall and swayed up to Raz, running a finger up his white jacket. "Baby, you know the rumors won't stop 'til you come back to me. I'll keep them going until you do. I know how lonely you must be, since everyone hates you. I can make it all go away; just say the word."

Raz's fists clenched at his side, and Rubric could hear his teeth grinding. "I've got some words for you, Dahlia: Fuck Off."

She glared. "I hope you both enjoyed your time with the queer here, because he won't want to be your boy-toy for much longer. And no girl will touch you ever again, I'll make sure of it."

Raz's fur fluffed out, and his spine stiffened. He backed into Rube, who wrapped him in his arms. "We don't need a girl, and we don't want you. We love Rubric, and he's way too good a person to believe your lies."

L-Love? His stomach burned again, this time from shame. He felt awful for doubting them; he knew the twins well enough to discount the rumor-mill for the lie-machine it was, and yet he'd still believed, somewhere inside, that they actually did those things. Never again; he'd be damned if he'd listen to rumors he knew weren't true, and if there was any doubt at all he'd speak up instead of chickening out and staying silent.

But he couldn't say any of that. Not here, not now. Instead, he looked this mental-case in the eye and confirmed the statement with a nod. "I don't care how much hate you spew, you lying dirt-bag. They've been my best friends for too long and I love them too much to abandon them over something as worthless as you."

She merely arched an eyebrow. "Oh really? You know, Tony's not the only man around here I have wrapped around my fingers. I have several pets willing to send someone to the hospital, with the right persuasion. And I don't care how many of them I have to ruin to get what's mine. Nobody tells me no, and if I have to lie to destroy you too, then whatever."

An evil grin stole onto Rubric's face, and he reached into his pocket before pushing Raz gently aside. "Thank you, Dahlia. That's just what I wanted to hear."

She squawked as he grabbed her around the waist and threw her over his shoulder. "C'mon, Raz. This ends now." He stalked his way back to the ballroom with the rabbit at his heels, and hauled her struggling carcass into the middle of the room and the center of attention. The crowd edged away, leaving an empty space around them under that damned disco ball.

He saw Jaron and Chaz more-or-less where he left them, though Chaz had somehow managed to wrap himself around the devil, who seemed stuck in a permanent eye-roll but wasn't objecting. He liked the sight, but now wasn't the time for daydreams. He waved them over. "Jaron, go tell the DJ to turn off the music please. I need to say something."

The devil (and everyone else) looked at him like a crazy man, but true to form Jaron nodded. "Okay, Rube. Whatever the hell this is, I've got your back." Which was one more reason he loved the man; he trusted Rubric whatever happened.

Unlike me, he thought bitterly. Well, it was high-time to rectify that mistake, and he would start here, no matter how uncomfortable he might be.

Chaz sidled up to his brother. "What's going on? What's she doing here?" he asked, his voice thick with disgust and loathing.

"I dunno, bro. But Spazz has something he wants to share with the rest of the class, and I have this sneaking suspicion that Dahlia's not going to like it much."

A moment later the music cut off and several spotlights pierced the gloom to shine down on Rube and the twins. "Nice touch," he muttered before unceremoniously dropping the 'coon to the wooden floor. One of her heels shattered, and the fall must've knocked the wind from her, because the shrieking stopped.

He took a deep breath and eased it out slowly, then spoke loud enough so the whole room could hear. "This piece of garbage lied to you, to all of us, and she used us to hurt the last people in the world to deserve it." He pulled the twins in close and held them there, standing tall. He didn't feel nervous or embarrassed in front of the crowd; the disgrace at having doubted them seared away everything else. Of course, the alcohol helped, as well. "She used lies and gossip to humiliate them, to ruin their reputations, so she could force them to do what she wanted.

"In fact, tonight she spread a particularly ugly rumor so her boyfriend and a group of his buddies would beat the hell out of them because they wouldn't cave. Thankfully, I got there soon enough to stop it. But all this time Raz and Chaz refused to give in to her bullying, or to anyone else's, no matter how much it hurt them.

"They're not the dirty little whores her stories made them out to be. In fact, they're two of the nicest guys I've ever met.

"Not everyone believed the lies, and for those that didn't, thank you. You should be proud. But the rest of us should take a close look at ourselves and realize how much damage we can do by our words and actions, and we should be ashamed of ourselves."

Dahlia pushed herself to her knees, the vindictive expression on her muzzle positively vicious. "And what kind of proof do you have for any of that? They've fucked everything they could get their paws on for the last four years! Everyone knows it!"

A wave of whispers moved through the crowd, and a female voice near the back of the crowd shouted, "I heard they raped a girl in Junior year, and did the same thing to the men's soccer players!"

He turned in that direction and glowered. "Whatever, Janelle. Pull your head out of your ass. Just because you're jealous of my boyfriends doesn't mean you can pull shit like this too. I'm gay and I have no interest in you. At all. You had a snowflake's chance in hell from the beginning; get over it."

Her strangled sobs didn't have the chance to fade before the slamming doors cut them off.

"As for proof?" He dug into his pocket and withdrew Raz's cell phone, fiddled with it a moment, then pressed 'Dial'. "It's right here."

"Message One, Recorded on Friday, March first, nine thirty-six pm."

"Aww, Raz. Tony didn't play with you like I asked him to?" The recording was a bit tinny, but it rang out loud and clear. He ran through the entire conversation between Raz and Dahlia, and he noticed ears folding in embarrassment throughout the crowd and eyes dropping to the floor. "...and if I have to lie to destroy you too, then whatever."

He flipped the phone shut. "This is the kind of crap they've had to put up with all through school. Everyone hates them because of this... this filth. And yet they face it down every day and still manage to smile."

He kissed each of them on the top of the head. "I'm so proud to call you my friends... and my boyfriends."

He looked up again and swept his gaze over the crowd. "So the next time you feel like spreading a nasty little rumor about someone, remember what happened here. After all, you could be next."

The bitch on the floor had, by this point, shriveled in on herself; gone were her self-satisfied smirks and superior attitude, replaced with the humiliation of having the whole school know exactly what she was. A number of students spat on her as they passed, which only rubbed the disgrace in harder. He and the twins had her beat and she knew it.

Rubric crouched next to her and spoke low enough that most of the crowd couldn't hear. "We told Anthony what you did, you know. His buddies were still pretty pissed-off when we left. You should go before they catch you alone."

She shot him a look full of loathing and opened her mouth in what he knew would be a threat, so he cut it off from the start by clamping her muzzle shut. "Oh, and I wouldn't think too hard about revenge, either; slander and conspiracy to commit assault carry fines and prison time, and I'm making copies of our little conversation as insurance."

The twins stood to either side of him, and each of them rested a hand on his shoulders. "So leave us alone."

"Or we'll tell."

FINAL STEP: AND FOUR'S A BEACH

Rube sat with the twins on the sand a few hundred feet from where the night started, but with everything that happened he felt light-years away. He couldn't have imagined back then how wonderful life would be in two short hours, and now he couldn't imagine anything better.

Well he could, but that wasn't happening, so he tried not to. But speaking of which...

They'd looked for Jaron after the debacle at the party and panicked a bit before a text message eased their worries; he didn't want to get in the way of their 'after-party celebration' and headed home early. Then Raz pulled rank as designated driver to bring them out here, not that anyone complained.

The night was warm, and they'd stripped down to their dress-pants, leaving the rest of their clothes in Rubric's car. The twins seemed fascinated with the panda's red fur and muscles, running their hands over him at every opportunity. He found it difficult to sit comfortably with their attentions focused on him, but he suspected his too-constrictive pants wouldn't be an issue for much longer.

Rube held both brothers in his lap as they held each other. He nuzzled against them, and they shivered despite the heat. "Things were really bad for you guys for a long time, weren't they?" It wasn't really a question. "I never knew. Why didn't you say something? Why didn't you put a stop to it in the beginning?"

"We tried."

"Nothing worked!"

"And protesting wouldn't have done any good."

"Yeah, complaining about it would just make it worse."

"So we just acted like it didn't matter and after awhile, it didn't."

"Not so much, anyway."

"We still couldn't get a date to save our lives."

"And we only had a couple of friends that didn't turn on us."

"But at least we know who really cares, right?"

"Right!" Followed by a squeeze from both sides as the twins turned and hugged him tight.

"Why didn't you tell me?"

They hugged him a little tighter and shivered again, but from an entirely different cause. "We know how much it hurts to get in Dahlia's way."

"We wanted to protect you."

He wrapped his tail around them and hugged them close. "Please don't do that again. You're my friends whatever happens, and I love you. Tell me if something's wrong, and I'll help however I can. Boyfriends protect each other, yes, but we also help each other, and I can't help if you don't tell me what's wrong. Promise me?"

The twins nuzzled into his embrace and he felt them nod, one after the other. "But it goes both ways, Spazz."

"You have to tell us, too."

"You were so miserable earlier, and if we hadn't pushed you'd still be sitting on this beach in pain."

"Fair enough." And now came time for the unvarnished truth, painful as it was. He sighed. "I guess there's one thing you need to know. One of the reasons I never told you I liked you was because I heard all those horrible rumors. I knew they weren't true, but the nagging doubt in the back of my head wouldn't shut up. I'm ashamed to admit it, but I wondered if I'd be just another conquest." He hugged them tighter as a couple of tears fell into their fur. "I'm so sorry I doubted you. I understand if you're upset; you have every right to be."

The twins stilled, and he wondered if they were about to stand up and leave. But then: "I'm not mad at you, Rube."

"Me neither."

"Some of those rumors were pretty bad, after all."

"And you made up for it tonight."

"As long as you don't have any more doubts, we're even."

He shook his head. "No more doubts."

"Good."

"And besides, boyfriends help each other, but we also forgive each other."

"Damned straight." And they giggled in the way that came so easily to them, then turned in his lap and pushed him to his back in the sand.

They crawled up and kissed both sides of his muzzle as one, and he ran his hands over those striking white pelts that glowed brilliantly under the moon. They were so beautiful, and the sight stole his breath. His hands wandered down their backs by themselves, and they cupped their rumps before pulling them against him. The sensation of both twins grinding on his fur brought a moan he couldn't have suppressed if he'd tried.

They pulled back wordlessly and he could only watch as they stood side-by-side and unfastened their slacks, dragging their zippers down in a slow, sensuous arc. Neither rabbit wore anything underneath, and as they stripped to the skin he mused to himself that this fact didn't surprise him at all.

They stood before him, demure but for their nudity and the shared look in their eyes. Their white fur took the edges off their gangly, long-limbed frames, but he could see hints of powerful runners' muscles under the fluff. Both were fully-erect, their long pink members slender and lovely, clearly visible in the light of the moon. Only the colors of their eyes distinguished one from the other, but somehow he knew which was which without effort, even in the dark. Maybe just as they knew him, he knew them, too.

He wanted them so hard it hurt. He reached for his own zipper, desperate to shed his clothing and liberate his painful erection from its cage of cloth, but he found the twins grabbing his hands before he could.

They each kissed the hand they took, and shook their heads in unison. "We've waited a long time for this, Rube."

"We wanna do it."

He nodded, and they stripped him with agonizing slowness. He groaned in relief when he finally sprang free into the night air. They tugged his pants all the way off and threw them aside, and he couldn't help but groan again as they stroked their nails over his length with a feather-light touch and fondled his balls.

Raz hesitated. "Crap." Then he nudged his brother. "I left the condoms in the car. They're in my backpack. Go get 'em, Chaz." "No way. You had him most of the evening, so you go. It's only fair."

Rubric propped himself on an elbow and raised an eyebrow. "You actually brought condoms?"

They grinned. "And lots and lots of lube!"

"We were Boy Scouts, you know."

"Always be prepared!"

"And as soon as Chaz gets our stash we can get this jamboree started."

"No way, Raz! You do it!"

He smirked at their squabbling. "Since you guys can't decide, I'll—" but he cut short as he heard the flumph of sand, and something landed next to him: a plastic bag full of condoms, and several bottles of XY Jelly. He froze.

The twins' eyes widened as they peered over his shoulder. "Oh!"

"Uh...hi Jaron."

"We were just...uh..."

The devil's voice rang hollow. "...about to have sex. Yes, I know." It sounded duller and more melancholy than Rube had ever heard, and it doused the mood as effectively as ice-cold water. "Rube, you really should lock your car doors."

Jaron shuffled into his line of sight and slumped to the sand in front of them, dressed in denim shorts and a dark-colored tee. He looked awful; the panda hadn't seen him this dejected since the day of his mother's murder. "I thought I'd find you here. Can I be a selfish bastard and interrupt?"

Rubric squirmed a bit; all three of them were naked, fully exposed, and erect as they could be, but the devil didn't seem to care. "This really isn't the best time, Jaron."

Jaron nodded glumly and pushed to his feet. "Okay. I just wanted to talk, but..."

He sounded so damned miserable that Rubric reached out and grabbed him by the wrist. "No, wait." He sighed. "I'm sorry, don't leave. What's wrong?"

Jaron looked down at him and nodded to himself before pulling the panda's hand into his and dropping to his knees in the sand. Raz and Chaz hesitated, but they each took one side of the devil and sat close, laying their arms across the devil's shoulders when he didn't object.

"Chaz, you spent half the night hanging all over me. It was... nice. And it got me to thinking.

"I... I've been watching you guys all evening. You all seem so happy. And I realized how damned lonely I've been. I mean, you guys are all I have since Mom died and Dad... Well, since he went away."

"I saw the way all of you looked at each other, and at me, and it made me realize how empty my life would be without you guys. I've tried my best to ignore it because I didn't want to lose what I have, but I can't avoid it anymore. I've been crushing on you so hard it's not even funny. All of you."

The twins' heads jerked up, their faces incredulous. "What?!"

Rube felt his eyes open wide enough to fall out of their sockets. Did he just hear what he thought he heard?

They sat there for what seemed an eternity, staring at the devil staring at the sand. Rubric had never seen anything that made Jare this uncomfortable, but now he looked almost scared. "W-well? You can't just clam up after something like that. Say something!"

"You...have a crush? On us? But I thought you were straight!"

"Not...exactly."

"So, you lied to us?"

"You're gay?"

"Or bi?"

"I never guessed."

"Me neither."

Jaron growled in frustration. "No. No, I'm not gay. Or bi. Or anything else. I just... don't like people. I mean, I know when a guy is good-looking, or when a girl is pretty, but they don't push my buttons.

"You guys... do. You've been my buds forever, and you were there for me when my parents— Well, you've been the best friends a guy could hope for, and—god, I can't believe I'm admitting this, but—I love you. I've loved all of you for a very long time."

He gave a nervous chuckle and nudged the bag of condoms with a foot. "So, mind if I use some of these?" He looked at the panda with a frightened half-smile. "I think you're gonna need someone to help you keep these hellions in line. Lead from the rear, so to speak."

Rube pushed to his knees and all three of them converged on the devil in a group-hug. Jaron looked ready to run, but relaxed after a moment before hugging them back. He laughed, and it was a happy sound. "I guess that's a yes."

Chaz nuzzled into Jaron's neck, kissing him gently. "Oh, yes."

Raz mirrored him on the other side. "Oh god, yes."

Rube pressed against him, his flagging erection immediately at full mast again. He kissed him full-on, leaving them both nose-to-nose, dizzy and smiling. "Definitely and without a doubt, yes."

He reached under Jaron's shirt and rubbed his hand over those washboard abs. God, he'd wanted to do that for so long. The devil's body was a compact wall of solid muscle, and his stomach was so damned hard.

He kissed his friend again, and found him more than willing to return the favor, with tongue.

His fingers brushed the twins' as they rubbed Jaron's ribs, and together they edged the shirt higher until he had to break the kiss so they could pull it off and cast it aside. He glanced at the brothers, and the three of them nodded together, then pushed Jaron to his back.

The devil landed on the sand with a muffled thud without protest. His shorts stripped off with little resistance. He was nervous but eager, his green eyes shining in the moonlight.

Christ, but this Tasmanian devil was a sexy beast. His fur was glossy black, with one symmetrical white splotch between his thighs that stretched over his groin and up to his belly-button, and another wrapped around his neck that trickled down into the hollows of his throat and coiled around under his armpits. They accentuated his oh-so-lean body in a way that made Rubric's mouth water, and he had to swallow hard to keep from drooling.

He wanted to take Jaron so badly, but—"Chaz, he's your date for the evening. Why don't you do the honors?" He wasn't the only one here, after all. And the rabbits were just as wonderful. He slid back and hugged Raz, nibbling his ear and giving him a grope for good measure.

Chaz looked from panda to devil, with a grin so big and broad it shone like the sun. "Really?"

Jaron nodded, his smile softer than any of them had ever seen. "I like the sound of that." He reached up and pulled Chaz down to him, nuzzling against his shoulder and kissing around his neck. "Sorry I ignored you all evening."

"S'okay. We're used to it."

The devil wrapped his arms around the rabbit and rolled the both of them over so he landed on top. Chaz squeaked in surprise, then giggled. Jaron's voice was a thick, husky growl. "Well get unused to it, because it's not going to happen again. And to make it up to you, I'm gonna give you a blowjob you'll never forget." And he slid down and licked that long thick tongue of his from the rabbit's tail-hole to the end of his bunnycock, leaving Chaz groaning beneath him.

Rubric ran his fingers under Raz's tail, and gave him a sly grin. "That looks fun." He held his hand out in invitation. "Shall we?"

Raz grinned back. "Let's."

They mirrored Chaz and Jaron, with Raz on his back next to his brother, and Rube above him, side-by-side with the devil. The brothers wrapped their arms around each other and kissed eagerly. It was hot as hell, and from the looks of things, this was something they'd done before. Often.

He and Jaron licked their respective twins in long, sure strokes, and they soon had them both panting heavily. It tasted funny, but not bad. He liked it quite a lot actually, all the more because Raz was obviously enjoying his end of things.

He changed his tactics a short way in, nibbling his way along in the places he figured would be the most sensitive, then licking the clear dribble off the end, engulfing as much of that pinkness as he could in his mouth, and sucking hard. Raz cried out, his hips bucking up and shoving even more of his cock into Rube's muzzle. He tasted the warm sticky squirts as his friend lost it; the semen was far sweeter than he thought it'd be, and he savored it for a few moments before swallowing the whole mouthful.

The rabbit panted in the lull, and his voice was hoarse when he spoke. "God, Spazz... You're good at that."

He licked his chops and raised an eyebrow. "Apparently. You didn't last long."

Raz dinged him on the ear. "We're rabbits, you dork! What we lack in stamina we make up for in speed." He looked around, then motioned Rube down and whispered as if he were imparting a secret. "No refractory period." He winked.

"You mean you're ready again?"

"For what you just did? Hell yeah."

Jaron pulled off of Chaz and looked up at them curiously. "What did he just do?"

Chaz sat up, clearly interested. Rubric looked from him to Jaron to Raz, and Raz gave a nod toward the devil. "Get to it." Chaz nodded emphatically. "Tell us!"

He grinned and pushed Jaron to his back. "I'd rather show than tell."

Before he could even start, Raz spoke up. "Wait a sec." He watched the rabbit scuttle behind his brother, then sit with his arms and legs wrapped around Chaz's body, spooning him so they could watch together. The sight of them touching so intimately looked right, as though both bodies were two halves of a whole, and holding each other made them one again. "That's better."

He repeated his entire performance, and couldn't help but notice Tasmanian devil tasted different from rabbit; stronger, muskier, but again not unpleasant. He earned a series of moans and a gush of salty slickness a few minutes later, though this time it was just pre.

Jaron panted like he'd just sprinted a mile. "Je-hesus, Rube! I thought you were a virgin! How'd you get so good at this?"

He took a long lick between Jaron's tail-hole and his tip, pausing on the way to play with the balls in their fuzzy pouch, and the body under him trembled. "Natural talent, I guess." He smiled wryly. "And lots of porn."

Chaz pulled away from his twin and nuzzled against Rube coyly. "My turn?"

He nodded with a smile. "Gladly." And he pushed him back to give his third blowjob of the evening.

His other two boyfriends (and god, it sounded good to say that, even in his head) made out hot and heavy, groping each other while waiting for him to finish. He heard Raz cum twice more (twice!) and it was a good sound. He loved watching them, even though he could only see them out of the corner of his eye. The white-on-black-on-white of his two friends was a beautiful sight, though he was careful not to let himself get too distracted from pleasuring friend number three.

Chaz tasted like his brother all the way through, though with a hint of alcohol. In the end he came hard, and again Rubric swallowed it after savoring the sweetness. He wondered idly how many times he could suck the three of them off before he got tired of it. More than he could count, probably.

Devil and rabbit ambushed him when it was clear he was done. Jaron pinned his shoulders to the sand, and Raz sat on his legs. Raz looked grave, but with the edges of a grin taking over his muzzle. "You're outnumbered. Come quietly, and no one gets hurt."

The devil leaned down so they touched nose-to-nose, and mock-glared into his eyes. "You're about to get what you deserve, you dirty cocksucker." He brushed some sand out of the panda's fur and grinned. "Though it looks like we'll all need a swim when this is over."

Chaz crawled over to them and rested a hand on his black and red stomach-fur, rubbing it around in erogenous little circles. "I am so not going to miss this." He reached down and cupped his hand around Rube's balls. "Karma sucks, doesn't it, Spazz?" And then Chaz slid his lips over the panda's dick.

Rube burbled something completely unintelligible as he shuddered, before pulling an unsteady breath. "Ohhh g-god, yes." The damp warmth felt so damned good, and it shot electric sparks all the way up his spine.

The twins worked him over, Chaz focusing on his all-too-sensitive tip, and Raz working his mouth over everything else. His back arched, and his hands scrabbled to hold onto something, to cling to something solid, but all they found was sand.

Jare clamped his mouth over Rubric's to swallow his groans, and clambered atop him without breaking the kiss. They kissed like it was their first, their last, and every one in between. The panda finally had something solid to hold, and they ran their hands over each other like he'd dreamed about for years. It felt every bit as electrifying as the twins giving him head. His fur stood on end as his body broke out in goose bumps, and he heard the twins giggle as he fluffed up.

He couldn't see what the twins were doing, but from the sounds of things he wasn't the only one they were pleasuring; from the periodic strangled groans, they must've blown their loads two or three times each. Raz wasn't kidding about rabbits being fast.

The fifth time he heard it, Jaron pulled away, and they both peered back to see what the twins were doing. What he saw left Rubric harder than ever: Raz mounting Chaz, pounding away amidst a bunch of scattered used condoms, Chaz still doing his best to swallow Rubric's groin whole. As they watched, Raz gave another strangled gasp and shuddered before pulling out, stripping off the old condom, and yanking a new one from the torn-open bag.

Jaron's erection throbbed, wedged between his hips and Rube's stomach. "Wow." Obviously Rubric wasn't the only one turned on by the sight, and he agreed with the sentiment wholeheartedly.

Raz grinned. "This is about the only thing we didn't do, according to all the rumors." He giggled. "If only they knew."

Rube sat up, holding Jaron against him so he wouldn't fall off. "Well, now that you've got a moment—"

Jaron grinned, finishing his thought for him. "—mind if we cut in?"

A few minutes later saw Raz and Chaz sandwiched together, with Rube on his knees mounting Raz on one end, and Jare mounting Chaz on the other. Both panda and devil were too large for the condoms the twins used, and they were grateful the brothers brought assorted sizes.

He and Jaron both began at a slow, even pace. Since both were inexperienced, the twins had explained how they needed to ease into the heavier thrusts, to stretch them out comfortably.

God, this was even better than the twins' fellatio. Raz's tail-hole was so tight as he eased his way in, and the feel of the rabbit's lube-slicked rear engulfing him made him hard enough to hurt. He'd been wary at first, but the twins assured him they were practiced enough to take it, assuming they were all careful and used plenty of lube.

Rube wondered if the look on his face was as goofily-blissful as Jaron's as he worked his hips back-and-forth. It was wonderful to see the devil happy after everything he'd been through. Just as good were the bubbly squeaks and giggles (and frequent gasps of release) of the twins as they sucked each other off to the staccato beat of hips-on-ass.

Rube leaned over, propping himself up with a hand on Raz's back, and reached forward to pull Jaron into another kiss (which was quickly becoming his most favorite hobby ever). He lost himself in the taste of his friend and the pounding of his body, and lost all track of time as they made love sweeter than he'd ever imagined. This setup just pushed all sorts of buttons, including several he never knew he had, and it left him hard as he'd ever been.

He had no idea how long it took, but he could tell the devil was getting close. He felt his own pressure building as he thrust faster by the second, his breath coming quick and hard, punctuated by choked grunts as he tried not to bellow his euphoria into the night. Jaron matched him, thrusting in a frenzy to put his cartoon-namesake to shame.

Whether through biological convergence or pure serendipity, panda and devil came together, crying out in shared orgasm. Rubric's entire body caught fire, and neither of them tried to bite back the screams of ecstasy which echoed weirdly in the surf.

Thirty blissful seconds later he was done, and his muscles turned to jelly. He collapsed to the side, and Jaron joined him after a moment, both too weak and winded to do anything else. He pulled the devil to him, and they held each other close as they watched the twins finish. It was amazing really, as first one would cry out, then the other, and they swallowed what looked to be copious amounts of semen.

And people said rabbits had no stamina.

Rube lay there basking in the afterglow, and wondered at how he could ever have been ashamed to tell these three how he felt about them. They'd just shared something amazing, and the love in his heart only swelled when he considered everything they meant to each other.

It wasn't much longer before the twins each gave one final cry and lay there, still and spent and gasping. It took a minute for them to catch their breaths before they pulled apart with a shared groan and crawled over to their spooning boyfriends. Raz slipped into Jaron's arms, whereas Chaz merely pushed himself up and lay on top all of them, turning it into a proverbial puppy-pile.

"So," Jaron rumbled after a few minutes, "was it as good for you guys as it was for me?"

The rabbits shifted against them lethargically, and their sighs were languid and content, a far cry from their normally-hyper selves. "You were fantastic, Jare."

"You too, Rube."

"Not bad at all for a couple of virgins."

"Well, not virgins anymore." And they tried to giggle, but it ended as more of a gurgle.

Rube squeezed the devil tight and nibbled the fuzz of his ear. "Oh yeah. That was incredible, Taz."

Jaron growled. "Don't you start that too. I get enough from these goofballs."

He grinned. "But aren't lovers supposed to have cutesy names for each other?"

"Sure, but not that one. Anything but that one."

"How about 'Binky'?"

"That's even worse!"

"'Fuzzy-Wuzzy Lumpkins'?"

Jaron huffed in exasperation. "Just stick with 'Taz,' you asshole."

Rubric could only chuckle.

EPILOGUE:

They held each other awhile, basking in the intense afterglow, the sound of the gentle waves under the moon, and the inner-warmth that comes from finally embracing those you love, and Rubric found himself again thinking sexy thoughts, though his body couldn't respond...yet.

So he allowed his mind to drift for a bit, and something occurred to him. "I wonder why Tony gave up so easily? He seemed pretty PO'd at you guys for 'spreading rumors' about him, after all."

The twins snuggled in deeper, their voices thick with sex-induced lethargy. "Oh, Tony's a good guy, once you get to know him."

"Yeah, it didn't take much to convince him to...uh..." Chaz trailed off suspiciously.

Rubric pulled himself up from the pile and frowned at them. "Raz, Chaz...what is it you're not telling me?"

His mates (and he felt a thrill of excitement at the word) glanced at each other, trepidation painted all over their nearly-identical faces. They lowered their eyes nervously. "Well..."

Their next string of sentences rushed by so quickly his head spun. "We kind of-" "-talked Tony into-" "-setting Dahlia up-" "-to clear our names-" "-and get even with her-" "-and we wanted to get you-" "-out of the closet-" "-and into us-" "-and we thought you might run away if you knew-" "-and it worked better than we thought possible-" "-so please please please don't be mad-" "-'cuz we love you-" "-and we just want you to be happy!"

Rubric stared agape for a moment, then he and Jaron both burst into side-splitting laughter. These two magnificent little bastards orchestrated the whole thing! They grabbed the rabbits and held them tight as they calmed down in fits and starts. "Oh god, that's rich!"

Jaron cocked his head in curiosity. "But...what would you've done if Rube hadn't recorded the conversation with your phone?"

Raz grabbed his pants, reached into the pocket, and pulled out Chaz's phone, which was identical to his but without the stickers. He grinned. "Plan B."

The panda couldn't help but laugh again. "Nice!"

The endorphins finally tipped the scales, and Rube found himself ready for another round. But before he could start anything, Jaron shifted, his gaze drifting between the three of them, his ears askew. "So...what happens now?"

Rubric considered the question a moment, as well as the motivation behind it, and gave him a gentle smile. "Now we graduate, then we hit college. I'd considered renting a house by myself, but... I think I'd rather we all room together, if that's okay."

The twins looked excited, like all their dreams had come true. "Oh, that's a great idea! I always did want a live-in maid!"

"I'm more excited about having live-in lovers."

"What about me, Raz?"

"Incest doesn't count, Chaz." Charles's whiskers twitched and his ears drooped more than normal.

"If you say so."

"I do."

Jaron's reaction was considerably less enthused. He grabbed a handful of sand and watched it slip through his fingers, then threw the rest away. "What about my place? I can't just leave it."

Rubric wrapped his arms, legs, and tail around the devil's body and snuggled close. "I think you've spent enough time alone in that huge empty house. Too many awful memories. You ought to sell it and get a new place where you can make a fresh start. Work on building a new life full of good memories."

The idea startled him. "I..." Jaron bit his lip as he considered it. "That might be a good idea, actually. I'll have to think about it."

"You're not the only one with bad memories, though." He reached out and gathered in the twins. "I think we all need to let go of the past. A new life will do us all good."

He squeezed them all tight. "So what do you say, guys? Are you ready to face life after high school? Together?"

His friends and lovers all looked at each other, then to him, and their voices rang out as one, as it should be. As it always should be. "Yeah. Together."

*Growing up, Peter's desires were shaped by sin-
gularly graphic story. Over the years of his life, he
is confronted with the all too real implications of his
fantasies.*

THE KEY

Metassus

THE END

It is just before dawn, a few minutes before six in the morning. Here lies Peter, close to death.

A hint of a smile crosses his thin, parched lips. He moans something unintelligible, lifting his hand weakly. The effort causes him to break into a dry hacking cough and, exhausted, he slowly slumps back down.

Peter is a cheetah: obviously so, for he is laying naked on his back upon the soiled white tiles of something that resembles a prison cell. It is, in fact, a cell, for the name and logo of a well known security manufacturer is embossed on a steel plate by the oversized lock. It fills one wall of a large, empty room. There are no windows here, and no way for Peter to know that outside, away from this fetid room, stars are fading and the fresh, bright sun is rising into cornflower blue skies. Several banks of fluorescent tubes provide an unemotional flat light, and lend a distant electric hum. Other than his laboured breathing, it is the only sound to break the silence.

In the gloom of the far stairwell, a crumpled figure sprawls in a broken heap, his rich dark blue business suit splashed with the congealed contents of a dinner tray. The tray itself lays by his head; a bear's head, his pelt a light honey shade of brown. The plastic

291

plate under his jaw is smeared with crusted food; a plastic glass, overturned and empty, is motionless against his nosepad. Small flies crawl into the food, or rummage through the dishevelled fur of the still bear, seeking a safe place to lay their eggs. It is not a pleasant sight.

Upstairs, beyond the sound-proof door, lies another world. Above the gloomy prison-like cellar is an airy home full of light, comfortable furnishings and appealing *objets d'art* that would charm the cognoscenti and aesthetically-inclined alike. Delicate french windows open upon a seductive garden that—though fallen from the heady heights of perfection—could readily return to an Eden-like state under the caring ministrations of one with a patient eye and a green thumb. Ivy-clad walls around the garden lend the mansion discreet privacy. A swimming pool beneath its patterned cover is strewn with last autumn's leaves. A fine estate owned by a careless, if wealthy, owner.

Scattered over a green leather writing pad on the antique bureau lies a scattering of personal letters and hand-delivered notes, each one more *urgent* and *critical* than the next, written in the unique gobbledegook of Business language, asking the CEO to consider his position and do the right thing for the shareholders to maintain the stock valuation.

One floor above, a selection of tasteful bedrooms link from a beautifully carpeted hallway, all spacious, with walk-in wardrobes and full en-suite—yet only one smaller room is in use. The master bedroom door is locked. This has been so for the past five years or more. The abandoned room is grey with accumulated dust, yet it retains the cheerful aspect it once had. There are no obvious signs as to why it has been locked away, like our friend Peter.

A selection of family photographs are displayed on the walls: a lion and his parents, from boyhood slimness to powerfully maned middle age; a sequence with the same lion and a young cheetah that is more casual and less stuffy, with smiles and laughs in interesting locations.

The room is abandoned and forgotten—as though one day the door was locked and never reopened.

CORRUPTION

Many years before, there was a shabby living room in a shabby house, filled with the wild kits of a shabby family. It was vibrant, full of life and sounds and smells and squeals of youthful exuberance. It was a happy home.

On a cold wet Saturday night, as the living room bustled with those squirming kits—all arguments and laughs; using crayon on books that were not meant to take color and ignoring those that should—the television, bright and warm, was the center of their world. Young Peter loved television. He was a little past his eleventh birthday, a big event for which he received a schoolbag as a gift from his parents. The straps were already ripped from it, thanks to a flying tackle by an older hyena at school, one day after his birthday.

The *Late Show* was on, even though a really good foreign thriller was on another channel. Peter's position in the family hierarchy meant he rarely got to choose the viewing. With three elder brothers and a young sister, his choices were limited. As a result, he became an amiable soul that enjoyed whatever was shown: a surprisingly omnivorous viewer for one of his delicate years. In an unfriendly world where cheetahs were treated with mild suspicion—being fast and lean, they had a reputation for banditry and nefarious dealings—watching the boob tube was better than being loose on the street, subject to the occasional mauling, both verbal and physical.

On this night, his parents had left the kits under the supervision of their eldest. He was a power-hungry bully and though he disliked the *Late Show*, he knew he would get his ears boxed if the younger ones went back to their father and reported even a flash of unclad fur. Dad could be vicious after draining his mug, and his ideas of morality were very traditional.

The show droned on, guest after guest touting new books or new records. The youngest kit had curled up and was fast asleep in the middle of the couch, kicking viciously whenever anyone moved her. Peter sat on the floor, bright-eyed with tiredness but focused on the screen. He was happy to be up late.

The next guest was a sinister, tough-looking human. Wiry and mean, he was announced as an infamous criminal: a man who had openly admitted in court that he killed "more than one" in his time. He was caught bang to rights and sentenced to life imprisonment for his deeds. He looked frightening to the young cheetah— exactly the type he hoped never to encounter in a darkened alley, or anywhere else for that matter.

He oozed aggression.

Blunt. To the point.

No attempts to explain a motive.

The ocelot hosting the show was a renowned interviewer, regarded by some as a national treasure. He looked suitably appalled and, using subtle verbalisms and overt body language, he guided his audience and viewers into a broad disgust for his guest. Still, he had little difficulty in getting this hoodlum to spill his guts on live television. There was a glint of triumph in the ocelot's eyes, a dead-give away that the show would be on the tongues of the people and the front pages of the country's papers the following morning.

And the audience, both in the studio and that living room, was enraptured. Peter leaned forward, elbows on knees, as he imagined the fiend pulling out a machine gun to kill everyone at the show. *Then they would show slow motion replays! That would be so cool!* He stared at the human—the sinister blue-ink tattoos on his bare arms, silver studs in his ears, *humans have such strange ears that can't even swivel*—and listened to every word.

"Ah wus wan o'th' moast dange'ris pris'nars en th' jail," growled the guest in a gravelly Scottish accent, far more scary in sound than when committed to the written word. He leaned towards the camera. Peter edged closer to the screen, receiving a smack on the head from his elder brother when he blocked the other's view of proceedings.

"I kept hurting people when in prison, so they put me in the Cages. They were in the cellars of the prison, a special confinement area for the wildest and craziest brutes. It can withstand any human-and any morph."

A ripple of nervous laughter passed through the studio audience as the larger morphs in the front rows-bulls, bears and the like-shifted self-consciously in their seats.

"They lock everyone up in these wee single cells in there, all in one big cellar. Stark naked like wild animals. And we were wild animals. Screws—that's what we called the prison guards—they had to deal with us somehow. They threw the food in at us. Hosed us down with cold water. They used the same hoses to clean the floors. And we fought. We fought the screws in our bare pelts and skin: we spat at them, we pissed through the bars at them and we even threw our own shit at them." There was a appalled gasp of disgust from the self-righteous in the studio audience. Peter's older brothers snorted and laughed. "When we got close enough to each other 'cross the gaps, we tore at each other. We were out to damage and wound anything we could... arms and legs and tails." He flashed a sinister grin, displaying a selection of gold teeth. "Of course, I didn't have much to fear about my tail getting caught."

"Guys with claws really had the best of it. I remember a wolf getting his arm ripped clean off him by a hyena in the next cage. Not an easy place, but I was tough. If we couldn't fight each other, we tore the mattresses apart to show our strength. And there was this one night when I nearly choked a polar bear to death with my own bare hands—"

Peter was glued to the screen, but it was not from the sheer brutalism of the description. A newly-formed nugget of yearning formed within his pre-pubescent mind, and grabbed at the first bizarre sexual concept he experienced. Deprived by his parent's fear of overt sexuality, he was open to anything that stuck in his head. A hot, uncomfortable sensation rippled through him; he felt hot and vaguely sick, excited and embarrassed. Aroused.

The rest of the interview went in one ear and out the other.

The thug found God. He woke one morning in that stinking room, the array of naked savages in cells, and found everything had changed inside his head. Overnight, he claimed, while he lay shivering on his torn mattress, as the growls, grunts and snores and farts of his fellow murderers and sadists echoed off the bare walls, he realised none of them would ever have an opportunity to better themselves—even get out of prison alive—without some form of help. With no one else to whom he could turn, he turned to God for support and guidance and was, as he called it, "born again". Whatever being *born again* entailed, it must have been a success, for he was free, supposedly safe enough to be let loose in a television studio without screws, cages or hoses.

He explained he became the founder and big cheese of the largest and most successful church to minister the word of God to prisoners, Saving Them From Recidivism and Bringing Them The Good News, work placements in society and Saving Their Souls. The ocelot, showman that he was, moved the audience to an appreciation of the human, using his powers of language and posture. When the interview ended, the audience gave the preacher a standing ovation.

Squirming uncomfortably on the couch, Peter's impressionable mind filled with twisted, raw images—cages full of naked men; morphs, humans and one young cheetah among them; locked away, hosed and abused, exposed, humiliated—and his brain neurones responded, creating permanent pathways of finest warp and kink, sealing the new concepts as fetishistic desires for a lifetime to come.

It could be argued that the God that led the former prisoner to the path of righteousness could be blamed for the moral corruption of a harmless kit, and be the direct cause for the terrible predicament he is now in.

FROM SCHOOL TO CITY

Bright schoolboy days did not pass easily for Peter. The old adage *cheetahs never prosper* was used for good reason. Though he was intelligent, friendly and filled with an easy charm, simply being a member of his species denied him that comfortable path more fortunate races enjoyed.

True, cheetahs fell into alcoholism more than most; they had a wanderlust that drove them from place to place; and yes, when they were rejected in one or other way, they took full advantage of their natural speed, deftness and worldliness to effect revenge. Many were small-time criminals or street hawkers. They were good at both trades. Sadly, even those who did not participate in the traditional businesses of the line were still tarred and feathered by the association.

Peter was slim and sporty, a natural athlete, with a good looking face offset only by the roguish aspects of his bloodline. He enjoyed school and learning, although he heartily disliked his teachers. His schoolmasters and schoolmarms loved to remind him that he would amount to nothing.

The badness is in the genes, they proclaimed.

No cheetah in history amounted to much, they assured him. His history teacher described one exception: the Roman slave Spartacus, but his claim to fame only proved the point, for his rebellion was defeated by the rightful leaders of the Republic and he was executed, along with six thousand of his fellow slaves, who would not have suffered such a cruel fate if the cheetah had behaved himself as he should. Cheetahs never prosper, not even when leading an uprising.

Teachers' mind games made little difference to a lad used to such abuse. Names could never hurt him. His fellow students were a different matter entirely, as they had sticks and stones to break his bones.

Jocks jealous of his sprinting prowess—big lumbering oxen, he called them—regularly gave him the dreaded swirly: flushing his head down a toilet bowl. To avoid it, Peter developed even greater pace and stamina and could soon outrun them all, only rarely getting trapped.

When Peter once complained to the Physical Education master about these abuses, he was told bluntly that he probably deserved it. When the jocks found he had squealed they battered him to a pulp behind the bicycle shed, pulled out his whiskers one by one, and hammered his face so thoroughly he could not see out of his left eye for a full week. Peter told his family he fell. Later, when the master insisted that Peter run for the school in the County Finals, the cheetah intentionally threw the race. The master seethed when he heard a rumour that Peter's brothers made an excellent return from some strategically placed wagers.

In the meantime, Peter's father had turned his paw to any and all legitimate work, yet was repeatedly rejected. Though scrupulous, decent, and gaining a grudging respect from those that knew him personally or lived locally, he was a violent man when drunk. Despite that failing, his children benefitted a little from his attitude, but the cut of a man's jib sets his sails and, no more than can a leopard, a cheetah is unable to change the spots on his pelt or the stripes on his cheeks.

The pressure eventually caused Peter to crack. In his sixteenth year, when school restarted after the summer break, he was not there. No more, he said, would jocks pick on him, girls shun him, geeks dislike him or nerds fear him. His father was deeply hurt by his son's decision to abandon what he believed was the only way he could lift his status. He drowned his sorrows in whiskey, and ended up in the County Jail for brawling. The neighbours gossiped that bad blood will always win out. His wife, Peter's mother, had learned over time how best to hide bruising from public view.

The day of reckoning was violent and noisy in the packed household. When the smoke cleared, the home was no longer a home for all. Peter had fled, his meager possessions thrust into a kit bag that he held tightly to his chest on the entire bus journey to the city, as tears filled his eyes.

For many days and nights thereafter, he regretted his hot-blooded action and dreamt of being back home, sitting on the couch with his siblings, Dad coming in at evening-time, Mother cooking, noise and bustle, *I didn't* and *you did*, cutlery jingling, and a warm bed in which to sleep. Those warm thoughts flooded his mind as he lay between soiled sheets with men who favored the pure blossom of innocent youth; corpulent abusers with moist palms and wet lips, wallets loaded with notes that staved off hunger, in return for a feeling that he would never again feel truly clean under his short pelt.

His bloodline ran true. Peter milked the johns for all he could, a new rent-boy for sale and hire under the shadowy bridges, and in the greasy cheap motel rooms of the big city.

FIGHTING FIRE WITH FIRE

The predations that Peter suffered to feed, clothe and keep himself were many and foul. It left him with souvenirs of unwanted encounters, such as the words "MIKE'S BITCH" tattooed (to his great shame) on the skin of his left buttock.

Fortunately, the tattooist employed to do the task saw a lack of enthusiasm in the face of the subject and far too much transitory lust in the one that held the cash, so thoughtfully inked an area that would be well hidden when the fur grew back on the youth's rump. Indeed, by the time the short pelt was restored the john was long gone and the money long spent. The tattoo remained, invisible to the eye, unless the cheetah was visited by a future diagnosis of alopecia or mange.

Peter had a regular meet arranged with a familiar client at the gates of the City Zoo. One week, the john, a well-padded old boar with an expansive wallet and taste for the feral, failed to arrive. An hour passed. Peter, annoyed, frustrated and broke, finally accepted that his meal ticket was a no-show and, with nothing else to do, gazed upon the posters of the animals—*Our Friends*—displayed on the outer walls. A variety of animals with faces just like real people, albeit expressionless or angry, wandered around on all fours, with oddly protruding spines, long tails and narrow chests; panting ignorantly through open mouths; unabashed and completely without social graces. The iron bars that held them at bay in their naked stupidity aroused Peter's secret fetish and made him shift uncomfortably to get some relief under his waistband.

A colourful hand-written poster near the ticket kiosk caught his eye.

"Assistant Keepers Wanted!!! Find Your Outer Animal!!! (Good pay and conditions—apply at office)"

His whiskers raised as he smiled, considering, not for the first time, a real job with a real future. He might even regain the respect of his family. He was, in truth, terribly lonely. Touting blow-jobs to curb-crawling closeted basket-cases gave him no pleasure and was certainly not conducive to any solid long-term relationship. It would appall his parents, whereas a weekly wage in a decent profession just might mollify them.

He grinned at the irony; to be treated as shit by sexual predators one day, to then clean out the shit of real predators the next.

Thus, after three tough, stimulating weeks of training, and dressed in a fresh green Zoo uniform, Pete the Rent Boy, former

Mike's Bitch and slut-around-town returned to Earth as *P. Hepardo, Trainee Assistant Keeper of the Feline House.*

He took to the job like a fish to water and swiftly impressed his colleagues. He bonded easily with both management and keepers, establishing a favourable reputation due mainly to hard work and a dogged refusal to shirk any task.

Everything would be right-as-rain, good-as-gold and easy-as-pie except for one particular manager: a rigid, unsmiling bull who habitually wore a perfectly pressed pin-stripe suit, for fear that he might be mistaken for a mere keeper. A married man, full of Family Values and a God-fearing churchgoer, he openly professed disgust at the *queers* that blighted the Zoo's entrance plaza by their presence. Curiously, his own preferred cruising spot was at a park several miles away, where he once had the pleasure of intimate contact with a certain young cheetah. Mildly panicked, the bull started a series of sinister rumours that their new boy was more—or less, depending on values and/or orientation—than he seemed. The stories came back to Peter indirectly, but he had no idea of how they started, for it had not been the bull's face that he serviced.

The unfairness of this smear campaign fired Peter's blood. He seethed with all the passion and anger expected from a cheetah. In a burst of wild pique, he chose to fight fire with explosives. And so, just before opening time one delightfully warm Tuesday morning, as several small puffy clouds dared the Sun to evaporate them (which it did with pleasure) a ripple of shock and awe spread from the feline house to the Zoo proper. Staff members, barely able to believe the crazy scenario described by their colleagues, left their tasks to see for themselves.

A sight to melt eyeballs was mucking out the empty tigers' enclosure. Clad in a pair of tight pink denim hot pants, a tie-dyed pink wife-beater bearing the slogan OUT AND PROUD, and sporting a large silver hoop through a fresh piercing in his right ear, stood Peter. Sweeping brush in his paws and a yellow hose at his feet, he ignored the gathering crowd while he completed his assigned work, as though he was the only one around. Gasps, giggles and an occasional huff of incredulity came from the viewers above. Peter was in his element. He stopped long enough to cool himself down with the hose, lewdly allowing the t-shirt soak through in a show worthy of a professional lap dancer. Fighting fire with fire was effective he knew, though he was fearful there would be nothing left for him but ashes after the flames burned out.

Senior management called a brief meeting for eleven o'clock. It was semi-formal and consciously over-polite. Peter agreed to avoid further displays of flamboyance. The Zoo director emphasised that the dismissal of an openly gay staff member subjected to unfair discrimination would cause a tremendous amount of bad press that the facility could not afford. The whispering campaign would end, he assured Peter, and it would serve little point for the anonymous instigator to continue, now that the matter was public knowledge. The bull sat among the management team, his wide face thunderous, but unable to defend his actions. As for Peter, he emerged from the office with a firm handshake from the Director, who let slip there might be a possibility of a wage rise if he performed up to par in the future.

He won!

Even if no further cash appeared, his *outing* allowed him a certain casual flare. While his colleagues sweated and panted through work days under the summer sun, burdened by official garb and their own pelts, Peter was the only one to fling off jacket and t-shirt and go bare to the waist. There was a noticeable increase in visitor numbers to the feline house through that hot summer, as aficionados of the body beautiful, the cohort of cruisers from outside and those that enjoyed a bit of rough all flocked to see if he was on view. Inevitably, a regional newspaper latched on to the story and, through a lead article in their lifestyle supplement, Peter's became a local cause célèbre. The story lauded the tolerance shown by management and staff towards "this young disadvantaged gay man." He revelled in it.

Nights drew in, the weather got colder and Peter headed home for winter break. It was nerve-wracking, for he had not contacted his family since the day he stormed off. But, he was hopeful and missed them dearly. As he rattled along on the train he imagined fond hugs from his mother, back-slaps and arm-punches from his dad, some good natured banter from his brothers… Little sis would ask shyly if he brought her a present from the big city. He had his old kit bag crammed with gifts—an entire month's salary blown on gaily-wrapped boxes. Home came the hero.

He was greeted in the hallway by his father, a photocopy of that newspaper article, a set of explicit photographs of him in lewd poses in a hotel room, and an anonymous letter about his "disgraceful history" as a "provider of sexual services". It was written by someone who appeared to know him well, who was "concerned that he has let his family down."

The newspaper headline was scrawled on the outside of the envelope: "Queen of the Beasts". That was his own fault. He had offered the line jokingly during the interview as he performed a faux-camp impression of a mincing keeper.

The envelope was dated two days after his fight with fire. The damage was done months before he went home. He won the battle and lost the war. That evening, he headed back to the city, his kit bag and gifts abandoned in a dumpster.

VINCE

The winter passed miserably for Peter. His letters home, feeble attempts to explain, all came back as *addressee unknown*.

In early spring, as the snow began to melt, he was observing his favourite animal, a beautiful sleek panther, tear her dinner apart. He jingled his keys at her and she spit-growled in response, eliciting a smile from him. Outwardly he is little changed, but his heart was torn from that pain one can only feel when rejected by the people who mean most. Though he bravely tried to not think about it, there were occasionally mornings where tears stained his pillows.

A gravelly voice buzzed in his ear, the mouth so close that the air from his breath made the cheetah's ear flick-flick. Startled, he spun around and almost toppled into the enclosure. The panther beneath growled and pulled her shank of meat further away from the walls. A large lion grabbed his arm and helped him regain his balance. He smoothed his crisp suit cuff casually, and made a comment about something or other.

"W-what did you say?"

"Gud look'n cat. In y'rr cage tharrr. Felis pan-therrr-ra if ah'm no' mistak'n."

The lion's distinctive voice gave Peter an immediate flashback—the burr was identical to that wild human thug-turned-preacher from so long ago—but this was no TV-bound fantasy with an attitude. Big, strong, impressive, certainly rich: this lion was real and hotter than a firecracker in a fuel tank. Peter stared stupidly at the maned head and big tawny flecked eyes until the lion broke him out of his reverie.

"D'ye have a naym for et?"

"Y-yes-I'm Peter."

The lion chuckled and shook his head, that amazing mane appearing to swirl in slow-mo. Expensive cologne flared the cheetah's nostrils.

"Ah'm Vince, and ah ment hem," he replied, pointing at the cage where the panther was crushing bones between her powerful jaws, "but tha' anssar 's bettar."

The rolling Rrrr of the lion's accent made the addled keeper go weak at the knees. He began to explain, somewhat distractedly, that the panther is female, but the lion-Vince-cut him off with an out-thrust paw and handshake, as he pulled the cheetah toward him in an elbow-deep half embrace.

"Ah think ah jus' go' me a sou'v'n'rrrr frrrom th' Zuh," he rumbled, making his purr so deep Peter felt it vibrate in the pit of his belly.

POSSESSIONS

Vince.

A force of nature. A strong personality. Vince was two hundred and fifty pounds of well-maintained muscle, wrapped in a golden pelt like a manicured lawn: groomed and buffed in a way that only the most wealthy can manage or afford. Vince described himself as a mere accountant at first, before finally admitting that he was the CEO of Shaer & Co., one of the most respected financial houses in the city.

Vince was humble, generous, caring, interesting; perfect, maybe. Peter could not understand why he chose to spend time and effort on one as "common" as he—every time Peter raised the question, Vince placed a perfectly manicured claw on his nose pad to shush him. The cheetah felt a magnetic attraction to the magnificence of his new friend, his easy ways and honest approach, although he finally came to understand it might have been partly due to the newspaper exposure. If so, it finally brought him some good fortune, even if his family continued to shun him.

Curiously, Vince displayed an complete lack of interest Peter's life prior to their first encounter, even while he recounted many entertaining tales of his own life and times to the younger feline. It wasn't a chore, for Peter could happily spend a lifetime listening to that wonderful voice.

Things moved quickly after that.

Within weeks Peter was resident in Vince's home—a real mansion by Peter's standards—and introduced publicly as the lion's new *personal assistant*. He rapidly learned the few tasks his new role required, not that they were overly taxing. He quietly resigned his position in the Zoo (to some further abusive comments from a certain manager who couldn't help himself) and moved his few possessions into his very own plush bedroom, down the hall from Vince.

One by one, the household staff were dismissed with decent severance pay, until only Peter remained, a Jack-of-all-trades: part cook, maid, cleaner, gardener, butler and "perrrrrsonal assistant." Oh, how his skin tingled when he heard the lion roll those Rrrrrs!

Deep inside, Peter felt a hint of Cinderella-ism. His handsome prince was the King of the Financial Jungle. There were no slippers, no pumpkins and no ugly sisters to ruin the story. It was easy to allow himself be carried along and enjoy life, being with Vince in the evenings after his word. It was undemanding. Convenient.

A perfect relationship, yet they slept in separate rooms. It became clear that Peter's role was to provide Vince with a comfortable, pressure-free home life, and gain the same in return. He had, he knew, become Vince's possession, just like his expensive

Mercedes-Benz, his cashmere jacket, or his diamond tie-pin. It was gentle and stable, and Peter was delightedly embarrassed when one of Vince's secretaries whispered to him that he was the best thing that ever happened to her boss.

In return, Peter needed little; his wants were limited to some decent clothes for when in public with the lion, a computer, and a TV. They enjoyed occasional intimate contact in the sauna, or the pool, but nothing too deep or tiring. Some evenings, Vince might arrive from work to relax and unwind, sharing a few beers or a bottle of wine as they chow down on some Chinese food, as the lion recounted the day's happenings in the world of high finance. Afterwards, a movie on the comfy leather couch and a snuggle.

Life was good, and life moved quickly.

Mother Dearest

Peter was working diligently in the living room, polishing the mahogany surfaces and the pleasing objet d'art upon them. The television was on and the french windows were open, allowing the sweet scent of blooms permeate the room.

Clad in just his jogging pants, he enjoyed the warmth of the day as he sang along with his favourite commercials while he waited for a tribute show. The well-loved host of the *Late Show* had passed away and his former station had been airing a retrospective of the ocelot's most notable interviews. Peter missed it on its first broadcast the previous night, an unusually frisky lion in the sauna distracted him. The show opened to the familiar theme tune, and then something he had not thought about for many years made his eyes pop, ears and whiskers vibrate, and jaw drop.

The interview—his fantasy interview—THE interview!

The colours were overly bright, the clothing dated, but the words were the very same. Peter could recall every single word. The Scottish human that caused his deepest lustful thought rumbled once more, rolling his Rrrrrs, and squatted belligerently in his brain. The young cheetah resurfaced, with the abilities of the current beast, and could not help himself. It was the source of his inner fire, it made every square inch of his pelt bristle with static, and his skin crawled with arousal.

He peeled off his leggings and flung them through the french window to land on a rose bush. Shaking, he knelt before the screen, one paw rubbing a nipple and clawing his chest fur, the other pistoning like crazy on his rock-hard shaft. He was a wild creature—*Our Friend The Cheetah*—about to burst as the voice told the story one more time.

The ex-prisoner growled his way through the tale of the cages, the locks, the hosing-down, being naked—

With a caterwaul of lust, his watery seed gushed high into the air; all over the screen, the carpet, the table, his chest and his face. He held the orgasmic rigour magnificently, every muscle taut for a full twenty seconds, until he sighed a long "ohhhhhhhhfuuuuuuck" and shuddered, collapsing onto his back and sprawling on the cream woollen carpet. The last of his semen seeped out to coat his groin stickily. Panting like a steam train, he closed his eyes and relaxed, savouring the pleasurable moment after climax.

A quiet cough came from behind. He leapt to his feet in a blind panic and stares at the entrance door.

Vince returned early. He stood there, a hopelessly unreadable expression on his muzzle. Supported by his right arm was an stern, elderly lioness, wearing gobs of expensive pearls and a real fur coat. The room temperature seemed to drop. Peter shivered in his pelt. The musky smell of semen filled the air as a dribble of it dripped from the end of his whiskers, to land with a tiny plish on his bare foot.

Vince coughed again and gestured at the lady.

"Peter," he said formally, "this is my mother. Ma, this is my P.A., Peter."

The following week was Peter's *Hour of Shame*. Mrs. Shaer did not speak one word to the "insane pervert" employed by her son. Peter could not blame her. He lost himself in gardening work when she was present. She refused point-blank to go into the living room, particularly after the embarrassed cheetah used industrial-strength bleach on the carpet and turned it from a rich cream to a blotchy white in under an hour. Vince quietly had the carpet replaced the following day.

She finally left that weekend. The front door slammed as Vince returned home, stomped into the living room and threw himself down on his favourite chair. He looked through Peter, or so the cheetah believed, as for one awful moment he believed he was about to be thrown out on his ear. He cautiously approached the big lion, ears pinned, eyes down and attempted to explain himself. Vince silenced him with a raised paw.

"Peter," Vince said slowly, "we've been living here together for a time now..."

Peter nodded. He fought back tears that were forming in his eyes.

"And all that time together I've never asked you what kind of things turn you on."

Peter blinked in surprise. One tear shook free and dropped onto the new carpet. He looked up, hardly able to believe his ears. He shook with emotion and threw himself onto the lion, blubbing like a baby. Vince wraps his arms around his friend and caresses his cheek gently with his paw. He speaks softly in his broadest accent.

"No' a great thang fer a mate t'do, eh?"

A DREAM FULFILLED

The large prison cage slotted perfectly into one end of the gym after Vince arranged a team of *building professionals* (as he called them) to move most of the equipment closer together. It was a genuine, government-grade cell, just like the one described by the prisoner-turned-preacher in the interview. Eight feet tall, ten wide and ten deep, it had a low shelf welded to one side that held a fixed foam mattress covered with a special liner that was "guaranteed rip-, scent- and stain-proof." The builders, their bemusement at why they were assembling a cell in the basement of a mansion diverted by the hush money added to their fee, ignore the lion and cheetah as they come down to inspect the work.

Who cares what big-shots do behind closed doors? Perverts, all of them. Come the revolution...

Clean white wall-tiles behind the cage matched the newly tiled floor, and sloped down to the newly installed drain, conveniently sited where the shower formerly stood. Peter waited for the last of the tradesmen to leave, just staring at the contraption, trembling with excitement. He was, he told the lion, filled with wild lust. Vince chuckled as he wrapped his muscular arm around his mate's bare shoulder and gave him a companionable squeeze.

"Are you still sure that this is really what you want most, my love?"

He spoke tenderly. Lovingly. He spoke in the hope that he would be able to prove to his mate that he cared and that he is treating him to his dream out of purest motives. At least that was what Peter hoped, unable to read another's mind, particular Vince's. His reply was little more than a nod and a grunt, however, the almost electrical excitement surging through his body and the growing wet patch in the front of his shorts expressing more than his voice ever could. He pulled the lion into a tight hug that is more akin to a lewd grope, as his bulge slid over the latter's pressed cotton slacks. Vince pushed him off with a laugh and a mock complaint that the sweaty and aroused cheetah would soil his clothes.

Vince slowly pulled Peter's shorts down, letting the erect cheetah maleness spring free. Crouching, he placed a lingering kiss atop the smaller feline's glans before he helped him step out of his only clothing, and kicked the used apparel off to one side. He squeezed the exposed rump and tugged his tail as he came upright again, then firmly guided Peter through the door of the new cell.

And then it was time. Vince closed the cage door, then locked it, leaving his mate imprisoned within it, with nothing more than the pelt in which he was born. Arousal pulsed through Peter. One single touch to his groin would probably have caused him to explode like a geyser.

Vince grinned as he looped the lanyard with the key over his neck. He shook his great mane and the lanyard was no longer visible.

"This," he told his new *prisoner*, "is the only copy of the key that's here. The spare is safe somewhere else, so I'll keep this with me all the time so I know where you are!"

The lion headed back upstairs to order a pizza, and Peter mused happily about how all this had come about. After all, it was only a month or two since the ill-fated visit of the dreaded Mrs. Shaer. Since that traumatic event, the two felines had moved to a new and distinctly better phase of the relationship. Vince watched another replay of the infamous TV interview and began to understand Peter's peculiar fetish. It had been hard for Peter to put his needs into words, to share something hidden away so long, but he had found in Vince an avid and interested listener.

His appalling timing had created that defining moment. They opened up to each other, allowing each other to see them as they were: unrepressed, kinky, horny sexual beings; creatures with needs and desires that they could discuss without shame or embarrassment. The change in Vince was remarkable. Though Peter had to extract—and occasionally manufacture—the lion's kinks and was more than willing to facilitate anything the lion could imagine (and then some), the latter's greatest pleasure seemed to come from making Peter's own warped fantasies come true.

He was finally sitting in his dream cage, content to be trapped, when he realised that he failed to wriggle one single original twisted or warped fetish from his mate. Vince was naturally dominant, claiming it to be his due as "King of Beasts". Chaos ensued from that, with Peter's screams of "Fuck me, Your Majesty!" echoing out of the mansion at moments of extreme pleasure.

Presently, Vince padded back down with a couple of pizza boxes and pushed one through the slot on the barred door.

"I want you to be happy, you know."

Peter knew. Peter really, truly knew.

Going Too Far

Vince played the part of official warder for two amazing, exciting, weeks. Locked into his cage, naked and alone, Peter only had the pleasure of his company twice a day, exactly as he instructed. First thing each morning, the lion hosed out the cage—and the cheetah—with cold water. Not having a proper toilet in the cell had embarrassed Peter at first, until he figured out how to time his needs with the floor sluicing, just as they did in the real prison. He thought it might be the one aspect of the fantasy at which his lion might balk, but the ever-accommodating Vince just shook his head slowly, shrugged, and played along. After the rinse-out, Peter obviously had nothing with which to dry his pelt and had to let it air-dry naturally—an alien sensation at first. He soon managed to comb his short fur with his own claws and even found out how to nibble at rough patches, just like his former charges in the Zoo. Vince, meanwhile, grinned widely each time he came down the stairs to the redesigned gym, as the tiles and most of his friend was usually covered in his own seed.

He couldn't help it! He was painfully aroused all the time, almost manic with his own sexuality, and there was little else to do. He insisted that no books, radio or TV should be available to him, for he was desperate to emulate the role of a real prisoner.

In the evening, Vince returned from work and carried down his prisoner's daily tray of food. The lion stood officiously by as the cheetah gobbled it down without cutlery or napkins, wiping his muzzle on his own arm. Then the warder would urinate through the bars, having refused point-blank to allow the prisoner pee out at him—there's no way y'git t'pish on mah gud duds! It wasn't much of a problem to Peter, however, as he would happily curl up in the puddle of his mate's scent. Arousal would flare once again and he would pump away until he found his release. At midnight Vince would roar a goodnight down the stairs with a stern lights out! and head to bed, leaving Peter to his own devices.

On the third week of the experience, and with the prisoner not showing any desire to be released, they had a small tiff. Vince wanted Peter to return to his usual self, rejoin the world and get with the plan on some of the housework that had been ignored.

"You've been here for a long while now, and I've been busy with work," Vince reasoned. "Can you not take a break for a day or two? Or a couple of months, maybe? I miss you being around, you know."

There should have been no reason for Peter to disagree with the honest request. Perhaps he should have been grateful for all the lion did to grant him his dearest wish. Perhaps Peter should have nodded and agreed, come out of the cell willingly and showered, done his duties and realised the cage was there for his fun at any time.

He should have, but didn't.

Peter stood defiantly inside the cage, growling and throwing shapes, and selfishly refused to come out. He grabbed himself and attempted to pee on the lion. Vince's expression hardened. He walked up the stairs without a word. Some minutes later the front door slammed shut, then came the growl of his Mercedes' engine. The car crunched the gravel as it drove away, leaving the cheetah where he wanted to be, naked and alone.

ABANDONED

Vince didn't return that evening.

Peter spent a long, lonely night in the cage. Despite having caused the argument, he was so angry that he would have spit fire at the lion. Hungry, smelly, and with his water jug almost empty, his sleep was disturbed. The ceiling lights burned all night. All of the eroticism he enjoyed had now disappeared. Only his trust in Vince keeping him from panic. It was unlike the noble and honourable lion. Soon after sunrise, he drained the last of the water. The hose was out of reach and, with no key other than the one hanging from Vince's neck he was trapped: horribly, terrifyingly trapped.

He sat on a corner of the rip-proof mattress, huddled up miserably, tail wrapped tightly around his feet. He wondered why on earth he had done what he had done; why had Vince abandoned him; how could Vince have left him like this? Peter wanted to hold and hug his lion and bawl sincere apologies. He wanted to jump on top of him and claw his eyes out. He wanted to kiss his face and beg his forgiveness, he wanted to punch him in the snout and demand answers…

He wanted good, he wanted bad. A thousand times his emotions flickered to and fro, as the day crawled past, punctuated only by the impotent rings of the unanswered telephone upstairs. He could hear muted voices as the answering machine kicked in each time.

Evening drew in. His stomach knotted with hunger pangs. He licked the last drops out of the jug. He wallowed in self pity.

I couldn't have insulted him that much... Could I? It wasn't even a fight! He didn't say anything!

The sun rose. He shivered all night and his tongue felt like a half-inflated balloon in his parched mouth. Out of desperation, he urinated into his water jug and downed it, but it was dark and bitter and gave him no relief. He started to yell, pointlessly he knew, for they had reduced all staff in the mansion to one single cheetah.

The sound of a car finally pulling up outside broke into Peter's lethargy. It was late in the afternoon. He unfolded stiffly from the shape into which he had huddled and clung to the bars, ready to hurl abuse at Vince for his ignorance and complete lack of regard for his safety. The front door opened. Peter gave a sigh of relief as he listened to the footsteps pad through to the kitchen. His empty gut rumbled and gurgled in anticipation.

Okay, he figured, he's probably as angry as I am... Still, he's making me something to eat! Peter's face broadened into a smile as he saw a haughty, stuffy lion descend the stairs in his mind's eye, holding a tray and a lovely fresh jug of water. He decided he would continue to play prisoner with Vince, and his penis firmed as he readied his mind and attitude.

I'll request a 'temporary' release and do all the housework. Fair is fair. But I'll make him suffer for leaving me like this! See if I don't!

Vince didn't come down immediately, frustrating Peter. He waited to hear the ding of the microwave. It didn't come, so he eventually rattled the door and roared for the warder. The sounds above stopped suddenly and moved towards the stairs. His sex-drive returning with a vengeance, Peter rolled around on the soiled floor, knowing that Vince would then have to spend more time washing him down as a result. He pawed himself up to a full erection and smacked his mouth to turn his spittle into foam for effect. It was a buzz, having his rank piss drip off his matted fur. He clung onto the bars, pushing his genitals through the bars lewdly, and yelled until a big-framed male appeared ...

It was not Vince.

Terry Arkoudas, Vince's legal advisor, tennis partner and best friend, was a bear with a rich honey-coloured pelt. A nice guy, he and Vince had gone to school together and, as Vince grew in stature with his business, Terry was pulled onwards and upwards in his career by his friend. Peter once asked Vince if he and Terry had ever been an item. Vince chuckled.

"I doubt Terry ever had a sexual thought in his entire life, Peter. Even in the locker rooms at school he would go purple if anyone saw him in the nip, or if he saw anyone himself. Even in the tennis club he goes home to shower."

Now, as he came into view, Peter made a startled eeep and covered himself up with his paws as best he could, feeling his throbbing maleness deflate under his fingers like a burst balloon. Terry's eyes bugged in shock as he gaped around the room, the big steel cage and, finally, at the filthy naked cheetah imprisoned in his best friend's gym. His wide brown eyes raked over Peter's frame and the bear shuddered visibly. Mortified, Peter felt utterly humiliated, embarrassed beyond measure before someone he only knew casually. It had to be, after the rejection by his parents, the second-worst feeling of his life.

Terry, surprisingly, didn't leave. He clapped his big paw over his forehead and groaned.

"Peter," he sighed, "what in hell's name are you doing?!"

Fired

"Peter... I have to go now. Are you sure you want me to go? Will you be okay until morning in there? Are you certain you don't want anything else?"

Peter, slumped on the padded shelf, slowly turned his puffy red eyes to Terry. His numbed mind gradually realised that the bear was addressing him.

"No. No, thank you, Terry. I'll—I'll be alright. You will be back, though? First thing?"

As he replied, the cheetah found himself reaching a paw out towards the bars. He knew it was a pathetic gesture but he could not will his arm to lower itself. Terry nodded, a piteous expression written on his features, and left. The front door slam was eerily reminiscent of when Vince left: it only felt like moments ago! Terry's car pulled away and the house grew perfectly still. Peter was alone again—terribly alone: without the lion, his lion, his friend; his only friend. He was gone, and lost forever.

Vince was dead.

The terrible silence of the room made his head swim. His waking nightmares revolved around the tale Terry had revealed in a voice cracking with emotion.

After he stormed away, Terry said, Vince headed back to his office. Mere minutes thereafter a serious fire broke out on the ground floor. The old redbrick building blazed—something had gone wrong with the sprinkler system—yet many of the office workers in the upper floors emerged unscathed, including Vince. Before the emergency services arrived, however, someone yelled that there were some people trapped in the restrooms on the third floor. Vince, ever brave and noble, and a horse that worked in a publicists nearby, ran to their rescue and broke the first rule of evacuations: never, ever go back in. The duo battled to the third floor. They were seen at a window. The flames were tremendous.

Fire crews arrived. They raised a ladder. Flames and smoke spewed from the building. Flammable furnishing and flame retardant carpeting melted with equal ferocity. The firemen fought back with equal force. They raised a ladder to the third floor, where the horse and lion could be see behind the insulated glass, banging on it with chairs. They smashed the window with their fire axes and the crowds below cheered. Just as the lead fireman grabbed at the window ledge a loud rumble began. He snatched at the nearest person he could reach, the horse, and heaved him onto the top of the ladder. Under Vince's feet, the floor and brick facade of the building had had enough and it crumbled, one heroic lion dragged along with it. He suffered an unspeakable end.

That was the tale Terry told. One miraculous rescue. One tragic loss. One cheetah, left alone.

Peter woke to the the click of Terry's claws on the tiled floor. In that first moment of confusion after sleep, he thought it was Vince and called out. The bear did not answer, and remained standing solemnly until Peter emerged from under the bed shelf and wiped his red eyes. During the night he had crawled off the bed to curled up on the floor beneath. The stoic bear, tears in his own eyes, reached into the cage. Peter crawled over, for he felt drained and had no energy, or desire, to stand. Terry gently rubbed his shoulder.

"I've had no luck with the manufacturer yet," he admitted with a nod at the big lock. "They are prohibited by law to provide any more than two coded keys per cell. Government regulations and all that shit. I got a company coming later to cut you out. I brought you some breakfast."

He fetched a tray with coffee and freshly baked croissants, and eased it through the slot. Peter, though he felt like he would never need to eat again, chewed on the flavourless food and drank the black drink without sensing its warmth. The croissants were light and crispy. Just as Vince liked them. The coffee was strong and rich. Just as Vince liked it. To Peter, it was ashes and mud. He started to weep.

"There, there. It's alright. It's alright," Terry crooned, again reaching in through the bars. "I miss him too."

He gently rubbed Peter's ears with his big soft paw. Peter sobbed his eyes out.

Requiem

The funeral was a vortex of solemn activity, ernest hand-shaking and "Reporting Live From the Funeral Of Vince Shaer, the hero of this week's tragic fire" television cameras. Vince had been a formidable figure in his field, a wealthy socialite and now a fallen hero, therefore coverage of his demise was of interest to the public, press and the elite that wanted to be connected to his heroics.

Peter kept his head down, unwilling to tarnish Vince's public memory by declaring who and what they were to each other. He chose a seat near the back of the church. Terry had to arrange permission for his attendance, for Vince's mother was still less than pleased he had not been dismissed by her "soft-hearted son". After the unmentionable scene where he embarrassed himself before her, Vince reported with obvious delight that his mother told him, "A servant who humiliates his betters in such a disgraceful and lewd manner should be whipped first, then dismissed!" The lion chuckled and waved his finger in a mock admonition. "Knowing you," he smirked, "you'd take the whipping and ask for more!"

His seat was almost as far from Vince's mother as possible. At one point before the memorial service she spotted him in the courtyard and pulled a face like she stepped in something foul, before insisting that she be taken to some other area "where the air is less tainted." Naturally, the majority of people around her looked directly at him, trying to fathom what was going on. To most everyone there, Peter was merely the P.A. or the handyman: a disposable cheetah and humble employee. Though Terry had loaded him into a respectable suit and tried in vain to get him to move closer to the bier, Peter felt as much an outsider as at any time in his life.

None of this mattered anyway, he thought miserably, for that burned shell in the wooden box up there was not his lion. He was gone.

After the service, the usual retinue of local politicians, personalities and other bigwigs clustered around Vince's mother to pay their respects. Their carefully crafted looks of compassion and concern disappeared once they got outside, where they chatted on their cellphones to plan where was best for a quick lunch in this drab neighbourhood. They turned Peter's stomach.

Vince's coffin was dumped into a cold, dark, fetid hole in the ground while a bored priest read meaningless archaic words from a old book covered in the long-dead skin of some unfortunate animal. The celebrities and politicos moved away to their limousines: the most worthy went immediately to a particularly well-known and exclusive restaurant called BEEF, where Vince's mother had arranged luncheon for those worthy of the honour. The graveyard emptied as rapidly as the gravediggers filled the hole. When they left, only two people remained. Terry said nothing: he just wrapped his big ursine arm around the cheetah as they stood by Vince's final resting place, each alone in their thoughts. The sun, matters of personal grief irrelevant to it, shone gaily in the warm blue sky. Birds sang in the trees.

"I suppose I should go clear up the gym." Peter wanted to escape his emotions with some mindless activity.

"I'll drive you there. I'm not doing much else on a day like this."

"You're not going to the dinner?"

Peter was surprised. Terry had sat in the place of honour beside Vince's mother in the church, but the bear shook his head and told him that he had a living friend who needed some support right now. Though he though he would never be able to cry again, Peter's eyes filled with tears. After a last quiet moment by the grave, they left.

When they arrived back at the house Peter changed into an old pair of shorts and a tired t-shirt, then went downstairs with some cleaning equipment. Terry headed straight for the kitchen to prepare some food.

The cage door dangled from its frame, for the guy with the cutting tools had sliced his way through the hinge. He was full of questions why a professional-grade prison cage was in the basement of a rich dude's house, and how could anyone be so dumb as to get locked inside without a key. Terry threatened to get some other tradesman if the questions didn't stop. Peter said nothing.

He placed his paw on the big lock. Even now he could feel the warmth that had soaked into the metal bars from the blue flame. He squeezed his eyes tightly as he tried to recall the excitement and joy he felt when Vince locked him up on that first evening. There was nothing. The laughter and smiles were there, but no emotion. He felt truly empty. The scenes that flashed through his mind's eye were just pictures and voices from another time. He imagined the dark emptiness would continue its course and remove all emotion from his mind, to leave him as an empty shell: blank inside and out; unable and unwilling to care about anything ever again.

Terry's clack-clack across the floor broke his dark introspection. He handed the cheetah a large ham sandwich on a plate and ordered him to eat it, then wolfed down his own huge snack. Peter picked at it wistfully for a time, until the smell of the soft fresh bread broke something in his mind and he had a mad rush of hunger. He gobbled it down.

"So… What are you planning to do, Pete?"

The most haunting question of all, and the one he did not want to face… What was he to do? He had moved his entire life and future hopes into this home, what he had come to call *our home*, but had no rights to anything within it—not even the cage that his beloved lion had bought just to satisfy his fetish. He stood motionless, tears welling up again as he faced down the awful reality that he was not only without his mate, but without a job and effectively homeless. Unable to answer, he stood and grabbed his cleaning kit.

Terry respected his pain and left him to some needed solitude. He carried the plates away and pottered off to do some paperwork for the estate. Peter finished his task, padded up to his room, then stuffed the very few items he could call his own into a black refuse sack. When he walked away from the house, Terry didn't even know he had left.

WHERE THERE'S A WILL

The Zoo director personally welcomed him back to his former position, although he did inform him that his wages would be cut by twenty percent because of his break in service. He found a clean single room to rent and lived there quietly, not talking to anyone, not going out. Peter withdrew, hoping it might help him gather all the pieces of his heart back together.

Nights were torturous infinities, haunted by dreams of Vince. They would be together, but not quite. Vince might be in the next room as Peter tried over and over to free himself from a bleached carpet into which his feet kept sinking, and all his cries for help were drowned out by an elderly lioness with a whip calling him a filthy animal. He might be in the cage, only able to see the lion's footpaws on the top step of the stairs as he slammed the front door, then the flames would start and he would see the house tumble down, carrying Vince with it, but he would never see his face. He would wake screaming in a tangle of sheets, soaked in sweat, heart pounding, with only the drudge of the next day awaiting him.

One rainy weekday he was clearing dung from the elephant pen when he heard a familiar voice. Terry stood at the gate, wearing a vast trenchcoat and carrying an umbrella. Peter leaned the sweeping brush he was using against the wall and went out to meet him.

"I won't shake hands if you don't mind, Terry. I'm a bit dirty, if you know what I mean." The cheetah's light conversation did not reflect the turmoil he felt at seeing Terry again. The memories of Vince that the bear brought back to life were overwhelming.

"Gods, Pete, you have no idea how hard it was to find you! I've been looking for you for months! What the hell did you sneak out like that for?"

There was no reason to discuss everything out in the rain, and the water from Terry's umbrella dripped down Peter's collar, so they ventured to the staff canteen. Discarded wrappers from lunchtime soiled the tables, and it smelled as musty and rank as the animals the staff tended. Terry shucked off his overcoat and sat opposite the cheetah, an earnest look on his face, the scent of expensive cologne drifting subtly, just as Vince on that first day—

"—you listening to a word I'm saying?"

"Oh, sorry, Terry. I was a million miles away."

"Well," he looked mildly offended, "you shouldn't have left like that. I had so much to discuss with you and, well—"

His paw slowly stretched out and covered the cheetah's. It didn't feel right. Peter pulled his paw back. Terry blinked with embarrassment and his ears flattened.

"Look, there's a lot you need to know. Firstly, I was appointed as Vince's executor. I have to look after everything to do with his estate, and his will."

Peter's heritage stuck a needle into his brain, waking up that part of him that he prayed he lacked. Did Vince possibly include him in his will? He had never considered himself greedy, but Vince was his lover after all, and he was very, very rich, and he should be entitled to something—

"He didn't mention you, I'm afraid. The last time he changed it was about five years ago."

"Oh."

"He was a man set in his ways. Slow to change, as you probably knew."

Peter nodded numbly. He had nothing before this conversation, he gained nothing because of it, except disappointment in someone he thought might have loved him. What did he lose?

"The estate went to his—his former partner. All of it."

Peter looked up in surprise, transfixing the ursine with a very yellow feline stare.

"His former partner? He never mentioned one!"

Another hurt from this one single conversation. Vince never shared anything about his past, his lovers, with the cheetah. How stupid could one cat be? Peter sagged inside. He felt even more worthless, realising darkly that he was nothing more than a convenient worker and possession for the lion; a useful bit of fluff with a good body, until something better came along. His fur bristled up and down his spine. It was unfair, all of it.

Terry cleared his throat. He gave an embarrassed smile.

"That former partner? Well, uh… That was me."

COLLARED

Terry ran his finger nervously around the inside of his shirt collar as he began to explain. His small round ears were pinned back and his obvious embarrassment made Peter feel compassionate towards his difficulty.

"We were together for ten years, he and I. His firm was funded by his mother. He looked after me and got me my position as legal officer. I was happy to be with him all the time because I—" he struggled with the words "I really loved him from the first day we met as kids. And I couldn't tell him that straight up."

Peter's mind was reeling. How could—they weren't—they didn't?

"…so one night at a party in his apartment, I got really drunk and fell asleep. All the other guests left, and I was alone with him. I woke up as he was trying to undress me, just my shoes and jacket, to put me to bed. I couldn't help myself. I got pretty wild. Then so did he. The following morning was something else, I can tell you.

"But when we realised we could both love each other as something more than friends, we promised we would keep it a secret between ourselves. He had a position in life that was more liberating than mine. I couldn't really handle anyone knowing anything about my… Uhm… My desires."

Peter thought back to Vince's comment about Terry never having sex. So that was a lie.

"We had good times and bad times, and he was a wonderful partner, in business and in—other ways. But after eight or nine years, we grew apart. I began to need more, see more, do more; but Vince… Well, he just stayed Vince. Two years ago, we came to realise there was no point in fooling ourselves anymore. Our time had ended and it was turning into something hurtful. Then you came along, Pete, and I think you made him happier than I ever did. Despite that, we remained best friends and business partners."

He leaned closer, more intimately, locking his eyes to Peter's.

"Vince spoke about you a lot. He really cared for you and he truly loved you. Do you know how you changed him? He never said that about another person, not even me. And you were only together for months! He and I were an item for a decade and never got to that level. He said he would do anything to make you happy, because… Well, he said you never asked for anything for yourself."

"There was the cage," Peter replied. Terry nodded.

"That there was. There's something I have to show you." The bear fished clumsily in his overcoat pocket and pulled out a crumpled paper bag. "I brought Vince's car back from where it was left when—" He sighed, and placed it respectfully on the table between them. "This was on the front seat. I believe it was a gift for you."

The bag bore the name of a pet store opposite Vince's office. Peter had been there many times, looking through the pets and paraphernalia, chatting with the staff about animal husbandry and his days at the Zoo. He opened the bag carefully. Inside was a wide leather collar, a matching lead, an identity disk and the receipt.

"This, I believe, is why Vince went to the office in the first place," said Terry solemnly.

Peter turned the disk over. The inscription read *DISOBE-DIENT CHEETAHS MUST OBEY THEIR LION*. So many emotions surged through him that he started to shake, before he broke down in long wailing sobs.

Vince loved me!

Terry got up heavily, came around to Peter's side of the table and hugged him close for a long time, until the cheetah could cry no more.

The Cage

That evening, Terry and Peter shared a chow mein at Terry's apartment. It cheered Peter greatly. Afterwards, they sat on the couch and talked for hours. Terry was a good listener and let the younger male share everything about life with Vince. It was cathartic: a true release. There were more tears, but the smiles and laughs grew greater in proportion.

Terry responded with wonderfully told tales of the shenanigans he and Vince managed to get into at college. Peter noticed that the bear did not talk about more recent times and assumed his romantic separation from Vince was just as painful as Vince's death. As the fire grew low and a couple of glasses of wine had slowed their conversation, they fell into a peaceful companionship.

Peter was beginning to drowse when Terry spoke with a sharper tone in his voice.

"Pete, that morning when—when I saw you in the cage… You know, stark naked, filthy, hard as a rock… Well, it was something else."

Peter swallowed hard and felt that mix of hurt and acute embarrassment again. It was the morning after Terry found out his former lover died.

"But—but I thought you looked… Well, you looked awesome locked in there and… I really fell for you. You know, when I was hosing you down and—and everything."

Peter was shocked out of his sleepiness. Just what exactly was Terry saying?

"I'm not trying to upset you, Pete. I just want to tell you how I feel. About you."

The comfortable mood in the room had evaporated. Terry looked distressed and reached out his paw, gripped the cheetah's wrist and held him in place.

"I'm moving into Vince's place next month, Pete. I'd love if you would consider staying there, but with me. And we can keep the cage there too! I got the key, look!"

Peter stared, horrified, as Terry pulled a pristine, undamaged key from under his shirt collar. It was hanging from a gold chain, eerily similar to the one Vince wore. The one that Vince would have had around his neck as he fell into the flames—

Terry held Peter's arm tighter as the cheetah pulled back from him, and spoke soothingly to reassure him.

"He gave the key to me," he smiled lovingly, searching Peter's face for a positive reaction. "Vince wanted me to have it and be happy with you. He loved you more than me, but I loved him so much! I want to love you too, if you're more than I am! He wanted me to love you too!"

Terry began to lose control. His eyes bulged as Peter tried in vain to pull away from him, but the bear was simply too big and powerful for the lean cheetah. Peter yelled at him to let go. The bear was past rational thought. Peter scratched his claws on Terry's arm, eliciting a gruff grunt from the bear. With one haymaker punch to the jaw, Terry knocked the cheetah to the ground, stood over him and stomped his ursine foot on Peter's slim chest.

All pretence of friendship vanished.

"He abandoned someone who loved him for a piece of shit animal that wanted to live naked in a fucking cage!" he screamed, spit flying from his hate-warped muzzle. "A pink t-shirted piece of rough from the wrong side of town!

"He abandoned me for this! He would have loved you forever and forgotten me completely! I knew he would play the hero, he always did!"

The breath was squeezed out of the dazed and confused cheetah's lungs by Terry's solid weight. He punctuated each syllable with a stomp. Peter scrabbled helplessly at his leg, claws shredding shred the bear's expensive slacks and ripping through his pelt. Even with the blood pouring from his calves, it was a mismatched fight that Peter could not win.

"I knew he bought the cage for you! He would never have done it himself! He asked to use my personal credit card so it wouldn't show up on his own accounts. His precious mother might have found out!"

A rib cracked. Lights popped brightly in Peter's field of vision. He managed one single word—*please*—in vain hopes the bear would relent.

"And when he set off to be the almighty hero, he gave me the key and told me to let you out! If he only knew I started the fire in the first place!"

He lifted his foot—Peter gasped in a lungful of air—and he stomped downwards with all his might. Everything went black.

When Peter awoke everything was still black. Woozily, he carefully felt about. It was hard to breathe. His chest was a mass of hurt. The too familiar padding of a plastic mattress was beneath him. Bandage-like strapping was wrapped tightly around his midriff, but otherwise he was naked. He struggled to his feet and fought to stay conscious as a coughing fit wracked his frame. He staggered around in the darkness, bumping into iron bars. His worst fear was realised, as he already knew he was back in the cage with the door locked.

He yelled until the room was suddenly flooded by the light of a single lightbulb, though when his eyes adjusted, it was obvious the flood was more of a trickle. What he could see under the low powered incandescent bulb was shocking. He was in the cage in the basement gym, but the long window facing the garden had been blocked up, save one small opening where a small panel was covered by newspaper and masking tape. The room was bare: all the gym equipment was gone. There was nothing except for the cage: freshly repaired and solidly locked, with Peter inside. The clacking of bear claws on the stairs heralded Terry's appearance. The bear smiled at his prisoner and leaned against the wall, a glass of brandy in his paw.

"I fixed your cage, Pete. Now you can live out your fantasy here with me. I boarded up the windows so as not to distract you, and soundproofed the walls and ceiling. You can roar your little lungs out without disturbing anyone upstairs. I even left you a little window so we can conserve a little energy during daylight. I like to think green. Good for the planet, you know. When the paint dries I'll pull off the newspapers. I did that myself, you know. I'm quite the tradesman."

He smiled and swirled the brandy in the snifter. Peter felt weak, scared and hungry, and had to sit down. This was certainly not erotic.

"I'll pop down every second day to feed you and hose your lovely dirty body down. If I've nothing better to do I'll watch you through the camera up there. It's got infra-red. I don't even need to leave the light on! Now, if you'll excuse me, I was watching a very good film on TV."

He walked up the stairs, switched off the light and shut the new soundproofed door. Peter, shocked and terrified beyond belief, screamed and pleaded until his voice and ribs gave out, and somehow fell into dark, disturbed dreams.

THE BEGINNING OF THE END

Peter scratches a mark for each day, and a line for every week, into the grey paint under the bunk. He has been trapped in the cell for at least the past five years, and nothing ever seems to change. Terry comes regularly to sit on the comfortable chair he brought from the living room, where he relaxes in the company of his prisoner. He chats to the cheetah sometimes, although he never mentions anything of note happening out in the real world. He tells Peter that the worries of the great big world are something he no longer has to deal with, and he should be happy for that.

Terry has stuck to his word about feeding times, for he only feeds his "pet" every second day, just as Peter fed the animals in the zoo. It's a healthy system, he tells the cheetah, and he should be grateful that someone is looking out for him. In return, the cheetah has to provide entertainment whenever the bear demands it. The naked pet might have to jerk himself off, or finger his own tailhole, or even kneel at the bars so Terry can urinate over him. Failure to obey loses him a meal, so his desire for rebellion faded after only a couple of months.

The bear often comes down to stare wordlessly at the naked cat, drink large amounts of brandy, and pass out on his chair. That is the worst time for Peter, as the bear will insist on pissing into his mouth before he goes back upstairs for the day.

He gives Peter scraps and left-overs from finer dinners, throwing them into the cage for the cheetah to eat from the floor. There was a time when doing that made Peter physically ill, but he has become inured to it over time and no longer cares.

Over the years, however, Terry has become obese and slow. Even his penis is beginning to get lost under the roll of ursine fat that hangs over it. Occasionally he pops a small white tablet under his tongue. He doesn't talk much anymore. Peter no longer cares. The bear looks unwell, yet Peter has little idea how he himself looks, for there are no mirrors or shiny surfaces available down in the private Zoo.

He tried several times to convince Terry to release him so he could, perhaps, tend to the needs of the house. Terry smiled knowingly and dismissed it out of paw. However, Peter is now at the point where he would be happy to do it honestly and without escaping. He would love to go upstairs again and help clean it. Watch TV. Perhaps tend to the garden. He would love to see the garden. The roses would be beautiful.

Terry opens the door at the top of the stairs. Peter's belly rumbles. The light snaps on and the cheetah blinks painfully, for there has been little light for the past two days, since his last feed. Both the cell is and its occupant are malodorous and he longs for the cold water hose to sluice his body and, in particular, beneath his tail, for he is soiled and uncomfortable. The smell of roast beef and vegetables freshens the dank air, but Terry doesn't come down immediately. Peter almost growls with anticipation for his food, and can't quite understand what the bear could be messing with up there.

No! My dinner! He's dropped it! It's gone all over the stairs and the floor. But something is really wrong. I hear him gasping. He's falling! He's falling!

And then, silence. Terry lies in a heap at the foot of the stairs, his open eyes staring emptily at the cell.

"T-terry? TERRY!!!"

It is just before dawn. A few minutes before six in the morning. Here lies Peter, close to death.

A hint of a smile crosses his thin, parched lips. He moans something that sounds like a name, a friend's name, a lion's name, and he lifts his hand weakly, caressing an invisible mane. The effort causes him to break into a dry hack and, exhausted, he slowly slumps back down.

AFTERWORD

Whyte Yoté has been writing erotic furry fiction since 1995 when he was probably far too young to be doing such a thing, and he has been seriously pursuing his craft since 2000. His works have appeared multiple times in FANG, and also in the anthologies ROAR, X The Fortune Teller's Poem and Holidays in addition to issues of Heat magazine. Never a Not Writer, he juggles multiple short-story projects as well as anthology and novel work.

Kansan by birth, South Dakotan by grace and Californian by convenience, Whyte Yoté currently lives in Sacramento. He shares his life with writer/ graphic designer Tym, his forever boyfriend since 2004. When he isn't writing, he enjoys fast driving, good food and all things anthropomorphic.

* * *

Sylvan Scott is the pen-name of a longtime member of the fandom who first discovered it in the pages of the Centaur's Gatherum Newsletter (back in the early 1990's). He has written a wide range of short stories and created the research for "Furry Sociology 101": one of the most widely-referenced, early studies on Furry Fandom. His first publishing credit was a tabletop gaming module for "Chill"; he is also a former journalist. Today, he splits his time between Web writing, coding, cooking, gaming, and partici-pating in speculative fiction fandom.

* * *

Tym Greene is 6'3" of awkward nerdy jackorn (jackal plus unicorn—my parents are a little

*strange). An aspiring author and artist who knows
that there is always more to learn. He has finally
graduated with a degree in Graphic Design, and is
trying to figure out post-college life. He lives with
his boyfriend Whyte Yoté and far too many books.
Tym dabbles in many things, including sculpture,
steampunk, painting, fursuit-making, and full time
jobs.*

* * *

*Toonces began writing furry porn in Pennsylvania's
Amish country, but has been living in the nation's
capital since leaving on Rumschpringe at age
seventeen. It is in the Pennsylvania heartland that
Toonces developed the work ethic to accomplish
timely, efficient erections, specializing at first in barn
frames. Of modern electric conveniences, these are
those most enjoyed by the author: the Automobile,
the Computer, the Television and Video Games;
Soda-Pop Fountains, the Train. On the Podcast,
which is like the Radio, but on the Computer,
Toonces discusses furry literature from an adult
perspective with SkipRudder. The Podcast can be
located at http://www.baddogbookclub.com/.*

* * *

*H. A. Kirsch usually (but not always) writes gay,
BDSM and fetish-themed erotic anthropomorphic
fiction. He can be found at http://www.hakirsch.com*

* * *

*Scott Maddix lives in Salt Lake City, Utah, but has
roots in Maine and California. He's been writing
since he was a wee leveret. He's self-published a book
-- Chunnel Surfer II -- and is nearly finished with a
second. In addition, he's worked as a journalist for
three different publications, and editor for a fourth.*

Scott currently lives with his boyfriend, another hare, and is working full-time on his writing. He did actually work fast food once, though the story is purely fictional.

* * *

Anima is a first-time submitter to FANG, or any other formal publication for that matter. A member of the furry community since 1998, he has been writing furry fiction for over a decade for himself and friends. Born in Michigan, Anima now resides in rural Ohio, using a weak DSL connection to terrorize the internet as an enormous black panther. Winner of Morphicon's ignominious Iron Author award two years running, he hopes to build a successful writing career regardless.

* * *

Lindskold Janis is a fan of Anne McAffery's Dragonriders of Pern, her son Tod's work in the same setting, The Wheel of Time by Robert Jordan, Uhura's Song by Janet Kagan, everything he's read so far by Brandon Sanderson, M. C. A. Hogarth's Spots: The Space Marine, Ursula Vernon's Digger, The Demon Cycle by Peter V. Brett, Carpe Diem by Graveyard Greg (whom he blames for a number of things), and, unsurprisingly, "Firekeeper's Saga" by Jane Lindskold. He distinctly dislikes A Song of Fire and Ice by George R. R. Martin.

The saarlooswolfhond has been happily attached to the same man since December 2002 and would love to fall out of the professional IT and government contractor fields and just write. When not writing or reading or working, Lindskold can generally be found playing D&D in both the DM and player roles, wishing he had more people to play board and card games with, and watching cartoons.

* * *

Tyler David Coltraine has been tooling around the fandom for somewhere close to two decades now, dabbling now and again in writing and the creative world of the word. This appearance is his first published work, but several pieces can be found around the internet on places like Fur Affinity.

Aside from creating adult works for the furry reader base, Tyler is an amateur musician, technocrat, and overly avid video gamer with a massive collection of retro gear. And yes, there may be more stories forthcoming...

* * *

Lycanthromancer lives in Kansas, also known as The State of Confusion. He's assisted other artists of prose with such works as Graveyard Greg's "Welcome to Cappuccinos," Alflor_Aalto's "Prince of Knaves," and WhyteYote's "The Leather's Always Blacker". You can find the few stories he's written at http://lycanthromancer.sofurry.com/.

* * *

Metassus has been composing short stories, microfiction, part-works and poetry for several years. He is also a keen photographer of (among other things) wolves and creepy-crawlies. If he had infinite power, he would move his island a little closer to the equator. Failing that, world dominance would be a decent fallback. Metassus lives in a mud-hut in Ireland with a pack of wild dogs and a duck. His website—www. metassus.com—features a wide selection of his works.